Mischief

Amanda Quick

piatkus

PIATKUS

First published in the US in 1996 by Bantam Books,
A Division of Random House, Inc
First published in Great Britain in 2008 by Piatkus Books
This paperback edition published in 2008 by Piatkus Books
Reprinted 2008, 2009, 2010

A CIP catalogue record for this book
is available from the British Library

ISBN 978-0-7499-3909-0

Data manipulation by Phoenix Photosetting, Chatham, Kent
www.phoenixphotosetting.co.uk
Printed and bound in Great Britain by Clays Ltd, St Ives plc

Papers used by Piatkus are natural, renewable and recyclable
products sourced from well-managed forests and certified
in accordance with the rules of the Forest Stewardship Council

Mixed Sources
Product group from well-managed
forests and other controlled sources
www.fsc.org Cert no. SGS-COC-004081
© 1996 Forest Stewardship Council
FSC

Piatkus
An imprint of
Little, Brown Book Group
100 Victoria Embankment
London EC4Y 0DY

An Hachette UK Company
www.hachette.co.uk

www.piatkus.co.uk

For my editor,
Beth de Guzman,
with thanks and appreciation.

Mischief

Prologue

The weak flame of the candle made little impact on the flood of darkness that filled the interior of the deserted mansion. It seemed to Matthias Marshall, Earl of Colchester, that the vast house had absorbed the very essence of the night. It had the aura of a tomb, a place where only ghosts would willingly reside.

The folds of Matthias's long, black greatcoat swirled around his mud-spattered boots as he climbed the stairs. He held the candle higher to light his path. No one had greeted him at the door when he had arrived a few minutes earlier, so he had let himself into the cavernous hall. It was clear now that there were no servants about, not even a maid or a footman. He had been obliged to take care of his horse himself, because no groom had come forth from the stables.

At the top of the stairs he paused to glance down over the railing into the ocean of night that filled the front hall. The candle could not begin to penetrate the waves of darkness that ebbed and flowed there.

Matthias walked down the gloom-filled corridor to

the first chamber on the left. He stopped in front of it and twisted the old knob. The door gave a groan of despair as it opened. He held the candle aloft and surveyed the bedchamber.

It resembled nothing so much as the interior of a mausoleum.

In the center of the chamber was an ancient stone sarcophagus. Matthias glanced at the inscriptions and carvings that adorned it. Roman, he thought. Quite ordinary.

He crossed the chamber to where the coffin stood beneath gauzy black hangings. The lid had been removed. The candlelight revealed the black velvet cushions that lined the inside of the sarcophagus.

Matthias put the candle on a table. He stripped off his riding gloves and dropped them beside the taper, then sat down on the edge of the coffin and removed his boots.

When he was ready, he wrapped himself in the folds of his greatcoat and settled onto the black cushions inside the sarcophagus.

It was nearly dawn, but Matthias knew that the heavy drapes that covered the windows would prevent the rays of the rising sun from invading the dark chamber.

Some might have had difficulty finding sleep in such sepulchral surroundings. Matthias knew that he would have no problem. He was accustomed to the company of ghosts.

Just before he closed his eyes he asked himself again why he had bothered to respond to the summons that had been issued by the mysterious Imogen Waterstone. But he knew the answer to that question. Long ago he had given his oath. His word was his bond.

Matthias always kept his promises. Doing so was the only way he could be certain that he would not become a ghost himself.

Chapter 1

Matthias was rudely awakened by a woman's blood-curdling scream.

A second female voice, this one as crisp as the green apples of ancient Zamar, interrupted the horrified cry.

"For heaven's sake, Bess," the apple-tart voice admonished. "Must you screech at the sight of every cobweb? It is extremely irritating. I am trying to accomplish a great deal this morning and I can hardly do so if you shriek at every turn."

Matthias opened his eyes, stretched, and sat up slowly in the sarcophagus. He glanced at the open door of the bedchamber just in time to see a young maid crumple to the floor in a deep swoon. The weak sunlight that seeped down the hall behind her told Matthias that it was late morning. He raked his fingers through his hair and then tested the stubble of his beard. He was not surprised that he'd scared the maid into a faint.

"Bess?" Crisp, fresh apples again. Light footsteps in the hall. "Bess, what on earth is wrong with you?"

Matthias rested one arm on the edge of the stone

coffin and watched with interest as a second figure appeared in the doorway. She did not see him at first. Her full attention was focused on the fallen maid.

There was no mistaking the fact that the second female was a lady. The long apron that she wore over her serviceable gray bombazine gown could not disguise the elegant line of her spine or the high, gently rounded curve of her breasts. The determined set of her shoulders bespoke an innate pride and a purposeful air that had been bred into her very bones.

Matthias contemplated the lady in growing fascination as she hovered above her maid. He swept a critical eye over her, cataloguing the various parts of her form much as he would assess the carving of a Zamarian statue.

She had made a valiant attempt to confine a voluminous mass of tawny brown hair beneath a practical little white cap. Several tendrils had escaped imprisonment, however, and bounced around her fine-boned face. That face was turned partially away from Matthias's view, but he could make out high cheekbones, long lashes, and a distinctive, arrogant nose.

A strong, striking face, he concluded. It conveyed the essence of the forceful spirit that obviously animated it.

The lady was no young chit fresh out of the schoolroom, but on the other hand, she was not nearly so ancient as himself. Then again, few people were. In truth he was thirty-four, but he felt centuries older. He estimated that Imogen was five and twenty.

He watched as she dropped a leather-bound journal onto the carpet and knelt impatiently beside her maid. There was no sign of a wedding ring on her hand. For some reason that fact pleased him. He suspected that the apple-tart voice and the commanding manner had had a great deal to do with her apparent status as a spinster.

It was a matter of taste, of course. Most of Matthias's male acquaintances preferred honey and chocolate. He, however, had always favored something with a bit of a bite when it came to after-dinner delicacies.

"Bess, that is quite enough. Open your eyes at once, do you hear me?" Imogen produced a vinaigrette and waved it briskly under the maid's nose. "I really cannot have you screaming and swooning every time you open a door in this house. I warned you that my uncle was a very odd man and that we were quite likely to come across some rather strange items when we inventoried his collection of sepulchral antiquities."

Bess moaned and rolled her head on the carpet. She did not open her eyes. "I seen it, ma'am. I swear it on me mother's grave."

"What did you see, Bess?"

"A ghost. Or maybe it were a vampire. I'm not sure which."

"Nonsense," Imogen said.

"What was that earsplitting noise?" another woman called from the top of the stairs. "Is something amiss down there, Imogen?"

"Bess has fainted, Aunt Horatia. It is really too much."

"Bess? Not like her." More footsteps in the hallway announced the impending arrival of the woman who had been addressed as Aunt Horatia. "Bess is a sturdy girl. Not at all prone to fainting spells."

"If she has not fainted, she is doing an excellent imitation of a lady suffering an attack of the vapors."

Bess's lashes fluttered. "Oh, Miss Imogen, it was dreadful. A body in a stone coffin. *It moved.*"

"Don't be ridiculous, Bess."

"But I seen it." Bess groaned again, raised her head, and glanced anxiously past Imogen into the shadows of the bedchamber.

Matthias winced as she caught sight of him and screamed again. Bess flopped back down onto the carpet with all the grace of a beached fish.

The third woman arrived in the hall outside the doorway. She was dressed in the same practical fashion as Imogen, a plain gown, apron, and cap. She was an inch or two shorter than her companion and considerably broader about the waist and hips. Her graying hair was pinned beneath her cap. She studied Bess through a pair of spectacles. "What on earth is upsetting the girl?"

"I have no notion." Imogen busied herself with the vinaigrette. "Bess has an imagination that is easily overheated."

"I warned you about the dangers of teaching her to read."

"I know you did, Aunt Horatia, but I cannot bear to see a sound mind go uneducated."

"You're just like your parents." Horatia shook her head. "Well, she's not going to be of much use if she continues to start at every unusual sight in this house. My brother's collection of funereal oddities is enough to give anyone a fit of the vapors."

"Nonsense. Uncle Selwyn's collection is a bit morbid, I admit, but rather fascinating in its way."

"This house is a mausoleum and well you know it," Horatia retorted. "Perhaps we ought to send Bess back downstairs. This was Selwyn's bedchamber. She was no doubt startled by the sight of the sarcophagus. Why my brother insisted on sleeping in that old Roman coffin is beyond me."

"It is a rather unusual sort of bed."

"Unusual? It would inspire nightmares in anyone possessed of normal sensibilities." Horatia turned to peer into the shadows of the darkened bedchamber.

Matthias decided that it was time to rise from the coffin. He stepped over the edge of the sarcophagus and pushed aside the thin black draperies. His greatcoat swirled around him, concealing the breeches and badly wrinkled shirt in which he had slept. He watched with amused resignation as Horatia's eyes widened in horror.

"Sweet God in heaven, Bess was right." Horatia's voice rose to a shriek. "There is something in Selwyn's coffin." She staggered back a step. "Run, Imogen, *run.*"

Imogen leaped to her feet. "Not you, too, Aunt Horatia." She whirled to glower into the darkened bedchamber. When she caught sight of Matthias standing in front of the coffin, her lips parted in amazement.

"Good heavens. There is someone in there."

"Told ye so, ma'am," Bess whispered hoarsely.

Matthias waited with keen curiosity to see if Imogen would scream or succumb to the vapors.

She did neither. Instead, she narrowed her eyes in unmistakable disapproval. "Who are you, sir, and what do you mean by frightening my aunt and my maid in this nasty fashion?"

"Vampire," Bess muttered weakly. "I heard tell of 'em, ma'am. Suck yer blood, he will. Run. Run while ye still can. Save yerself."

"There is no such thing as a vampire," Imogen announced without bothering to glance down at the stricken maid.

"A ghost, then. Flee for yer life, ma'am."

"She's right." Horatia plucked at Imogen's sleeve. "We must get away from here."

"Don't be ridiculous." Imogen drew herself up and regarded Matthias down the length of her very fine nose. "Well, sir? What have you to say for yourself? Speak up, or I shall summon the local magistrate and have you clapped in irons."

Matthias walked slowly toward her, his eyes fixed on her face. She did not retreat. Instead, she fitted her hands to her waist and began to tap the toe of one half-boot.

An odd but unmistakable sense of awareness, almost a thrill of recognition, went through him. *Impossible.* But when he was close enough to see the intense clarity of Imogen's wide blue-green eyes, eyes the color of the seas that surrounded the lost island kingdom of Zamar, he suddenly understood. For some whimsical reason he could not explain, she made him think of Anizamara, the legendary Zamarian Goddess of the Day. The mythical lady dominated much of the lore of ancient Zamar and a great deal of its art. She was a creature of warmth, life, truth, energy. Her power had been equaled only by Zamaris, the Lord of the Night. Only Zamaris could embrace her brilliant spirit.

"Good day to you, madam." Matthias pulled his fanciful thoughts back under control and inclined his head. "I am Colchester."

"*Colchester.*" Horatia took another startled step back and came up against the wall. Her eyes went to his hair. She swallowed heavily. "Cold-blooded Colchester?"

Matthias knew that she was staring at the icy white streak that lanced through his black hair. Most people recognized it immediately. It had identified the men of his family for four generations. "As I said, I am Colchester, madam."

He had been Viscount Colchester when he had earned the appellation of *Cold-blooded.* The fact that both of the family titles went by the same name, Colchester, had made things convenient for the gossips in the ton, he thought bitterly. There had been no need to lose the alliteration.

Horatia's mouth worked. "What are you doing here in Upper Stickleford, sir?"

"He is here because I sent for him." Imogen favored him with a blindingly bright smile. "I must say, it's high time you arrived, my lord. I dispatched my message more than a month ago. What kept you?"

"My father died several months ago, but I was delayed returning to England. When I arrived, there were a number of matters pertaining to his estate that required my attention."

"Yes, of course." Imogen was acutely embarrassed. "Forgive me, my lord. My condolences on the death of your parent."

"Thank you," Matthias said. "But we were not close. Is there anything to eat in the kitchens? I am feeling quite famished."

○   ○   ○

The first thing one noticed about the Earl of Colchester, Imogen decided, was the swath of silver in his midnight-dark hair. It burned in a cold white flame through the unfashionably long black mane.

The second thing one noticed was his gaze. His eyes were colder than the icy silver in his hair.

The fourth Earl of Colchester was magnificent, she thought as she waved him to a chair in the library. He would have been altogether perfect had it not been for those eyes. They glittered in his hard, ascetic face with the chillingly emotionless light of an intelligent and very dangerous ghost.

With the exception of those spectral gray eyes, Colchester was exactly as she had envisioned. His brilliant articles in the *Zamarian Review* had accurately reflected his intellect as well as a character forged by years of harsh travel in strange lands.

Any man who could calmly lie down to sleep in a sarcophagus was a man who possessed nerves of iron. Just what she needed, Imogen thought ebulliently.

"Allow me to introduce myself and my aunt properly, my lord." Imogen seized the teapot and prepared to pour. She was so excited to have Colchester at hand that she could scarcely contain herself. Wistfully she toyed with the notion of blurting out the whole truth concerning her identity. But caution prevailed. She could not, after all, be entirely certain how he would react, and at the moment she needed his willing cooperation. "As you have no doubt concluded, I am Imogen Waterstone. This is Mrs. Horatia Elibank, my late uncle's sister. She was recently widowed and has kindly consented to become my companion."

"Mrs. Elibank." Matthias nodded once to acknowledge the introduction.

"Your lordship." Horatia, perched stiffly on the edge of her chair, darted an uneasy, decidedly disapproving glance at Imogen.

Imogen frowned. Now that the initial fright had

passed and proper introductions had been made, there
was no reason for Horatia to look so anxious. Colchester
was an earl, after all. More significantly, at least so far as
Imogen was concerned, he was Colchester of Zamar; the
distinguished discoverer of that ancient, long-lost island
kingdom, founder of the Zamarian Institution and the
prestigious *Zamarian Review,* and trustee of the Zamarian
Society. Even by Horatia's high standards, he should have
been eminently acceptable.

For her part, it was all Imogen could do not to stare
at him. She still could not quite bring herself to believe
that Colchester of Zamar was sitting there in the library,
taking tea as though he were an ordinary man.

But not much else was ordinary about him, she
thought.

Tall, lean, and powerfully built, Colchester was imbued with a sinewy masculine grace. The years of arduous
travel in search of Zamar had no doubt honed his phy-
sique to its present admirable state, Imogen reasoned.

She reminded herself that Colchester's impressive
physical attributes were hardly unique. She had seen any
number of well-muscled men. She lived in the country,
after all. Most of her neighbors were farmers who worked
in their own fields. Many of them had developed broad
shoulders and strong legs. In addition, she was not entirely without experience when it came to the male of the
species. First, there had been Philippe D'Artois, her dancing instructor. Philippe had been as graceful as a bird in
flight. And then there had been Alastair Drake. Athletic
and handsome, he had certainly not required any help
from his tailor in order to do justice to his attire.

But Colchester was as different from those men as
night was from day. The strength that emanated from him
had nothing to do with his sleekly muscled shoulders and
thighs. It radiated from some inner core of inflexible steel.
The force of his will was palpable.

There was also a great stillness about him that belonged more properly to the shadows than to the daylight.

It was the patient stillness of the predator. Imogen tried to imagine him as he must have looked on that fateful day when he finally mastered the labyrinth beneath the ruined city of Zamar and discovered the hidden library. She would have sold her soul to have been with him on that memorable occasion.

Colchester turned his head at that moment and gave her an inquiring, slightly amused glance. It was as though he had read her thoughts. Imogen felt a wave of embarrassed warmth go through her. The teacup she was holding rattled on its saucer.

The dark library was chilly, but Colchester had obligingly built a fire on the hearth. The room, which was crowded with a variety of bizarre sepulchral artifacts, would soon warm.

Once she had been assured that Colchester was not a ghost or a vampire, Bess had recovered sufficiently to retreat to the deserted kitchens. There she had prepared a pot of tea and a cold collation. The simple meal consisted only of leftover salmon pie, some bread pudding, and a bit of ham, but Colchester seemed content with it.

Imogen certainly hoped he was satisfied. The food had not come from the mansion's empty cupboards. It had been packed in a hamper early that morning and brought along to sustain the women as they went about the business of cataloguing Selwyn Waterstone's collection. Judging by the efficient manner in which Colchester was demolishing the repast, Imogen doubted that there would be much left over for Horatia, Bess, or herself.

"I am, of course, delighted to make your acquaintance," Matthias said.

Imogen suddenly realized that his voice had an extremely odd effect on her senses. There was a dark, subtle power in it that threatened to envelop her. It made her think of mysterious seas and strange lands.

"More tea, my lord?" Imogen asked quickly.

"Thank you." His long, elegant fingers brushed hers as he accepted the cup.

A curious sensation began at the point where he had touched her. It traveled along Imogen's hand, rendering her skin unaccountably warm. It was as though she sat too close to the fire. Imogen hastily set the pot down before she dropped it.

"I am very sorry that there was no one here to greet you when you arrived last night, sir," she said. "I sent the servants to their own homes for a few days while my aunt and I conduct the inventory." She frowned as a thought struck her. "I was quite certain that I directed you to come to Waterstone Cottage, not Waterstone Manor."

"No doubt you did," Matthias said softly. "But then, there were a great many instructions in your letter. I may have forgotten one or two along the way."

Horatia glared at Imogen. "Letter? What letter? Really, Imogen, I must have an explanation."

"I shall explain everything," Imogen assured her aunt. She eyed Matthias warily. The cool mockery in his eyes was unmistakable. It cut her to the quick. "My lord, I fail to see anything amusing about the contents of my letter."

"I was not particularly amused by it last night," Matthias admitted. "The hour was late. It was raining. My horse was exhausted. I saw no point wasting time in an attempt to locate a small cottage, when I had this vast house at my disposal."

"I see." Imogen gave him a determined smile. "I must say, you appear remarkably unruffled by a night spent in a sarcophagus. My aunt and I have often remarked that Uncle Selwyn's notion of a proper bed was certainly not to everyone's taste."

"I have slept in worse places." Matthias helped himself to the last of the ham and surveyed his surroundings with a considering expression. "I had heard tales of Selwyn Waterstone's collection. The reality is even more unexpected than the rumors implied."

Briefly distracted, Horatia peered at him over the rims of her spectacles. "I expect you are aware that my brother had an abiding interest in sepulchral art and tomb antiquities, sir."

Matthias's arresting eyes lingered thoughtfully on an Egyptian mummy case propped in the corner. "Yes."

"It is all mine now," Imogen told him proudly. "Uncle Selwyn left his entire collection to me along with the house."

Matthias gave her a speculative glance. "You are interested in sepulchral art?"

"Only that which is Zamarian," she said. "Uncle Selwyn claimed that he owned a few Zamarian artifacts and I have every hope that he did. But it will take time to find them." She gestured to indicate the heap of antiquities and funereal oddities that littered the library. "As you can see, my uncle had no sense of organization. He never bothered to catalogue the items in his collection. There may be any number of rare treasures waiting to be unearthed in this house."

"It will certainly take a great deal of work to find them," Matthias said.

"Yes, it will. As I said, I plan to keep any antiquities that I can positively identify as Zamarian in origin. I shall offer the remainder to other collectors or perhaps give them to a museum."

"I see." Matthias sipped tea and studied the library more closely.

Imogen followed his gaze. There was no denying that her eccentric uncle had possessed a very strange taste for artifacts associated with death.

Ancient swords and armor taken from Roman and Etruscan burial chambers were strewn about in a careless fashion. Sphinxes, chimeras, and crocodile motifs copied from Egyptian tombs adorned the furniture. Bits of statuary and cloudy glass bottles that had been discovered in antique sepulchral monuments reposed in the cupboards. Grim death masks stared down from walls.

The bookcases were stuffed with dozens of worn volumes that dealt with ancient entombment practices and the embalming arts. Several large crates were stacked on the far side of the room. Imogen had not yet opened them. She had no idea what was inside.

The situation was no better in the upstairs chambers, all of which were crammed with the tomb antiquities that Selwyn Waterstone had spent his life acquiring.

Matthias finished his brief survey and looked at Imogen. "What you choose to do with Waterstone's oddities is your affair, of course. Let us return to the business at hand. Would you mind telling me why you sent for me?"

Horatia uttered a small, faint gasp. She whirled to confront Imogen. "I cannot believe that you have done this. Why on earth didn't you tell me?"

Imogen gave her a placating smile. "The thing is, I sent for his lordship a few days before you arrived here in Upper Stickleford. I was not entirely certain he would put in an appearance, so I saw no reason to mention it."

"This is folly," Horatia snapped. Now that the initial shock had passed, she was apparently regaining her usual spirits. "Do you realize who this is, Imogen?"

"Of course I know who he is." Imogen lowered her voice to a properly reverential tone. "He is Colchester of Zamar."

Matthias raised his brows but made no comment.

"As you said, my lord," Imogen continued, "it is time to get to the heart of the matter. You were a good friend of Uncle Selwyn's, I believe."

"Was I?" Matthias asked. "That is certainly news to me. I was not aware that Selwyn Waterstone had any friends."

Alarm shot through Imogen. "But I was led to believe that you owed him a great favor. He claimed that you had vowed to repay him if it were ever possible to do so."

Matthias regarded her in silence for a moment. "Yes."

Imogen was vastly relieved. "Excellent. For a second there I thought I might have made a dreadful mistake."

"Do you make many such mistakes, Miss Waterstone?" Matthias asked gently.

"Almost never," she assured him. "My parents were great believers in education, you see. I was trained in logic and philosophy, among other subjects, from the cradle. My father always said that when one thinks clearly, one rarely makes mistakes."

"Indeed," Matthias murmured. "As to your uncle, it's true that I considered myself to have been in his debt."

"Something to do with an ancient text, was it not?"

"Years ago he came across a very old Greek volume in the course of his travels," Matthias said. "It contained some oblique references to a lost island kingdom. Those references, together with others I had discovered, gave me some of the clues I needed to locate Zamar."

"That is just what Uncle Selwyn told me."

"I regret that he died before I could repay him," Matthias said.

"You are in luck, sir." Imogen smiled. "As it happens, there is a way for you to fulfill your promise."

Matthias regarded her with an unreadable expression. "I fear that I do not entirely grasp your meaning, Miss Waterstone. You have just told me that your uncle is dead."

"He is. But in addition to his collection of tomb artifacts, my uncle also left me a respectable inheritance and the promise that you owed him."

There was a heartbeat of silence. Horatia stared at Imogen as if she had gone mad.

Matthias watched her with enigmatic eyes. "I beg your pardon?"

Imogen cleared her throat delicately. "Uncle Selwyn bequeathed me the promise that he claimed you made to him. It is quite clear in his will."

"It is?"

This was not going as smoothly as she had hoped, Imogen reflected. She braced herself. "I wish to collect on that promise."

"Oh, dear," Horatia whispered. She sounded resigned to a dreadful fate.

"Just how do you propose to collect the debt that I owed to your uncle, Miss Waterstone?" Matthias finally asked.

"Well, as to that," Imogen said, "it is somewhat complicated."

"Somehow that does not surprise me."

Imogen pretended not to hear that unencouraging remark. "Are you acquainted with Lord Vanneck, sir?"

Matthias hesitated. Cold disdain appeared briefly in his gaze. "He is a collector of Zamarian antiquities."

"He was also the husband of my good friend Lucy Haconby."

"Lady Vanneck died some time ago, did she not?"

"Yes, my lord. Three years ago, to be precise. And I am convinced that she was murdered."

"Murdered?" For the first time, Matthias actually showed a trace of surprise.

"Oh, Imogen, surely you do not intend—" Horatia broke off and closed her eyes in dismay.

"I believe she was murdered by her husband, Lord Vanneck," Imogen said forcefully. "But there is no way to prove it. With your help, sir, I intend to see that justice is done."

Matthias said nothing. He did not take his eyes off Imogen's face.

Horatia rallied. "My lord, surely you will talk her out of this wild scheme."

Imogen scowled at Horatia. "I dare not wait. An acquaintance has written to tell me that Vanneck is preparing to marry again. He has apparently suffered some serious financial reverses."

Matthias shrugged. "That much is true. A few months ago Vanneck was forced to sell his large town house and move into a much smaller residence. But he still manages to keep up appearances."

"I suspect that he is even now prowling the ballrooms

and drawing rooms of London in search of a wealthy young heiress," Imogen said. "He might very well murder her too, once he has his hands on her fortune."

"Imogen, really," Horatia said weakly. "You must not make such accusations. You have absolutely no proof."

"I know that Lucy feared Vanneck," Imogen insisted. "And I know that Vanneck was frequently cruel to her. When I visited Lucy in London just before her death, she confided to me that she was afraid he might someday murder her. She said that he was insanely jealous."

Matthias set his cup down and rested his elbows on his thighs. He loosely clasped his hands between his knees and regarded Imogen with an expression of reluctant interest. "Just how do you intend to carry out your scheme, Miss Waterstone?"

Horatia was horrified. "Good heavens, you must not encourage her, my lord."

"I find myself somewhat curious," Matthias said dryly. "I would like to hear the details of this plan."

"Then all is lost," Horatia muttered. "Imogen has a way of sweeping others up into her schemes."

"I promise you that I am not easily swept along by much of anything unless I so choose," Matthias assured her.

"I pray you will remember those bold words later, sir," Horatia muttered.

"My aunt is inclined to be overanxious at times, my lord," Imogen said. "Do not worry, I have planned this out very carefully. I know what I am doing. Now then, as you just observed, Lord Vanneck is an extremely zealous collector of all things Zamarian."

"So?" Matthias's mouth twisted humorlessly. "Vanneck may fancy himself an expert, but in truth he would not know a genuine Zamarian artifact from the hindquarters of a horse. Even I. A. Stone displays more perception."

Horatia set her cup down with a small crash. Her eyes darted from Matthias to Imogen and back again.

Imogen took a very deep breath and composed herself. "You have frequently argued with I. A. Stone's conclusions in the pages of the *Zamarian Review*, I believe."

Matthias was politely amused. "You have kept up with our little squabbles?"

"Oh, yes. I have maintained a subscription to the *Review* for several years, my lord. I always find your articles extremely enlightening."

"Thank you."

"But I also find I. A. Stone's writings to be quite thought-provoking," she added with what she hoped was a bland smile.

Horatia frowned in warning. "Imogen, we seem to be straying from the subject. Not that I am particularly desirous of returning to that other topic, however—"

"I. A. Stone has never even been to Zamar," Matthias said through his teeth. A flare of genuine emotion lit his ghostly eyes for the first time that morning. "He has no firsthand knowledge of his subject, yet he feels free to make observations and reach conclusions based upon my work."

"And the work of Mr. Rutledge," Imogen pointed out hastily.

The warm emotion died in Matthias's eyes as swiftly as it had appeared. "Rutledge died four years ago on his last trip to Zamar. Everyone knows that. His old writings are sadly out of date. I. A. Stone should know better than to use them in his researches."

"I was under the impression that I. A. Stone's papers were quite well received by the members of the Zamarian Society," Imogen said tentatively.

"I will admit that Stone has a certain superficial familiarity with Zamar," Matthias allowed with gracious arrogance. "But it is the sort of knowledge one gleans from studying the work of a more informed expert."

"Such as yourself, my lord?" Imogen asked politely.

"Precisely. It is obvious that Stone has read virtually everything I've written on Zamar. And then he has the incredible gall to disagree with me on any number of points."

Horatia coughed discreetly. "Er, Imogen?"

Imogen resisted the urge to pursue the matter. Horatia was right. She had other priorities. "Yes, well, back to Vanneck. Regardless of his intellectual limitations, you must admit that he is known to be consumed with a passion for Zamarian artifacts."

Matthias looked as though he would have preferred to continue the heated discussion of I. A. Stone's lack of expertise. But he allowed himself to be drawn back to the subject of Vanneck. "He covets anything said to be from ancient Zamar."

Imogen steeled herself. "I shall be blunt, sir. Rumor has it that you are of a like-minded nature. The difference between the two of you is that you are the undisputed authority on Zamarian antiquities. I'm sure you collect with exquisite taste and discretion."

"I allow only the finest, rarest, and most interesting Zamarian artifacts under my roof." Matthias watched Imogen with an unblinking gaze. "In other words, only those that I personally unearthed. What of it?"

Imogen was astonished by the tiny chill that went down her spine. There were very few things that could unsettle her nerves, but some quality in Matthias's voice did just that on occasion. She took a deep breath. "As I told you, I have no proof with which to accuse Vanneck of murder. But I owe Lucy too much to allow her killer to go entirely unpunished. For three years I have tried to devise a plan to accomplish my goal, but it was not until Uncle Selwyn died that I finally saw a way to avenge Lucy."

"What, exactly, do you intend to do to Vanneck?"

"I have hit upon a way to destroy him in the eyes of the ton. When I have finished, Vanneck will be in no position to prey on innocent women such as Lucy."

"You are quite serious about this, are you not?"

"Yes, my lord." Imogen lifted her chin and met his eyes without flinching. "I am extremely serious. I intend to set a trap for Vanneck, one that will ruin him financially and socially."

"A trap requires bait," Matthias pointed out softly.

"Quite right, my lord. The lure I intend to use is the Great Seal of the Queen of Zamar."

Matthias stared at her. "Are you claiming to possess the Queen's Seal?"

Imogen frowned. "Of course not. You of all people should know that the seal has never been found. But shortly before he disappeared, Rutledge sent a letter to the *Zamarian Review* informing the editors that he believed he was on the trail of the seal. The rumors that he died in the underground labyrinth while searching for the thing inspired the Rutledge Curse."

"Which is rubbish." Matthias lifted one shoulder in an elegant shrug. "That damned notion of a curse persists only because the seal was said to be extremely valuable. Legends always abound concerning objects of great worth."

"Your own researches claim that the seal is fashioned of a very pure gold and encrusted with valuable gems," Imogen reminded him. "You wrote that you had seen inscriptions that described it."

Matthias's jaw tightened. "The true value of the seal lies in the fact that it is an object fashioned by the finest artisans of a vanished people. If the seal exists, it is priceless, not because it is made of jewels and gold but because of the tales it can tell us of ancient Zamar."

Imogen smiled. "I comprehend your feelings, sir. I would expect you to take just such a scholarly view of the seal. But I can assure you that a man of Vanneck's base nature will be far more intrigued by the financial value of the thing. Especially in his present reduced circumstances."

Matthias's smile was unpleasant. "You are no doubt correct. What has that to do with your scheme?"

"My plan is simple. I shall travel to London with Aunt Horatia and work my way into Vanneck's social circles. Thanks to Uncle Selwyn, I have the money to do so. And thanks to Aunt Horatia, I also have the proper connections."

Horatia stirred uneasily in her chair. She gave Matthias an apologetic glance. "I am distantly related to the Marquess of Blanchford on my mother's side."

Matthias frowned. "Blanchford is traveling abroad, is he not?"

"I believe so," Horatia admitted. "He usually is. It is no secret that he cannot abide Society."

"He and I have something in common on that point," Matthias said.

Imogen ignored that. "Blanchford rarely puts in an appearance during the Season. But that is no reason Aunt Horatia and I should not do so."

"In other words," Matthias said, "you are going to trade on your aunt's connections in order to carry out this mad scheme."

Horatia rolled her eyes toward the heavens and made a tut-tutting sound.

Imogen glowered at Matthias. "It is not a mad scheme. It is very clever. I have been working on it for weeks. Once I am in the proper social circles, I shall drop little hints concerning the Queen's Seal."

Matthias raised laconic brows. "What sort of hints?"

"I shall let it be known that while conducting an inventory of my uncle's collection, I happened across a map that contains clues to the location of the seal."

"Hell's teeth," Matthias muttered. "You intend to convince Vanneck that this nonexistent map can lead him to a fabulous artifact?"

"Precisely."

"I do not believe what I am hearing." Matthias finally looked at Horatia for support.

"I did try to warn you, my lord," she murmured.

Imogen leaned forward eagerly. "I shall convince Vanneck that I intend to share the clues to the seal with whoever will help finance an expedition to retrieve it."

Matthias gave her a quizzical look. "What good will that do?"

"Isn't it obvious? Vanneck will be unable to resist the notion of going after the seal. But as his finances are in a bad way at the moment, and he has not yet found himself an heiress, he lacks the funds to underwrite an expedition himself. I shall encourage him to form a consortium of investors."

Matthias eyed her thoughtfully. "Allow me to hazard a guess. You intend to draw Vanneck out on a financial limb and then cut off the limb, do you not?"

"I knew you would understand." Imogen was pleased that he was finally beginning to perceive the true genius of the plan. "That is exactly what I intend. It should be no great trick to convince Vanneck to put together a consortium to finance the expedition."

"And when he has spent the consortium's money to hire a ship and a crew and to purchase the expensive equipment needed for the expedition, you will provide him with a useless map."

"And off he will go on a fool's voyage," Imogen concluded with a satisfaction she did not bother to conceal. "Vanneck will never find the Queen's Seal. The expedition will collapse when the money runs out. The members of the consortium will be furious. There will be rumors that it was all a great fraud perpetrated upon innocent investors. Another South Seas Bubble. Vanneck will not dare to return to London. His creditors will hound him for years. If and when he does come back, he will certainly not be able to take his previous place in the ton. His chances of recouping his fortunes with an heiress will be thin indeed."

Matthias looked bemused. "I do not know what to say, Miss Waterstone. You take my breath."

There was a certain satisfaction to be derived from having such an electrifying effect on Colchester of Zamar, Imogen thought. "It is a clever plan, is it not? And you are a perfect partner for me, sir."

Horatia appealed to Matthias. "My lord, pray tell her that it is a mad, dangerous, reckless, foolish plan."

Matthias glanced briefly at Horatia and then returned his cold gaze to Imogen. "Your aunt is quite right. It is all of those things and more."

Imogen was stunned. "Nonsense. It will work. I am sure of it."

"I know that I shall regret asking, Miss Waterstone, but morbid curiosity compels me. What role have you created for me in this grand scheme?"

"Isn't it obvious, my lord? You are the acknowledged authority on all things Zamarian. With the possible exception of I. A. Stone, there is no finer scholar on the subject."

"There is *no* exception," Matthias corrected her grimly. "Especially not I. A. Stone."

"If you insist, my lord," Imogen murmured. "Every member of the Zamarian Society is aware of your qualifications."

Matthias brushed aside the obvious. "So?"

"I would have thought it self-evident, sir. The simplest and most effective way to convince Vanneck that I have a genuine map to the Queen's Seal is for you to indicate that you believe I possess such a map."

A short, sharp silence gripped the library.

"Damnation." Matthias sounded almost awed. "You want me to persuade Vanneck and the rest of the ton that I believe your uncle left you a map of ancient Zamar that shows the location of the seal?"

"Yes, my lord." Imogen was relieved that he had finally grasped the essentials of the scheme. "Your interest in the map will lend the necessary credibility to my tale."

"And just how am I expected to display this interest?"

"That is the easy part, my lord. You will pretend to seduce me."

Matthias said nothing.

"Oh, dear," Horatia whispered. "I believe I feel a trifle faint."

Matthias gazed at Imogen with expressionless eyes. "I am to seduce you?"

"It will be a pretense, of course," she assured him. "All of Society will notice that you are pursuing me. Vanneck will conclude that there is only one reason you would do so."

"He will think that I am after the Queen's Seal," Matthias said.

"Precisely."

Horatia heaved another heartfelt sigh. "We are doomed."

Matthias tapped one finger very gently against the rim of his teacup. "Why should Vanneck or anyone else conclude that I am intent only on seduction? Everyone knows that I have recently returned to England in order to assume my responsibilities to the title. Society will expect me to be hunting a wife this Season, not a mistress."

Imogen sputtered on a swallow of tea. "Do not concern yourself, my lord. You run no risk of finding yourself inadvertently engaged to me. No one will expect you to make me an offer."

Matthias searched her face. "What of your reputation?"

Imogen set her cup down with great precision. "I see you do not know who I am. Not surprising, I suppose. You have been out of the country a good deal of the time during the past few years."

"Perhaps you will enlighten me as to your true identity?" Matthias growled.

"Three years ago when I visited my friend Lucy in London, I acquired the nickname Immodest Imogen." She hesitated. "My reputation was compromised beyond repair."

Matthias's brows came together in a dark line. He glanced at Horatia.

"It's quite true, my lord," Horatia said quietly.

Matthias looked at Imogen. "Who was the man?"

"Lord Vanneck," Imogen said.

"Bloody hell," he said softly. "No wonder you want revenge."

Imogen straightened. "That incident has nothing to do with this. I do not give a fig for my own reputation. It is Lucy's murder that must be avenged. I told you the story because I want you to understand that Society does not consider me a suitable candidate for marriage. No one would expect a man of your position to pursue me for anything other than a brief affair or the opportunity to acquire something valuable."

"Such as the Queen's Seal." Matthias shook his head. "Bloody hell."

Imogen stood up briskly and gave him an encouraging smile. "I believe you have the gist of the thing now, my lord. We can go over the details of my plan this evening at supper. In the meantime, we have an inventory to complete. As you are here, and there is really nothing else for you to do, perhaps you would care to assist us?"

Chapter 2

Horatia sidled closer to Matthias as soon as they were alone in the library. "My lord, you have got to do something."

"Do I?"

Horatia's anxious expression congealed into one of stern disapproval. "Sir, I am well aware of just who you are and what you are. As it happens, ten years ago I lived in London."

"Indeed?"

"I did not move in your circles, my lord. But then, few respectable people did. However, I know how and why you earned the name Cold-blooded Colchester. My niece knows you only as Colchester of Zamar. She has admired you for years. She is not acquainted with your more notorious activities."

"Why don't you inform her of them, Mrs. Elibank?" Matthias asked very softly.

Horatia took a quick step back, as though she expected him to spring at her with bared fangs. "It would do no good. She would dismiss the tales as malicious gos-

sip. I know her. She would assume that your reputation was unjustly shredded, just as hers was. She would no doubt become your strongest ally and staunchest supporter."

"Do you really think so?" Matthias gazed thoughtfully at the doorway. "I have never had very many of those."

Horatia glared at him. "Very many of what?"

"Strong allies and staunch supporters."

"I think we both know that there are some very good reasons for that, my lord," Horatia snapped.

"As you say."

"Colchester, I realize that I have no claim on your consideration, but I am quite desperate. My niece is determined upon this rash plan. You are my only hope."

"What the devil do you expect me to do?" Matthias glanced over his shoulder to make certain Imogen had not reappeared in the doorway. "No offense, madam, but I have never encountered a female quite like Miss Waterstone. She leaves a man feeling as if he had just been trampled by the hunt."

"I know what you mean, sir, but you must do something or we shall all find ourselves enmeshed in this grand scheme of revenge that she has concocted."

"We?" Matthias plucked a leather-bound volume off the nearest shelf.

"I assure you, Imogen will not give up her scheme if you refuse to cooperate. She will merely find another means to implement it."

"Strictly speaking, that is not my problem."

"How can you say that?" Horatia looked desperate. "You did make that promise to my brother, sir. It was in Selwyn's will. It is said that you always keep your promises. Even your worst enemies, and I understand that there are any number of them, do not deny that."

"It's true, madam, I always keep my promises. But I do so in my own fashion. In any event, my debt was to Selwyn Waterstone, not to his niece."

"Sir, if you would repay that debt to my dear, departed brother, you must keep Imogen from coming to grief."

"Imogen expects another sort of assistance entirely from me, madam. She seems hell-bent on coming to grief and, given her fortitude and determination, I expect she will achieve her goal."

"She is amazingly strong-minded," Horatia admitted.

"She puts both Napoleon and Wellington to shame." He inclined his head toward the shelves full of books. "Take my present occupation, for example. I have no clear notion of precisely how I come to find myself assisting Miss Waterstone with the inventory of her uncle's collection."

"That sort of thing happens frequently around my niece," Horatia said ruefully. "She has a tendency to take charge of a situation."

"I see." Matthias glanced at the title of the book in his hand. *An Account of the Strange and Unusual Objects Found in Tombs Discovered in Certain South Seas Islands.* "I believe this goes on your list."

"Books on tomb artifacts, do you mean?" Horatia bustled over to the desk and frowned at a page in the open journal. She dipped a quill into the ink and made a note of the book. "Very well, you may put it with the others."

Matthias set the volume down on top of a growing pile of similar titles. He surveyed the remaining volumes absently, his brain busy with the more important problem of Imogen Waterstone. He told himself that he needed information before he could decide upon a course of action.

"How did Vanneck compromise your niece, madam?"

Horatia's mouth tightened. "It is a very unpleasant story."

"If I am to take any sort of action, I must know the facts of the matter."

Horatia eyed him with some hope. "I suppose you may as well hear the details from me rather than one of the London gossips. And it is not as though you were not saddled with a somewhat nasty reputation yourself, is it, my lord?"

Matthias met her eyes. "That is very true, Mrs. Elibank. Your niece and I have that much in common."

Horatia suddenly became keenly interested in an ancient Etruscan death mask. "Yes, well, three years ago Lucy asked Imogen to come to see her in London. Lady Vanneck had been married for over a year at that point, but that was the first time she had bothered to invite Imogen to visit."

"Did Imogen stay with Lord and Lady Vanneck?"

"No. Lucy claimed that she could not invite her to stay in the mansion because Lord Vanneck would not tolerate guests in the household. She suggested that Imogen take a small house for a few weeks. Lucy made all the arrangements."

Matthias frowned. "Imogen went off to London by herself?"

"Yes. I was unable to join her because my husband was extremely ill at the time. Not that Imogen considered that she needed a companion, of course. She has a very independent nature."

"I noticed."

"I lay the blame squarely at the feet of her parents, God rest their souls." Horatia sighed. "They loved her dearly and meant to do their best, but I fear that they gave her an extremely unconventional upbringing."

"How is that?" Matthias asked.

"My brother and his wife were considerably advanced in years when Imogen was born. Indeed, they had both abandoned any hope of having children. When Imogen came along, they were thrilled."

"She has no brothers or sisters?"

"No. Her father, John, who was my eldest brother, was a philosopher who had radical notions concerning the education of young people. He saw in Imogen a golden opportunity to test his theories."

"And her mother?"

Horatia grimaced. "Alethea was a most unusual lady. She created something of a stir in her younger days. Wrote a book that seriously questioned the value of marriage to females. My brother fell in love with her the instant he read it. They were wed immediately."

"In spite of the lady's views on marriage?"

"Alethea always said that John was the only man in the entire world who could have made her a suitable husband." Horatia hesitated. "She was right. In any event, Alethea also had developed a host of strange notions about the education of females. Indeed, she wrote another book describing them."

Matthias was briefly amused. "In other words, Imogen is the product of a radical philosophical experiment?"

"I fear that is precisely the case."

"What happened to your brother and his wife?"

"They both succumbed to lung infections the year Imogen turned eighteen." Horatia shook her head. "I had often warned them that their habit of smoking that vile American tobacco was most unhealthy. Fortunately, Imogen did not adopt the practice."

"You were about to tell me what happened three years ago when Imogen went to London." Matthias paused at the sound of brisk footsteps in the hall.

Imogen stuck her head around the edge of the door and gave Matthias and Horatia an inquiring look. "How is the inventory going in here?"

Matthias held up a bound volume of the *Quarterly Review of Antiquities* which he had just come across. "I believe we are making satisfactory progress, Miss Waterstone."

"Excellent." Imogen glanced down at a list in her hand. "I have devised a schedule which, if we adhere to it, should see us finished with the inventory of the first floor before we leave for London on Thursday. Aunt Horatia and I will finish the rest of the house at our leisure when we return in a few weeks' time. Keep up the good work." She lifted one hand in a cheerful wave and hurried off down the hall.

Matthias gazed thoughtfully after her. "What an amazing creature."

"I fear that nothing can dissuade her from her purpose, my lord," Horatia said forlornly.

Matthias set the *Quarterly Review of Antiquities* down on a table. "You were telling me about how she came to be compromised three years ago."

"If only I had been able to join her in London. Imogen considers herself a woman of the world, but you know as well as I do, sir, that after a lifetime spent here in Upper Stickleford, she was woefully unprepared for London Society. Furthermore, her parents both detested the Polite World. They taught her a great many useless subjects such as Greek and Latin and logic, but they did not teach her anything helpful such as how to survive in Society."

"A lamb among wolves," Matthias murmured. "But a lamb with some teeth, I think."

"Her friend Lucy was certainly no help," Horatia said bitterly. "Lady Vanneck definitely bore some of the responsibility for the incident. But that was Lucy for you. I know Imogen counted her a dear friend, but the truth is, Lucy never cared a jot for anyone but herself."

"You knew Lucy?"

"I met her on occasion when I visited my brother and his family. She was very beautiful and she could be charming. But she used her beauty and charm to manipulate others. She broke the hearts of several of the young farmers here in Upper Stickleford. As far as I'm concerned, she became friends with Imogen only because there were no other young ladies in the vicinity. She did not even bother to correspond with Imogen after she moved to London until a full year had passed. And then, out of the blue, she sent for Imogen."

"What happened in London?"

"For a time all went well. Imogen got involved in the Zamarian Society. She has been passionate about Zamar since the age of seventeen. That was the year you and Rutledge returned from your first expedition. She joined the Zamarian Society shortly after it was formed, but she had not had an opportunity to meet any of the members until she went to London."

"I regret to say that the Zamarian Society is composed largely of amateurs and dilettantes." Matthias set his jaw. "Unfortunately, Zamar has become fashionable."

"Perhaps. But for the first time, Imogen was able to mingle with others who shared her interests. She was very excited. You must remember that she was alone following the death of her parents. Lucy had been her only friend, and after Lucy went off to London and married Vanneck, Imogen was very lonely. I fear that the study of Zamar became everything to her. Meeting others of a like-minded nature was very exciting for her."

"Whom, precisely, did she meet?" Matthias asked warily. The fascination with Zamar had brought into the ranks of the Zamarian Society an assortment of dangerously bored young bloods, debauched rakes, and others seeking excitement.

"Lucy introduced Imogen to a nice young man named Alastair Drake." Horatia hesitated. "It was the only truly decent thing Lucy ever did for Imogen. Mr. Drake shared Imogen's enthusiasm for ancient Zamar."

"Did he, indeed?"

"The pair got along famously from all accounts. I heard from friends that Mr. Drake developed a *tendre* for Imogen. There was even talk of an offer of marriage. But then the disaster struck."

Matthias abandoned any pretense of continuing with the inventory. He propped one shoulder against the bookshelf and folded his arms. "Disaster in the form of Lord Vanneck, I presume?"

Horatia's eyes were bleak behind the lenses of her

spectacles. "Yes. Imogen had not the faintest notion of how to deal with a hardened rakehell bent on seduction. There was no one to guide her or advise her." She stopped talking abruptly, yanked a hankie from the pocket of her apron, and dabbed at her eyes. "It is difficult to even speak of the incident."

"I must ask you to finish the tale, madam," Matthias said ruthlessly. "I cannot decide how to proceed until I know everything there is to know about this situation."

Horatia slanted him an uncertain glance and then appeared to come to a decision. She stuffed the hankie back into a pocket. "Very well, sir. It is no secret after all. Everyone in Town knew of the incident, and when Imogen returns, the gossip will no doubt be resurrected. The long and the short of it is that Imogen was discovered in a bedchamber with Vanneck."

For some reason, Matthias felt as though he had just been kicked in the stomach. He was puzzled by the violent reaction. It took him a moment to realize that he had not been expecting to hear quite such a dramatic ending to the tale.

He had imagined something a good deal more innocent. After all, it took very little to ruin a young woman's reputation in Society. An indiscreet kiss, venturing out alone to shop or ride without a maid, too many waltzes with the wrong man, any number of such harmless lapses could make a woman notorious. Appearances were everything among the ton.

But being discovered in a bedchamber with a man, any man, let alone one of Vanneck's stripe, was more than a minor indiscretion, Matthias thought. Immodest Imogen had apparently earned her title. She was fortunate that the epithet had not been worse.

"Was it Vanneck's bedchamber?" Matthias made himself ask. "Or did she invite him to her house?"

"Of course not." Horatia averted her gaze. "But in the end it might have been better if the incident had occurred at some such private location. Unfortunately, Imogen and Vanneck were discovered together in an upstairs bedchamber during the course of a ball given by Lord and Lady Sandown."

"I see." Matthias had to exert an effort to quell the whip of anger that had uncurled in him. What the devil was wrong with him? He barely knew the lady. "Your niece certainly does not do things by halves, does she?"

"It was not her fault," Horatia said with touching loyalty. "Vanneck lured her to that bedchamber."

"Who discovered them?"

Horatia heaved another sigh of regret. "Mr. Drake, the nice young man who was on the verge of making an offer. He was accompanied by a companion. Naturally, there was no more talk of marriage after the incident. One could hardly blame Mr. Drake for losing interest."

"Drake could at least have kept his mouth shut about what he had seen."

"I expect he did," Horatia said. "But as I said, he had a companion with him that night. The other man was obviously not such a gentleman."

Matthias released a deep breath that he had not realized he had been holding. "I take it the incident, as you term it, put an end to the friendship between Miss Waterstone and Lady Vanneck?"

"Lucy took her own life the day after Vanneck was discovered with Imogen. She left a note saying that she could not endure the knowledge that her best friend had betrayed her with her husband."

Matthias considered that briefly. "How did she kill herself?"

"She took a great quantity of laudanum."

"Then there is no question but that she committed suicide?"

"None so far as the rest of the world is concerned. Imogen is the only one who believes that Vanneck murdered Lucy. I fear my niece's view of the matter is clouded by her own dreadful experience at his hands. Perhaps she feels a measure of guilt. But what happened in that bed-chamber was Vanneck's fault. I have no doubt of that."

Matthias glanced at the empty doorway of the library. "And now, three years later, Miss Waterstone has hit upon this crazed notion of avenging her friend."

"I thought she had put it all behind her," Horatia confided. "But through her membership in the Zamarian Society, she corresponds with a vast number of people. A few weeks ago one of them conveyed the information that Lord Vanneck was hanging out for an heiress. My brother had just died and left Imogen this house and its contents and your, er, promise to him. Imogen was suddenly inspired."

"*Inspired* is not quite the word I would have chosen." Matthias straightened away from the bookcase. He paused as he caught sight of a recent volume of the *Zamarian Review*. He scowled when he noticed the date. "Damnation."

"Is something wrong, my lord?"

"No." He picked up the copy of the *Review* and flipped through the pages. "This just happens to be the issue in which the editors published two articles on the interpretation of Zamarian inscriptions. One written by me and one by I. A. Stone. The fellow haunts me."

"I see." Horatia busied herself with a funeral urn.

"For some reason, the editors gave Stone's article considerable attention even though any dolt can see that he is completely wrongheaded in his conclusions. I shall speak to them about it."

"You're going to speak to the editors about publishing I. A. Stone's papers?"

"Why not? I founded that damned journal. I have a responsibility to ensure that only the most scholarly articles are printed in it."

"I take it I. A. Stone's conclusions about Zamarian inscriptions did not agree with your own, my lord?" Horatia asked very dryly.

"No, they did not. It was especially irritating because,

as usual, Stone based his conclusions on the results of my own published researches." Matthias took a grip on his outrage. He generally regarded the work of other Zamarian scholars with complete disinterest and disdain. He knew better than anyone else that since Rutledge's disappearance, he had no equal in the field.

There had been no real challenge to Matthias's authority on the subject until I. A. Stone had exploded upon the scene eighteen months earlier in the pages of the *Review*.

To Matthias's increasing annoyance and total bemusement, I. A. Stone was proving to be the first person in years who was capable of kindling any kind of strong response in him. He did not understand it. He had never even met Stone. Thus far, Matthias knew his new rival only by his writings. Soon, he promised himself, he would track Stone down and have a word with the upstart.

"My lord?" Horatia said cautiously. "About our little problem?"

"Forgive me, madam, Stone is a sore point with me."

"I can see that, sir."

"Ever since I returned to England a few months ago I have been made increasingly aware of his encroaching articles in the *Review*. Members of the Zamarian Society actually take sides now when Stone and I disagree in print."

"I can certainly understand your feelings on the subject, sir, given your unquestioned position in the field," Horatia said diplomatically.

"Unquestioned position? I. A. Stone questions my position at every opportunity. But that is another issue. It is Imogen and her mad scheme that we are discussing."

Horatia searched his face. "Yes, it is."

"I suppose it is unlikely that the incident three years ago will make it impossible for her to reenter Society?"

"Do not pin your hopes on the possibility that she will not receive the proper invitations," Horatia advised. "I fear Society will find her vastly entertaining. The combination of my connection to Blanchford, her own respectable inheritance from Selwyn, and her tale of a map that will lead someone to a Zamarian treasure will all combine to captivate the jaded interest of the ton."

"She will not be considered marriageable, but she will definitely be entertaining," Matthias said softly.

"I fear that sums it up rather nicely."

"It is a recipe for disaster."

"Yes, my lord. You are my only hope. If you do not find a way to alter her course, Imogen will surely sail straight into the sea of catastrophe." Horatia paused just long enough to add weight to her next words. "It seems to me that if you truly mean to repay your debt to my brother, you must save Imogen. That is what Selwyn would have wanted."

Matthias raised his brows. "You have a rather concise way of summing up matters yourself, Mrs. Elibank."

"I am desperate, sir."

"You must be, if you think to manipulate me toward your own ends with that promise that I gave your brother."

Horatia gasped, but she held her ground. "My lord, I beg you will prevent my niece from pursuing this folly."

Matthias held her eyes with his own. "You claim to be acquainted with my reputation, Mrs. Elibank. If that is so, then you must know that I am more inclined to destroy others than to save them."

"I am well aware of that, sir." Horatia spread her hands. "But there is no one else. She will not listen to me. And you did make that promise to my brother. The whole world knows that Cold-blooded Colchester always keeps his promises."

Matthias turned away without responding. He walked out the door and crossed the hall to the staircase. He took the steps two at a time.

When he reached the landing he stopped to listen. A loud crash followed by several muffled thumps told him that his quarry was working in the east wing. He went down the corridor with long, determined strides.

Imogen Waterstone had already caused enough commotion in his life, he decided. It was time he took control of his own fate. He always fulfilled his promises, but, as he had warned Horatia, he did so on his own terms.

A series of thuds guided him to the open door of a bedchamber on the left side of the passageway. Matthias halted in the opening and surveyed the interior.

The chamber was a dark, shadowed room that had been decorated in the same funereal style as the rest of the house. Heavy black curtains had been tied back from the windows, but the light that entered had little impact on the overall gloom. The bed was shrouded in colors suitable to mourning. Black and maroon hangings cascaded from the ceiling.

Far and away the most interesting sight in the chamber was Imogen's nicely rounded backside. Matthias felt a sharp tug in the vicinity of his groin.

The lush curve of Imogen's derriere was displayed in a provocative manner due to her somewhat awkward position. She was bent over at the waist, attempting to haul a large iron-bound trunk out from under the black-draped bed. The skirts of her bombazine gown had risen several inches in back to reveal elegantly shaped calves clad in white stockings. Matthias had a sudden, nearly overwhelming desire to explore the territory above the tops of the stockings.

The powerful wave of desire that rolled through him took him by surprise. He drew a long breath and forced himself to concentrate on the problem at hand.

"Miss Waterstone?"

"What in the world?" Imogen came upright with a quick, startled movement. She whirled around, her face flushed from her recent exertions. Her hand swept out and struck a small, ugly statue of a tomb deity standing on a nearby table. The little clay monstrosity crashed to the floor and shattered.

"Oh, dear." Imogen frowned at the broken statue.

"Don't waste any regrets on it," Matthias advised after a single glance at the remains of the statue. "It's not Zamarian."

"No, it isn't, is it?" Imogen reached up to straighten her little white cap, which had listed to one side. "I did not hear you coming down the hall, my lord. You cannot possibly be finished with the library?"

"No, madam, I have barely even begun. I have come up here to discuss something more important."

She brightened. "Our plans to trap Vanneck?"

"Your plans, not mine, Miss Waterstone. Mrs. Elibank and I have discussed the matter in some detail, and we are both of the same opinion. Your scheme is ill-advised, rash, and possibly quite dangerous."

Imogen stared at him, dismay darkening her eyes. "Sir, you cannot stop me."

"I was almost certain you would say that." He studied her for a moment. "What will you do if I refuse to assist you by playing the role that you have assigned to me?"

She eyed him uncertainly. "You refuse to keep your promise to my uncle?"

"Miss Waterstone, the promise I made to Selwyn was rather vague in nature. It is open to interpretation, and since I made the promise, I shall interpret it."

"Hmm." She put her hands on her hips and began to tap her toe. "You intend to default on your promise, do you not?"

"No. I always keep my promises, Miss Waterstone, and this one will be no exception." Matthias realized he was growing angry. "I have concluded that the best way I can repay my debt to your uncle, however, is to keep you out of dangerous mischief."

"I warn you, sir, you may refuse to aid me, but you cannot stop me from carrying out my plan. I will admit that your support would be invaluable, but I am certain that I can attract Vanneck's attention without you."

"Is that so?" Matthias took a step into the chamber. "And just how will you do that, Miss Waterstone? Will you meet him in a private bedchamber again as you did three years ago? I must admit, such an offer will no doubt capture his interest."

Imogen looked dumbfounded for an instant. Then outrage lit her eyes. "How dare you, sir?"

Chagrin lanced through Matthias. He suppressed it. The ends justified the means in this case, he assured himself. He clamped his teeth together. "I apologize for bringing up the incident, Miss Waterstone."

"As well you should."

"But," he continued relentlessly, "I fail to see how either of us can ignore the past. Facts are facts. If Vanneck seduced you once, he will surely attempt to do so again. And unless you intend to use your very charming person to lure him into your plot—"

"*Bloody hell.* Vanneck did not seduce me three years ago, sir. He compromised me. There is a vast difference."

"There is?"

"One is reality, the other is merely a matter of appearances." Imogen sniffed disdainfully. "I would have thought that a man of your intelligence would have been able to detect the essential distinction between the two."

Matthias's temper flared without warning. "Very well, split hairs, if you will. It changes nothing. The problem remains. You are not going to find it easy to handle a man of Vanneck's nature."

"I assure you, I can and will handle him. But I am beginning to think that you are correct in one regard, sir. Perhaps I do not require your services. When I initially formed my plan, I thought you would be extremely useful, but now I begin to wonder if you might prove more of a hindrance than a help."

For some reason that Matthias could not fathom, Imogen's scathing retort served only to further fan the flames of his anger. "Indeed?"

"Obviously you are not the man I had believed you to be, my lord."

"Hell and damnation. Just what sort of man did you believe me to be?"

"I had assumed, incorrectly it seems, that you were a man of action, the sort of man who does not flinch from danger. A man capable of going forth into adventure without a second's hesitation."

"Where did you gain that peculiar notion?"

"From your articles on ancient Zamar. I concluded from the thrilling accounts of your travels and explorations that you had actually lived through those adventures." She gave him a scornful smile. "Perhaps I was mistaken."

"Miss Waterstone, are you implying that I base my articles on secondhand researches, as that damnable I. A. Stone does?"

"I. A. Stone is entirely honest about the sources of *his* information, sir. He does not claim to have observed firsthand all that he writes about. You do. You pass yourself off as a man of action, but now it seems that you are not that sort of man at all."

"I do not pass myself off as anything but what I am, you exasperating little—"

"Apparently you write fiction rather than fact, sir. Bad enough that I thought you to be a clever, resourceful gentleman given to feats of daring. I have also been laboring under the equally mistaken assumption that you are a man who would put matters of honor ahead of petty considerations of inconvenience."

"Are you calling my honor as well as my manhood into question?"

"Why shouldn't I? You are clearly indebted to me, sir, yet you obviously wish to avoid making payment on that debt."

"I was indebted to your uncle, not to you."

"I have explained to you that I inherited the debt," she retorted.

Matthias took another gliding step into the grim chamber. "Miss Waterstone, you try my patience."

"I would not dream of doing so," she said, her voice dangerously sweet. "I have concluded that you will not do at all as an associate in my scheme. I hereby release you from your promise. Begone, sir."

"Bloody hell, woman. You are not going to get rid of me so easily." Matthias crossed the remaining distance between them with two long strides and clamped his hands around her shoulders.

Touching her was a mistake. Anger metamorphosed into desire in the wink of an eye.

For an instant he could not move. His insides seemed to have been seized by a powerful fist. Matthias tried to breathe, but Imogen's scent filled his head, clouding his brain. He looked down into the bottomless depths of her blue-green eyes and wondered if he would drown. He opened his mouth to conclude the argument with a suitably repressive remark, but the words died in his throat.

The outrage vanished from Imogen's gaze. It was replaced by sudden concern. "My lord? Is something wrong?"

"Yes." It was all he could do to get the word past his teeth.

"What is it?" She began to look alarmed. "Are you ill?"

"Quite possibly."

"Good heavens. I had not realized. That no doubt explains your odd behavior."

"No doubt."

"Would you care to lie down on the bed for a few minutes?"

"I do not think that would be a wise move at this juncture." She was so soft. He could feel the warmth of her skin through the sleeves of her prim, practical gown. He realized that he longed to discover if she made love with the same impassioned spirit she displayed in an argument. He forced himself to remove his hands from her shoulders. "We had best finish this discussion at some other time."

"Nonsense," she said bracingly. "I do not believe in putting matters off, my lord."

Matthias shut his eyes for the space of two or three seconds and took a deep breath. When he lifted his lashes he saw that Imogen was watching him with a fascinated expression. "Miss Waterstone," he began with grim determination. "I am trying to employ reason here."

"You're going to help me, aren't you?" She started to smile.

"I beg your pardon?"

"You've changed your mind, haven't you? Your sense of honor has won out." Her eyes glowed. "Thank you, my lord. I knew you would assist me in my plans." She gave him an approving little pat on the arm. "And you must not concern yourself with the other matter."

"What other matter?"

"Why, your lack of direct experience with bold feats and daring adventure. I quite understand. You need not be embarrassed by the fact that you are not a man of action, sir."

"Miss Waterstone—"

"Not everyone can be an intrepid sort, after all," she continued blithely. "You need have no fear. If anything dangerous occurs in the course of my scheme, I shall deal with it."

"The very thought of you taking charge of a dangerous situation is enough to freeze the marrow in my bones."

"Obviously you suffer from a certain weakness of the nerves. But we shall contrive to muddle through. Try not to succumb to the terrors of the imagination, my lord. I know you must be extremely anxious about what lies ahead, but I assure you, I will be at your side every step of the way."

"Will you, indeed?" He felt dazed.

"I shall protect you." Without any warning, Imogen

put her arms around him and gave him what was no doubt meant to be a quick, reassuring hug.

The tattered leash Matthias was using to hold on to his self-control snapped. Before Imogen could pull away, he wrapped her close.

"Sir?" Her eyes widened with surprise.

"The only aspect of this situation that truly alarms me, Miss Waterstone," he said roughly, "is the question of who will protect me from you."

Before she could reply, he crushed her mouth beneath his own.

Chapter 3

Imogen stilled. For an instant all her senses seemed to collide, producing a dazzling chaos. She had always prided herself on the strength of her nerves. She had never suffered from an attack of the vapors, never felt faint, never succumbed to light-headedness or a giddy sensation. But at that moment she felt utterly dazed.

Her breath caught in her throat. Her palms were suddenly damp. Her thoughts, which had been quite lucid only a second before, were now in a shambles. Everything around her appeared to have gone suddenly askew. She shivered and then felt a delicious, almost feverish warmth spread through her.

If she had not been positive that she enjoyed excellent health, she would have thought she was ill.

Matthias groaned and deepened the kiss, crushing her closer to his hard, unyielding body. She felt his tongue trace her lips and realized with a shock that he wanted her to open her mouth for him. Intense curiosity swept over her. Tentatively, she parted her lips. Matthias's tongue surged between them.

Shocked by the intimate kiss, Imogen went weak at the knees. The world spun around her. She gripped Matthias's shoulders very tightly, afraid that she would fall if he were to release her.

But Matthias made no move to set her free. Instead, his arms tightened around her, pulling her so close that she could feel the alarming bulge in his snug breeches. She knew that he must surely be aware of her breasts pressed against his broad chest. He shifted slightly, bending her backward. One of his booted feet slid between her legs. She could feel the fierce strength in his thigh.

Sensations flowed through Imogen, wild, turbulent feelings that were unlike any she had ever known. She was not entirely without experience, she reminded herself in a desperate bid for sanity. But there was no denying that not even Philippe D'Artois's practiced kisses or Alastair Drake's chaste embraces had tumbled her senses into such shimmering disarray.

Passion. This was true passion at long last. A thrill of fiery excitement unfurled within Imogen.

With a soft, wordless exclamation of delight that was somewhat muffled by the pressure of Matthias's demanding mouth, she tightened her arms around his neck.

"Imogen." Matthias raised his head. His austere face was taut. His eyes were no longer an emotionless, ghostly gray. They burned. It was as though he looked into an oracle glass in search of answers to some unknown question. "What the devil am I doing?"

Reality returned with a shattering effect. Imogen gazed at Matthias, aware that he regretted the rash impulse that had made him take her into his arms.

Ruthlessly Imogen squelched the keen sense of loss that welled up within her. She fought for composure while she desperately sought appropriate words for a most inappropriate situation.

"Calm yourself, my lord." She struggled to adjust her cap. "This was not your fault."

"It wasn't?"

"No, indeed," she assured him breathlessly. "This sort of thing can happen when the darker passions are aroused. My parents had the very same problem. Any argument that flared between them always ended in this fashion."

"I see."

"You and I were quarreling a moment ago and I expect the emotions of the moment temporarily overcame your self-mastery."

"I knew I could depend upon you for an intelligent explanation, Miss Waterstone." Matthias's eyes gleamed. "Are you ever at a loss for words?"

Uncertainty tingled deep within her. Surely he was not mocking her. "I expect there are occasions when even the most articulate person might be unable to find just the right word, my lord."

"And other occasions when only action will suffice." He cradled the back of her head in one powerful hand, held her still, and slowly bent his head to kiss her again.

This time the kiss was deliberate, calculated, and devastating. Imogen went limp in Matthias's arms. She heard her cap fall to the carpet with a soft plop. Her hair tumbled free. Matthias buried one hand in it.

Imogen swayed. The world around her became fluid and began to dissolve. The only solid thing left in it was Matthias. And he was very solid, indeed. The strength in him at once overwhelmed and enthralled her. A sweet hunger swept through her. She locked her arms around Matthias's neck again and held on with all her might.

"You offer one surprise after another," Matthias whispered against her mouth. "Not unlike Zamar."

"My lord." She was dazzled by his words. To be compared to ancient Zamar was beyond anything. No one had ever paid her such a profound compliment.

Matthias eased her back one step and then another. She came up against the wardrobe without any warning. Matthias captured her wrists in his hands and pinned them to the carved mahogany door behind her head.

Holding her there, he freed her mouth to trace a scorching series of kisses down her throat. At the same time, he drew his thigh up between her legs. The skirts of her gown foamed over his breeches.

"Good heavens." Imogen sucked in her breath. Matthias's leg moved higher between her thighs. "I cannot think—"

"Neither can I at the moment." He released her wrists. His powerful, elegant hands settled around her throat. He tipped her head back.

Imogen grabbed awkwardly at the handle of the wardrobe to steady herself. But at that exact instant Matthias whirled her away toward the bed.

Imogen forgot to let go of the handle. The wardrobe door came open with a jarring crash. The large object sitting on the middle shelf shuddered beneath the impact and started to topple forward.

Matthias tore his mouth away from Imogen's throat. "What the devil . . . ?"

Imogen watched in horror as the bowl slipped over the edge of the shelf and plummeted downward. *"Oh, no."*

Matthias moved with startling, graceful speed. He released Imogen, stepped around her, and caught the bowl in a single lithe movement.

"Bloody hell." Matthias gazed at the bowl cradled in his hands.

Imogen breathed a sigh of relief. "That was a very near thing, my lord. You move quite quickly."

"When there's a good reason to do so." He smiled slightly as he studied the bowl.

His eyes still gleamed, Imogen noted, but not precisely the same way they had a moment earlier. She took a closer look at the bowl. It was delicately sculpted from a translucent blue-green stone. The stone was unique to Zamarian artifacts. Imogen had been told by one of her correspondents that the fashionable had labeled the color Zamarian green. The bowl was inscribed with words written in a flowing script that was as elegant as the vessel itself. Imogen recognized the language immediately.

"Zamarian." She gazed at the bowl with wonder. "Uncle Selwyn told me that he had some Zamarian artifacts, but I did not realize that he possessed anything so lovely."

"It probably came from a Zamarian tomb."

"Yes." She leaned closer to examine the bowl. "This is a very fine piece, is it not? Look at the words. Informal script rather than formal. A personal offering left in the burial chamber of a loved one, if I am not mistaken."

Matthias tore his gaze away from the bowl long enough to give her an assessing glance. "You recognize the script?"

"Yes, of course." Gingerly she took the sea-green bowl from him and turned it slowly in her hands, marveling at the beautiful workmanship. "*As Zamaris embraces Anizamara at day's end, our two spirits shall be joined for all time.* Isn't that a lovely sentiment, my lord?"

"Hell's teeth." Matthias stared at her with a dark intensity even greater than that with which he had gazed at the bowl. "There is only one person other than myself in all of England who could have translated that line of informal Zamarian script so quickly and so flawlessly."

Too late, Imogen realized what she had just done. "Oh, dear."

"I presume that I have just had the pleasure of kissing I. A. Stone?"

"My lord, I assure you, I never intended to deceive you."

"No?"

"Well, perhaps just a trifle. I was going to explain everything."

"Eventually?"

"Yes. Eventually. At the proper time." She tried to summon up what she hoped was a placating smile. "We have been so busy since you arrived, what with one thing and another, that there simply has not been an opportunity."

Matthias ignored the weak excuse. "The first initial is plain enough. And it's obvious where the Stone came from, Miss Water*stone*. But what does the middle initial stand for?"

"Augusta," Imogen confessed with a small sigh. "Sir, please understand. I have kept my identity a secret because I knew that the editors of the *Review* would never publish my researches if they learned that they had been written by a woman."

"Indeed."

"I intended to reveal the truth to you as soon as we were properly introduced. But you made it clear straight off that you considered I. A. Stone a rival. I did not want that view to cloud your perception of me or my scheme."

"A rival?" Matthias raised his brows. "Nonsense. I do not consider I. A. Stone a rival. The word *rival* implies someone who is on an equal footing. I. A. Stone is a presumptuous little scribbler who bases her ridiculous conclusions on my articles."

Imogen was stung. "May I remind you, sir, that good, solid interpretation of facts is every bit as important as firsthand experience."

"There is no substitute for firsthand knowledge of a subject."

"Rubbish. In the past you have leaped to a number of conclusions about Zamarian antiquities that were unwarranted by the evidence that you yourself discovered."

"Such as?"

Imogen lifted her chin. "Such as those entirely unsupported assumptions concerning Zamarian wedding rituals that you detailed in your latest article in the *Review*."

"I never make unsupported assumptions. I arrive at logical conclusions based upon firsthand discovery and research."

"Indeed?" Imogen fixed him with a challenging glare. "You claimed that the bride had no say in her marriage contract, when it is obvious to even an amateur that Zamarian brides had a great many rights and privileges. A Zamarian lady could even dissolve her marriage if she wished."

"Only under extremely limited conditions."

Imogen smiled coolly. "She could do so if her husband proved to be either cruel or impotent. That covers a great deal of ground, my lord. Furthermore, she retained control of her own property and income after marriage. That certainly puts ancient Zamarian law well ahead of modern English law."

"Do not be too certain of that," Matthias said. "When it came to marriage, the Zamarians were not so vastly different from the English. The man was the master in his own home. His wife was expected to be an obedient, compliant companion who saw to the running of the household and to her husband's comfort. He in turn assumed the responsibility of protecting his wife and children."

"There you go, making unwarranted assumptions again. After a thorough investigation of your writings, I have concluded that Zamarian marriages were based on mutual affection and intellectual respect."

"Only a fevered imagination and a complete lack of firsthand familiarity with your subject could lead you to make such an outrageous statement. Zamarian marriages were based on property, social standing, and business considerations, just as most English marriages are."

"That is not true," Imogen shot back. "Mutual affection was the most important element in Zamarian marriages. What about the poetry you discovered in the ruins of the Zamarian library?"

"Very well, so a few Zamarian poets wrote a few silly romantic verses." Matthias ran a hand through his hair in a gesture of exasperated disgust. "That proves nothing. Marriage was a business matter in ancient Zamar, just as it is here in England."

"Are you claiming that the Zamarians did not believe in the power of love, my lord?"

"*Love* is a fine word for lust, which I'll wager was well known to the Zamarians. They were a very intelligent people, after all."

"Love is not the same thing as lust."

"But it is, Miss Waterstone." Matthias's jaw tightened. "I assure you, I have drawn that particular conclusion from firsthand observation, just as I draw all my conclusions. Unlike some people."

Imogen was outraged. "I am not entirely without some firsthand experience of the subject, sir, and I have drawn different conclusions."

Matthias's smile was cold. "You've had firsthand experience of lust? Would you care to go into detail, Miss Waterstone?"

"No, I would not. Such things are of a private nature."

"Indeed. Well, allow me to give you a few of my own firsthand observations on the subject of love and lust. I am the product of a union that began in the fires of a grand, lusty passion. But when that lust cooled, it left only bitterness, anger, and regret in its wake."

Shocked sympathy doused the smoldering embers of Imogen's temper. She took a quick step closer to Matthias and then halted uncertainly. "Forgive me, my lord, I did not understand that this was such a personal matter for you."

"Unfortunately it was too late for either of the two parties involved to escape." All inflection had vanished from Matthias's voice. "My mother was pregnant with me. Her family demanded marriage. My father's family wanted my mother's inheritance. It was a match made in hell. My father never forgave my mother. He claimed she had tricked him into marriage. For her part, my mother never forgave my father for seducing her and then turning against her."

"What a dreadful experience your childhood must have been."

An icy amusement appeared in his eyes. "On the contrary, I consider that experience to have been a salutary one, Miss Waterstone. I learned a great deal from it."

"No doubt you feel you learned a terrible lesson." Imogen suppressed a pang of sadness. Then a thought struck her. "You mentioned that you will be expected to wed now that you have come into the title. Surely you will seek happiness in your own alliance?"

"You may be certain of that," Matthias said grimly. "I intend to contract a marriage based on a far more substantial foundation than one built on foolish romantic passions and lust."

"Yes, of course," Imogen murmured.

Matthias took the glowing blue-green bowl from her hands and gazed at it with deep contemplation. "I seek a bride endowed with common sense rather than one who has muddled her brains with romantic poetry. An intelligent female who is ruled by an educated mind. One whose sense of honor will ensure that she does not develop a passion for every dark-eyed poet who comes along."

"I see." It was difficult to comprehend how she could have been so wrong about this man, she thought wistfully. The Colchester of Zamar she had conjured in her mind was imbued with the very essence of romance. The real Colchester was obviously a bit of a stick-in-the-mud. "It is very odd, sir, but when I sent for you, I had convinced myself that we had much in common."

"Had you?"

"Yes. But now I see that I was quite mistaken. We are as opposite as two people can be, are we not, my lord?"

He looked abruptly cautious. "In some respects, perhaps."

"In every important respect, so far as I can see." Imogen gave him a wan smile. "I hereby release you from your promise, my lord."

He scowled. "I beg your pardon?"

"It was wrong of me to expect you to assist me in my scheme." Imogen studied the manner in which his sensitive, long-fingered hands cradled the Zamarian bowl. "You have quite convinced me that you are not cut out for this type of adventure and that I have no right to insist on your services."

"I thought I made it clear that you are not going to get rid of me quite so easily, Miss Waterstone."

"Sir?"

"I shall assist you in your plot. I may not be the man you believed me to be, Miss Waterstone, but I find myself consumed by a desire to prove myself something more than a milksop."

Imogen was horrified. "Sir, I never meant to imply that I thought you a . . . a milks—"

He held up one hand to cut off her protest. "You have made yourself clear. You perceive me to be possessed of an overanxious, fainthearted temperament. I do not deny that there is some truth to that perception, but I'll be damned if I will have you label me an out-and-out coward."

"Sir, I would never have dreamed of labeling you a coward. A certain tendency toward nervous weakness is not something that should cause shame. It is no doubt a family trait, rather like that blaze of white in your hair. It is something over which you have no control, my lord."

"Too late, Miss Waterstone. I have decided that I must fulfill my promise to your uncle. It is the only way I can retain even a few shreds of my pride."

"*I* was appalled, if you must know the truth," Imogen confided to Horatia two days later as they set out for London in a post-chaise. They were alone in the carriage because Matthias had left the previous day with the list of instructions that she had given him. "He is doing this to prove that he is not lacking in nerve. I fear I wounded his

pride. I never meant to do it, but you know how I sometimes get carried away when I feel strongly about a matter."

"I wouldn't worry overmuch about Colchester's
pride," Horatia said crisply. "He has more than enough
arrogance to last him a lifetime."

"I wish I could believe that, but I'm convinced he is
possessed of rather delicate sensibilities."

"Delicate sensibilities? Colchester?"

"I wore out my tongue attempting to dissuade him
from assisting me, but as you saw, I had no success."

"Colchester certainly seems determined to help you
pursue this mad scheme. I wonder what he is about."

"I just told you what he is about. He is attempting to
prove himself a man of action. Anyone can see that he is
no such thing."

"Hmm." Horatia adjusted the skirts of her carriage
dress and leaned back against the cushions. She fixed Imogen with a thoughtful gaze. "In the beginning, I told you
that your plan was dangerous in the extreme because I
feared Lord Vanneck's reaction. But I am now persuaded
that involving Colchester is an even more reckless move."

"Colchester is not dangerous." Imogen wrinkled her
nose. "Indeed, I only wish he were. I would not be so
concerned. As it is, in addition to managing the details of
my scheme, I shall be obliged to keep an eye on him. I
must make certain that in his enthusiasm to prove himself,
he does not get into trouble."

Horatia stared at her niece askance. "You are going
to watch over Colchester?"

"It is the least I can do under the circumstances."
Imogen gazed glumly out the window. "He is not at all
what I expected, Aunt Horatia."

"You keep saying that. Be honest, Imogen, your expectations were built upon a fantasy that you had concocted out of vapor and smoke."

"That is not true. I developed my notion of his lordship's temperament from the articles he wrote for the

Zamarian Review. It only goes to prove that one cannot put much credence in everything one reads."

Horatia peered at Imogen through her spectacles. "My dear, you do not understand about Colchester. I have tried to tell you that his reputation was firmly established nearly a decade ago when he was in his early twenties. I know you will not believe this, but the truth is that he was considered extremely dangerous and utterly cold-blooded."

Imogen grimaced. "Nonsense. One cannot know him for even five minutes without realizing that such a reputation is completely at odds with the true nature of the man. He is obviously the victim of nasty gossip, just as I was three years ago."

"He certainly seems to have convinced you of that," Horatia muttered. "I wonder why."

"I appear to be stuck with his assistance," Imogen said, resigned to the situation. "He will no doubt prove to be more trouble than he is worth."

"I would not be surprised if he is saying precisely the same thing about you at this very moment, my dear."

Imogen did not respond. She turned her attention back to the countryside that was passing by outside the carriage window. Fragments of the dream that had awakened her in the middle of the night returned. She'd had similar dreams for the past several weeks, but last night's imaginings had been the clearest and most disturbing.

She was standing in the library of Uncle Selwyn's mansion. It was midnight. Pale moonlight slanted through the windows. Shadows bathed the chamber and its sepulchral furnishings.

She turned slowly, searching for the man she knew was there. She could not see him. She had never seen him. But she sensed his presence. He was waiting, cloaked in deepest night.

Something or someone stirred in the darkest corner of the chamber. She watched with trepidation as a figure detached himself from the surrounding shadow and walked slowly toward her. His face was concealed by the gloom, but when he moved through a patch of moonlight she saw the glint of cold silver in his hair.

Zamaris, Lord of the Night. Powerful, seductive. And very dangerous.

He came closer, his hand outstretched.

Not Zamaris, she realized. Colchester.

Impossible.

But for some reason, she could not seem to differentiate between the two. Colchester and Zamaris had coalesced into one single creature of the night.

She looked at the hand that he held out to her and saw blood dripping from his long, elegant fingers.

*H*e was going to regret becoming involved with Miss Imogen Waterstone, Matthias told himself for what was no doubt the thousandth time since he had arrived in London. She was already having a damaging effect on his powers of concentration.

He set down his quill and gazed unseeingly at the notes he was making for his next article in the *Review*. Thus far he had covered less than half of a sheet of foolscap with his speculations on Zamarian rituals. Thoughts of Imogen's imminent arrival in Town kept intruding.

She and Horatia were due to arrive that day. Her wild, reckless plan would no doubt be set in motion shortly thereafter. All she required were a few invitations to the right levees and balls. Horatia seemed convinced they could be obtained.

Matthias rose from his chair and walked around the corner of his vast ebony desk. He went to stand in front of the fire, aware of a deep, gnawing restlessness. It had been troubling him since he had returned to London.

He was a fool to become embroiled in Imogen's mad scheme. The only positive note that he could see in the murky picture was that the damnable plot was highly unlikely to work. Unfortunately, there would doubtless be some extremely trying moments ahead before Imogen would be convinced to give up her grand plan of vengeance. Matthias glumly contemplated the fact that it would be up to him to keep her out of trouble until she accepted defeat.

She was determined to set forth on a path fraught with the threat of scandal and danger. Matthias considered her scheme once more, attempting to be objective. He did not believe that Vanneck had actually murdered his wife. Vanneck was a sly, dissipated, unprincipled rake who had an unpleasant reputation in the brothels and hells, but he did not strike Matthias as a killer. The ruthless seduction of an innocent, naive young lady such as Imogen was more Vanneck's style. Matthias's hand flexed into a tight fist at his side.

He closed his eyes and thought about the way Imogen had responded to him when he had taken her into his arms. A wave of sweet, searing heat went through him, stoking the fire that had been smoldering in his loins since he had left Upper Stickleford. He could not remember the last time a woman's kiss had produced such a lingering effect on his senses. He tried to will away the desire that had flared within him. When that failed, he pictured Imogen with Vanneck in the bedchamber above the Sandowns' ballroom. His gut turned to ice.

Matthias knew what was happening, and it worried him as nothing else had for a long while. He wanted Imogen for himself. The vision of her in Vanneck's debauched embrace was almost enough to make him contemplate murder.

He took a deep breath, gazed into the heart of the fire, and searched for the ghosts. They were there, as they always were, reaching out for him as though to draw him down into the flames to join them. So damn many of them.

Matthias had been ten years old when his father, Thomas, had raged through the house for the last time, shouting at Elizabeth, who was, as usual, in tears.

Matthias had witnessed the final battle through the posts of the upstairs balustrade. The awareness of his own inability to stop the dreadful words or stem the flood of his mother's tears had made his hands shake. He wanted to run and hide. Instead, he had made himself watch as the father he had never been able to please did battle with the mother he could never comfort.

He had heard the same terrible accusations hurled back and forth between his parents many times, but this was the first occasion on which he had actually understood them.

After all these years the words still burned in his brain.

"You trapped me, you conniving, coldhearted bitch," Thomas had shouted as he faced his wife in the front hall. "You used your body to seduce me and then you deliberately got yourself pregnant."

"You told me that you loved me," Elizabeth had flung back. "I was an innocent, but you had no scruples about bedding me, did you?"

"You lied to me. You told me that you knew how to keep from getting yourself with child. Damn you, I never intended to marry you. I never felt anything but a fleeting lust for you. No more than I would feel for a whore."

"You talked of love," Elizabeth wailed.

"Bah. I have had enough of this loveless marriage. You wanted the title, well, you have it, but, by God, Elizabeth, that is all you shall have from me."

"You cannot leave me, Thomas."

"I cannot rid myself of you by any legal means. Divorce is out of the question. But I refuse to condemn myself to a lifetime of unhappiness. Enjoy the title you used your body to obtain. You shall have this house and an allowance, but I shall never step foot in this hall again. I shall take up residence in London. If you must communicate with me about any matter of grave importance, you will do so through my solicitors."

"What of Matthias?" Elizabeth asked desperately. "He is your son and heir."

"I have only your word for that," Thomas said harshly. "For all I know, you slept with half the members of my club."

"He's your son, you bloody bastard. The law will not allow you to deny it."

"I am well aware of that, madam," Thomas said. "But one day I shall learn the truth concerning just how badly I was deceived. Every man in my family develops a streak in his hair by the age of twenty."

"So will Matthias. You'll see. In the meantime, you cannot ignore him."

"I shall do my duty by him," Thomas vowed. "It is past time that Matthias was sent away to school. If he stays in this house a moment longer, you will no doubt bind him to you so tightly with your damned tears and apron strings that he will never become a man."

"You cannot send him away. He is all I have. I will not allow it."

"You have no choice, madam," Thomas had retorted. "I have already made the arrangements. His tutor has been dismissed. With any luck Eton and Oxford will undo the damage you have tried to inflict."

School had not been altogether unpleasant. Having spent the first ten years of his life attempting to please his father, Matthias continued the futile effort. He had thrown himself into his studies.

Thomas had paid little attention to the boy's scholarly successes, but something unusual did occur during those years. Unlike the majority of his companions, Matthias had actually become enthralled by the classical texts that formed the core of the curriculum. As he grew older they continued to draw him with an inexplicable power. He sensed the secrets hidden deep within them.

Long, melancholic letters from Elizabeth had kept him informed of her endless complaints about his father's selfish, tight-fisted ways, the house parties she had planned, and her illnesses. Matthias dreaded going home between terms, but he did so because something inside him told him that it was his duty. As the years passed, he saw enough of his mother to realize that between house parties she had begun to treat her depressed spirits with increasing quantities of wine and laudanum.

The letters from his father had been few and far between. They were concerned primarily with the high cost of Matthias's school expenses and angry diatribes about the relentless financial demands Elizabeth made through the solicitor.

Elizabeth drowned in an estate pond the winter of Matthias's fourteenth year. The servants said that she had had a great deal of wine at dinner that night and several glasses of brandy afterward. She had told her staff that she wished to take an evening walk alone.

Her death had been declared an accident, but Matthias sometimes wondered if his mother had committed suicide. Either way, he was doomed to bear a measure of guilt for the rest of his life because he had not been there to save her. His mother would have wanted it that way, he thought wryly.

He could still see his father standing on the other side of Elizabeth's grave. It was a memorable occasion for many reasons, not the least of which was that Matthias had made his first serious promise to himself that day. He had looked into his father's face and silently vowed that he would never again bother to try to please him. A coldness had settled somewhere inside him that day. It had never disappeared.

Thomas had been blithely unaware of Matthias's mood. He had taken him aside immediately after the funeral and jubilantly announced his intention to wed again. Thomas's relief at being free of Elizabeth and his happy anticipation of his forthcoming nuptials had stood in sharp contrast to the colors of mourning that surrounded them.

"Her name is Charlotte Poole, Matthias. She is lovely

and gracious and pure. A noble paragon of womanhood. She will bring me a happiness I have never known."

"How nice for you, sir."

Matthias had turned on his heel and walked away from his mother's grave. He had known then that her ghost would follow him.

The letter from Thomas announcing the birth of a daughter, Patricia, had come a year after the earl's marriage to Charlotte. Matthias had carefully read the joyful, glowing words his father had penned describing his "deep and abiding affection" for his infant daughter and her mother. When he was finished, Matthias had consigned the birth announcement to the hearth. As he watched the letter burn, he thought he saw his mother's ghost in the flames. Hers proved to be the first of many.

The streak of silver appeared in Matthias's hair almost overnight. Thomas began to send increasingly earnest letters to his son, inviting him to visit his new family. Matthias ignored them.

By the time he had finished his studies, Matthias was well steeped in Greek, Latin, hazard, and whist. Regular trips down to London with his friends had given him an intimate familiarity with the worst gaming hells and with the contents of the British Museum.

It was in the museum that he had first encountered the clues to lost Zamar. It was there, too, that he had met George Rutledge, a highly respected scholar and an expert on antiquities. Rutledge had invited Matthias to make use of his private library.

Rutledge's impressive library contained more evidence of the existence of the lost island kingdom. Rutledge was as enthusiastic as Matthias about the possibility of discovering Zamar. The only problem that loomed on the horizon was that of obtaining the money for an expedition. Matthias solved that difficulty in a unique manner, one that scandalized Society and outraged his father.

He opened a gaming hell.

In the years that followed Matthias's discovery of

Zamar, there were several notes from Lord Colchester inviting him to visit his small family at their country home. Matthias had politely declined. He had managed to avoid meeting his stepmother and his half sister.

He had been en route home from Zamar a few months earlier when Thomas and Charlotte had been killed in a carriage accident. The funeral was held several weeks before he reached England. Patricia had gone to live with an uncle on her mother's side immediately after her parents had been buried.

Matthias had arrived in London to discover that he had assumed the earldom and a few more ghosts.

Chapter 4

If things got out of hand, he would play the one card he held, Matthias promised himself Tuesday evening as he walked into the glittering ballroom. There was a possibility that once Imogen's scheme was launched, he might be able to sink it by making it clear to Vanneck and the ton that he had concluded her uncle's map was a fraud.

It would be risky. There was no guarantee such a tactic would work. Imogen was I. A. Stone, after all. She was determined to keep her identity a secret, but she was perfectly free to quote Stone's opinions at great length. If I. A. Stone, who had attracted an enthusiastic and devoted following who respected her opinions, let it be known that he considered the map to be genuine, Vanneck might very well go for the bait regardless of Matthias's opinion. There were many in Society who would very much like to see Matthias proved wrong.

He disregarded the speculative glances and covert stares directed at him as he moved through the large room. He pretended not to hear the whispered comments that ebbed and flowed around him.

Cold-blooded Colchester.

He had never lived down the reputation he had acquired a decade before. Then again, he had never made any effort to do so. He'd had more important things to accomplish in the intervening years. Lost Zamar had consumed him body and soul. At least it had until Imogen Waterstone dragged him into this outlandish scheme.

For the most part, Matthias ignored the Polite World. He made no secret of his disdain for the frivolous fashions and vicious gossip that were its lifeblood. As a consequence, the ton thought him fascinating.

Matthias exchanged cool nods with an acquaintance and helped himself to a glass of champagne from a passing tray. He lounged against one of the appallingly overwrought, heavily gilded columns that decorated the ballroom and drew his watch from his pocket. Nearly eleven. Curtain time.

In an extremely detailed note that had arrived very early at his town house that morning, Imogen had given him his instructions for his role in tonight's performance. She had gone so far as to supply him with a short script designed to guide him through their first conversation together in front of the ton. He had been ordered to act as though he were being introduced to her for the first time.

After a cursory glance at the ridiculous lines of dialogue that he was supposed to memorize, Matthias had tossed the sheet of foolscap into the fire. He was no Edmund Kean, and Lady Blunt's ballroom was not Drury Lane. Nevertheless, he was there.

And he was intrigued, in spite of himself.

Imogen's little charade was outlandish, outrageous, and crazed in the extreme. He would no doubt live to rue his part in it. But he could not deny the sense of anticipation he felt.

It occurred to him that in the short while since he had known her he had experienced any number of unfamiliar sensations, everything from disbelief to a disturbing degree of desire. In between, he had suffered irritation, astonishment, and bemusement, more sensations, in short, than he had been obliged to deal with in the past decade. The lady was dangerous.

"Good evening, Colchester. This is certainly a surprise. Something interesting must be scheduled to occur here in Lady Blunt's ballroom this evening. I cannot imagine any other reason for you to have condescended to accept an invitation."

At the sound of the familiar, throaty tones, Matthias turned to glance at the woman who had come up beside him. He inclined his head slightly. "Selena." He raised his glass in a small toast. "My compliments. Spectacular, as always, madam."

"Thank you, sir. One does one's best."

"And in your case, one always succeeds."

If Selena, Lady Lyndhurst, was aware of the hint of mockery in his words, she did not allow it to show. She merely smiled with cool acceptance of the obvious. She *was* spectacular. Everyone in Town acknowledged that fact.

Selena was in her late twenties. She had taken up residence in London four years earlier following the death of her elderly husband. She had shown no inclination to remarry, but her name was occasionally linked, albeit discreetly, with certain gentlemen of the ton. Beautiful, stylish, and clever, she took advantage of the unique freedom she enjoyed as a wealthy widow.

Selena had joined the Zamarian Society, but in Matthias's opinion her interest in antiquities would be short-lived. She was certainly intelligent enough to study the subject, but, as was the case with a majority of the members, her concern with ancient Zamar was a matter of fashion rather than scholarly fascination. When Zamar ceased to be amusing, she would move on to some other entertainment.

Selena's pale gold hair, sky-blue eyes, and strong tendency to favor celestial blue in her gowns had earned her the sobriquet the Angel. The young bloods of the ton

wrote odes to her "heavenly aspect" and "ethereal aura."
The older, more jaded gentlemen concentrated on trying
to charm her into their beds. From what he had heard,
Matthias knew that few were successful. Selena was extremely selective when it came to choosing her paramours.

His instincts told him that she was the sort of woman
whose charm and beauty inspired passion in others but
who was not strongly affected by it herself.

Tonight she was dressed in her customary hue of
blue. The gown, which exposed a vast expanse of snowy
bosom, was trimmed with a net of iridescent gold. The
fine threads glittered in the light of the chandeliers. Gold
plumes danced in her hair. Her hands were sheathed in
long blue gloves. Blue satin slippers adorned her feet. The
very picture of an angel, Matthias thought. He wondered
what had become of her wings.

A brief vision of Imogen's tawny hair and lively sea-
colored eyes danced in his head. There was nothing ethereal about Imogen Waterstone. She was vivid and sharp
and bright. The very opposite of the ghosts he saw in the
fire. Any passion she indulged would be very real, not a
practiced imitation of the emotion. The memory of the
kiss they had shared flashed through Matthias's head.

His mouth twisted ruefully as he took a sip of champagne. He was not particularly attracted to angels, but he
seemed to have developed a taste for a certain lady who
had a bit of the devil in her.

"Come, Colchester, tell me what it is that brings you
here tonight." Selena surveyed the room. "Is it true that
you have decided to do your duty by your new title? Have
you descended upon Society this Season to hunt for a
bride?"

"Is that what the gossips say?"

"It is the prevailing theory at the moment," she admitted. "Tell me, do you have your eye on one of the
young ladies in this crowd?"

"And if I do?"

Selena uttered a laugh that was reminiscent of the

chime of crystal on crystal. "If you are truly shopping for a suitable bride, sir, I may be able to assist you."

"In what way?"

"With introductions, of course. You may have heard that I have formed a small salon to amuse myself. We gather in my drawing room twice a week for the purpose of studying ancient Zamar. I invite only young ladies of the finest families to attend. Tell me what you seek in the way of looks, address, age, and inheritance, and I shall select one or two for your consideration."

Matthias smiled humorlessly. "You sound as if you were employed in the auction yard at Tattersall's, Selena."

"Selecting a wife is not so very different from choosing a fine horse, is it, my lord?"

"I wouldn't know." Matthias swept a second glass of champagne off a tray and handed it to her. "I've never gone through the process. Tell me about your Zamarian salon, Selena. It does not sound quite your style. What possible amusement can you take from entertaining a group of young ladies twice a week?"

Selena's eyes glinted above the rim of her glass. "Does it not occur to you that I might simply enjoy instructing others in the mysteries of ancient Zamar?"

"No," he said bluntly. "I suspect it is far more likely that you have discovered that the naive young ladies are an excellent source of fresh gossip concerning the highest-ranking families in Society."

"I am, of course, crushed by your low opinion."

"Don't take it personally, Selena. I have a low opinion of most of the games played by the ton."

"You are hardly in a position to criticize, Colchester. Given that only a few years ago you established a gaming hell for the specific purpose of divesting gentlemen of the ton of their inheritances." Selena laughed softly. "And to think that you accuse me of playing games, sir. Your notion of entertainment takes away one's very breath."

No man had ever lost his entire inheritance at the gaming tables of The Lost Soul, Matthias reflected. He had made certain of it. But he saw no reason to explain that to Selena. She was highly unlikely to believe him, in any event. Certainly no one else in Society believed it. Even after all these years, gossip maintained that he had destroyed any number of fortunes during the years he had owned the hell.

"I prefer to find my amusements in other ways these days." Matthias surveyed the crowd, searching for Imogen. She should have arrived by then.

"Looking for someone in particular?" Selena asked. "Perhaps I should warn you that I noticed Theodosia Slott among the guests tonight."

Matthias suppressed a groan and kept his tone entirely devoid of inflection. "Indeed."

"Someday you really must tell me what actually happened when you shot her lover at that dawn meeting."

"I have no notion of what you're talking about," Matthias said smoothly. He would give Imogen another fifteen minutes, he decided. If she had not put in an appearance by then, he would abandon her to her own devices.

But he had no sooner made that firm resolve than he hastily changed his mind. The thought of Imogen left to her own devices was enough to chill his blood.

Selena slanted him a curious glance. "So you still refuse to discuss the duel even though it occurred several years ago? How very disappointing. Still, I cannot say that I am surprised. You are notorious for refusing to converse about anything other than ancient Zamar."

"There is little else in Society that is worth a lengthy conversation."

"I fear you are somewhat cynical, my lord." Selena paused as a small commotion broke out at the far end of the ballroom. "Well, well. It appears that someone interesting other than yourself has arrived."

Matthias followed Selena's glance. There was no mistaking the sly, eager buzz of the murmurs that rippled through the crowd. The anticipation reminded him of the atmosphere that hovered around a pack of hounds shortly before the start of the hunt. The scent of blood was in the air.

A name rode the crest of the conversational wave that splashed across the ballroom. Matthias caught it as it flowed past him.

"Immodest Imogen. The Waterstone chit. Do you not recall, my dear?"

"Don't know the details m'self. Happened three years back. All hushed up because of the family connection to the Marquess of Blanchford. Understand she came into a respectable portion when her uncle died."

"Her name was linked to Vanneck's in a most unpleasant fashion. Found together in a bedchamber at Sandowns', you know. Lady Vanneck killed herself because of the incident."

"Indeed. And she's still received in polite circles?"

"Immodest Imogen is nothing if not amusing, my dear. And her aunt is connected to Blanchford."

Selena fluttered her blue-and-gilt fan. "Immodest Imogen. I had almost forgotten her. Well, this should certainly prove amusing, my lord."

"Do you think so?"

"Yes, indeed. You were not in Town three years ago when she caused such a stir. An Original, to say the least. Quite the blue-stocking." Selena smiled. "You will appreciate this, Colchester. She was absolutely impassioned about ancient Zamar."

"Was she?"

"As I recall, she had no taste and absolutely no notion of style. I wonder if she ever learned to waltz properly."

Matthias slanted her a glance. "Did you know her well?"

"*Everyone* knew of her after the incident with Vanneck. It was the talk of the Season. I cannot see her from where I stand, sir. You are tall enough. Can you catch a glimpse of her over the heads of the crowd?"

"Yes," Matthias said softly. "I can see her quite clearly."

He watched Imogen's progress with mingled fascination and amused respect. Whether she intended to or not, she was certainly cutting a swath through the ballroom.

She was dressed in a high-waisted gown of Zamarian green. The color alone was not what made it distinctive, Matthias thought. After all, Zamarian green was popular this Season. It was the dolphin-and-shell design that trimmed the low neckline and the three tiers of flounces on her skirts that made one look twice. He smiled faintly. The motifs were certainly characteristic of Zamarian art, but the dolphins and shells looked rather odd on a ball gown.

Imogen wore a rather large Zamarian-green turban that concealed all but a few stray curls. The style was more suited to an elderly matron. A gold dolphin pin decorated the front of the imposing headdress.

Horatia, resplendent in a silver damask gown, was at Imogen's side. She had substituted an elegant lorgnette for her usual pair of spectacles.

Matthias swallowed a grin as he watched Imogen progress through the crowd. She did not walk with the tiny, airy steps that most of the other women had practiced so diligently. Rather, she strode forward with energetic enthusiasm.

As he watched her, it seemed to Matthias that his senses suddenly became more acute. He was aware of the flowery scents of the garden that wafted through the open French doors behind him. The candles massed in the huge chandeliers blazed a little brighter. The hum of conversation was harsher than it had been a few minutes before. And every other man in the crowd suddenly appeared predatory. Matthias knew that last observation was not solely a figment of his overheated imagination.

"I wonder if she thinks to find a husband," Selena mused. "Perhaps her aunt has convinced her that the inheritance she received recently will be enough to induce some desperate gentleman to make an offer. Which is quite possible."

Matthias brought his teeth together in an almost audible snap. Imogen had to know that the scandal of three years past had been resurrected in a matter of minutes. The Waterstone family's distant connection to the Marquess of Blanchford could get her back into Society, but it could not keep Society from gossiping. The whispers must have reached her by then, just as they had reached him.

He studied her closely. From where he stood she appeared unfazed by the talk that was roiling around her. It only went to prove that there was little that could intimidate Imogen.

He watched her with increasing admiration as she and Horatia made their way across the floor. He knew full well what it was like to enter a ballroom and hear an unpleasant epithet attached to one's name. It took courage to walk through this lot. How the devil was he to discourage her from carrying out her reckless scheme, when she demonstrated such a degree of raw nerve? he wondered.

"Colchester?"

Matthias pulled his attention back to Selena, who was watching him with an odd expression. "Sorry, I didn't catch that. What did you say?"

"I asked if there was something wrong."

"Wrong? Not at all." Matthias set his half-finished champagne glass down on a nearby tray. "Please excuse me, I have an urge to discover whether or not Miss Waterstone is, indeed, searching for a husband."

Selena's lovely mouth fell open in shock. Matthias realized that he had never seen such a startled expression on her face. He almost laughed aloud.

"Colchester, you cannot be serious!" Selena recovered her poise with some difficulty. "What on earth are you about? Never say that you are interested in Imogen Waterstone as a potential wife. My lord, I just told you, the gossip about her is most unpleasant."

"I rarely listen to gossip, Selena. I have heard far too much of it about myself to put any credence in it."

"But, Colchester, she was caught in a bedchamber with Vanneck, for God's sake. No man in your position would possibly consider making an offer for Immodest Imogen. It's not as though you need her money. Everyone knows you're as rich as Croesus these days."

"If you will excuse me, Selena, I must see about arranging an introduction."

He turned on his heel and strode straight into the first of several tightly wound skeins of people that cluttered the room. The knots in his path unraveled as if by magic as he approached. Matthias felt the riveted gazes follow him in avid speculation as he charted a clear course toward Imogen and Horatia.

He arrived at the edge of the growing circle that surrounded the pair at the same moment that Fletcher, Lord Vanneck, reached it.

Vanneck was so intent on Imogen that he did not see Matthias until he nearly trod on the toe of one of Matthias's brilliantly polished Hessians.

"Beg your pardon," Vanneck muttered as he maneuvered for a better vantage point. Then he recognized Matthias. Surprise flared in his heavily lidded eyes. "Colchester." Wary curiosity replaced the initial startled expression on his face. "Heard you were in Town. What the devil brings you here? Thought you couldn't stand this sort of affair."

"Everyone seems to be asking me the same question tonight. I am beginning to find it monotonous."

Vanneck flushed. His thin mouth tightened angrily at the rebuff. "Sorry."

"Pay me no mind, Vanneck. I am preoccupied with another matter this evening."

"Indeed."

Matthias ignored the deepening speculation in Vanneck's eyes. He had never cared for the man. Their paths crossed on occasion not only because Vanneck was a member of the Zamarian Society but because he also belonged to one or two of Matthias's clubs.

Matthias knew that Vanneck had once been accounted a handsome man by the ladies of the ton. But he was in his mid-forties now and the years of heavy drinking and debauched living had taken their toll. He had grown thick around the middle and jowls had softened his formerly square jaw.

Matthias watched as Imogen was introduced to their hostess, the plump, cheerful Letitia, Lady Blunt. It was obvious that Horatia and Letty were old friends. The two women were bubbling together like two pots on a stove. Letty was clearly thrilled at the stir she had created with her unexpected guests. Her ball would be on everyone's lips in the morning. Horatia had chosen the first invitation well.

"Imogen Waterstone," Vanneck offered. "Hasn't been in Town for some three years now. She was a friend of my late wife's."

Matthias slanted him a brief glance. "So I've heard."

Vanneck scowled. "You know her?"

"Let's just say that I know enough about her to seek an introduction."

"Can't imagine why," Vanneck muttered. "Woman's an oddity."

Matthias had a vision of this dissipated, self-indulgent bastard luring Imogen to a bedchamber and had to repress an almost overpowering urge to plant a fist in Vanneck's meaty face. He made himself turn away and push through the last circle of onlookers.

Imogen, who had been listening politely as Horatia and Letty exchanged news, brightened at the sight of him. Matthias smiled faintly.

"Colchester." Letty beamed at him. His presence there was a great coup, and she was well aware of what she owed him. In a single stroke he had made her a hostess to be reckoned with.

"Letty." Matthias bowed over her plump, gloved hand. "My congratulations on a most entertaining affair.

May I impose upon you for an introduction to your new guests?"

Letty's round face glowed with delight. "But of course, my lord. Allow me to present my great, good friend, Mrs. Horatia Elibank, and her niece, Imogen Waterstone. Ladies, the Earl of Colchester."

Matthias smiled reassuringly into Horatia's anxious eyes as he bowed over her hand. "A pleasure, Mrs. Elibank." He let his gaze glide across Imogen's eager face.

"My lord." Horatia cleared her throat. "You'll be interested to learn that my niece is a student of ancient Zamar."

"Indeed." Matthias took Imogen's gloved hand. He recalled the script Imogen had provided in her morning note. "What a coincidence. So am I."

Imogen's eyes danced in triumphant approval as he quoted the proper opening lines. "Sir, are you by any chance the Lord Colchester who discovered lost Zamar and made it more fashionable than ancient Egypt?"

"I am certainly Colchester." Matthias decided it was time to depart from the script. "As for Zamar, I can only say that it came into fashion simply because it is Zamar."

Imogen's gaze narrowed slightly at his improvised lines, but she stuck determinedly to her own role. "I am delighted to meet you, my lord. I believe we have much to discuss."

"There is no better time than now to begin the conversation. Will you honor me with this dance?"

She blinked in surprise. "Oh, yes, of course, sir."

With a nod to Horatia, Matthias reached out to take hold of Imogen's arm. He missed by several inches, as she had already started off through the crowd. He managed to catch up with her just as she reached the crowded dance floor.

Imogen turned smartly, stepped into his arms, and immediately swept him into an energetic waltz.

"It has begun." Excitement lit her eyes. "I was greatly relieved to see you here tonight, sir."

"I merely followed instructions."

"Yes, I know, but I confess I was a trifle concerned that you might have succumbed to your doubts about my scheme."

"I was rather hoping that you might have had a few qualms yourself by now, Imogen."

"Not at all." She cast a quick, searching glance from side to side and then steered him toward a quieter corner of the floor. "Have you seen Vanneck?"

"He's here." Being led about the dance floor by his partner was something of a novelty, Matthias reflected.

"Excellent." Imogen's hand tightened around Matthias's fingers. "Then he will have taken note of your sudden interest in me?"

"He and everyone else in the room. I do not generally make it a habit to be seen at this sort of thing."

"All the better. Aunt Horatia is planting the tale of the Queen's Seal in Lady Blunt's ear even as we speak. She will inform her that Uncle Selwyn left the map to me. Word will spread quickly. I expect Vanneck will hear the rumors tonight, or tomorrow at the very latest."

"No doubt, given the way gossip moves through Society," Matthias agreed grimly.

"As soon as he learns that I possess the key to the Queen's Seal, he will recall how you seized upon the opportunity to gain an introduction to me at the earliest opportunity." Imogen smiled with satisfaction. "He will immediately wonder why you would bother to do so. He will then conclude that there is only one obvious reason you would make it a point to meet me so quickly."

"The Queen's Seal."

"Precisely."

Matthias studied her obliquely. "There is another reason for my seeking an introduction tonight, you know."

She gave him a baffled look. "What is that, my lord?"

"I told you, Society believes me to be hunting for a wife."

Her face cleared. "Oh, yes. You did mention something along those lines. But no one is likely to conclude that you have fixed your interest on me for that reason."

"Why not?"

She frowned. "Don't be dense, Colchester. No one will expect you to be seriously interested in me as a wife. Do not concern yourself, sir. Society will assume exactly what we wish it to assume. You are after my map."

"If you say so." Conscious of their audience, Matthias smiled to conceal his exasperation. "I suppose there is no hope of talking you out of this plan?"

"None whatsoever, my lord. Indeed, I am very pleased with the way the thing has begun. Try not to fret. I shall see to it that you are not placed in any danger."

"If there is no possibility of convincing you to give up your scheme, is there any chance that I can persuade you to let me lead?"

"I beg your pardon?"

"I know it is somewhat boring and conventional, but I was taught to lead when I waltz with a lady."

"Oh." Imogen blushed a vivid shade of pink. "Forgive me, my lord. I am somewhat out of practice. I hired an instructor three years ago. He was French. The French are very skilled at that sort of thing."

"So I've heard." Out of the corner of his eye Matthias saw Vanneck hovering on the fringes of the crowd. He was watching Imogen with unmistakable interest.

"Philippe said that I had a natural aptitude for assuming the lead on the dance floor."

"Philippe?"

"Philippe D'Artois, my French dancing instructor," Imogen explained.

"Ah, yes. The dancing instructor."

Imogen demurely lowered her lashes. "Philippe said he found it quite thrilling to have the lady take the lead."

"Indeed?"

She cleared her throat discreetly. "He said it heated the blood in his veins. The French are inclined to be romantic, you know."

"Indeed."

Matthias was suddenly consumed by a fierce desire to know a great deal more about Imogen. He needed to find a place where they could have a private conversation, he decided. The gardens, perhaps.

By dint of brute strength, he managed to bring her to a halt at the edge of the floor. "Can I interest you in a breath of fresh air, Miss Waterstone?"

"Thank you, but I do not feel the need of any fresh air."

"Nonsense." He wrapped his fingers very firmly around her elbow and propelled her forcibly in the direction of the doors that opened onto the gardens. "It is quite warm in here."

"Truly, sir, I am not at all overheated."

"I am."

"I beg your pardon?"

"I expect it was the thrill of having you take the lead on the dance floor. You did tell me that it has a tendency to overheat the blood."

"Oh." Comprehension dawned on her face. "Yes, indeed. I quite understand. Fresh air is exactly what you require, sir."

Matthias plowed through the crowd with Imogen in tow. Just before he reached the doors, he was obliged to veer left to avoid an encounter with a cluster of curious onlookers.

It was the sudden change of direction that apparently caused the small disaster. Imogen was unprepared. She collided with a footman carrying a tray of champagne glasses.

There was a sharp exclamation from the footman. The tray slipped from his hands and fell to the floor. Glasses crashed and shattered. Champagne sprayed the gowns of the ladies who stood closest to the scene of the accident.

One of the ladies, Matthias saw, was Theodosia Slott.

Her eyes widened at the sight of him. Her mouth parted in shock. She put a hand to her full bosom.

"Colchester." Theodosia gave a muffled gasp, went quite pale, and slid to the floor in a graceful swoon.

"Bloody hell," Matthias said.

An uproar ensued. The gentlemen looked non-plussed. They glanced from the fallen Theodosia to Matthias and back again with confused expressions. Several ladies sprang into action. They reached for their vinai-grettes even as they turned their deliciously horrified gazes on Matthias.

"On second thought, Miss Waterstone—" Matthias paused when he saw that Imogen had gone to her knees to help the footman pick up the broken glass. He hauled her effortlessly upright again. "I believe it's time to leave. This affair is about to become exceedingly dull. Let's find your aunt and call your carriage."

"But I've only just arrived." Imogen peered back over her shoulder as Matthias marched her away from the shat-tered glass and the fallen woman. "Who is that odd lady? I do believe she fainted at the sight of you, sir."

"My unfortunate reputation sometimes has that effect on people."

Chapter 5

Matthias leaned into the carriage just before the footman closed the door. He pinned Imogen in the glow of the carriage lamps, his gaze grim with frustration. "I wish to speak with you, Miss Waterstone. Obviously that is not possible tonight." He cast a brief, irritated glance over his shoulder at Lady Blunt's crowded front steps, where guests were arriving and departing in a scene of mild chaos. "I shall call on you tomorrow at eleven. Make certain that you are at home."

Imogen raised her brows at his cool presumption, but she told herself that she must make allowances. It had obviously been a trying evening for him, although for her part she thought things had gone rather well. "I shall look forward to your visit, my lord."

She gave him an encouraging smile, hoping to bolster his flagging spirits, but the expression in his eyes merely darkened in response. He inclined his head in a brusquely civil farewell. The lamplight iced the streak of silver in his hair.

"I shall bid you both good evening." He stepped back and turned away. The footman closed the door.

Imogen watched Matthias disappear into the shadows that gathered in the street. Then she glanced at the front door of the large town house. Vanneck emerged onto the front step. His eyes met hers for an instant before the movement of the carriage broke the connection.

Imogen sat very still against the cushions. This was the first glimpse she'd had of Vanneck since the funeral. Three additional years of intemperate living had not been kind. He appeared to have grown more malevolent.

"I must say, nothing is ever dull when Colchester is in the vicinity." Horatia raised her lorgnette to peer at Imogen. "And as the same can be said of you, my dear, I suspect we are in for a lively time of it." She did not appear pleased by the prospect.

Imogen drew her thoughts back from the problem of Vanneck. "Who was the lady who fainted at the sight of Colchester?"

"He does have a peculiar effect on certain females, does he not? First Bess, and now Theodosia Slott."

"Bess's reaction was understandable, given the circumstances. She took him for a ghost or a vampire. But what of this Theodosia Slott? What is her excuse?"

Horatia gazed out into the crowded street. "It's an old tale and, as is the case with so many of the old stories concerning Colchester, I have no notion of how much of it is true and how much is fiction."

"Tell me what you know, Aunt Horatia."

Horatia glanced at her. "I thought you did not wish to hear gossip about his lordship."

"I have begun to wonder if perhaps it would be wiser to be more fully informed. It is difficult to know how to respond to a situation when one does not know what is going on."

"I see." Horatia settled back with a thoughtful expression. "Theodosia Slott was the reigning belle of her Season. She contracted an excellent marriage to Mr. Harold Slott. His family was in shipping, I believe. Mr. Slott was somewhat elderly, as I recall."

Imogen grew impatient. "Yes, yes. Do go on. What happened?"

"Nothing all that unusual. Theodosia did her duty by her husband. Gave him an heir. And then she promptly formed a connection with a dashing young man named Jonathan Exelby."

"Are you saying Theodosia and Exelby were lovers?"

"Yes. Exelby frequented the most notorious gaming hells. One in particular, The Lost Soul, was said to be his favorite haunt. It was very popular with the young bloods of the ton. Still is, for that matter. In any event, one night he encountered Colchester there and the two men got into a violent quarrel. A dawn meeting was arranged."

Imogen was horrified. "Colchester was in a duel?"

"That is the story." Horatia made a small, dismissing movement with one hand. "No one will ever confirm it, of course. Dueling is illegal. The parties involved rarely discuss the matter."

"But he could have been killed."

"From all accounts, it was Exelby who was killed."

"I don't believe it." Imogen felt her mouth go dry.

Horatia gave a small shrug. "To my knowledge, Exelby was never seen again following the events of that dawn. He simply disappeared. Dead and buried in an unmarked grave, people say. He had no family to raise questions."

"There must be more to the story."

"There is, actually." Horatia warmed to her tale. "Theodosia claims that to add insult to injury, Colchester showed up on her doorstep later that same morning to claim her favors."

"*What?*"

"Colchester apparently told her that she had been the subject of the quarrel and, as he had won the duel, he naturally expected to take her lover's place in her bed. She claims she had him thrown out into the street."

Imogen was speechless for a second. When she managed to pull herself together, she exploded in protest. "Outrageous."

"I assure you, it was the *on-dit* of the Season. I recall it well because the scandal even replaced the dreadful story of the Demon Twins of Dunstoke Castle which had been on everyone's lips that year."

Imogen was briefly distracted. "Demon Twins?"

"A brother and sister who conspired to burn down a house in the north. It happened shortly before the Season began," Horatia explained. "Apparently the sister's aged husband was in his bed at the time. Charred him to a cinder. The Demon Twins were said to have made off with the husband's hoard of gems."

"Were the twins ever caught?"

"No. They disappeared along with the fortune. For a time everyone wondered if they would show up in London and attempt to seduce and murder another wealthy old man, but they never appeared. Left for the Continent, no doubt. In any event, as I said, people stopped talking about the Demon Twins after the Colchester affair."

Imogen frowned. "Colchester would never have gotten involved in such a thing."

"Well, as he has never bothered to confirm or deny the tale, it stands to this day. And Theodosia still dines out on it. As you can see, she works hard to keep the drama alive."

Imogen wrinkled her nose. "She certainly does. That was a fine bit of theater she staged tonight. But it is too ridiculous to be true. Colchester would never engage in a duel, let alone kill his opponent and then attempt to seduce the poor man's lover."

"You did not know Colchester in those days, my dear." Horatia paused. "In point of fact, you do not know him very well today either."

"On the contrary, I am beginning to believe that I am better acquainted with him than with anyone else in Town."

Horatia was amazed. "What makes you think that?"

"We have so much in common," Imogen said. "And I can assure you that he is far too sensible to allow himself to be drawn into a silly quarrel over a female such as Theodosia Slott. His nerves would never survive a violent encounter. Furthermore, I cannot for one moment imagine Colchester frequenting sordid gaming hells."

"No?"

"Of course not," Imogen said. "He is a man of delicate sensibilities and refined taste. He is simply not the sort to seek his entertainments in gaming hells."

"My dear, Colchester owned the hell in question."

*I*mogen would not escape so easily the next time, Matthias promised himself as he alighted from his carriage. He went up the steps of his town house with a sense of resolve. He would get the answers to his questions tomorrow when he called upon her. One way or another, he intended to find out exactly what had happened between Vanneck and Imogen three years ago. At the moment he was inclined to believe that Society's version was not entirely accurate. It seldom was.

Ufton opened the door with perfect timing. His entirely bald head gleamed in the light of the wall sconces. He regarded Matthias with his customary air of unflappable composure. "I trust you had a pleasant evening, sir."

Matthias stripped off his gloves and tossed them to the butler. "I had an interesting evening."

"Indeed. I fear it is about to become even more so, my lord."

Matthias paused halfway across the hall and turned to glance back over his shoulder. He and Ufton had known each other a very long time. "What the devil does that mean?"

"You have guests, my lord."

"At this hour? Who is it? Felix? Plummer?"

"Your, uh, sister, my lord. And her companion."

"If this is your notion of a joke, Ufton, allow me to inform you that you are growing senile."

Ufton drew himself up and contrived to appear mortally offended. "I assure you, sir, I do not jest. Indeed, I never jest. You should know that. You have told me often enough that I have absolutely no sense of humor."

"Damnation, man, I haven't got a sister—" Matthias broke off abruptly. He stared at Ufton. "Bloody hell. You cannot mean my half sister?"

"Lady Patricia Marshall, sir." Ufton's eyes held a certain sympathy. "And her companion, a Miss Grice." Reaching around Matthias, he silently opened the library door.

Matthias went cold as he gazed into the firelit chamber. The library was his sanctum sanctorum, his retreat, his lair. No one should be in this room without his personal invitation.

Many found the chamber strange and oppressive with its Zamarian decoration and exotic hues. Others thought it fascinating, although some said it made them uneasy. Matthias was not concerned with the opinions of his visitors. The library had been created to remind him of ancient Zamar.

Every time he walked into this room, he strode into another world, a place where the long-lost past enveloped him and locked out the present and the future. There, among the ghosts of an ancient people, he could occasionally forget the ghosts of his own past. He spent hours at a time in this chamber, engaged in the task of unraveling the clues left by those who had inhabited mysterious Zamar.

Years earlier Matthias had discovered that if he concentrated sufficiently on the quest to understand ancient Zamar, he could ignore the unanswerable need that seethed deep beneath the ice inside him.

This chamber was a perfect replica of his most astounding discovery, the great library he had found hidden in the labyrinth beneath the ruins of the lost city.

Rich, heavily fringed hangings of Zamarian green and gold were suspended from the ceiling. The floor was covered in matching carpet. Elaborately carved and gilded columns jutted out from the walls of the room, giving the impression of an ancient colonnade.

The bookcases were crammed with volumes of all shapes and sizes. Greek, Latin, and other far more obscure texts filled their pages. Inscribed clay tablets and documents written on rolls of a material that resembled papyrus but had proved more durable over the centuries were stacked on several shelves. Matthias had brought the tablets and the scrolls out of the secret library as though they had been fashioned of solid gold and priceless gems. Indeed, their true value to him had been far higher than the glittering treasures Rutledge had craved.

Painted scenes of the ruins of Zamar decorated the walls between the elaborate columns. Stone statues depicting Zamaris and Anizamara loomed in opposite corners. The furniture was ornamented with the dolphins and shells that were so prevalent in Zamarian art.

Matthias walked slowly into the firelit chamber.

Two women, one young, one of middle years, sat stiffly on the dolphin sofa in front of the hearth. They hovered close together, evidently intimidated by their surroundings.

Both women were garbed in dusty traveling gowns. There was an air of weariness and apprehension about them. Each gave a start when Matthias entered the library, as if the time they had spent waiting for him had unnerved them. The younger one turned an anxious face toward Matthias.

He found himself looking into silvery-gray eyes that were mirror images of his own. She would have been quite pretty if she had not looked so desperate, he thought dispassionately. A classical nose and an elegant chin promised a hint of backbone beneath the nervous expression.

Her hair was somewhat lighter than his, a dark brown hue that had no doubt come from her mother. She was willowy and graceful. He was surprised to note that her gown was somewhat worn and shabby.

This was Patricia, the half sister he had never met, never wanted to meet. This was his father's other offspring, the beloved daughter who had been wanted, adored, sheltered, and protected; the babe whose mother had not been obliged to coerce her seducer into marriage.

This was the daughter of the woman who had played her cards far more cautiously than his own mother had played hers, Matthias thought. The daughter of the paragon.

He came to a halt in the center of the library. "Good evening. I am Colchester. It's rather late. May I ask what brings you here?" Matthias kept his voice very even. It was an old trick, one he had developed before he was twenty and which had become a habit over the years. It effectively concealed all emotion, all doubt, all hope. It asked no quarter and it promised none.

Patricia was apparently struck speechless by his icy greeting. She gazed at him with huge, frantic eyes, looking as if she were about to burst into tears.

It was the older woman, the one with years of bitterness and resignation etched into her face, who drew herself up and regarded him with a degree of determination. "My lord, I am Miss Grice," she announced. "I accompanied your sister on her journey to London. She informed me that you would reimburse me for my expenses and pay me a fee for my services as her companion."

"Did she?" Matthias crossed the room to the brandy table. He removed the top of the crystal decanter and deliberately poured himself a healthy dose of the contents. "And why does she not pay you herself? My solicitor informs me that she is well provided for according to the terms of my father's will."

"I cannot pay her because I haven't got any money," Patricia burst out. "Every time my quarterly allowance arrives, my uncle takes it all and spends it on his hounds and his horses and his gaming. I was obliged to pawn my mother's necklace to purchase a ticket on the stage."

Matthias paused with the glass halfway to his mouth. "Your uncle?" He recalled the name his solicitor had mentioned. Someone on her mother's side. "That would be Poole?"

"Yes. He is in charge of my inheritance and he is stealing it. Last year Mama and Papa gave me my first Season. Mama said I was to have another this year, but my uncle refuses to pay for it. I realize that he does not want me to marry and thereby escape his household. As long as I am forced to live in his home, he will have control of my money. I have been trapped in Devon since my dear parents died."

"Trapped? That sounds something of an exaggeration," Matthias muttered.

"It's the truth." Patricia snatched a hankie from her reticule and began to sob into the little square of linen. "When I protest my uncle's treatment of me, he laughs. He tells me that he deserves the money because he was the only one who was willing to give me a home after Mama and Papa died. He reminds me that you want nothing to do with me, my lord. I know that is true, but now I must throw myself on your mercy."

At the sight of her tears, bleak memories howled across Matthias's soul. He hated tears in a woman. They never failed to bring back those occasions on which he had been expected to deal with his mother's periodic bouts of weeping. He had always felt helpless to comfort her and at the same time consumed by rage because his father had walked out and left him to handle the situation.

"I shall have my solicitor look into the matter of your finances." Matthias downed a large swallow of the brandy and waited for the heat of it to warm him. "Something can be worked out."

"It will do no good. My lord, I beg you, do not send me back to my uncle's house." Patricia clenched her hands in her lap. "You do not know what it is like there. I *cannot* go back. I'm afraid, my lord."

"Of what, for God's sake?" Matthias narrowed his eyes as an unpalatable thought occurred to him. "Your uncle?"

Patricia shook her head quickly. "No, my lord. He ignores me for the most part. He is interested only in my inheritance. But two months ago my cousin Nevil came to stay with us after he was sent down from Oxford." She lowered her gaze to her tightly clasped hands. "He frightens me, sir. He is always watching me."

Matthias scowled. "Watching you? What the devil are you talking about?"

Miss Grice cleared her throat and fixed him with a steely gaze. "I trust you can hazard a guess, my lord. You are a man of the world. Think of it. A young man with a distinctly unsavory reputation moves into the household. The young lady of the house does not feel well protected from unwanted advances. I'm sure that there is no need to go into details. I myself was in a similar situation at one time in my younger days. Very difficult."

"I see." Matthias rested an arm along the black marble mantel and tried to marshal his thoughts. "Surely you must have other relatives, Patricia? Someone else on your mother's side?"

"No one else who will take me in, sir."

Matthias drummed his fingers on the cool marble. "Something can be arranged." He looked at Miss Grice, seeking inspiration.

"Lady Patricia informs me that you are her brother, my lord," Miss Grice said as if that summed up the entire matter. "You will, of course, want to provide her with a proper home." She glanced around dubiously at her surroundings.

Matthias could read the woman's thoughts as clearly as if she spoke aloud. Miss Grice was not at all certain that this household constituted a proper home.

Patricia ignored the fantastical room. She watched

Matthias with the sort of hope that only the young and the naive can successfully conjure. "Please, my lord. I throw myself on your mercy. I beseech you not to toss me out into the streets. Papa told me that you promised him you would give me a home if it became necessary."

"Bloody hell," Matthias said.

"*T*here be a gentleman to see ye, Miss Waterstone."

Imogen looked up quickly from the copy of the *Zamarian Review* she was reading. Mrs. Vine, the house-keeper, who also happened to be the landlord, hovered in the doorway of the drawing room. The gentleman she referred to must be Vanneck. The rumors must have reached him quickly, just as she had hoped. But now that the moment was upon her, she felt fear flash through her veins. She suddenly wished that Matthias were with her.

Nonsense, she told herself in the next instant. This was her scheme. She was in command and she was responsible for making it work properly. Matthias had warned her that he was not a man of action.

Slowly she put down the *Review*. "Send him in, Mrs. Vine. And then please inform my aunt that we have company."

"Aye, madam." Mrs. Vine was a tall, dour woman of indeterminate years. She nodded in a long-suffering fashion, as though the task of ushering a guest into the parlor was a great imposition.

It seemed to Imogen that Mrs. Vine's position as both landlord and housekeeper gave her a distinctly skewed view of the proper relationship between herself and her tenants.

Footsteps sounded in the hall. Imogen braced herself. This first encounter with Vanneck was critical to the success of her plans. She must keep her wits about her. Once again she thought wistfully of Matthias. He might not be the adventurous sort, but he was extremely clever. He would prove a useful ally in a situation such as this.

Mrs. Vine reappeared in the doorway, looking more put upon than ever. "Mr. Alastair Drake to see you, ma'am."

"Alastair." Imogen leaped to her feet so quickly that she knocked over her teacup. Fortunately the cup was empty. It bounced harmlessly on the carpet. "I was not expecting you," she said as she stooped to pick up the cup. "Please, sit down." She straightened quickly, set the cup back in the saucer, and summoned up a smile for the handsome man in the doorway. Old, wistful memories tumbled through her mind.

"Good day, Imogen." A slow smile curved Alastair's sensual mouth. "It's been a long while, has it not?"

"Yes, it has." She stared at him, searching for any changes the past three years had made.

If anything, Alastair was more attractive than she remembered. He was nearly thirty now, she realized. Experience had rendered his face more interesting. His light brown hair was cut short and crimped in the latest fashion. His blue eyes still held that beguiling expression that was a combination of little-boy-lost and man-of-the-world. Lucy had once told him it was his most charming quality.

Alastair sauntered into the room. "Sorry to surprise you. Were you anticipating a visit from someone more interesting perhaps? Colchester, for example? I hear that he fastened himself on to you last night at the Blunts' ball."

"Don't be ridiculous." Imogen gave him what she hoped was a bright, convincing smile. "I was startled to see you because my housekeeper did not mention the identity of my caller. Would you care for tea?"

"Thank you." Alastair studied her from beneath his lashes. "I can well comprehend that after the unfortunate manner in which we parted three years ago, you have no reason to greet me with any warmth today."

"Nonsense, sir. I am delighted to see you again." Now that she had recovered from her initial shock, Imo-

gen was pleased to feel her pulse slow to a more normal
rate.

Lucy had once remarked that Alastair was the good-
natured older brother every woman wished she had. Imogen had never seen him as a brother, however. He had
drifted into Lucy's social sphere three years earlier when
the pair had met at a meeting of the Zamarian Society.
When Imogen had arrived in Town to visit, Lucy had
introduced her to Alastair. The three of them had become
inseparable.

Alastair had been welcome initially because he could
be counted upon to serve as an escort. Vanneck was rarely
available to take Lucy and Imogen about in the evenings.
He preferred to spend his time at his club or with his
mistress. Lucy had confided to Imogen that she was grateful that her husband spent his time with another woman.
She had dreaded the nights that he came to her bedchamber.

More memories washed through Imogen. There was a
time when she had thought that Alastair might be falling
in love with her. He had kissed her as if she were made of
fragile silk.

There had been only a handful of such embraces,
most of them stolen in dark gardens or on shadowed ter-
races during the course of a soiree or ball. Imogen had
quite enjoyed them. Alastair had not been as good at that
sort of thing as Philippe D'Artois, her dancing instructor,
but then, Philippe was French. Not that the comparison
mattered now, she thought. The frail ghosts of the kisses
she had received from both men had been well and truly
incinerated a few days before in the blaze of Matthias's
fiery embrace.

Although she was unable to summon up more than
the tattered remnants of the warm feelings she'd once had
for Alastair, she could not help but note that he looked
very fine. His coat and trousers were expertly cut and his
cravat was folded in the stylish manner she thought she
recognized as the Waterfall. His blue waistcoat comple-

mented his eyes. Alastair had always been in the first stare of fashion.

"I could scarcely believe my ears when I learned that you were in Town, Imogen." Alastair took the cup and saucer from her. His eyes were eloquent. "It's good to see you again, my dear. My God, how I have missed you."

"Indeed." Imogen had a sudden vivid recollection of the shock and outrage that had marked his face the night he had discovered her with Vanneck. Alastair had never given her a chance to explain. "I have certainly missed Lucy."

"Ah, yes. Poor Lucy." Alastair shook his head. "Such a sad situation. I often think about the wonderful times the three of us shared together." He paused meaningfully. "But I must confess, my fondest memories are of you, Imogen."

"Really?" She took a breath. "Then why did you never write, sir? I had rather hoped to hear from you after Lucy's funeral. I thought that we were friends, at least."

"Friends?" His voice abruptly hardened. "We were more than friends. I shall be perfectly honest with you, Imogen. After the incident, I could not bear to reopen the wounds."

"Wounds? What wounds?"

"I was . . . hurt." His mouth tightened. "Shattered, if you must know the truth. It took me a very long time to get over the sight of you in Vanneck's arms."

"I was not in his arms," she said tartly. "I, oh, never mind. It's all in the past now and it would no doubt be best to leave it there. May I ask why you chose to call upon me today?"

"Isn't it obvious?" Alastair put down his cup and rose. "I came to see you because when I learned you were in Town I realized that what I had once felt for you had not entirely died." He took her hand and pulled her to her feet.

"Alastair, please." Imogen was so shaken by his declaration that she could not think of a graceful way to retrieve her hand from his.

"There is something I must tell you. Something that has been plaguing me for three long years. I want you to know that I forgive you for what happened that dreadful night."

"Forgive me?" She glowered at him. "Well, that is very kind of you, sir, but I assure you, I do not require your forgiveness."

"You need not explain, my dear. It no longer matters. The whole world knows what sort of man Vanneck is. He took advantage of your innocence and naiveté. I myself was much younger in those days. I let Society's opinions influence me."

"Do not concern yourself." Imogen braced her hands against his shoulders. "I comprehend perfectly well why you leaped to the conclusion that I was Vanneck's paramour. Indeed, any gentleman in your position would have believed the worst."

"I was so shocked that I could not think clearly. And by the time I came to my senses, it was too late. Lucy was dead. You were gone."

"Yes, yes, I understand." Imogen pushed against his shoulders.

"We are both older and wiser now, my dear. Mature adults who know the ways of the world." He bent his head to kiss her.

Imogen ducked his searching mouth and shoved hard. "Pray, release me, sir."

"Surely you have not forgotten how it was between us? Those warm embraces that we shared? Those intimate little chats about lost Zamar. Your eyes lit with such passion whenever you talked of Zamar, my dear."

A large, dark shadow blotted out the light in the doorway. "Am I interrupting anything?" Matthias asked in a voice that could have frozen the fires of the second Zamarian hell.

"What the devil?" Alastair released Imogen and hurriedly stepped back. *"Colchester."*

Imogen whirled around, flustered and breathless from the small tussle. "Do come in, my lord," she said in a loud, firm tone. "Mr. Drake was just leaving."

Chapter 6

"What was Drake doing here?" Matthias asked much too softly as he lowered himself into the chair Alastair had just vacated.

"He's an old acquaintance." Imogen reached for the teapot. She was vastly relieved to have Alastair gone, but she was not certain that Matthias would prove to be a significant improvement. He did not appear to be in good spirits. "A friend from three years ago."

"A close friend." Matthias regarded her with a shuttered gaze.

"Of both Lucy and myself," she said pointedly.

"I believe your aunt did mention him."

"Vanneck could never be bothered to escort his wife to the theater or to soirees and parties, and Lucy did so love to attend such affairs."

"Having acquired her, he ignored her, is that it?"

"I believe he would have locked her away in a storage chamber along with the rest of his collection if he could have managed such a thing. Lucy joined the Zamarian

Society in an effort to please him, but he ridiculed her interest. She met Alastair there, however."

"And introduced him to you, I believe Mrs. Elibank said," Matthias murmured.

"Yes. As I said, the three of us went about together. Alastair was very gallant. He was happy to serve as our escort."

"I see." Matthias took the cup and saucer into his elegant hands and leaned back in his chair. He stretched his legs out in front of him and contemplated Imogen with an unreadable gaze. "Pray, continue."

She gazed at him blankly. "Continue with what?"

"With the rest of the tale."

"There is nothing else of interest to relate, my lord. Last night Alastair learned that I was in Town for the Season. He paid a call on me just now to renew our acquaintance. That is all there is to it."

"Imogen, it is true that I have spent most of the past few years in Zamar, and when I was in London I made it a practice to avoid what is amusingly termed Polite Society." Matthias gave her a thin smile. "But I am not a complete idiot. When I walked in here just now you were in Drake's arms. Therefore, I very cleverly deduce that there is more to your tale."

"What of it? I told you, we are old friends."

"I realize from what your aunt told me that you hold excessively liberal views on relations between the sexes. But I would have thought such an impassioned greeting went a bit too far, even for old friends. Having been obliged to witness the event, I feel I am entitled to an explanation."

Imogen bristled. "My connection with Alastair need not concern you, my lord. It has no bearing on my scheme."

"I disagree. If I am to assist you, I must be kept fully informed."

"Calm yourself, my lord. I shall keep you apprised of everything you need to know."

"You obviously have no conception of how complex this sort of thing can become," Matthias said. "What if Drake takes a notion to involve himself in this situation?"

She stared at him in astonishment. "Why on earth would he do that?"

"He may decide that he would like to obtain the Queen's Seal himself."

Imogen gave a ladylike sniff. "Highly unlikely. I assure you, Alastair's interest in Zamarian antiquities is superficial, at best. He is a fashionable dilettante, not a true scholar. He does not even collect artifacts. Alastair will not pose a problem in that regard."

Matthias's gaze narrowed. "Then perhaps he will conclude that having enjoyed an intimate connection with you three years ago, it would be pleasant to, shall we say, renew the association?"

"I do not intend to allow that to happen," Imogen said grimly.

"Indeed?"

"What are you implying, Colchester?"

"That you had best do a more convincing job of discouraging Drake than the one I saw you doing a few minutes ago."

"Why are you so very concerned with this subject?" Imogen demanded. "It is none of your affair, I assure you. I shall deal with Alastair."

Matthias drummed his fingers on the arm of his chair. He looked as if he were searching for another approach to the subject. "Imogen, I must insist on complete honesty between us when it comes to any matter that touches on this damnable plan of yours."

"It is not a damnable plan. It is a very clever scheme."

"It is a crazed notion, and if I am to be a part of it, I will have honesty from you. You owe me that much in exchange for my assistance. There are risks involved in this thing. Serious risks."

Comprehension dawned at last. Imogen heaved a disgruntled sigh and sank back into the corner of the sofa.

"So now we come to the heart of the matter. You are growing overanxious again."

"One could say that."

"No offense, my lord, but it is unfortunate that you are not a more daring sort."

"I comfort myself with the knowledge that we all have our strengths and weaknesses. Perhaps I shall prove useful in the end."

"Hmm." She considered him from beneath half-lowered lids. There were times when she could not escape the nasty suspicion that Matthias found her amusing. "Very well, if it will settle your nerves, I shall tell you about my association with Alastair Drake."

"I doubt that your explanation will have a soothing effect on my nerves, but I think I'd better hear it."

"The long and the short of the matter is that Alastair was the gentleman who discovered Vanneck and me together in a bedchamber three years ago."

"Your aunt already told me as much."

"Then why the devil are you asking me all these silly questions?" Imogen snapped.

"I want to hear your version of the tale."

Imogen glowered. "Alastair saw me in a compromising situation and assumed the worst. That is all there is to it."

Matthias contemplated his teacup as though it were an interesting Zamarian relic. "A man may be forgiven certain assumptions when he discovers two people in bed together."

"Bloody hell, I was not in bed with Vanneck," Imogen exploded. "I was in the bedchamber with him. There is a difference, sir."

Matthias glanced up from the teacup. "Is there?"

"Of course there is. It was all a terrible misunderstanding. Or so I thought at the time." Imogen nibbled on her lower lip as more memories returned. "Then Lucy died. There was talk of a note she had written. People said she had taken her own life because her husband and best friend had betrayed her. For a time everything was muddled."

"No doubt."

Imogen jumped to her feet, clasped her hands behind her back, and began to pace the parlor. "When I could think clearly again, it occurred to me that perhaps Vanneck had deliberately lured me to the bedchamber that night, knowing that we would be discovered."

"So that when Lucy died, the rumors of betrayal and suicide would conceal the truth? It seems a bit farfetched, Imogen."

"You must admit it has a certain logic. Vanneck is a very clever man. He would not have wanted anyone to cry murder. He wanted Lucy's death to appear a suicide. That meant he had to supply a plausible reason for her to kill herself."

"Why did you go to that bedchamber to meet him?" Matthias asked.

"I did not intend to meet him. I went there because I had received an urgent note asking me to go to the bedchamber."

"Who sent the note?"

"Lucy. Or so I thought at the time. Now I believe that Vanneck himself wrote the note and signed her name. When I walked into the bedchamber, I found him there. He was—" Imogen broke off, blushing furiously.

"He was what?"

She cleared her throat. "He was partially undressed, if you must know. He had removed his shirt and boots and was in the process of taking off his breeches when I arrived."

Matthias set the cup and saucer down with great precision. "I see."

"Vanneck pretended to be as astonished to see me as I was to see him. I turned at once to leave the bedchamber, of course. But at that very moment Alastair and his friend came along the hallway. They passed the open door of the bedchamber and saw Vanneck and me together inside."

"And promptly dashed off to their club to inform their cronies that Vanneck had seduced you?" Matthias asked dryly.

"Alastair did no such thing." Imogen glared at him. "He is a gentleman. But his companion was not so discreet. Naturally, Alastair did his best to protect my reputation."

"Naturally."

Imogen shot him a quick searching glance, uncertain of his tone. Was he mocking her again? She decided to ignore it. "But it was impossible to stop the gossip, especially after Lucy died."

"Tell me, Imogen, did you explain the situation to Drake?"

Imogen paused in front of the window and gazed out into the street. "Alastair was distraught at the time. Quite overset by what he thought he had seen. He hurried off before I could tell him the truth. Later there was no opportunity to do so."

"I see. Drake did not challenge Vanneck, then?"

Imogen flushed. "Of course not. A duel would have been out of the question. I would never have permitted such a thing."

Matthias said nothing.

"Nor would it have done any good," Imogen said quietly. "It is just as my parents said, the Polite World cares only about appearances, not about truth. Which is precisely why Vanneck found it so easy to deceive Society when he murdered Lucy. He gave them the appearance of suicide and they believed him."

Matthias hesitated. "Perhaps it's time to move on to more productive subjects."

"By all means, sir." Greatly relieved by that suggestion, Imogen swung away from the window and went briskly back to the sofa.

Horatia appeared in the doorway. She gazed in surprise at Matthias. "What's this? I did not realize we had guests. I really must have a talk with our housekeeper. She failed to inform me that anyone had arrived."

"Imogen and I were just discussing her plans." Matthias rose to greet Horatia.

"I see." Horatia bustled into the room and gave her hand to Matthias. "This scheme of Imogen's has made me exceedingly anxious."

"I am relieved to know that I am not alone in my qualms." Matthias slanted a laconic glance at Imogen. "Those of us who lack stalwart nerves must join forces."

Imogen fixed both of them with a reproving look. "All will be well. I have everything under control."

"One can only hope." Matthias took his seat. "But as it happens, I have another problem on my hands."

Imogen frowned. "What is that?"

"My half sister arrived on my doorstep last night. She announced that she has nowhere else to turn and must take up residence with me."

Imogen blinked. "I did not know that you had a sister."

Matthias's eyes were devoid of expression. "My father remarried after my mother died. Patricia is his daughter by his second wife. To be blunt, I do not know what to do with her. She arrived with a companion, but the woman could not stay."

"How old is Patricia?" Imogen asked.

"Nineteen."

"Then she is of an age to enjoy the Season," Horatia observed.

"How the blazes am I supposed to arrange for her to participate in the Season?" Matthias grumbled. "Firing a young lady off into the ton requires gowns, proper invitations, a chaperone, and God knows what else."

"Put your mind at ease, Colchester," Imogen said. "Aunt Horatia is an expert on social matters. We shall turn Patricia over to her."

Horatia's eyes widened slightly behind the lenses of her spectacles.

Matthias's gaze slid from Imogen to Horatia and back again. His relief was obvious. "It is a great deal to ask."

"Nonsense." Imogen glanced at Horatia. "Well, Aunt? Are you game to guide a young lady through a Season?"

"It will be great fun," Horatia said cheerfully. "Nothing I fancy more than ordering vast quantities of beautiful clothes and sending the bills to someone else."

*T*here was definitely much to be said for a female who was inclined to take charge, Matthias thought three days later as he walked into his club. In the blink of an eye Imogen had assumed command of the pressing problem of Patricia. With any luck he would get his sister married off this Season and thereby fulfill his promise to his father.

That promise had been made here in this very club, he reflected as he handed his hat and gloves to the elderly porter. Two years ago Thomas had cornered him in the coffee room. Perhaps he'd had some premonition of his own impending death, Matthias thought.

"I wish to speak with you," Thomas had said as he sat down across from Matthias.

"Of course, sir." Matthias was always careful to keep his tone cool and unfailingly polite whenever he spoke with his father. "Is something amiss?"

"I am concerned with the future."

"Aren't we all? Personally, I've discovered that it is best to ignore it."

"I've noticed. Damnation, your irresponsible attitude does you no credit. You have created nothing but scandal since the day you came down from university." Thomas propped his elbows on the arms of the chair, steepled his hands, and made an obvious effort to control his anger. "But as it happens, that is not what I wished to discuss

today. I seek to make provisions for Patricia in the event
that anything should happen to me and my wife."

"Solicitors generally handle that sort of thing, I believe."

"I have already taken care of the financial side of
matters. Patricia has been well provided for in my will.
But her mother and I are concerned with her happiness."

"Ah, yes. Happiness."

Thomas frowned. "That is something that is not so
easy to provide."

"I have noticed that, sir."

Thomas's mouth compressed into a thin line. "Should
anything happen to Charlotte and me, arrangements have
been made for Patricia to live in the home of relatives on
Charlotte's side of the family."

"So?"

Thomas met his eyes. "If that arrangement does not
work out for any reason, I want your word that you will
take care of Patricia."

Matthias stilled. "What are you asking me to do?"

"Your duty." Thomas wearily closed his eyes and
then opened them to pin Matthias. "God knows, you have
mocked your responsibilities as my heir for your entire
adult life, but you will not avoid this one. Patricia is your
sister. You will take care of her should anything happen to
me. Is that understood? I want your oath on this."

"What makes you think that you can rely upon me to
keep such a promise?"

"You disgraced your heritage when you established
that damned gaming hell. You went off in search of ancient Zamar instead of contracting a good marriage and
giving me a grandson to ensure the title. Some suspect
that you were responsible for Rutledge's death. There is
talk that you killed a man in a duel over a married
woman." Thomas bunched his hands into fists on the
arms of the chair. "But it is said that you have never
broken a promise. I want your promise on this."

Matthias contemplated him for a moment. "I know

how difficult this must have been for you, sir. You must love Patricia very much."

"She and her mother are the light of my life."

"And every time you look at me, you can see only the darkness that your marriage to my mother brought you," Matthias concluded softly.

Thomas stiffened. His eyes went to the icy streak in Matthias's black hair, a mirror image of the one that marked him. "God help me, every time I look at you, I see my son and heir."

Matthias smiled humorlessly. "How very unpleasant that must be for you, sir."

"You have done nothing to make it pleasant, damn your eyes." The anger in Thomas faded into a bleak weariness. "You will not believe this after all that has passed between us, but I regret that you and I did not spend more time together when you were younger. Perhaps I could have instilled a stronger sense of duty in you."

Matthias said nothing.

Thomas watched him with palpable intensity. "Do I have your word that you will look after Patricia if anything happens to me?"

"Yes." Matthias picked up the paper he had been reading.

Thomas frowned. "Is that all you have to say?"

"I gave you my word concerning Patricia." Matthias glanced at him. "Was there something else you wanted from me, sir?"

"No." Thomas got slowly, heavily, to his feet. "No. There is nothing else." He hesitated. "That's not true. There is one other thing."

"What is that, sir?"

"Do you ever intend to wed? Or will you have your revenge against me by allowing the line to die out?"

"Why would I seek such revenge, sir?"

"Bloody hell. We both know that you blame me for your mother's unhappiness. But you are old enough now to understand that there are two sides to any story. If you ever find yourself in my shoes, you will realize why I acted as I did."

"Then I must make very certain that I never find myself in your position," Matthias said gently. "Good day, sir."

Thomas hesitated, as though there were something else he wanted to say. When he could not find the words, he turned and started to walk away.

Matthias watched him go. He was startled to see how old his father looked. Out of nowhere the long-suppressed wish to gain Thomas's approval surfaced.

"Sir?"

Thomas turned back. "What is it?"

Matthias hesitated. "I intend to do my duty by the title one of these days. I will not allow the line to die with me, if I can help it."

Something that might have been relief, even gratitude, appeared in Thomas's face. "Thank you. I regret that I . . . Never mind. It is no longer important."

"What do you regret, sir?"

"That I did not give you the money you needed to fund your first expedition to Zamar." Thomas paused. "I know how much the venture meant to you."

Matthias knew that he and his father had come as close as they ever had to a reconciliation that day in this club. He closed the door on the old memories and went into the coffee room.

He nodded at one or two acquaintances, picked up a copy of *The Times,* and settled into a large, overstuffed chair near the hearth. The newspaper was camouflage. He did not wish to read it. He wanted to think without being interrupted. In the past few days his calm, orderly existence had been thrown into an uproar.

He gazed unseeingly at the front page of the paper and considered Imogen's tale of how she had been compromised by Vanneck. Then he forced himself to recall the sharp, unpleasant sensation he had experienced when he had seen Imogen in Drake's arms. It was not jealousy he had felt, he assured himself, merely irritation. He had every right to be annoyed under the circumstances.

Imogen, Vanneck, and Alastair Drake. The three were linked together and the connection among them disturbed Matthias as nothing else had in a very long time. *Damn it to hell,* he thought. *Maybe I have developed a case of weak nerves.*

He forced himself to conjure up the unpalatable vision of Imogen in a bedchamber together with a half-dressed Vanneck and a distraught Alastair Drake. He reminded himself that Imogen was the daughter of unconventional parents. His fingers clenched around the edge of the newspaper, crumpling it.

"Colchester. I thought I saw you come in a few minutes ago."

Matthias slowly lowered his paper and looked at the tight-lipped young man standing in front of him. "Have we been introduced?"

"Hugo Bagshaw." A defiant glitter lit Hugo's eyes. "Arthur Bagshaw's son."

"I see. As you obviously know my identity, perhaps we can end this conversation. I wish to finish reading the paper." Matthias made to raise *The Times.*

"If I had realized that you were a member of this club, sir, I would have joined another."

"Don't let me stop you from canceling your membership here."

"Damnation, sir. Do you know who I am?"

Matthias reluctantly folded the paper and regarded Hugo's angrily flushed face. Bagshaw was an earnest-looking young man with blunt, sturdy features and a strong, athletic build. His crimped brown hair, extravagantly tied cravat, and snug-fitting coat marked him as a man of fashion. The seething expression in his serious brown eyes was not the poetic smoldering affected by so many of the young bloods of the ton, however. It was quite genuine.

"Hugo Bagshaw, I believe you said," Matthias murmured.

"Arthur Bagshaw's son."

"You've already mentioned the connection."

"You killed my father, Colchester. Just as surely as if you'd put a gun to his head."

A great stillness descended on the coffee room.

"I was under the impression that your father was responsible for his own death."

"How dare you, sir." Hugo's hands flexed into fists at his sides. His face worked furiously. "He shot himself after he lost everything playing cards in that damned hell you operated ten years ago."

"That is not quite the way I recall the tale."

Hugo ignored him. "I was only fourteen years old at the time. Too young to avenge him. But one of these days I will find a way to do so, Colchester. One of these days you will pay for what you did to my family."

Hugo spun around on his heel and stalked off toward the door. None of the other men in the coffee room looked up from their newspapers, but Matthias knew they had all overheard Bagshaw's accusation. He exhaled slowly. So much for finding a quiet place to think.

He gazed into the flames on the hearth and contemplated the ghost of Arthur Bagshaw.

"Young Bagshaw has only recently arrived in Town," Vanneck drawled from behind Matthias's chair. "A distant relative died and left him some money. Do you think we were inclined to be so emotional in our younger days, Colchester? Or is it the influence of the new poets on this generation of young men that makes them so damnably melodramatic?"

"Personally, I can scarcely recall being that young, and what bits and pieces I do recollect are not inspiring."

"I am of a similar opinion regarding my own youth." Vanneck strolled around the chair and came to a halt in front of the fire. "A word of warning, Colchester. Bagshaw bears you a great deal of ill will and could be dangerous. I hear that he is taking boxing lessons at Shrimpton's and practicing his aim at Manton's. He is accounted a decent shot."

"Young Bagshaw's skills in such matters are of no great concern to me. I have other, more pressing interests at the moment."

"I see." Vanneck made a show of warming his hands at the fire. "And would those other interests be connected to Miss Waterstone and a certain Zamarian artifact?"

Matthias gave Vanneck a quizzical glance. "Wherever did you gain that notion? I am not in the market for antiquities just now. I have other plans. I fear I must find myself a wife this Season."

"I am well aware that you have come into your title, sir. You have your obligations to see to, as do I, devil take it."

"I heard you were in search of a wife, yourself."

Vanneck snorted. "My first wife could not be bothered to give me my heir. She cared only about parties and balls and clothes. Just between you and me, she was a cold fish in bed. Married me for my title. And I was fool enough to let it happen."

"You surprise me, Vanneck. I would not have thought you the sort to be charmed by a pretty face."

"You never saw Lucy." Vanneck paused. "She was really quite spectacular. But not a penny to her name. I got nothing out of that damned bargain. Made my life a living hell. Believe me, I shall not make that mistake again."

"Indeed."

Vanneck gave him a sidelong glance. "We were discussing you, sir."

"Were we?"

"You cannot convince me that you seriously consider Miss Waterstone a suitable candidate for a wife."

"Why do you find that so difficult to believe?"

"Come, sir, what do you take me for?" Vanneck gave him a man-to-man look. "Miss Waterstone is five and twenty years of age. Sitting rather high on the shelf, wouldn't you say? One can hardly envision her as a blushing bride."

"Personally, I prefer mature women." Matthias turned the page of his newspaper. "They tend to have more interesting conversation."

Vanneck frowned. "Even if her age is a virtue in your eyes, there are rumors to the effect that she lacks virtue of another sort. They call her Immodest Imogen, you know."

Matthias put down his paper and looked straight at Vanneck. "Anyone who refers to her in those terms in my presence had best be prepared to finish the discussion over a brace of pistols."

Vanneck flinched. "See here, Colchester, don't expect me to believe that you actually intend to make an offer for Imogen Waterstone. If you're pursuing her, it's got to be for another reason. And I can think of only one possibility."

Matthias rose to his feet. "You may believe whatever you wish, Vanneck." He smiled faintly. "But I would advise you to be extremely careful about what you say."

*P*atricia glanced uneasily around the interior of the bookshop. "Are you quite certain my brother will not object if I make a purchase?"

"Leave Colchester to me," Imogen said firmly. "I shall deal with him if he raises any objections. But I doubt that he will. The cost of a book or two will be so paltry compared to the bills for your gowns that I daresay he will not even notice it."

Patricia paled. "I knew your aunt went too far at the modiste's. So many gowns. And such expensive fabrics. Colchester will be furious when he discovers how much we spent."

"Nonsense. I shall explain matters to him if necessary." Imogen gave Patricia a reassuring smile. "Now, run along and browse a bit. I want to inquire whether or not Garrison's new book on antiquities is available. By the time we are finished, Aunt Horatia will have concluded her conversation with Mrs. Horton. She will be waiting for us in the carriage."

Patricia looked doubtful, but she obediently moved off to study the titles on a nearby shelf. Imogen crossed to the counter. While she waited for the shopkeeper to finish with another customer, she idly examined several volumes lying on a nearby table. When the shop bell tinkled behind her, she glanced absently over her shoulder to see who had entered.

She chilled at the sight of Vanneck standing in the doorway. It was the first time she had run into him since she had seen him at Lady Blunt's ball.

His appearance in the bookshop could be a coincidence, she told herself. But it was far more likely that he had finally taken the bait. *About time,* she thought.

"Miss Waterstone." Vanneck gave her an oily smile as he walked toward the counter. "What a pleasant surprise. It has been three years, has it not?"

"I believe it has."

"Are you looking for a particular book?" Vanneck inquired politely.

Imogen summoned what she hoped was a serene smile. "I am hoping to find something on Zamarian antiquities."

"Naturally. It does not surprise me that you have retained your interest in ancient Zamar. You were quite passionate about the subject, as I recall." Vanneck casually propped himself against the counter and surveyed her with ill-concealed eagerness. "There is a rumor going round that you have recently come into a most interesting inheritance."

"I was very fortunate. In addition to a pleasant income, my uncle left me his entire collection of antiquities. There are some fascinating items in it."

Vanneck glanced around quickly and then edged closer. "Including a certain map that purports to show the location of an extremely valuable Zamarian artifact, I understand."

"Word travels swiftly here in Town." She had to force herself to stand still. The urge to step away from Vanneck was almost overwhelming.

"It's true, then?" Vanneck searched her face with an avid expression. "You believe this map can lead you to the Queen's Seal?"

Imogen shrugged lightly. "Quite possibly, though it is of little use to me at the moment. I cannot afford to mount an expedition to search for the seal. But I have hopes that my financial problems will soon be remedied."

"You refer to Colchester, do you not?"

"He has been kind enough to take an interest."

"Damnation. So I was right." Vanneck's hand clenched on the counter. "I thought that was why he'd attached himself to you. The whole Town's talking about it, you know."

Imogen looked down the length of her nose. "Indeed, sir?"

"He thinks to get his hands on your map. Colchester would do anything to find the Queen's Seal."

"It's certainly common knowledge that his lordship is a great collector of the finest Zamarian antiquities," Imogen allowed.

Vanneck bent his head and lowered his voice. "I know that you harbor a certain degree of ill will toward me because of that unfortunate incident three years ago. But I assure you that I was just as much a victim of circumstance as you yourself were."

"There is something I have always wondered about that incident, sir. Just what were you doing in that bedchamber?"

"If you must know, I was waiting for someone. A lovely widow whose name I will not mention for obvious reasons. I was certainly not expecting you. It was all a dreadful mistake."

"A mistake that cost poor Lucy her life."

Vanneck looked confused. "Lucy?"

"You remember her, my lord? She was your wife."

"Don't be ridiculous." Vanneck ran a finger between the towering folds of his cravat and his neck. "Of course I remember her. But she has been dead some three years now and a man must get on with his life."

"Indeed." Imogen's hand tightened on the book she held. She forced herself to stay calm. She would jeopardize the entire scheme if she gave in to her rage.

Vanneck scowled. "You and Lucy were friends, Miss Waterstone. Surely it did not escape your notice that my wife was often possessed of an unstable temperament? It took very little to depress her spirits. You must not blame yourself for her death."

Imogen sucked in her breath *I blame you,* she thought. *Not myself.* But was that true? she wondered suddenly. Was it possible that her quest to punish Vanneck had its roots in her own sense of guilt about what had occurred that night? She shivered.

"There is no point dwelling on the past," Vanneck continued forcefully. "As you and I were once acquainted because of your friendship with my wife, I feel a certain responsibility to advise you."

Imogen stilled. "Advise me?"

"I must warn you against forming any sort of connection with Colchester."

So he has, indeed, taken the lure. Imogen gave him a brittle smile. "But I am determined to find the Queen's Seal, sir. Colchester can help fund an expedition."

"Forming a business alliance with Colchester would be akin to dancing with the devil himself."

"Nonsense. Surely you exaggerate, sir."

"I'm telling you the truth," Vanneck spat out. "The man is called Cold-blooded Colchester for good reason. If he agrees to finance an expedition to search for the seal, it will be only because he expects to possess it when it's discovered."

"I'm sure the two of us can work out a mutually satisfying arrangement."

"Bah. That is undoubtedly what poor Rutledge thought. We all know what happened to him."

"Do we?"

"He never returned from lost Zamar," Vanneck snapped. "There are those who think that Colchester knows exactly how he died."

"I do not believe that ridiculous gossip for one moment. Colchester is a gentleman to his fingertips. He had nothing to do with Rutledge's death."

"A gentleman? Colchester?" Vanneck's eyes widened and then slitted with sudden understanding. "Good God. Surely you haven't allowed him to convince you that he's developed a genuine *tendre* for you, Miss Waterstone. You cannot be that naive. Not at your age."

There was no need for Vanneck to look quite so incredulous at the notion of Matthias falling in love with her, Imogen thought. "My relationship with Colchester is a private matter."

"Forgive me, but I would be remiss in my responsibility as an old friend if I did not warn you that Colchester may attempt to seduce you in order to get his hands on the map."

"Rubbish. I resent that, sir."

He stared at her with disbelief. "You surely don't think that a man in Colchester's position would make an honorable offer to a woman of your years and, uh, unfortunate reputation?"

Imogen planted her hands on her hips and began to tap her toe. "To be perfectly honest, sir, I am not nearly so interested in marriage as I am in finding someone who can help me finance my expedition. At the moment I do not see a lot of alternatives to Lord Colchester. He is the only gentleman I know who can afford to mount an expedition and who has an interest in doing so."

"There are other methods of financing an expedition," Vanneck said quickly. "Methods that would be far less dangerous than dealing with Cold-blooded Colchester."

Imogen pursed her lips. "Do you think so? I did consider forming a consortium at one time, but I do not have the knowledge or connections to forge such a complex business arrangement."

Vanneck blinked. A gleam of excitement glowed in his eye. "Forming a consortium would be child's play for me, Miss Waterstone. I have extensive experience in matters of business."

"Really? How interesting." Good Lord, was she going to have to steer him every step of the way through this tricky waltz? Imogen wondered. She made a show of studying the face of the little watch pinned to her pelisse. "It is getting late. If you will excuse me, sir, I am in a hurry. My aunt is waiting for me."

Vanneck frowned. "I shall see you tonight, I trust?"

"Perhaps. We have a number of invitations. I am not certain yet which ones we shall accept." Imogen smiled vaguely and moved away from the counter. "Good day to you, sir."

"Until tonight." Vanneck nodded brusquely. He turned and strode to the door with a determined expression.

"Miss Waterstone?" Patricia came up to her, a volume in her gloved hand. "I have made my selection."

"Excellent." Imogen watched the door close behind Vanneck. Then she glanced out the window. "I believe I see Aunt Horatia being handed into the carriage. Let us be off. We must get you home so that you can unpack your purchases. The gown you are to wear tonight is to be delivered at five o'clock. There is much to do before it arrives."

"Do you really think the dress will be ready on time?" Patricia asked. "We gave the modiste such short notice."

Imogen grinned. "Aunt Horatia promised Madame Maud a king's ransom. You may be assured it will arrive on time."

Patricia did not appear reassured. In fact, she looked more worried than ever. "Are you quite certain that my brother will not be furious when he learns how much money we have spent today?"

"You seem inordinately concerned about Colchester's attitude toward your expenses. What makes you think that he will be angry?"

"Because he hates me," Patricia whispered.

Imogen stared at her. "Impossible."

"It's true, Miss Waterstone. He holds me in the lowest regard because I am the daughter of our father's second wife."

"Surely not."

"Mama explained it all to me the day she told me that I had an older brother. She said I must never expect anything from Colchester. She told me that he was very dangerous and that he possessed none of the more refined emotions."

"Rubbish. For heaven's sake, Patricia, that's ridiculous."

"She told me that he was given the name Cold-blooded Colchester when he was barely four and twenty."

"I assure you, Colchester is the victim of malicious gossip."

Patricia struggled with a hankie. "Two years ago Papa told me that if anything ever happened to him and Mama and if I felt I would not be happy in my uncle's house, I must call on Colchester. Papa said he had promised to take care of me."

"And so he shall."

"Papa said that the only good thing about Matthias was that he had a reputation for keeping his promises."

"Very true."

"But I know he does not want me in his home, Miss Waterstone. He will seek any excuse to be rid of me.

When he receives the bills for my gowns, he may very well decide that I am too expensive. And then where will I go? I dare not go back to my uncle's house. I shall surely end in the workhouse or worse. Perhaps I shall be forced to sell myself on the streets."

"Somehow I don't think it will come to that," Imogen muttered.

"Oh, Miss Waterstone, I miss Mama and Papa so much."

Sympathy surged through Imogen. She had been the same age as Patricia when she had lost her own dearly loved parents. She recalled the loneliness and the sense of loss far too well. There had been little comfort from anyone except Lucy. Horatia had been unable to visit often because the demands of her sickly husband had kept her trapped in Yorkshire. Her uncle, Selwyn, had been consumed by his sepulchral interests. Yes, Imogen thought. She knew precisely what Patricia felt.

Ignoring the disapproving glances of the bookshop patrons, Imogen put her arm around Patricia and gave her a quick, warm hug. "Things will be different now, Patricia. You are no longer alone."

Chapter 7

The commotion in the hall brought Matthias to the door of the library. He lounged there and watched, bemused, as the intrepid shoppers returned from their whirlwind tour of Pall Mall and Oxford Street.

Boxes and bundles of every description were in the process of being unloaded from the carriage. Ufton stationed himself to one side, a stoic expression on his stony face as Imogen assumed command. She stood on the front step, looking very cheerful in a Zamarian-green sprigged walking dress and a huge bonnet trimmed with shells.

She issued instructions to the footmen with the crisp precision of a military officer. Horatia fluttered about, checking the packages as they were brought into the hall. Patricia hovered, her expression anxious, as usual. She kept shooting uneasy glances in Matthias's direction.

His sister had been in the house for only a matter of days, and already he had grown weary of her nervous manner and her tendency to weep at the least provocation. She reminded him of a frightened rabbit.

"Yes, yes, bring everything inside." Imogen motioned

briskly with her dolphin-handled parasol. "And then take the whole lot upstairs to Lady Patricia's bedchamber. My aunt will accompany you and see to the unpacking. She knows about the proper care and storage of fine materials and such." She glanced at Horatia. "You will handle that end of things, will you not? I wish to have a word with Colchester."

"Yes, of course." Horatia smiled with satisfaction. "We must also set out the things that will be needed for Patricia's first appearance tonight." She beckoned toward Patricia. "Come along, my dear. We have a great deal to accomplish."

Horatia started toward the stairs. Patricia gave Matthias one last skittish glance and then scurried after her.

Imogen turned to Colchester with a determined air. "May I speak with you in private for a moment, my lord? There is something I wish to discuss."

"I am at your service, Miss Waterstone." Matthias moved politely out of the doorway. "As always."

"Thank you, sir." Imogen untied the strings of her oversized bonnet as she strode past him into the library. "This will not take long. A slight misunderstanding I wish to correct."

"Another one?"

"This one has to do with your sister." Imogen broke off on a sharp gasp of delighted astonishment. She gazed in rapt fascination at the interior of the library. "Good heavens. This is amazing."

Matthias watched as she came to an abrupt halt just inside the door. He realized he had been awaiting her reaction. This was, after all, I. A. Stone, the only other person in all of England who could properly appreciate what he had created in this room. Her expression of unabashed wonder was deeply gratifying.

"Do you like it?" he inquired offhandedly as Ufton softly closed the door behind him.

"It is really quite wonderful," Imogen whispered. She

tipped her head back to study the green and gold ceiling hangings. "Extraordinary."

Slowly she began to walk through the room, pausing here and there to examine the exotic landscape scenes on the walls and the vases sitting on the carved pedestals.

"You have captured the very essence of ancient Zamar. I vow, its spirit lives and breathes in this room." She stopped in front of the towering statue of Anizamara, Goddess of the Day. "Exquisite."

"I brought it back with me on my last trip. I discovered her and the statue of Zamaris in a prince's tomb."

"It is fantastic, my lord." She ran her gloved hand lovingly along the back of one of the twin dolphins that supported the sofa. "Absolutely fantastic. How I envy you."

"I would not go so far as to say that it is a perfect copy of the Zamarian library." Matthias tried to maintain a semblance of modesty, but it was not easy. He leaned back against the edge of his desk, crossed his booted ankles, and folded his arms. "But I admit that I am pleased with the way it turned out."

"Incredible," Imogen murmured. "Absolutely incredible."

Matthias had a sudden vision of Imogen lying nude on the dolphin sofa. The vision was excruciatingly clear. He could see her tawny hair tumbled around her shoulders, her gentle curves bathed in firelight, one knee gracefully raised. He felt his lower body harden with a desire that was almost painful.

"You are fortunate to have been able to re-create this wonderful setting for yourself, my lord." Imogen stooped to study the script on a clay tablet. "A bit of verse. How unusual."

"I discovered it in a tomb. Most of the Zamarian clay tablets that are floating around London these days are rather dull records of business transactions. Rutledge arranged to send hundreds of them back to England. He thought he would make a tidy fortune selling them. And so he did."

"Speaking of financial matters, I have a question to put to you." Imogen glanced at him with perceptive eyes. "Tell me, Colchester, did you establish The Lost Soul in order to pay for your venture to Zamar?"

He raised his brows. "As a matter of fact, yes."

She nodded with evident satisfaction. "I thought that might be the reason. Well, that explains everything, of course."

"I asked my father for the funds," Matthias said slowly. It was the only thing he had ever asked of his father in his adult life. "He refused. So I opened the hell."

"Perfectly natural. You had to find a way to come up with the money. Zamar was simply too important."

"Yes."

Imogen touched a vase with delicate fingers. "About Mrs. Slott."

Matthias grimaced. "I caught her lover, Jonathan Exelby, cheating at cards one night in The Lost Soul. I told him he would have to leave. He was outraged. Said I had impugned his honor, which I certainly had. He challenged me to a duel but thought better of it once he grew sober. He decided to seek his fortunes in America instead. He never appeared in London again, but the rumors of his death were legion."

Imogen gave him a serene smile. "I thought it must have been something along those lines. Well, then, on to other matters. I wish to discuss your sister, sir."

Matthias frowned. "What about her?"

"For some odd reason, she appears to feel unwelcome in your household. Indeed, she is living in a state of near terror."

"Don't be ridiculous. Why should she be terrified?"

"Perhaps nervous weakness runs in your family, sir. It is not uncommon to observe families in which each generation reflects a certain temperament just as they often reflect a chin or a nose or"—she glanced at the icy streak in his hair—"other physical attributes received from a parent."

"Nervous weakness?" Matthias decided he was tired of listening to Imogen's theories concerning his temperament. "Where the devil did you come up with such an idiotic notion?"

"Lady Patricia certainly seems to have inherited your tendency toward anxious forebodings and uncertainties."

"That is quite enough on the subject of my sister," he said coldly. "You need not concern yourself with anything other than getting her launched into her second Season."

Imogen ignored him. She clasped her hands behind her back and began to pace thoughtfully across the green and gold carpet. "I am of the opinion that you must make more of an effort to encourage her to feel at home. The poor girl believes that she is here on sufferance. As if she did not have a legitimate claim on your assistance."

Anger flashed without warning deep inside Matthias. It went through him with the force of a storm, overcoming his self-mastery before he realized what had happened. He unfolded his arms and straightened away from the desk. "I do not want your advice on this matter."

This time his tone of voice had some impact on Imogen. She stopped pacing and turned to stare at him. "But, my lord, you do not appear to comprehend Patricia's anxious nature. I am merely attempting to explain that she, too, possesses extremely delicate sensibilities, just as you yourself do and that she—"

"I do not give a damn about her nerves," Matthias said through his teeth. "I have done my duty by my half sister. I have provided her with a roof over her head. From what I saw out there in the hall a short while ago, I shall very shortly be paying some extremely large bills. I am prepared to settle a suitable portion on her when she marries. You cannot ask any more of me."

"But, sir, you speak only of your financial obligations. I grant you that they are important, but not nearly so crucial as kindness and brotherly affection. That is what your sister needs most at the moment."

"Then she should not have thrown herself on my mercy."

"But surely you feel some degree of warmth toward her."

"I made her acquaintance for the first time a few days ago," Matthias said. "I barely even know her."

"Well, she knows entirely too much about you, sir, and it appears that everything she has learned is wrong." Imogen gave a tiny snort of disgust. "She actually believes that there is some foundation for that outrageous nickname you acquired. Can you imagine? It is up to you to correct her false impression."

Matthias needed to move. He forced himself to walk slowly, deliberately, to the window. When he reached it, he stood there, staring blindly out into the garden. "What makes you so bloody certain that it is a false impression?"

"Don't be ridiculous, my lord. You are Colchester of Zamar." She waved a hand to indicate the library and its treasures. "Any man who possesses your elevated taste in artifacts, your keen perception of the history of ancient Zamar, your passion for its wonders . . . well. Such a man cannot possibly be lacking the warmer emotions and delicate sensibilities."

He swung around to face her. "I give you fair warning. You do not know me nearly so well as you seem to think you do. A lack of knowledge can be extremely dangerous."

Imogen looked confused rather than dismayed by his harsh words. Then her eyes softened. "I can see that this is a painful subject for you, sir."

"Not painful. Boring."

She smiled wryly. "As you wish. But I urge you to bear in mind that your sister is extremely distraught. From our conversation today, I collect that she is all alone in the world. You are the only person to whom she can turn. I would have you remember two things, my lord."

"I have a feeling that I shall not escape this damnable conversation until you have spelled those two things out for me in detail. Get on with it."

"First, I would have you recall that regardless of whatever happened, Patricia is innocent. As you are yourself. Second, bear in mind that just as you are the only close relation she has in the world, she is the only one you have, my lord. The two of you must stick together."

"Bloody hell. Who told you about the history of my family?"

"I do not know a great deal about it," Imogen said. "But I assume from what Patricia said this afternoon that there was a rift between you and your father following the death of your mother."

"You are correct, Imogen. You know nothing at all about the matter. I suggest you do not interfere. I have fulfilled the promise I made to my father, and that is the end of it."

"You are both very fortunate to have each other, you know," Imogen said quietly. "In the months following the death of my parents, I would have sold my soul for a brother or a sister."

"Imogen—"

She turned and walked to the door, where she halted again briefly, her hand on the knob. "I almost forgot. There is one other thing I intended to tell you."

Matthias watched her with brooding fascination. "Pray, do not contain yourself another second, Miss Waterstone."

"I encountered Vanneck in a bookshop today. I can safely report that he has taken the bait. He is even now planning to form a consortium. My scheme is afoot."

She went out the door. Ufton closed it behind her.

Matthias shut his eyes and groaned. His delicate nerves were not going to survive this affair unscathed. He would be fortunate if he did not find himself locked away in Bedlam before the thing was finished.

○   ○   ○

$\mathcal{M}$atthias walked to the balcony rail and looked down at the crowded ballroom. It was nearly midnight and the soiree was at high tide. The chandeliers cast a brilliant light over the elegantly dressed men and women below. His mouth twisted in mild disgust. He had no use for Society.

It took him only a moment to locate Imogen among the dancers. His eye went to her as if she were the only woman in the room. For a moment he allowed himself to enjoy the vision. The green silk skirts of her gown flirted about her ankles. She wore matching dancing slippers and long green gloves. Ringlets of tawny hair peeked out from beneath a towering evening turban.

She would have been a riveting sight, Matthias thought, if it were not for the fact that she was in the arms of Alastair Drake. The only consolation was that Drake was obviously having difficulty maintaining his balance. Even from where he stood, Matthias could see that Imogen was charting the course across the floor. He grinned briefly and felt his mood lighten.

He pulled his attention away from Imogen and searched for his sister. He was surprised to see Patricia in the center of a cluster of male admirers. She looked flushed and excited. Her pink and white gown was all that was proper for a well-bred, stylish young lady.

Horatia stood dutifully nearby, smiling with the air of a proud hen presenting her only chick. She was chatting with Selena, Lady Lyndhurst, who was her customary celestial self in a pale blue gown.

Well, that took care of one problem, Matthias thought. Thanks to Imogen and Horatia, his sister was a success. With any luck, his solicitor would be drawing up marriage settlement papers by June.

His sense of satisfaction vanished when he noticed that Hugo Bagshaw was making his way through the crowd toward Patricia. His hand tightened around the balcony rail. He made a note to warn his sister that Bagshaw's attentions were not to be encouraged.

Matthias glanced again at Imogen, who had just finished the waltz with Drake. He could tell that she was waxing enthusiastic on some subject, most likely lost Zamar. She motioned energetically with her fan as she made a point. She was so involved with her subject that she failed to see a nearby footman who carried a tray full of glasses. Unfortunately, Drake did not notice the impending disaster either until it was too late.

Matthias winced as Imogen swept her fan out in a wide arc and dashed several glasses of champagne to the floor. Then he leaned forward to watch the animated spectacle that ensued. The hapless guests in the immediate vicinity hopped quickly aside.

The footman cast a reproachful look at Imogen and then went to his knees to retrieve the bits of broken glass. Imogen, looking extremely distressed, stooped to assist him. She was forcibly constrained from doing so by Drake, who hastily whisked her away from the scene.

It was all over in a matter of moments. Matthias smiled to himself as he turned and strode toward the staircase.

It took several minutes to reach Imogen, who now stood with Patricia, Horatia, and Selena. When he arrived, the young men gathered in the vicinity quickly edged aside to allow him to make his way to the center of the circle. He could see Hugo watching him from the outer perimeter.

Imogen spotted Matthias first. "Ah, there you are, Colchester. We have been waiting for you. Patricia is a huge success. Horatia and I have been obliged to beat off her admirers with a large stick."

Several of the young gentlemen laughed uneasily, their wary gazes on Matthias.

"Indeed." Matthias surveyed Patricia, who smiled at him rather anxiously, as though she awaited his verdict. Imogen kicked Matthias's ankle with the toe of her dancing slipper. He glanced at her and saw from her expression that he was supposed to say something more. "I can certainly comprehend why Miss Waterstone and her aunt have had to protect you. Congratulations, Patricia. You are a diamond of the first water tonight."

Patricia blinked in surprise. Her cheeks turned pink and relief shone in her eyes. She visibly regained a measure of confidence. "Thank you, sir."

Selena gave a husky laugh. "The *on-dit* is that your charming sister has promised every dance, Colchester."

"Excellent." Matthias looked at Imogen. "Well, then, that's that. May I have this dance, Miss Waterstone?"

"Of course, my lord. I would be delighted." Imogen swung around and led the way toward the dance floor.

With a sigh, Matthias reached out, seized hold of her elbow, and dragged her to a halt. She gave him a startled glance.

"Is there something amiss, my lord? Did you change your mind?"

"Not at all. I merely thought it might be pleasant to walk out onto the floor at your side rather than to follow you as if I were a hound on a leash."

"Oh. Sorry. Take your time, sir. I did not mean to rush you. Occasionally I forget that yours is not an athletic nature."

"I am grateful for your understanding." Matthias guided her to the dance floor with a firm grip and took her into his arms. "You appear to be in fine form tonight."

"I enjoy excellent health, sir. Always have."

"I am delighted to hear that." Matthias applied sufficient force to take charge of the waltz. It was a challenge. "I was, however, referring to your looks rather than your health. That gown is extremely attractive on you."

Imogen glanced down as if she had forgotten what she was wearing. "It is quite lovely, isn't it? Madame Maud made it. Horatia tells me that she is very exclusive." She looked up. "I'm sure you'll be pleased to learn that Horatia thinks Patricia has been well received tonight. The invitations will no doubt pour in tomorrow."

"I owe you and your aunt a debt of gratitude for taking charge of Patricia's social life."

"It was no trouble at all, sir. Horatia tells me that Lady Lyndhurst has invited Patricia to attend her Zamarian salon which meets tomorrow. Quite a coup. She will meet any number of young ladies her own age there."

"I doubt that she'll learn much about ancient Zamar, however," Matthias said dryly. "Selena's salon is nothing more than a fashionable amusement."

"I see." Imogen's brows drew together in a frown of concentration as she attempted to steer him in a different direction. "Well, there is no great harm in that, my lord." She sounded a trifle breathless from her exertions.

"Perhaps not." Matthias glanced past her shoulder and saw that Hugo had led Patricia out onto the floor. "But there may be a problem with young Bagshaw's attentions. I shall speak to Patricia tomorrow about him."

Imogen's eyes widened. "What on earth is wrong with Mr. Bagshaw? He seems a very respectable gentleman."

"I suspect his interest in Patricia is motivated more by his wish to avenge himself against me than it is pure admiration of my sister."

"What in the world are you talking about, sir?"

"It's a long story." Matthias whirled her around in a wide, sweeping circle that brought them close to the French doors. "Suffice it to say that young Bagshaw holds me accountable for his father's decision to blow his brains across the wall of his study."

"You cannot be serious. What happened?"

"Arthur Bagshaw lost most of his fortune in a shipping venture that failed. The night he learned of the loss he came to The Lost Soul. He was very drunk and sunk in melancholy. I suppose he had some notion of recouping his losses at my gaming tables. I refused to let him play."

"That was very decent of you, sir. Bagshaw obviously could not afford to lose whatever money he had left."

"I don't know how decent my action was," Matthias

said dryly. "Bagshaw and I quarreled. He went home and took out his pistol. That is all there is to the tale."

"Dear God," Imogen whispered. "Poor Hugo."

Matthias brought her to a halt. "Hugo blames me for what happened. He believes that his father lost his fortune in The Lost Soul."

"You must set him straight at once, sir."

"Some other time."

"But, Matthias, this is really too—"

"I said I'll take care of the matter some other time. At the moment I wish to speak to you."

"Certainly, my lord." Imogen unfurled her fan. She began to wave it industriously. "It is a trifle warm in here, is it not?"

"Have a care with that weapon." Matthias drew her out through the terrace doors. "I have recently witnessed its destructive capability."

"What?" She frowned at the fan and then her face cleared. "Oh, I collect you saw my unfortunate little mishap a few minutes ago. It was not my fault, sir. The footman was standing directly behind me. We never saw each other until it was too late. Just one of those things. That's why they call them mishaps."

"Indeed." Matthias eyed the colorful lanterns that decorated the terrace and then elected to steer Imogen down the steps and deep into the night-shrouded gardens.

"Well, sir? What did you wish to discuss?" she asked when he brought her to a halt behind a tall hedge.

Matthias hesitated, listening closely to make certain that they were alone in this portion of the vast gardens. "I have just come from my club. You were right about Vanneck. He has indeed taken your bait. There are rumors of a consortium being formed to find the Queen's Seal."

"But that is wonderful, sir. Why are you so anxious?"

"Imogen, I don't like it. Vanneck is being extremely secretive."

"Well, naturally. Just as one would expect. He will

not want such a project being bandied about all over Town."

"The only reason I learned of his plans is that he approached an acquaintance of mine who told me what was afoot. I suspect Vanneck is deliberately attempting to keep me in the dark."

"Calm yourself, Colchester." Imogen tapped the sleeve of his coat with her folded fan in a gesture that was no doubt intended to reassure him and shore up his nerve. "Everything is well in hand."

"You keep saying that."

"Because it's true. My scheme is unfolding just as I envisioned it would." Her eyes gleamed with satisfaction.

Matthias studied her face in the moonlight and felt the hunger rise within him. "Imogen, is there any chance that I can make you see how dangerous this scheme is? Any possibility of talking you out of going forward with it?"

"I'm sorry, Colchester," she said gently. "I know how nervous you are, but I have come too far. For Lucy's sake, I cannot abandon my quest for justice."

"Lucy meant a great deal to you, did she not?"

"She was my best friend," Imogen said simply. "Indeed, after my parents died, she was my only friend."

"What of Drake?" he made himself ask.

She blinked. "I beg your pardon?"

He cradled her face between his hands. "He was your friend too. Do you sometimes dream of him? Do you wonder what might have been between the two of you if he had not seen you in that bedchamber with Vanneck?"

She stilled. "No. Never."

"Are you certain?"

"Whatever feelings I had for Alastair died the night he turned away from me in disgust because of what he thought he'd seen." Her eyes narrowed. "He never gave me a chance to explain. He never once questioned his own conclusions. I could never, ever feel any warm emotions for a man who had so little faith in me."

Matthias tipped her head back so that he could see her moonlit eyes. "Do you think that you could ever learn to feel some warm emotions for me?"

Her lips parted in shock. "Matthias? What are you saying?"

"Too much, I suspect. Perhaps it is past time for talk." He bent his head and covered her mouth with his own.

The need that had been simmering inside him exploded without warning.

Her mouth tasted as exotic and sweet as the effervescent springs of Zamar must have. Matthias crushed her close, abruptly desperate to feel the soft, firm curves of her thighs pressed against him.

Imogen gave a small, muffled cry. "Matthias."

For an instant he feared she would push herself away from him. He was seized by a terrible desperation, gripped by a need that emanated from the darkest, coldest regions inside him.

It seemed to Matthias that in that shattering moment his fate hung in the balance.

And then her arms went eagerly around his neck. Relief surged through him. He freed her mouth long enough to gaze into her eyes. A familiar sensation roared through him. This was what he had felt when he discovered the great columns that marked the entrance to the ancient ruins of lost Zamar.

"Imogen?"

She smiled at him with longing and feminine promise.

He brushed his mouth against hers. She trembled and returned the kiss with an enthusiasm that threatened to deprive him of breath. The music and the laughter from the ballroom receded into the distance. Matthias's concentration narrowed until the only thing that mattered was Imogen.

Without releasing her lips, he stripped off his gloves and dropped them heedlessly on the ground. Then he curved his hands around her shoulders and slowly eased the tiny sleeves of her gown aside.

She shivered when the small, high-waisted bodice slipped downward, freeing her elegant breasts.

"Matthias?"

"You are beautiful," he whispered. "You remind me of the pictures of Anizamara painted on the walls of the library of Zamar. Full of life and warmth."

She gave a shaky laugh and buried her face against his shoulder. "You will not believe this, sir, but I have had the oddest dreams of late. In them, you seem to become Zamaris or he becomes you. I cannot tell which."

"It would seem that we share our interest in Zamar even in our dreams." He fitted his hands to her waist and lifted her straight up off the ground. The movement brought her breasts to the level of his mouth. He took one firm nipple between his teeth and sucked gently.

"Matthias." She clutched at his shoulders and held on as if for dear life. "What are you doing?" Her voice rose as he circled her nipple with the tip of his tongue and then bit down very gently. "This is . . . surely this is . . ." She floundered into breathless silence.

He released the dainty fruit and turned his attention to the other nipple. He felt her fingers dig into his shoulders. The moan that went through her aroused him as nothing else had ever done.

Imogen began to rain frantic little kisses in his hair.

Matthias glanced around and spotted a garden seat. He carried Imogen to the stone bench and sat down with her in his arms. Her skirts tumbled over his breeches. He tugged the flounced hem of her gown up above her knees.

"Whatever are you about, sir?" Imogen demanded as he slid one hand between her warm thighs. "Is this some strange Zamarian lovemaking technique?"

"What?" The scent of her filled his head. He could not seem to concentrate on her words.

"In one of your articles in the *Zamarian Review* you

alluded to a scroll that you discovered that described certain customs of the Zamarian matrimonial bedchamber."

"Could we discuss this later, my sweet?" He kissed her throat.

"Yes, of course." Imogen turned her face into his coat and clung to his lapels. "It's just that this all feels so odd."

"On the contrary." He nibbled on her earlobe. "It feels incredible."

"I have often wished that you had published more detailed information of your discoveries on the subject of Zamarian marital relations. I read several times the one article that you wrote, but I was always left to wonder just what you meant when you hinted that the Zamarians were quite uninhibited."

"Kiss me, Imogen."

"Oh. Yes, of course." She lifted her head and parted her lips.

He took her mouth again and at the same moment cupped the hot, damp flesh between her legs.

Imogen screamed softly in surprise. Matthias swallowed the sound. She awkwardly tried to close her legs, but she succeeded only in trapping his hand. He probed carefully and she relaxed against him in a rush of pulsing excitement.

He eased one finger into her softness. "You are so warm and tight."

She shivered in his arms. Tiny muscles clenched gently against his finger. He thought that he would lose what little remained of his self-control.

"Matthias, this is so . . . so . . ." She sipped air and tightened herself. Her head fell back. Her turban slipped off and dropped to the grass.

Over and over again Matthias drove his finger deep, pushing through the constricting, glovelike passage. At the same time, he used his thumb on her small, hidden jewel.

With a startled cry Imogen convulsed and came apart in his arms.

He held her close, glorying in her response. He was on the brink of exploding inside his breeches, but he managed to hold himself in check. Later, he promised himself as he cradled her fiercely to him. His turn would come later. Right now the only thing that mattered was that she had found her satisfaction in his arms.

After a moment Imogen stopped trembling, although she still gripped the edges of his coat with such force that he knew the expensive fabric would be crushed. He absently noted that his cravat had somehow come undone. Imogen's hair spilled around her shoulders.

Matthias realized that although he ached with unsatisfied desire, he felt young and free, as he had not felt in years.

Imogen slowly raised her head to gaze at him with eyes made huge by sensual wonder. She smiled up at him from the curve of his arm. "That was the most astounding thing that I have ever—"

Voices, those of a man and a woman, interrupted whatever it was Imogen had been about to say. The reality of their precarious situation hit Matthias with the force of freezing rain. He realized that the other couple was only a few feet away. All that stood between Imogen and discovery was the tall hedge.

"Hell and damnation," he whispered.

He stood up with Imogen in his arms and quickly set her on her feet. There was no need to warn her. He could see that she had heard the voices. She grabbed futilely at her drooping bodice.

The voices moved closer. Soft laughter from the woman. A murmured comment from the man.

Matthias started to reach down to scoop up his gloves and then realized Imogen was having trouble adjusting her gown.

"Here, let me do that." He managed to drag the tiny sleeves back up onto her shoulders. Her breasts disappeared. There was nothing he could do about her loosened hair, however, or the turban that had fallen to the grass. She was the very picture of a woman who had just been locked in an abandoned sensual embrace.

"Come." He took her hand, intent on getting her away from the scene before the other couple came around the corner of the hedge. Imogen stumbled as she clutched his hand.

"Colchester." Selena, followed by Alastair Drake, rounded the hedge at that moment. "And Miss Waterstone. What are you two doing . . . ? Oh, dear." A slow, knowing smile curved her lips. "Never mind. I can see perfectly well what you are doing."

"Imogen." Alastair stared at her with a shocked expression.

Matthias stepped in front of Imogen in a vain effort to conceal her, but he knew the damage had been done. He saw Alastair's eyes go to a dainty dancing slipper and the turban that lay next to his discarded gloves.

Selena gazed at Matthias's loosened cravat and gave a rich, amused chuckle. "Well, well, well. I do believe that we have interrupted some very interesting researches into the subject of ancient Zamar, Mr. Drake."

Alastair was tight-lipped. "So it would seem."

"You have indeed interrupted something quite interesting," Matthias said. "But it was not a scholarly investigation. Miss Waterstone has just consented to become engaged to me. You may be the first to congratulate us."

Chapter 8

She was standing in her uncle's sepulchral library. This time she could feel a chill wind. She saw that the window was open, allowing the night to flow into the chamber. A stone sarcophagus loomed in the shadows. She was certain that it had not been there the last time. The lid had been removed. There was something inside. Something dangerous.

She started toward the sarcophagus and then paused when she felt the hair on the nape of her neck stir. She knew that he was in the room with her again. She turned slowly and saw Matthias/Zamaris. The moonlight gleamed on the icy silver in his hair. His austere features were in deep shadow.

He held out one elegant hand. Blood glistened on his fingers. "Lies," he whispered in a darkly sensual voice. "Do not believe the lies. Come to me."

"*I*t is a disaster." Imogen shoved aside the memories of her latest disturbing dream and forced herself to

concentrate on the crisis. "He has ruined everything. My entire scheme is in a shambles."

"Calm yourself, dear." Horatia, seated in a chair with her embroidery, peered at her over the rims of her spectacles. "I'm certain Colchester knows what he is about."

"Rubbish." Imogen threw her hands up into the air and stormed across the study. "It's a bloody disaster, I tell you. This morning everyone in Polite Society believes that Colchester and I are engaged."

"You *are* engaged, dear. The announcement last night made it quite official."

Imogen flung out a hand and accidentally struck a scented sweet jar off its stand. It bounced on the carpet and rolled under the desk. The dried herbs and flowers that had been inside fluttered to the floor. She paused briefly to glower at the small heap of faded roses and bay leaves.

"How could he do this to me?" she demanded of the universe at large.

Horatia considered that. "He obviously felt he had no choice. The situation was an extremely compromising one for you. Much worse than last time because Lady Lyndhurst witnessed it in addition to that nice Mr. Drake. Selena thrives on that sort of gossip. There was no possibility of hushing things up."

Imogen winced. "I suppose not."

She was fairly certain that Alastair could have been persuaded to keep his mouth closed. He was an old acquaintance who had once been something more than a friend. But there was no reason to believe that Lady Lyndhurst would have been discreet.

"Colchester did the only thing a true gentleman could do under the circumstances." Horatia frowned. "I must say, I'm rather amazed. His reputation is not such that one would expect noble behavior."

"You are wrong, Aunt Horatia. Colchester is exactly the sort of gentleman who would try to salvage my reputation. But I fear he did not stop to consider the results of his actions." Imogen resumed her pacing.

"You are being very hard on him, my dear." Horatia set a stitch in her embroidery. "This cannot be any easier on Colchester than it is on you."

"But it is my plans that are in ruins. A broken engagement will finish me so far as Society is concerned. You know the lady always takes the blame in such situations."

"I know, dear."

"If I end the engagement, I will put myself beyond the pale. I will not receive any further invitations."

"Yes, dear."

"And then how will I carry out my plans to trap Vanneck?"

"I have no notion, dear."

"Exactly. I am trapped." Imogen slammed a palm down on her desk as she went past it. The inkstand trembled. "One would almost think that Colchester did this deliberately."

Horatia's needle hovered in midair. "Deliberately?"

"You know very well that he has been opposed to my scheme from the start."

"Well, he admitted at the beginning that he was extremely anxious about the thing," Horatia conceded.

"Precisely." Imogen frowned. "Mayhap his nerves were so frayed from the pressure of his role in this affair that he decided to put an end to my scheme in this underhanded fashion."

"As I am forever telling you, Imogen, Colchester is not the sort to suffer from frayed nerves."

"And as I am forever explaining to you, he is possessed of very delicate sensibilities. That sort often suffers from a weakness of the nerves." Imogen narrowed her eyes as the suspicion built within her. "Last night, just before the disaster, he told me that Vanneck was attempting to form a secret consortium. My scheme was coming to fruition. I could see that the news had clearly shaken

Colchester. Evidently I failed to understand just how overset he was."

"Indeed."

"He must have panicked."

"Panicked? Colchester?"

"Perhaps he was so disturbed and anxious that he took drastic action to crush my scheme before it could go any further."

Horatia contemplated that notion. "I suppose this engagement does complicate your plans."

"It has made a complete tangle of them," Imogen snapped. "The idea was to make Vanneck believe that he was in competition with Colchester."

"I know."

"I wanted him to think that I was willing to form a partnership with whomever would finance an expedition to Zamar. I wanted Vanneck to believe that he had every chance of convincing me to let him become my partner." Imogen swept out a hand and missed a vase of flowers by inches. "Now he will likely abandon any notion of forming his consortium."

"True. Under the circumstances, Vanneck will naturally assume that he no longer has a chance at the Queen's Seal. Colchester has cut him out very neatly, has he not? No lady can form a business partnership of the sort you intend with one man when she is engaged to marry another. It isn't done."

"Precisely." Imogen came to a halt beside her desk and drummed her fingers on the polished surface. "It isn't done. The lady's loyalty must lie with her future husband, who will control her business affairs. Colchester knows that. Which is why I strongly suspect that this is a desperate ploy on his part. I fear it may have worked. He has effectively destroyed my scheme."

Horatia glanced at Imogen over her spectacles. "You make this sound as if it were all Colchester's fault. A nefarious plot to ruin your plans."

"I suspect that is just what it was."

"May I ask how he managed to compromise you on his own? Did he lure you into a secluded portion of the garden and force his attentions upon you?"

Imogen blushed furiously. "Not exactly."

The memories of Matthias's lovemaking had kept her awake for the better part of the night. The emotions that she had experienced in his arms had left her feeling unsettled and dazed. The mixture of excitement and unaccustomed sensations had been almost too much even for her strong nerves.

She had gazed at the ceiling for hours, wondering what sort of impact those strange sensations had had on Matthias. She was not altogether certain that he had felt anything particularly unusual. He had seemed very much in command of himself when Lady Lyndhurst and Alastair had appeared.

Imogen stifled a small sigh. She feared that whatever emotion Matthias had experienced last night had not been of a deeply stirring nature, as hers had most definitely been. The dream shortly before dawn had not helped settle her uneasy emotions.

Dawn, however, had brought a clearer head and a full realization of just what had been lost. And Horatia's gentle accusation of complicity only made matters worse. Very well, she had kissed Matthias willingly, Imogen thought. But matters would have ended right there if he had not employed exotic Zamarian lovemaking techniques to seduce her senses.

"Well, dear?" Horatia prompted.

Imogen cleared her throat and straightened her shoulders. "I told you, we went out into the garden to discuss the progress of my plans. We were discovered together by Lady Lyndhurst and Alastair Drake."

"Merely being discovered together in the garden would not have necessitated an engagement announcement. Not at your age, my dear."

"I am aware of that." Imogen sought for a way to change the subject. She did not want to go into detail about the events of last night. "I fear Lady Lyndhurst and Alastair assumed the worst."

"The gossip that went through the ballroom indicated that they discovered you in a state of complete dishabille," Horatia said with rare ruthlessness. "I heard that your hair was down about your shoulders. Your dress was rumpled and one of your shoes had come off. The bodice of your gown appeared to have come partially undone. According to one report, Colchester's gloves and your turban were lying on the grass."

Imogen was horrified. "You heard all those lurid details?"

"And more." Horatia sighed. "A great deal more. They are calling you Immodest Imogen again, my dear. You would have been ruined this morning if Colchester had not waved a magic wand and declared that the pair of you were engaged."

Imogen collapsed into the chair behind her desk and covered her face with her hands. She tried to school her thoughts so that she could think logically and coherently. But her brain had gone to mush.

"Bloody hell," she muttered. "What am I to do now?"

"You really must watch your language while we are in Town, dear," Horatia chided. "I realize that you learned the habit of swearing from your mother, but I must remind you that she was considered unconventional."

Imogen glared at Horatia through her fingers. "I beg your pardon, Aunt. But *bloody hell* seems to be the only adequate expression I can find at the moment."

"Nonsense. A lady can always find the appropriate words for any occasion."

A brief peremptory knock interrupted Imogen before she could think of a suitable response. Mrs. Vine opened the study door. Her heavy face was set in its customary morose lines.

"A message for ye, Miss Waterstone." She held a

folded piece of paper in one work-worn fist. "A lad brought it round to the kitchen a few minutes ago."

Imogen quickly lowered her hands and folded them on top of her desk. "Let me have it, please, Mrs. Vine."

The housekeeper trudged into the room and put the note on the desk. Then she turned around and lumbered back toward the door.

"Hold a moment, Mrs. Vine." Imogen picked up the paper and unfolded it. "I may wish to send a reply."

"As you wish, ma'am." Mrs. Vine waited stoically in the doorway.

Imogen glanced at the short message.

My Dear Imogen:
    I shall arrive at five this afternoon to collect you for a drive in the park. I look forward to seeing you. Do not allow yourself to become overwrought about recent events. We shall find a satisfactory way to deal with matters.
                    Yrs.
                    Colchester

It was too much. "Overwrought?" Imogen growled. "Me? I am not the one with weak nerves."

Horatia gave her an inquiring look. "I beg your pardon?"

"Never mind." Imogen crumpled the note in her hand. "Yes, Mrs. Vine, I definitely wish to send a reply."

Imogen snatched a sheet of foolscap from the drawer, dipped a quill in ink, and scrawled a hasty message.

Colchester:
    I received your note. I regret that I will be unable to join you for a drive in the park today. I am otherwise engaged.
                    Yrs.
                    I. A. Waterstone.
P.S. Unlike some people who are troubled by

nervous weakness, my own temperament is not the sort that becomes overwrought by unfortunate events.

Imogen carefully folded and sealed the letter and then held it out to Mrs. Vine.

"Please see that this is delivered immediately."

"Aye." Mrs. Vine shook her head as she took the letter. "Messages comin' and goin', goin' and comin'. Puts me in mind of another tenant I had a few years back. A little demi-rep. Member of the fancy set her up here for a few months. The two of 'em was always sendin' messages back and forth. When they weren't tumblin' about in the bed, that is."

Imogen was briefly distracted. "Someone's mistress once lived in this house, Mrs. Vine?"

"Charming little thing, she was. But she was French, y'know. Took a lover on the side. Another one of the fancy." Mrs. Vine sighed. "She had good taste, I'll say that for her. But her first lover, the one what paid the rent, found the pair of 'em in bed. Had a fit. Pulled a pistol out of her reticule and shot the bit o' muslin in the shoulder. Terrible mess on the sheets. Next thing I know, her other lover—"

"One moment here, Mrs. Vine." Horatia eyed her intently. "Are you saying that the member of the ton who paid the rent for the little demi-rep was a lady?"

"Aye. Lady Petry. Always paid the rent on time, she did."

"What happened?" Imogen asked, fascinated.

"Well, the little demi-rep weren't bad hurt. I fixed her up and then all three of 'em started cryin' and apologizin' and carryin' on. The next thing I know they asked me to bring 'em a tray of tea in the parlor. By the time I got back from the kitchen, everything was settled."

"Settled?" Horatia asked.

"Turns out that Lady Petry and Lady Arlon, that's the

lady who was in bed with Lady Petry's bit o' muslin, had both secretly been in love with each other for years."

"Good heavens," Horatia breathed. "Lady Petry and Lady Arlon?"

"Neither of 'em had ever told the other," Mrs. Vine explained. "Well, in the end they gave the bit o' muslin a nice sum of money and sent her on her way. She was happy enough with what she got out of the whole thing. Set herself up in business as a dressmaker. Madame Maud, she calls herself. Very exclusive."

*T*he second note from Colchester arrived within the hour. When Mrs. Vine brought it into the study, Imogen eyed it askance. Something told her that she did not want to read it. Slowly she unfolded the crisp paper.

Dear Imogen:
      I advise you to cancel the afternoon appointment that you mentioned in your note. If you are not at home when I call for you at five o'clock, I will assume that you have suffered some terrible misfortune. Those of us plagued by weak nerves and grave forebodings always assume the worst. Indeed, I shall be unable to rest until I have located you and assured myself that you are safe. Believe me, I will find you, even if I am obliged to search the whole of London.

                                        Yrs.
                                        Colchester

Horatia looked up expectantly. "From his lordship?"

"Yes." Imogen crushed the second note in her fist. "Who would have thought that a man who suffered from a weakness of the nerves would be so good at intimidation?"

o   o   o

Patricia returned from her first round of social calls at four-thirty that afternoon. Matthias was in his library. He was in the process of concluding some notes for a lecture he was scheduled to deliver to an audience at the Zamarian Society. He heard Ufton open the front door and greet his sister.

A moment later Ufton rapped once on the library door. Matthias put down his quill. "Enter."

Ufton opened the door. Patricia, dressed in one of her new afternoon gowns, hurried into the room. She looked distraught.

"Matthias, I must speak with you."

"Can it wait? I'm about to leave for an appointment. Miss Waterstone and I are to drive in the park this afternoon."

"It is Miss Waterstone I wish to discuss," Patricia said with surprising firmness.

Matthias leaned back in his chair and surveyed his sister. "You no doubt have some questions pertaining to my engagement."

"In a manner of speaking." Patricia removed her bonnet and clutched it very tightly in front of her with both hands. "I have just come from Lady Lyndhurst's. She was kind enough to invite me to call upon her this afternoon."

"I know. I trust you enjoyed yourself."

"Very much. She conducts a salon, you know. The members are studying Zamar. It is really quite interesting. I have been asked to join them."

"Indeed."

"But that is not what I wish to speak to you about." Patricia took a deep breath, obviously bracing herself for what she had to say next. "I must tell you, sir, that today I heard some extremely distressing news about Miss Waterstone."

Matthias stilled. "I beg your pardon?"

"I am sorry to tell you this, Colchester, but Miss

Waterstone was a topic of conversation at the salon. I felt you should know."

"A topic of conversation." Matthias wrapped his hands around the carved arms of his chair. "Do you mean to say that you listened to gossip about my fiancée?"

Patricia blanched at his tone. "I thought you should know that her name is on everyone's lips. Apparently she has a certain history. You will not believe it, but they actually call her Immodest Imogen."

"No one calls her that in my presence."

"Matthias, everyone is saying that you felt obliged to announce your engagement because Miss Waterstone compromised herself with you last night."

"What transpired between Miss Waterstone and myself last night is no one else's business but our own," Matthias said very softly.

"I don't understand." Patricia looked genuinely baffled. "I thought you would be as shocked as I am by the news that Miss Waterstone has a blemished reputation."

"As far as I'm concerned, her honor is untarnished and anyone who says otherwise will answer to me. Is that quite clear?"

Patricia took an uneasy step back, but she raised her chin. "Very well, you must do as you see fit."

"Precisely." Matthias got to his feet and started around the corner of the desk.

"If you wish to be engaged to a woman of questionable virtue, that is your affair," Patricia said defiantly. "But you cannot expect me to continue to go about with Miss Waterstone and her aunt. I have my own reputation to consider."

Anger flashed through Matthias. "As long as you choose to remain under my roof, you will show respect to Miss Waterstone and her aunt."

"But, Matthias—"

"By the bye, since we seem to be dealing with the subject of suitable associations, I may as well tell you that

I do not want you to become friends with Hugo Bagshaw. Do not encourage him."

Patricia was stunned. "Mr. Bagshaw is a perfect gentleman. He is entirely above reproach."

"Hugo Bagshaw hates me. He may very well attempt to use you to take revenge on me for something he believes that I did years ago. Stay away from him, Patricia."

"But—"

Matthias was already at the door. "You must excuse me. I have an appointment."

*I*mogen was seething. Matthias wondered that she did not set fire to his coat as she fumed beside him in the carriage. He smiled ruefully to himself as he drove the well-matched grays through the stone pillars that marked the entrance to the park.

The paths were already crowded with elegant equipages. Five o'clock was the fashionable hour to see and be seen. Matthias did not enjoy Society, but he knew its ways. He understood, even if Imogen did not, that it was crucial for the two of them to appear together that afternoon. The entire ton would be watching for them.

"I trust you appreciate precisely what your anxious nature has done to my plans," Imogen said brusquely.

"I regret any inconvenience our engagement has caused you."

She shot him a fulminating look. "Do you, sir? I wonder. It has occurred to me that last night's debacle might very well have been deliberately perpetrated by you. A blatant attempt to nip my plans in the bud."

"What makes you think that?" Matthias inclined his head a bare half inch at an acquaintance in a passing carriage.

"It is very simple. I came to that conclusion when I realized that you had practiced secret Zamarian methods of lovemaking upon my person."

Matthias nearly dropped the reins. "What the bloody hell are you talking about?"

"Do not try to cozen me, my lord. It will not work." Imogen's gloved hands clenched fiercely around her folded fan. She stared straight ahead. "I am not a fool. I am well aware that you used certain mysterious techniques designed to throw my senses into complete disarray."

"I see. And you believe I learned these, uh, exotic techniques in the course of my study of ancient Zamar?"

"Where else? They were certainly not normal methods of lovemaking. I perceived that fact immediately."

A reluctant fascination took root in Matthias. "Is that so? What makes you so certain?"

She shot him a disgruntled look. "I am not without experience, my lord."

"Indeed."

"I have been kissed any number of times and I know that your kisses are not the normal sort."

"Precisely how do my kisses differ from the others you have experienced?"

"You know very well how they differ, sir." Imogen's tone turned distinctly frosty. "They affected my knees so that I could scarcely stand. And they made my pulse race in a most unnatural manner. Furthermore, I am certain that they induced a temporary fever."

"A fever?" Matthias thought wistfully of the way she had shivered in his arms.

"I felt much too warm." She scowled ferociously at him. "But the most damning evidence is that your kisses completely destroyed my capacity to think logically. One moment I was feeling perfectly rational, concentrating on my plans to trap Vanneck, and the next, my brain was in chaos."

Matthias gazed at the tips of his horses' ears. "You say you have never experienced these same reactions when other men have kissed you?"

"Absolutely not."

"How many men have kissed you, Imogen?"

"That is a personal matter, sir. I would not dream of giving you a number. A lady does not discuss such things."

"Forgive me. I respect the fact that you are not the type to kiss and tell. But if you're using Alastair Drake as your only basis of comparison, I feel I must tell you—"

"Mr. Drake is not my only basis of comparison." Imogen whirled about on the seat. "For your information, my lord, I have been kissed by another man."

"Have you, indeed?"

"And he was a Frenchman," she added triumphantly.

"I see."

"The whole world knows that the French are very skilled in lovemaking."

"How did you meet this Frenchman?" Matthias asked.

"If you must know, it was Philippe D'Artois, my dancing master."

"Ah, yes, the dancing master. That does put a slightly different face on the matter. I suppose I shall have to concede that you do have some basis for comparison."

"I certainly do," Imogen retorted. "And I know perfectly well that the strong feelings I experienced last night were not the result of ordinary lovemaking methods. Admit it, sir. You used exotic Zamarian techniques to disorder my senses."

"Imogen—" There was a sharp crack. Matthias broke off to glance at her fan. He saw that she had been gripping it so tightly that she had accidentally snapped the delicate sticks. "I was about to say that there is another explanation for the strong feelings you say you experienced last night."

"Rubbish. What would that other explanation be?"

"It's possible that the reason you reacted as you did was that you have developed what Society likes to call a *tendre* for me," he suggested gently. "In other words, a degree of passion has developed between us."

"Nonsense." She suddenly became extremely interested in a passing carriage. "How could there be such a . . . an intense degree of passion without love?"

"That is an extremely naive thing to say, Imogen."

Hooves clattered on the path. Vanneck came up alongside the phaeton. Out of the corner of his eye Matthias saw Imogen paste a strained smile on her face.

"Good day to you both," Vanneck said grimly. He tightened the reins of his prancing bay stallion. The horse flattened its ears as the bit ravaged its mouth. "I understand that congratulations are in order."

"They are," Matthias said.

"Thank you, Lord Vanneck," Imogen murmured stiffly. She began to tap the broken fan against her knee.

Vanneck's smile was thin. The expression did not reach his eyes, which flicked back and forth between Matthias and Imogen. There was an element of sly, hungry watchfulness in that gaze. He reminded Matthias of a ferret.

"Some are saying that your future bride brings a most interesting dowry, Colchester," Vanneck observed.

"Miss Waterstone does not need a dowry to make her interesting," Matthias said. "She is quite riveting all on her own."

"I have no doubt of that. Until later, sir." Vanneck nodded brusquely and cantered off down the path.

"Hell's teeth," Imogen whispered. "I was so close. He had fallen into my trap. It remained only to shut the door on him."

Matthias scowled. "Give it up, Imogen. It's finished."

"Not necessarily," she said slowly.

Matthias was suddenly wary of the new expression in her eyes. "Imogen—"

"It has just struck me, Colchester. Mayhap there is a way to salvage something of my initial plan."

"Impossible. You cannot form a partnership with Vanneck now that you are engaged to me. Such things are not done."

"It's true that you have ruined my first scheme."

"I am sorry, Imogen, but I feel it was for the best."

"All is not lost," she said as though she had not heard him. "I have this very moment come up with another plan."

"Bloody hell."

"It is true that I am no longer in a position to form a partnership with Vanneck, but in the role of my fiancé, you can certainly do so."

"What the devil are you talking about now?"

"It is quite simple, my lord." She gave him a blinding smile. "You will tell Vanneck that you do not wish to risk a large portion of your own funds to finance an expedition. You will, however, allow him to become your partner. *If he can come up with the money to secure his share of the bargain.*"

"Good God." Matthias was awed in spite of himself.

"Don't you see? The effect will be the same as I had originally intended. Vanneck will still need to form a consortium to get his hands on the money he needs. And he will still be ruined when the expedition fails."

Matthias gazed at her in bemused wonder. "Do you ever give up, Imogen?"

"Never, my lord. My parents taught me to persevere."

Chapter 9

"I shall not beat about the bush, my lord." Light glinted angrily on the lenses of Horatia's spectacles as she confronted Matthias from the other side of his desk. "I came here today to find out just what sort of game you are playing with my niece."

Matthias steepled his fingers and gave her a deliberately quizzical smile. "Game?"

"What would you call this announcement of an engagement?"

"I thought you would be pleased, madam. The engagement will put an end to her dangerous scheme. Is that not what you wanted?"

"Do not be so certain that it will end the matter," Horatia retorted. "You know very well that she is already devising a way to go forward with her plans to ruin Vanneck."

"Yes, but her latest scheme requires more than just my assistance. It requires my complete cooperation in a false business venture. I do not intend to provide it."

Horatia frowned. "What do you mean?"

"I have no intention of luring Vanneck into a partnership. I doubt that he would consider such an alliance, even if I were willing to offer it. Not even for the sake of the Queen's Seal. We are natural enemies, Vanneck and I, not allies. Calm yourself. All will be well."

"Don't tell me to calm myself. You sound just like Imogen when you say that."

Matthias shrugged. "The thing ends here, Horatia."

"Ends? For God's sake, you have announced a formal engagement, Colchester. You know what that means. Where does that leave Imogen?"

"Engaged."

She stared at him in mounting fury. "Do not jest with me, sir. We are speaking of a young woman whose reputation has been savaged enough as it is. How do you think she will fare when you call off the engagement?"

"Something tells me that Imogen would survive the end of our engagement quite nicely. She is never without resources, is she? But as it happens, I do not intend to call it off. Nor do I plan to allow her to do so."

Horatia's mouth opened and closed. And then it firmed into a straight line. "Are you implying that your intentions are . . . are—"

"Honorable?"

"Well?" she challenged. "Are they?"

"You needn't look so stunned. The answer is yes." Matthias briefly glanced down at the Zamarian scroll that he had been studying when Horatia was shown into the library a few minutes earlier. Then he met Horatia's eyes. "I do believe they are."

"You intend to wed Imogen?"

"Why does that surprise you?"

"Sir, in spite of your unfortunate past and your even more unpleasant reputation, you are the Earl of Colchester. Everyone knows you possess a vast income and an impeccable lineage. To be blunt, you can look a good deal higher than a young woman of Imogen's birth and fortune when you set out to find a wife."

"You have assured me that through you she is connected to the Marquess of Blanchford."

"Don't be ridiculous." Horatia snorted. "That connection is extremely remote and well you know it. She is not in line for a single penny of his money. Furthermore, thanks to her eccentric parents, she lacks the social skills one expects in a countess. And on top of everything else, she has been thoroughly compromised, first by Vanneck and now by you. How can you expect me to believe that you are serious?"

"I think she will make me an excellent wife. The only difficulty that I can see lies in convincing her of that fact."

Horatia stared at him, clearly baffled. "I don't understand you, sir."

"Then you must trust me. I give you my oath that I intend to marry Imogen. The engagement is not a charade. At least, not on my part."

"Is this another one of your famous promises, sir?" Horatia asked with deep suspicion. "The sort you are said to keep at all costs?"

"Yes. It is." Matthias felt the conviction in his bones.

*H*e waited until the library door closed behind Horatia before he got to his feet. He carefully rerolled the scroll and set it aside. Then he walked around the edge of his desk and crossed the room to where the brandy decanter stood on the small inlaid table.

He splashed brandy into a glass and raised it in a mocking toast to the statue of Zamaris. "It won't be easy, you know. She has no intention of marrying me at the moment. But I have one clear advantage over her. I have very few scruples to hinder me and almost no gentlemanly instincts. Just ask anyone."

Zamaris looked down on him with the complete understanding that only one male who lives in the shadows, surrounded by ghosts, could offer to another.

Matthias went to stand in front of the fire. He did not

know precisely when the notion of marrying Imogen had formed in his mind. He only knew that he wanted her with a passion that was equaled only by his feelings for lost Zamar.

Imogen was his Anizamara, his lady of sunlight, life, and warmth. She was the one who could hold the ghosts at bay.

"And thus my investigations have shown that while there were certainly some Greek and Roman influences on the manners and customs of ancient Zamar, much of the literature and architecture of the people of that island was unique."

Matthias tossed aside the last of his notes with a sense of relief. He gripped the edges of the podium and looked out over the large audience that had gathered to hear him. "That concludes my talk on lost Zamar." He forced himself to add politely, "I shall be happy to answer a few questions."

Polite applause rang out across the crowded lecture hall. With the exception of Imogen, who sat in the front row, no one clapped with a great deal of enthusiasm. Matthias was not surprised. He had not gone there to entertain. He had been intent only on impressing the one person in the crowd who could appreciate his research and conclusions: I. A. Stone.

Imogen, he noted, was applauding with gratifying energy.

As a rule, Matthias dreaded these events. Ever since Zamar had become fashionable, the crowd that gathered to hear him speak had been increasingly composed of the dabblers, amateurs, and dilettantes he detested. He was well aware that the interest of the vast majority of the people sitting in front of him was superficial, at best. But that day he had lectured to a worthy rival, and Matthias was already anticipating Imogen's rebuttal.

He glanced down at her as the applause diminished.

She glowed in her seat, a bright, lively beacon in a chamber filled with dim, sputtering candles. Desire crashed through Matthias with the force of lightning. He would have her for his own. All he had to do was play his cards carefully. In her innocence and naiveté, she stood no more chance of evading him than Anizamara did of eluding Zamaris. He took a deep breath. His hands flexed on the sides of the podium. He would take the lead in this waltz. Whatever happiness he was fated to discover in life depended upon it.

Imogen was wearing another of her Zamarian-green gowns and a matching green pelisse trimmed with dolphins and shells. Her heavy hair was anchored beneath a massive green bonnet.

Matthias allowed himself to bask in the admiration he saw in her wide, intelligent eyes. *Intelligent, but so innocent.* He reflected on the fascinating accusations she had made during the drive through the park yesterday. Rather than admit to the passion that flared between them whenever they kissed, Imogen had actually convinced herself that he had employed secret Zamarian lovemaking techniques.

The last of the applause finally dissolved. Imogen leaned forward slightly in her chair, clasped her hands in her lap, and watched Matthias with rapt attention as he prepared to take questions from the audience. He had a fleeting, highly imaginative vision of her gazing up at him with a similar expression from the depths of the Zamarian dolphin sofa in his library. He was abruptly and profoundly grateful for the large wooden podium that shielded the lower portion of his anatomy from the view of the audience.

A portly man seated toward the back of the room hove to his feet and cleared his throat very loudly. "Lord Colchester, I have an inquiry."

Matthias stifled a groan. "Yes?"

"You said nothing in the course of your lecture on the

possible influence of Chinese society on the manners and customs of ancient Zamar."

Matthias saw Imogen roll her eyes. He knew precisely how she felt. Few things were more annoying than foolish questions.

"That is because there is no discernible influence," he said unequivocally.

"But wouldn't you say, sir, that the characteristics of the Zamarian script bear a striking resemblance to Chinese writing?"

"None whatsoever."

The questioner grumbled and sat down.

Another man rose. He scowled at Matthias. "Lord Colchester, I could not help but notice that you failed to discuss the notion put forth by Watley that Zamar was actually an ancient English colony."

Matthias endeavored to hold on to his patience. It was not easy. "Sir, the theory that Zamar was a lost English colony is as misguided, wrongheaded, and idiotic as the notion that Egypt was also an ancient outpost of this nation. No respectable scholar gives credence to either of those two opinions."

Imogen jumped to her feet. Her elbow caught the large reticule of the lady seated next to her and sent it flying. Matthias watched with interest as a brief flurry of activity ensued in the front row.

"Oh, dear," Imogen muttered. She bent down to retrieve the fallen reticule. "Do forgive me, madam."

"Quite all right," the lady said. "Quite all right."

Imogen straightened and turned her attention back to Matthias. Her eyes gleamed with determination. "Lord Colchester, I wish to ask a question."

"Of course, Miss Waterstone." Matthias leaned negligently against the podium and smiled down at her with anticipation. "What is it you wish to ask?"

"In your book on the manners and customs of ancient Zamar you include several sketches which you copied from the walls of the Zamarian library."

"Indeed."

"One of those sketches distinctly shows a wedding ritual. In it the bride and groom appear to be receiving tablets inscribed with poetry. Would you say that the scene implies that Zamarian marriages were founded upon a notion of true equality between the sexes and that a strong metaphysical communion existed between husbands and wives?"

"No, Miss Waterstone, I would not draw any such conclusion," Matthias said. "The scene on the wall of the Zamarian library was a metaphorical painting of the Zamarian goddess of wisdom giving the gift of writing to the ancient Zamarians."

"Are you quite certain that it was not a wedding ritual? It seems to me that the inscription on the tablets in the lady's hand constitute a wedding contract of some sort."

"As it happens, Miss Waterstone, I was fortunate enough to discover an actual Zamarian marriage scroll."

A murmur of interest went through the crowd.

Imogen's eyes widened with excitement. "What was contained in the scroll, sir?"

Matthias smiled. "The inscriptions were more in the nature of instructions. They were accompanied by some extremely detailed drawings."

Imogen's brows drew together in a quizzical frown. "Instructions? On the respective rights and obligations of husbands and wives, do you mean?"

"Not exactly," Matthias said. "The text provides directions and practical advice on certain delicate matters pertaining to the intimate side of the married state. Personal matters, if you take my meaning, madam."

Titters, chuckles, and a few embarrassed laughs broke out across the crowd. Several older ladies frowned. A number of younger ones displayed a fresh interest in the discussion.

Imogen fitted her hands to her hips and began to tap the toe of one little kid half-boot. She glowered at those around her and then at Matthias. "No, my lord, I do not take your meaning. Precisely what sort of advice is on that scroll?"

"The inscriptions advise married couples on specific techniques designed to ensure that both husband and wife find happiness and satisfaction in the marital bedchamber. And that is all I intend to say on the matter, Miss Waterstone."

There were several shocked gasps from the crowd. The titters and chuckles in the back row grew louder. Imogen lowered her brows and looked as if she were preparing to fire another question. Matthias moved quickly to forestall it.

He drew his watch from his waistcoat pocket and surveyed the time with an air of surprise. "Ah, I see that the hour is concluded. I thank you all for your kind attention." He scooped up his notes and started to descend from the podium.

Imogen met him as he reached the last step. Her eyes were sparkling with determination. "A very exciting talk, my lord."

"Thank you. I'm glad you enjoyed it."

"Oh, I did. Immensely. I was particularly taken with your observations concerning the pictures on the walls of the Zamarian library. How I wish I could have accompanied you when you discovered it."

"I would have liked to have had your opinions," he said honestly.

"About that marriage scroll you mentioned, I would very much like to view it, if I may."

"I have never made it available to other scholars," he said with slow deliberation. "But I might be willing to make an exception in your case."

Imogen brightened. "Would you, Matthias? That would be wonderful. When may I see it?"

"I'll let you know when it's convenient."

Her face fell. "I trust you will not delay too long, sir. I am impatient to study it."

"A charming thought."

"I beg your pardon?"

"Never mind." Matthias smiled. "In the meantime, you might find a private tour of the Zamarian Society's museum interesting."

"Extremely interesting," Imogen said. "But it has been closed to the public since I arrived in London."

"That is because the trustees of the Zamarian Society are preparing to move the collection into a larger chamber. At the moment the museum is actually more of a storage room. But I have a key. I shall be happy to serve as your guide."

Imogen's face lit up once more. "That would be thrilling."

He glanced around the rapidly emptying room. Only a handful of people remained and those few would soon be gone. He removed a key from his pocket.

"I see no reason why we cannot tour the museum now." He paused. "If you are free, that is."

"Yes, indeed. Perfectly free, sir."

"The door to the museum is just around the corner." Matthias indicated the direction with a slight inclination of his head. "Beneath the staircase."

"How exciting." Imogen set off toward the museum entrance at such a brisk pace that the skirts of her gown whipped about her ankles.

Matthias barely managed to grab hold of her arm before she vanished around the corner. "I fear you must wait for me, my dear. I've got the key."

"I hope you will not dawdle, sir."

"No, but neither do I intend to gallop across the hall."

She sighed. "I keep forgetting that you are not inclined toward athletic activity."

"I try to compensate in other areas." Matthias guided her around the corner and beneath the broad staircase that gave access to the upper floors of the Zamarian Institution.

When they reached the door to the museum, he drew Imogen to a halt and inserted the key into the lock. Then he opened the door and stepped back.

He watched Imogen's expressive face as she gazed into the gloom-filled interior. He was not disappointed. Her eyes filled with wonder and her lips parted as though in expectation of a lover's kiss. Only Imogen could have been counted upon to react in such a fashion to a chamber crowded with dusty artifacts and the ghosts of a long-lost people.

"This is wonderful." Imogen stepped into the room and gazed around at the array of objects that loomed in the shadows. "Did you bring most of these antiquities back from Zamar yourself?"

"No. I confess that I kept the pieces I brought back. They are in my library." Matthias lit a wall sconce. "The items you see here are those that Rutledge chose to transport back to England after our first journey to Zamar. As you can see, he favored size over delicacy."

Imogen tugged a shroud off a ten-foot-tall statue of Zamaris and blinked when she found herself at eye level with the god's oversized genitals. "I see what you mean." She hastily raised her gaze. "Oh, dear, it appears that the arm was broken off at the shoulder and repaired."

"Unfortunately, much of what Rutledge found was damaged due to his poor excavation techniques. He had no engineering skills." Matthias stroked the jagged edge of a broken column. "And little interest in the subtle details of the artifacts we uncovered. He was after treasure or items he believed he could sell to collectors."

"Poor Rutledge." Imogen walked around a vase that was as tall as she was. "Such a tragic ending. And so very mysterious."

"I trust you are not going to tell me that you believe in that ridiculous business of the Rutledge Curse."

"Of course not. But there is no getting around the fact that Rutledge did not survive his last trip to Zamar."

Matthias flattened his hand on the column. "There is

nothing mysterious about his death, Imogen. He grew careless during his explorations of the labyrinth. He broke his neck when he fell down a stone staircase that he had apparently failed to notice in the darkness. I was the one who found him."

She gave him a searching glance. "How terrible that must have been for you."

A chill went through Matthias. He knew then beyond a shadow of a doubt that she sensed that there was more to the story. "Yes. It was."

The questioning expression in Imogen's eyes was instantly replaced by sympathy. Matthias breathed a small sigh of relief as she moved on to a large sarcophagus.

"Have the items in this collection been properly catalogued?" Imogen asked as she studied an inscription on the lid of the sarcophagus.

"No. I'm the only one who has the knowledge and skill to do it properly, and I have not had the time to take on the task." *Or the inclination,* he added silently. Everything in this chamber was connected to Rutledge.

Imogen straightened and looked at him with an expression of gathering excitement. "I could do it, Matthias."

"Catalogue the collection?" He hesitated. "Yes, you could. It might be interesting to have I. A. Stone's opinions on these items."

"Do you think the trustees would allow me to study and record the artifacts in this chamber?"

"I control the trustees," Matthias said. "They will do as I say. But it would mean revealing your identity as I. A. Stone."

She considered that. "Perhaps the time has come." Then she sighed. "But first things first. I came to London to deal with Vanneck. I must get on with it. Have you given any thought to my new plan to lure him into a partnership, Matthias?"

"No."

"I cannot waste any more time, sir." Imogen

crouched down to inspect a large clay mask that was propped against the coffin. "I want to implement my new scheme as quickly as possible. Before everyone learns our engagement is a sham."

Matthias moved closer to her and found himself gazing down at the top of her bonnet. "Imogen, has it occurred to you that our engagement need not be a sham?"

"I beg your pardon?" Imogen shot to her feet in startled surprise.

Matthias stepped back quickly and just managed to avoid being struck by the brim of her bonnet. Off balance, Imogen flung out a hand with the apparent intention of catching hold of the edge of the sarcophagus. Unfortunately she grabbed the top of a tall vase instead. It started to topple.

"Oh, no," Imogen wailed.

Matthias caught the vase before it shattered on the floor. He righted it carefully. Then he turned back to Imogen. She was gazing at him with a dumbfounded expression.

"I don't think I heard you correctly, my lord," she said weakly.

"I think that we would make an excellent match." He reached for her and drew her into his arms.

She seized the lapels of his coat. "Matthias, what are you doing? There has been no talk of love between us."

"What we share is stronger and more enduring than any such metaphysical nonsense." He untied the strings of her bonnet and tossed it aside.

She searched his face with a desperate expression that threatened to tear asunder something deep inside him. He had the terrible sense that he hovered on the brink of one of the five Zamarian hells.

"What . . . what do we share?" she asked.

"Passion and Zamar." He bent his head and took her mouth with all the fierce longing that had been growing inside him for days.

Imogen gave a muffled cry and wrapped her arms

around his waist. She pressed herself against him and parted her lips beneath his. He felt the storm rise within her even as the thunder rolled through his own veins.

He threw himself recklessly into the gathering gale. Imogen tightened her hold on him. Her soft hips nestled intimately against his rigid shaft. When he broke off the fevered kiss to explore the secret, scented place at the nape of her neck, she shivered.

"Matthias, I do not comprehend what you do to me," she said breathlessly. "I vow, it is the most amazing sensation."

A cold rain swirled out of the tempest, chilling the fire in his blood. Matthias dragged his mouth away from the silken skin at the base of her neck. "No. I will not have you this way."

"What is it? What's wrong?"

He caught her face in his hands and forced her to meet his eyes. "When this is finished, I will not stand accused of employing secret Zamarian lovemaking methods to seduce you."

"But, Matthias—"

"I want you more than I have wanted anything since I went in search of Zamar. But unless you feel an equal passion for me, this embrace goes no further."

"Oh, Matthias. You feel toward me what you felt for Zamar?"

"Yes."

She went very still in his arms. Her long lashes lowered to conceal her gaze. For a shattering moment Matthias thought that he had lost her. He knew then which of the Zamarian hells it was that yawned at his feet. It was the third hell, the one in which a man faced a thousand years of living alone with only phantoms for company.

Imogen lifted her eyes to meet his. She smiled tremulously. "It was grossly unfair of me to accuse you of employing Zamarian lovemaking secrets to seduce me. I apologize. I was angry because you had ruined my plans with your announcement of an engagement."

"I know."

"In truth, I have only myself to blame for what happened in the garden the other night." She hesitated. "I wanted you to make love to me then and I want you to make love to me now."

Matthias realized that he could breathe again. "Are you certain?"

She stood on tiptoe and wound her arms around his neck. "I have never been more certain of anything in my life."

"*Imogen.*" His arms tightened fiercely around her. He started to lower his head.

Imogen halted him by the simple expedient of putting her fingertips against his lips. "My lord, let me clarify this matter."

"Clarify?"

"We are agreed that we venture into this embrace with complete understanding between us."

"Yes."

"Your fears that I will hurl accusations at you afterward have been put to rest?"

"Most assuredly." He began to nibble on her fingertips.

Her eyes glowed. "Then, under the circumstances, I do not see any reason why you cannot teach me one or two ancient Zamarian lovemaking secrets, do you?"

Relief and laughter welled up inside him. "No reason at all." He caught her hand before she could remove it from his lips and kissed her palm.

Imogen sighed and leaned into him. Her fingers curled around his. Matthias moved his mouth down to her vulnerable wrist and gloried in the small quiver of desire that went through her.

She stood on tiptoe and returned his kiss with unabashed enthusiasm. He moved his mouth up along the curve of her cheek to her ear. She speared her fingers through his hair. He shuddered.

"We'll take this slowly," he promised.

"If that is your wish." She unwound his cravat.

"We shall savor every moment. We shall drain each second of all sensation before we move on to the next."

"You remind me of one of the new poets, sir." She began to pry at the fastenings of his shirt. "Or is that Zamarian verse that you are spouting?"

"I would have you remember this occasion for the rest of your life," he said earnestly.

"I am hardly likely to forget it." Imogen yanked impatiently at his shirt. The sound of the fine linen being ripped apart was very loud in the dusty chamber. "Oh, dear."

Matthias grinned into her hair.

"I seem to have torn your shirt, sir. I am most dreadfully sorry."

A light-headed feeling came over him. "Forget the shirt, madam. I have a vast number of them."

"How fortunate."

Matthias tipped her face up again and gazed at her soft, full mouth. At that moment he dismissed his plans to make slow, deliberate love to her. A fever was upon him. He burned, and from the looks of his shirt, so did she.

He swept Imogen into his arms and carried her through the ghostly remains of ancient Zamar to a bench that had been positioned against the far wall.

A cloud of dust rose as he settled Imogen on the shrouded cushions. Matthias winced, but she did not seem to notice. She looked up at him with glowing eyes. There was a great deal to be said for a lover who shared his intellectual interests, Matthias told himself. He had very likely discovered the only woman in all of England who would not complain about being seduced in a gritty, grimy museum.

He kissed the tip of her nose and then straightened to rid himself of the dangling neck cloth. He flung it over a sarcophagus and then swiftly freed himself of his coat, waistcoat, and the damaged shirt. He smiled briefly at the sight of the tear in the expensive linen.

He tossed the garment aside and looked down to find Imogen watching him intently. There was a sweet yearning in her expression that made him catch his breath. The tip of her small pink tongue appeared at the corner of her parted lips.

"You are quite beautiful, my lord," she whispered in a soft, husky voice. "Indeed, I . . . I have never seen the like."

Matthias gave a hoarse laugh. "You are the only truly beautiful creature in this room." He lowered himself into the sea of green muslin skirts. His head spun as he sank beneath the waves.

"Matthias." Imogen clutched at his bare shoulders.

He gathered her to him and kissed her until Imogen shivered and her head fell back over his arm. Then he reluctantly freed her mouth to follow the beckoning line of her throat. She twisted beneath him, lifting herself until he could feel her breasts crushed against his chest.

When his kisses reached the decorous neckline of her gown, he reached around to unfasten the bodice. It fell away, revealing a linen chemise that was so thin, he could see the outlines of two rosy nipples through it. His whole body clenched.

He lowered his head and kissed her breasts until he had dampened the fabric that covered them. Imogen cried out and began to kiss his shoulder with a frantic eagerness.

Matthias reached down, grabbed a fistful of her skirts and the hem of the chemise. He hauled the whole lot up to Imogen's waist, revealing the triangle of tawny curls that shielded her secrets.

With a husky groan he bent his head and planted a kiss on the inside of one silken thigh. The scent of sunlight on a Zamarian sea filled his head. Very reverently he closed his hand around her, cupping her warmth.

Imogen's soft gasp was intoxicating. He felt her turn to liquid against his palm and thought that nothing had ever thrilled him so much in his entire life.

"This is beyond anything." Imogen's nails sank into his shoulders. Shiver after shiver rippled through her. "My lord, I do not care a fig if you employ every secret Zamarian lovemaking technique that you have ever discovered. I would learn them all this afternoon."

"Unfortunately, I do not possess the patience to run through the entire repertoire." Matthias fumbled with his breeches, freeing himself. "But I promise that eventually we will practice every single one. Wrap your legs around me, my sweet."

"My legs?"

"I need to be inside you." He raised one stocking-clad knee and eased it into position around his waist. "I will go mad if I wait any longer."

Imogen obediently circled him with her thighs. "Matthias, this feels very strange. Did you learn this position from that ancient Zamarian marital scroll you mentioned?"

He stroked her gently. "Some things are universal."

He felt her soften and open for him. His hand was slick with the dew he had coaxed forth from her snug passage. He used the moisture to lubricate the dainty pearl that throbbed above the entrance. Imogen moaned.

"Good heavens, I don't . . . I cannot . . ." Imogen swallowed the rest of whatever it was she had tried to say.

Matthias raised his head to look down into her passion-dazed face. "Look at me, Imogen. Open your eyes and look at me."

Her lashes fluttered and then lifted. She smiled slowly up at him, a smile that contained more mysteries than the ruins of lost Zamar.

Matthias surrendered to the powerful need that consumed him. Parting her carefully, he fitted himself to her and forged slowly into her hot, clinging passage.

Imogen froze in his arms. "Perhaps you have not got it right, sir. Your translation may have been faulty."

He clung to his sanity and his control with every vestige of his strength. "What are you talking about?"

"This particular Zamarian lovemaking technique obviously is not suited to a man of your proportions, Matthias. We must try another."

"You're a virgin," he whispered against her nose.

"What the devil does that have to do with your poor translation of the Zamarian instructions for this method?"

"Nothing," he admitted.

"I am not suggesting that we stop. I merely wish to try another technique."

"We must master this one before we go on." He brushed his mouth against hers. "Do you recall how it was for you the other night in the garden?"

She looked up at him with anxious eyes. "Yes. But this is entirely different."

"Wait and see." He started to ease himself slowly out of her clinging channel. The sensation was an indescribable, exquisite torment. "Take a deep breath." He reached down between their bodies and stroked her firm little jewel. He was rewarded with a tiny tremor of response.

Imogen inhaled sharply. And then she began to soften around him. She was just as tight as she had been a moment earlier, but some of the tension in her body began to dissipate. Matthias sank himself slowly, carefully, back into her.

Imogen sighed and scored his back with her nails.

He withdrew partway again and kissed her chemise-covered nipples. "Better?" he whispered.

"Yes. Yes, I . . . I believe this particular method may work after all. Have I got it right?"

"Perfect." Matthias clenched his teeth and fought to hold himself in check as he thrust slowly back into her warmth. "Absolutely perfect."

"*Matthias.*" Without warning, she trembled and convulsed beneath him.

Sensation tore through Matthias. He was alive and he was bathed in sunlight. At that moment no ghost could touch him.

Chapter 10

The following evening Matthias arrived at the theater just before the last act of *Othello*. Imogen, seated with Horatia and a sulking Patricia, gave him a reproving frown as he walked into the plush box. It was the first time she had seen him since he had made love to her in the Zamarian Institution.

"My lord, we had almost given up on you," Imogen whispered as he took her hand. "You have missed most of the play."

Matthias's mouth curved faintly. She saw the intimate memories of yesterday in his ghost-gray eyes. "I trust you will never give up on me, my dear." He kissed her gloved hand and turned to greet Horatia and Patricia. "Good evening, ladies. You are both looking very lovely this evening."

Horatia inclined her head. "My lord."

Patricia gave him a fulminating look. "You said you would meet us here, Matthias."

"And so I have."

Patricia flicked her fan. "The performance is nearly finished."

"I have discovered that a small dose of theatrics goes a long way." Matthias took the chair next to Imogen. "I pray you will not attempt to outdo Kean this evening, Patricia. You would not stand a chance of competing against him. Even drunk, he is the better actor."

Patricia flinched and then turned away with a small, angry flounce. She gazed grimly at the glittering crowd seated in the boxes across the way.

Imogen swallowed a small sigh, aware that she was the cause of the new hostility between Matthias and Patricia. For some unfathomable reason, Imogen's relationship with Patricia had deteriorated swiftly during the past few days. That evening it had been clear that Patricia had resented being forced to sit with Imogen and Horatia in her brother's box.

Imogen did not comprehend what had caused the change in Patricia's attitude, but it worried her. She intended to discuss the matter with Matthias at the earliest opportunity. But first there was another, more pressing item on her agenda. She had begun to suspect that Matthias was deliberately avoiding her. And she was fairly certain she knew why.

Imogen leaned toward Matthias and began fanning herself vigorously in order to make it appear to onlookers that her conversation was of an inconsequential nature. She trusted to the noise of the gossiping crowd and the rowdy cries from the pit to ensure that no one nearby overheard.

"Sir, I am delighted that you finally deigned to put in an appearance. It is about time you showed up."

"I have missed you too," Matthias murmured. "It seems as though an eon has passed since you had such an elevating effect on my spirits."

"Matthias, for heaven's sake, hush." Imogen blushed furiously and glanced wildly about to make certain that no one had heard him. "That is not what I wished to discuss with you, and well you know it."

"I am devastated." His eyes gleamed. He caught her hand and kissed her fingertips. "I assure you, our tryst amid the ruins of ancient Zamar has been the only thing on my mind for the past night and day. Indeed, since that magical time, all rational thought has flown."

She glowered at him. "What on earth is the matter with you, my lord?"

"You have inspired me, my sweet. I am thinking of abandoning my scholarly studies in favor of becoming a romantic poet. How do you think I would look with crimped hair?"

Imogen narrowed her eyes. "You are attempting to avoid the subject, are you not, sir?"

"What subject?"

"The subject of my new scheme to trap Vanneck," she hissed behind her fan.

"I would prefer to see the subject closed."

"Yes, I know you would, but I have no intention of putting aside my plans simply because we are engaged."

Matthias's brows rose. "You deem our engagement a mere bagatelle, then? I am crushed."

Another wave of heat went through her. Imogen increased the velocity of the fan. "You know very well that is not what I meant, sir."

"Have a care with that fan, madam. You are creating a draft. We romantic-poet types are very prone to chills."

She ignored him. "Matthias, I am very serious about this matter. I want your word that you will assist me in trapping Vanneck."

"This is not the time to discuss it."

"But—" A small commotion rose above the general din of the crowd. Imogen broke off and turned to glance out over the audience. "What is it? Has something happened?"

"Perhaps Kean is so far into his cups that he cannot take the stage," Horatia suggested. She leaned forward with an expression of great interest and raised her opera glass to her eye.

It was Patricia who spotted the source of the new wave of excitement that was rippling through the crowd. "It's Mrs. Slott. I believe she has fainted."

Horatia swung her opera glass toward Theodosia Slott's box, which was directly opposite Matthias's. "Yes, indeed. Theodosia appears to have collapsed in her chair. Lady Carlsback is waving a vinaigrette under her nose."

Imogen lowered her fan to peer at the small group milling about in Theodosia's box. "Whatever is the matter with that woman?"

Patricia cast an accusing look at Matthias. "Lady Lyndhurst says Mrs. Slott frequently falls into a swoon whenever Matthias appears. She says something dreadful happened in the past and Mrs. Slott has never recovered from the shock."

"Bloody hell," Matthias said wearily.

Imogen scowled. "What utter nonsense." She realized that heads across the way were turning toward the Colchester box. Speculation rumbled through the theater.

She folded her fan with a snap. Determined to make it clear to one and all that Matthias did not face the gossiping tongues of the ton alone, she leaped to her feet. Taking hold of the arm of her spindly little chair, she started to shove it closer to Matthias's chair.

He glanced at her, saw what she intended, and belatedly started to get to his feet. "Imogen, allow me to deal with your chair."

"Quite all right." Imogen gritted her teeth and pushed against the arm. "It seems to be stuck, but I can manage, my lord."

"Imogen, wait—"

The chair was heavier than it looked. Irritated, Imogen shoved harder. One delicate wooden leg suddenly cracked and gave way.

The small chair toppled over onto the red carpet. Imogen lost her balance and shot forward. She landed in

Matthias's lap. He caught her easily and grinned as she clutched wildly at his shoulders to steady herself.

Her dolphin-trimmed satin evening turban came free and went sailing over the rail of the box. It fluttered down into the cheap seats far below. A great shout went up from the boisterous young men who inhabited the lower regions of the theater.

"I've got it."

"It's mine. I saw it first."

"What, ho, I seem to have netted a dolphin."

"Hand it over. It's mine by right of salvage."

Horatia looked over the side of the box. "I do believe they are fighting over your turban, Imogen."

Laughter roared through the theater.

Patricia looked as if she were about to break into tears. "I am mortified. Absolutely mortified. I could die right here in this horrid box. How shall I face my friends at Lady Lyndhurst's salon tomorrow?"

"I'm sure you'll manage," Matthias said heartlessly. He stood and settled Imogen on her feet.

"I apologize to all of you," Imogen muttered as she brushed out her skirts. "I did not mean to cause such a ridiculous scene."

"No apology is necessary." Matthias grinned. "I assure you, this is the most entertaining evening I have spent at the theater in years. And since the performance on the stage is unlikely to match this one, I suggest that we all take our leave."

A short while later Imogen stood with Patricia amid the crowd that clogged the theater lobby. Matthias had gone outside to hail his carriage, which was one of many in a long row that snaked down the street. Horatia had turned aside to chat with an acquaintance.

Imogen glanced at the silent, sullen Patricia and decided to seize the opportunity. She took a step closer.

"Is there aught amiss, Patricia? I sincerely regret that

unfortunate scene a few minutes ago. However, I must point out that you seemed annoyed with me even before that occurred."

Patricia's face turned a dull red. She did not meet Imogen's eyes. "I have no notion of what you are talking about."

"Rubbish. I thought you and I were getting along rather well together. You appeared to take pleasure in our shopping expeditions. You seemed delighted with your success in Society. But during the past couple of days you have come very close to giving me what the Polite World calls the cut direct."

Patricia edged back a step and gazed fixedly at the lobby doors. "I cannot imagine what you mean, Miss Waterstone."

"So it's Miss Waterstone again, is it?" Imogen put her hands on her hips and began to tap one toe. "I thought we had agreed that you would call me by my Christian name."

"Must you tap your toe in that offensive manner?" Patricia asked through set teeth.

"I beg your pardon?"

"Everyone is staring at you."

"Nonsense." Imogen glanced around. "No one is watching me."

"How can they help but stare?" Patricia shot back. "You have the manners of a country hoyden. Look at your unladylike posture. Indeed, it is embarrassing to be seen with you when you stand with your hands in that immodest position and tap your toe in that common way. You lack all ladylike refinement and grace."

"Oh." Imogen blushed and quickly took her hands off her hips. "Sorry. I took dancing lessons a few years ago, but other than that I have never bothered to study the niceties of proper ladylike behavior."

"That," Patricia said tightly, "is obvious."

"My parents thought such instruction was unimportant." Imogen shrugged. "And to be perfectly truthful, I have had a great many other, more interesting things to learn."

"Apparently so." Patricia whirled about to confront Imogen directly. Her eyes glittered with tears of humiliation and anger. "I vow, I do not comprehend what my brother sees in you. I cannot imagine why he has asked you to marry him. You are aware, I assume, that people call you Immodest Imogen?"

"I know. I can explain how that unpleasant name came about."

"You do not have to explain. I have heard all of the sordid details concerning your past."

Imogen eyed her closely. "You have?"

"You were discovered in a bedchamber with Lord Vanneck."

"Who told you that?"

"A friend." Patricia bit her lip. "Someone I met at Lady Lyndhurst's salon. Everyone there talks about you. They say that Matthias was obliged to become engaged to you because you compromised yourself with him the other night."

"Hmm."

"They say that you have done to him what his dreadful mother did to my poor papa all those years ago. You have trapped him."

"What on earth are you talking about?"

Patricia blinked owlishly and took a step back. She seemed to realize that she had gone too far. "I'm sure you know very well, Miss Waterstone. It seems to be no great secret here in Town that my father was forced to marry Matthias's mother after she deliberately arranged to compromise herself with him."

Imogen frowned. "And you believe that Matthias has been snared in the same sort of web?"

"I cannot imagine any other explanation for why he would choose you to be his countess," Patricia whispered. "Everyone at Lady Lyndhurst's salon says that Matthias could have his choice of the young ladies on the Marriage

Mart this Season. He could have selected a woman with an unblemished reputation. Someone who is not known to all and as sundry as Immodest Imogen. Dear heaven, it is so humiliating.''

"I can see this is all very difficult for you," Imogen said dryly.

The theater door opened and Matthias strode into the warm lobby. He caught sight of Imogen and started toward her. Patricia suddenly looked very anxious. She cast an uneasy sidelong glance at Imogen.

Matthias frowned at his sister. "Are you feeling ill, Patricia? You look a bit peaked."

"I'm quite all right," she muttered. "Please. I just want to go home."

Imogen smiled blandly. "I fear that Lady Patricia is a bit overwrought from the events of the evening, my lord. She suffers from the tendency toward nervous weakness that runs in your family."

*I*mogen stalked into her study the moment she and Horatia arrived home. She tossed her evening cloak across a chair, stripped off her long kid gloves, and kicked off her shoes. Then she collapsed onto the sofa and glowered at her aunt from beneath lowered brows.

"Tell me everything you know about his parents' marriage, Aunt Horatia. I cannot deal with a problem if I do not have all the facts."

"There is not much to tell." Horatia helped herself to a bit of sherry from the decanter that sat on a small table. "It is very old news. Some thirty-five years old, to be precise. I was a young woman myself at the time."

"Were you acquainted with Colchester's mother?"

"I had met Elizabeth Dabney, but we did not move in the same circles." Horatia sat down near the fire and took a sip of sherry. "Elizabeth was considered a trifle fast, if you must know the truth. She got away with it because she was beautiful and charming and her father was an extremely wealthy and powerful man. Her parents had indulged her since the day she was born. She got whatever she wished."

"And she decided that she wanted Matthias's father?"

"So everyone said." Horatia's smile was wry. "But as I always say, it takes two. His name was Thomas and he was a viscount at the time. He had not yet come into the title because his father was still alive. He was just as spoiled as Elizabeth. He was also very arrogant and very handsome. Quite the rake that Season. I'm sure he did not think that he would have to pay a price for dallying with Elizabeth. I doubt that Thomas had ever paid for anything in his young life."

Imogen scowled. "That brings up an interesting question. Why did he have to pay? Thomas was the heir to an earldom. Surely he could have escaped Elizabeth's net had he truly wished to do so."

"The title was bankrupt." Horatia gazed thoughtfully into the fire. "No one knew it at the time. From all accounts, the old earl was delighted when his son was discovered in a compromising position with Elizabeth. He badly needed her inheritance to replenish the family coffers. And Dabney desperately yearned for a title for his only daughter. It was actually a good match from almost everyone's point of view."

"Except that of young Thomas?"

"Yes. But he did not dare defy his father for fear of being cut off entirely. He married Elizabeth. It was not a happy marriage, as you can guess. But then, how many are?"

"My parents were happy," Imogen said softly.

"True. I fear that you grew up with a very distorted sense of reality, my dear. In any event, there were no more children after Matthias was born. Thomas and Elizabeth lived apart most of the time. For several years Thomas kept a string of mistresses here in Town. Elizabeth contented herself with lavish house parties at the Colchester country estate. The year she died, Thomas apparently fell in love with a young widow named Charlotte Poole. They were married soon after Elizabeth's death."

Imogen rested her arms along the back of the sofa and gazed into the fire. "And Patricia was born."

"Yes."

"Patricia told me tonight that everyone is saying that Matthias is doomed to the same fate as his father," Imogen said quietly.

Horatia glanced at her. "Patricia is a very young lady who has had little experience of the world."

"I, on the other hand, am a mature woman who knows very well what she is about."

"Meaning?"

Imogen met Horatia's eyes. "Meaning that I cannot allow Matthias to marry me if he does not truly love me. I could not bear to live with the knowledge that I had forced him to repeat his father's mistake."

A sad comprehension appeared in Horatia's eyes. "How long have you been in love with Colchester, my dear?"

Imogen smiled ruefully "Since I read his first article in the *Zamarian Review,* I suspect."

"What a tangle this has all become."

"Yes." Imogen took a deep breath. "And as I am the one who created this Gordian knot, it is up to me to unravel it."

*T*wo nights later Imogen stood unnoticed behind a massive potted fern in Lord and Lady Wellstead's ballroom and watched Patricia slip out into the hall.

Imogen frowned, wishing that Matthias were present to deal with this new dilemma. Unfortunately he had again managed to avoid putting in an appearance. His dislike of social events was swiftly becoming a problem because Patricia resented the chaperones he had assigned to her.

Patricia had grudgingly consented to being accompanied by Imogen and Horatia to and from various social affairs because Matthias gave her no choice. But once she had arrived at a soiree or ball she made it a point to put as much distance between herself and her companions as possible. It was clear that she was embarrassed by her brother's fiancée, and some of that attitude spilled over to include Horatia.

Imogen sighed as she watched her charge leave the ballroom. There was nothing for it, she would have to go after Patricia.

Imogen put down the glass of lemonade she had just taken from a passing tray. There was no reason to be overly concerned, she told herself. It was not as if Patricia had gone out into Wellstead's extensive gardens, where a young, innocent lady might conceivably get herself into serious trouble. A number of couples had already vanished into that shadowy world of high hedges and dark paths.

Imogen made her way along the wall to the door through which Matthias's sister had escaped. It was possible that Patricia was merely seeking respite from the huge crowd and the overheated atmosphere. But there had been something distinctly furtive about the way she had carefully glanced around before disappearing. It was as if Patricia feared she might be followed.

She certainly would not thank Imogen for coming after her. Unfortunately, Imogen's sense of duty would not allow her to ignore the situation. The mansions of the ton were dangerous places for young ladies who strayed from the protection of the crowd. Imogen had learned that lesson three years earlier.

She went through the door and found herself in a narrow servants' passage. It was empty except for a cart laden with lobster tarts. She went past it, turned a corner, and went down another hall. At the end of the corridor she discovered a cramped staircase that twisted around itself.

Imogen paused to search for another exit, but there was none. She realized that Patricia must have climbed the winding stairs to the next floor. Imogen felt a tingle of real alarm.

It was obvious that Patricia had known where she was going. If she had simply stepped out of the ballroom for fresh air, she would have retreated immediately once she had realized that she had wandered into a servants' passage. This departure had all the marks of a planned assignation.

Imogen lifted her skirts and quickly went up the narrow steps. Her soft dancing slippers made no sound on the wooden treads.

There was just enough light from a wall sconce to make out a door at the top of the stairs. Imogen opened it cautiously and peered around the corner. She saw nothing but dense shadow dimly lit at regular intervals by shafts of moonlight that filtered through a row of tall windows.

She went through the door and closed it quietly behind her. It took a few seconds for her eyes to adjust to the darkness. When they did, she was barely able to make out the glint of heavy gilded squares hanging on the wall. Dozens of them. She realized that she was in a picture gallery that stretched the entire length of the big house.

Imogen gazed about, searching the shadows for some sign of Patricia. A small sound at the far end of the long gallery made her whirl around. She caught sight of a wisp of pale skirts just before they vanished into an alcove.

"Patricia? Is that you?" Imogen strode forward briskly.

And promptly rammed a toe into the claw-footed leg of a chair she had not noticed in the darkness.

"Bloody hell." She winced and bent down to massage her injured toe.

A man stepped out of the shadows. "Miss Waterstone?"

"Who in the world—?" Startled, Imogen stepped back quickly and stared at the figure who was coming toward her. She recognized him as he passed through a shaft of moonlight. "Lord Vanneck."

"I regret this melodramatic arrangement." Vanneck came to a halt and stood looking down at her with unpleasant intensity. "But I had to speak to you in private. I've had a devil of a time arranging this meeting."

"Where is Lady Patricia?"

"She is already on her way back to the ballroom accompanied by a respectable lady. Patricia is quite safe, I assure you. Her reputation is in no jeopardy."

"Then there is no need for me to remain here." Imogen seized her skirts and made to dart around Vanneck.

"Wait." Vanneck grabbed her arm as she went past him, forcing her to stop. "I've gone to a deal of trouble to arrange this meeting, and I mean to talk to you."

"Let me go."

"Not until you've heard me out." Vanneck paused. "For Lucy's sake, you must listen to me."

"*Lucy's sake.*" Imogen froze. "What does this have to do with poor Lucy?"

"You were her friend."

"What of it?"

"Damnation, Miss Waterstone, hear me out. Lucy would have wanted me to protect you. You never did know how to defend yourself in Society."

"I don't need your protection, sir."

Vanneck's hand tightened on her arm. "Surely you realize that Colchester deliberately compromised you so that he could announce an engagement."

"He did no such thing."

"He's after the Queen's Seal. Have you given him the map?"

"No, I have not."

"I thought not," Vanneck said with grim satisfaction. "If you had, he would have terminated the engagement. Don't you see what he's doing? He will cast you aside the moment he gets his hands on the map."

Imogen smiled coolly. "You could not be more mistaken, sir."

Fury and desperation sparked in Vanneck's face. His fingers bit into her skin. "I want that damned seal, Miss Waterstone. Rutledge wrote that it is worth a fortune. Practically priceless."

"You're hurting my arm."

He paid no attention. "A few days ago I began to put together a consortium to finance an expedition to Zamar. Unfortunately, the potential members lost interest when they learned of your engagement to Colchester. In that single stroke he ruined my plans."

Something in his tone stirred the hair on the back of Imogen's neck. "I really cannot stand here discussing this with you tonight. I must return to the ballroom."

"End the engagement," Vanneck said fiercely. "End it quickly. It is the only way. If you get rid of Colchester, I will establish the consortium. You and I will become partners. We will be rich when we find the Queen's Seal."

It was exactly what she wanted, but at that moment Imogen saw the seething, unhealthy intensity in him and was suddenly afraid.

"I must go," she said quickly. "Perhaps we can discuss this some other time. It might be possible for you to form a business arrangement with Colchester."

"With *Colchester*?"

Too late she realized that she had said the wrong thing. "Perhaps—"

"Impossible," Vanneck snarled. "Colchester would never agree to such an arrangement. The whole world knows he murdered Rutledge. He would likely do the same to me if I were to form a partnership with him. You must end the engagement before you give him the map. It is the only way."

Anger replaced caution. Imogen drew herself up to her full height. "I will do as I wish, sir. Kindly release me."

"I will not be cheated out of the Queen's Seal by a

woman's whim. If you will not end the engagement, I shall do it for you."

It was as if something had snapped within him. Imogen realized the danger she was in and struggled desperately to free herself. She could not escape.

Vanneck used his grip on her arm to push her down onto a nearby sofa. He flung himself on top of her with such force that he knocked the breath from her body. Imogen was stunned for an instant. She could not believe what was happening. Fear arced through her. She raked him with her nails.

"Damn you, you little bitch." Vanneck clawed at her skirts. "When I am finished, you will beg me to finance your expedition."

"Is this how you treated Lucy?" Imogen demanded as she fought back. "Did you rape her before you fed her the laudanum?"

"Lucy? Are you mad? I didn't give her the laudanum." Vanneck's eyes were as hard as stones in the shadows. "She drank it herself. The damned woman was always complaining about her nerves."

"Why bother to lie to me? I have reasoned it all out. I know that you arranged for me to be discovered with you in a compromising position so that people would believe Lucy committed suicide because she felt betrayed. I know you killed her. I know everything."

"You know nothing." Vanneck heaved himself up on his elbows. "What is going on here? Are you accusing me of murder?"

"Yes, I am."

"You're mad. I didn't kill Lucy." Vanneck slitted his eyes. "Although God knows I considered it often enough. I might have gotten around to it eventually. But as it happens, she did not die by my hand."

"I don't believe you."

"I don't give a damn what you believe. The only thing I want from you is that map. And I'll have it if it's the last thing I do."

He was consumed by rage and desperation, Imogen realized. He thought to control her by forcing himself upon her. She choked on a scream when she felt his clammy hand on her bare leg. He covered her mouth with a damp palm. Panic threatened to consume her. She glanced up at the wall behind the sofa and saw the gleam of a gilded frame.

As Vanneck struggled with her skirts, trying to scrape them up above her thighs, she flung out a hand and managed to grab the edge of the picture frame.

For one terrifying moment she feared that the thing would not come free of the wall. She wrenched at it even as Vanneck yanked at her gown.

The picture fell from its hooks. It was so heavy that Imogen could not control its descent. She tried to guide it as it slammed downward. It struck Vanneck's head and shoulders with an impact that reverberated through her own body.

Vanneck shuddered, groaned, and then collapsed on top of Imogen. She shoved at him, frantically trying to push him onto the floor. Before she could free herself from his crushing weight, other hands seized hold of Vanneck.

"Bastard." Matthias loomed, an avenging demon in the shadows. He hauled Vanneck off the sofa and dropped him at his feet.

Vanneck sprawled on the floor. He opened his eyes and gazed at Matthias with bleary recognition. "Colchester? Christ, what are you doing here?"

Matthias peeled off one glove and dropped it on Vanneck's chest. "My seconds will call upon yours tomorrow. I'm certain that an appointment can be arranged for the day after."

"Seconds? *Seconds.*" Vanneck tried to lever himself up on one elbow. He shook his head as though attempting to clear it. "You cannot be serious."

Matthias scooped Imogen up off the sofa and held

her close. "I assure you, I have never been more serious in my life." He turned and started down the gallery.

"But you never intended to marry her." Vanneck's desperate cry echoed off the wall of the long hall. "Everyone knows that the engagement is a ploy. All you care about is the map. Damn your eyes, Colchester, she's not worth a duel. This is a business matter."

Matthias said nothing. Imogen looked up into his face as he carried her through the shadowed gallery. A shiver went through her that had nothing to do with her recent struggle.

At that moment she recognized him as the dark, mysterious figure of her dreams. She was in the arms of Zamaris, Lord of the Night.

Chapter 11

Imogen could not stop shivering. She huddled against
Matthias, seeking his strength and warmth as he carried
her down a flight of stairs and along a hallway. She kept
her face pressed against his shoulder, her eyes squeezed
shut in a vain attempt to stop the tears.

Voices, some laced with genuine concern, others with
bored curiosity, floated past as Matthias strode swiftly
toward the door of the mansion.

"I say, Colchester, something wrong with Miss Waterstone?" a man asked.

"She is not feeling well," Matthias said without inflection. "Her nerves are overwrought. The excitement of the
engagement, you know."

The man chuckled. "Of course. Expect you'll be able
to come up with something to ease her fears."

Imogen wanted to protest that her nerves were much
too strong to be overset by something so mundane as an
engagement, but she did not dare raise her face from Matthias's shoulder. The man would see her tears.

"Shall I summon a doctor, sir?" a footman inquired.

"No, I shall escort her home. All she needs is rest."

"I'll see to your carriage, my lord."

"Thank you."

Imogen felt cool air against her skin. They were outside at last. In another moment she would be safely enclosed in Matthias's carriage.

Hooves and wheels clattered on the cobblestones. There was the sound of a coach door being opened. Matthias stepped into the cab with Imogen in his arms. He lowered himself onto the cushioned seat and cradled her against him.

"Calm yourself." He held her very tightly as the carriage set off into the night. "It's all right, my dear. It's over. You are safe."

"But you are not." Safe from prying eyes at last, Imogen erupted from the circle of his arms. She seized his shoulders and tried to shake him. "What in God's name have you done, Matthias?"

Matthias did not move. He did not even seem to notice her fingers crushing the fine fabric of his black greatcoat. He watched her with gleaming, unreadable eyes. "I was about to ask you the same question."

She ignored that, her attention fixed on the dire situation at hand. "You challenged Vanneck to a duel. Dear heaven, Matthias, how could you do such a thing?"

"Under the circumstances, it seemed the only appropriate response."

"But I am unhurt."

Matthias took her chin in his hand. "For which I can only thank God and your own brave heart. You are really quite amazing, my dear. I do believe you came close to killing Vanneck with that picture frame."

"Then surely there was no need to challenge him," she said desperately.

Matthias stroked the corner of her mouth with his thumb. His eyes gleamed in the shadows. "The fact that you managed to save yourself does not mean that I can allow Vanneck to go unchallenged. Indeed, I have no choice."

"That is not true." More tears welled up in Imogen's eyes. She dashed the back of her hand against them. "He is not worth it, my lord. I cannot allow you to risk your life in a duel. I refuse to let you meet him."

Matthias tipped her chin up slightly and searched her wet face with an oddly bemused expression. "I do believe these tears are for me."

"Why else would I be crying?" she demanded crossly.

"It would be understandable if you wept because of what happened to you tonight. Even a lady with your strong nerves would have every reason to succumb to—"

"Rubbish. I am far more concerned with what may happen to you because of this idiotic challenge." She reached up to catch his face between her hands. "Matthias, you must not do this, do you hear me? I cannot allow it."

He wrapped his fingers around one of her wrists and squeezed gently. "It's all right, Imogen. All will be well."

"You could be killed."

He smiled faintly. "Obviously the thought distresses you."

"Hell and damnation, Matthias, the thought will drive me mad."

"Why?"

Frustration and fear overwhelmed her. *"Because I love you."*

A great stillness settled on the interior of the carriage. It was as if a magician had worked a spell, freezing the moment. Imogen was dimly aware of distant voices and the din of carriage wheels and horses' hooves in the street. Lamps from passing coaches occasionally winked in the darkness. Outside the carriage the world was in motion. But inside nothing moved.

"You love me?" Matthias repeated very softly.

"Yes."

"Then marry me tomorrow by special license."

Imogen's mouth dropped open. "How can you talk about marriage when your life is at stake?"

"Somehow," Matthias said as he gathered her back into his arms, "marriage is the only thing that seems important enough to discuss at the moment."

"But, Matthias—"

"Say you will wed me before I go to meet my fate." He brushed a kiss across her damp eyes and dropped another into her tangled hair. "It is all I ask, my sweet."

"I will give you anything you want if you will cancel your dawn appointment."

"I cannot do that, Imogen. I can only assure you that I expect to live through it and join you for breakfast afterward."

Imogen heard the implacable note in his words and knew that further protest was useless. She pummeled his shoulders with small fists. "Matthias, I beg you—"

"Marry me. Tomorrow."

She subsided against him, exhausted by her own helpless outrage. She turned her face into his coat to blot the new flood of tears. "If that is truly your wish."

"It is my only wish. It is all I ask."

She could deny him nothing at that moment. "Very well." Her voice was muffled by his coat. "I will marry you tomorrow."

"You do not have to sound as though you are about to be transported to the colonies."

"Oh, Matthias."

"I know." He stroked her loosened hair. "I understand."

Another silence descended. Imogen allowed herself or a moment more to wallow in despair. Oddly soothed he feel of his powerful hands in her hair, she composed herself and turned her attention in a more productive direction. She had to devise a plan to stop the duel.

But before she could conceive of anything clever enough to be effective, her thoughts were distracted by something even more pressing.

"Good heavens, I almost forgot." She straightened so quickly that the top of her head collided with Matthias's jaw. "Ouch."

"Vanneck never really stood a chance, did he?" Matthias winced and rubbed his jaw. "If you had not brained him with the picture frame, I'm sure you would have found another way to save yourself."

"Sir, I am so sorry. I did not mean to hurt you."

"I know." His teeth flashed in a brief, startlingly playful grin. "Now then, what was it that you suddenly recalled?"

"Patricia. Where is she?"

"Patricia is safe and sound with Horatia. I saw them both just before I went upstairs to the picture gallery to find you. I shall send the carriage back for them after I get you safely home."

"Your sister is with my aunt?"

"Yes."

A grim realization dawned on Imogen. "Sir, how did you know to search for me in the picture gallery?"

"Patricia told me that she had noticed you going upstairs to view the paintings."

"I see," Imogen whispered.

She mulled that over as the carriage rumbled through the streets. There was nothing to be gained by confiding her new suspicions to Matthias. He had enough to concern him at the moment. It would only overset his already strained nerves to learn that his sister had very likely conspired with Vanneck to lead her into the picture gallery.

Imogen leaned against Matthias and stared out the carriage window, her thoughts in fresh turmoil. She decided to make one more attempt to talk Matthias out of the duel.

"Sir, promise me that you will reconsider this ill-conceived notion of meeting Lord Vanneck. I comprehend that some gentlemen feel that a duel is the only way for men to resolve a point of honor, but I believe it to be the height of idiocy. And you are surely no idiot. Therefore—"

"Enough, Imogen," he said very quietly. "The business is settled. Furthermore, you are not to speak of this to anyone, do you understand?"

"But—"

"This is a matter for men. The gentlemen involved are obligated to keep the entire thing a secret. You are not to turn it into a tidbit of gossip for the ton."

Imogen was appalled. "I would not dream of gossiping about such a . . . a featherbrained, addlepated, nonsensical piece of masculine stupidity."

"Excellent." He wound his fist into her tumbled hair. "I knew I could rely upon you to keep your mouth closed, my dear."

"*I*mogen, must you pace so?" Horatia poured tea into two cups. "I vow, you make me quite dizzy."

"What else am I to do?" Imogen reached the window of her study and paused to gaze moodily out into the small, rainswept garden. "I feel as if I were a bundle of fireworks about to explode over Vauxhall Gardens. It is a dreadful sensation."

"Nerves, my dear. Your first real case of overwrought nerves, I suspect."

"Rubbish. You know very well that I am not prone to nervous weakness."

"You have never before faced the prospect of marriage." Horatia made a tut-tutting noise. "I do not know why his lordship is insisting upon going about things in this hurried fashion, but I suppose, given the situation, he feels it's for the best."

"Situation?" Imogen got out in a strangled voice. For a moment she wondered if Horatia knew about the duel. "What do you mean?"

"No offense, my dear, but one does not plan a large, fashionable wedding under these circumstances. And his lordship is not much interested in such social affairs, in any event."

Imogen relaxed slightly. "No, he is not."

She continued to gaze out into the garden. The entire world seemed to have turned gray overnight. A heavy fog had blanketed the streets at dawn. Her fitful sleep had been shattered by another of the disturbing dreams that plagued her of late. In it she had been attempting to save Matthias from some unseen peril, but time had run out. She had found him in the stone sarcophagus. There had been blood everywhere.

Panic nibbled at the edges of her brain as she studied the mist-shrouded garden. She had less than a day to find a way to stop the madness.

"Imogen?"

"I beg your pardon?" Imogen glanced at her aunt over her shoulder. "What did you say?"

"I asked if you had instructed your maid to see to the packing."

"I must have said something to her. I'm sure I did." Imogen scowled. "But, in truth, I have been thinking of other things. Now that you mention it, I am not certain that I told her that I would be moving into Colchester's town house this evening."

Horatia gave her a reassuring smile as she got to her feet. "Sit down and have your tea, dear. I shall go upstairs and deal with the maid."

"Thank you." Imogen went across the room to where the tea waited on a small table. She seized the cup and took a large, fortifying swallow.

The door closed behind Horatia, leaving Imogen alone in the study. The ticking of the tall clock was very loud in the quiet room. When Imogen could not abide the sound any longer, she started to pace again.

Over the years she had heard occasional rumors of duels. She had not paid much attention, having had no reason to concern herself with the subject. She was fairly certain that there were a number of people involved in addition to the two principals. The gentlemen's seconds and sometimes a doctor were present, according to one account Imogen had heard. And there had to be others, she thought. The men who drove the carriages. Perhaps a groom or two. Gentlemen rarely did anything alone in Society. They were always accompanied by coachmen and grooms and one or two close friends.

Mrs. Vine knocked once and opened the door. "There be a lady to see you, Miss Waterstone."

Imogen swung around so quickly that tea sloshed over the edge of the cup into the saucer. "Who is it?"

"Lady Patricia Marshall, she calls herself, ma'am."

Imogen put down her cup with a bang. "Send her in at once, Mrs. Vine."

"Yes, ma'am." Mrs. Vine heaved a sigh and took herself off.

A moment later Patricia appeared. She hovered in the doorway, looking very different from the vivacious young lady she had been last night. Her pretty face was drawn taut with tension. Her gray eyes were filled with anxiety. She was obviously close to tears.

"I must speak with you," Patricia whispered as Mrs. Vine closed the study door.

"Sit down," Imogen said brusquely. She went behind her desk and sank into her own chair. She folded her hands on the polished mahogany and regarded Patricia closely. "What is it you wish to say?"

"Matthias told me at breakfast that he is going to marry you today."

"Did he?"

"Yes. And tomorrow morning he intends to risk his life in a duel." Patricia's voice broke on a sob. She groped for a hankie in her small reticule. "It was not supposed to happen like that."

Imogen was dumbfounded. "How did you learn of the duel?"

"I have just come from Lady Lyndhurst's house." Patricia sniffed into the hankie. "She told me that the news is all over Town."

So much for the supposed ability of the gentlemen

involved to keep their ridiculous secrets, Imogen thought. Someone had obviously talked. Perhaps one of the seconds, whose task it was to arrange the details of the dawn appointment.

"And they have the gall to complain that women are inclined to gossip," Imogen muttered.

Patricia gave her a quizzical look. "I beg your pardon?"

"Never mind. Patricia, since you seem to be fully apprised of the dire straits in which we find ourselves, perhaps you will be good enough to tell me *what the bloody hell you were doing last night?*"

Patricia flinched. Then a resentful anger pinched the corners of her mouth. "I was only trying to save my brother from your clutches. But it all went wrong somehow."

"Ah." Imogen closed her eyes and sagged back in her chair. "I wondered if that might have been your goal. It all begins to fall into place now."

"Lady Lyndhurst said that if Colchester discovered you in a compromising position with another man, he would have grounds to end the engagement. She said it would be simple to arrange."

"Indeed. So this was Lady Lyndhurst's notion?"

Patricia blew into her hankie and then raised furious eyes to meet Imogen's gaze. "I did precisely as I was instructed. I knew you would follow me from the ballroom up to the gallery. You are always attempting to play the chaperone even though you yourself have no more notion of proper behavior than a . . . a flea."

"A flea?"

"I led you to the gallery and then made my way back to the ballroom with Lady Lyndhurst. When Matthias arrived and inquired after you, I told him you were viewing the pictures. He went in search of you. Lady Lyndhurst said that everything transpired just as we planned it." Patricia's voice rose. "But Matthias did not end the engagement as she said he would."

"You silly twit." Imogen shot to her feet and slammed her palms flat on the desk. "Have you any idea of the harm you have done?"

"But I was only trying to save him." Fresh tears flowed down Patricia's cheeks. "I did not want him to suffer the same fate that Papa suffered. I did not want him to ruin his life."

"I trust you are satisfied with the damage you have wrought." Imogen came around the edge of the desk. "It would appear that your good friend Lady Lyndhurst must share a large portion of the blame."

"She was only trying to help me."

"Rubbish. Something tells me that Lady Lyndhurst is not the type to go out of her way to help anyone but herself. She is playing some game."

"That is not true. She has been most kind to me. I consider her a true friend."

"She has certainly proved herself to be a very unusual sort of friend." Imogen pondered the implications. "I wonder what there is in this to interest her. Perhaps she, too, is after the seal."

"I have no notion of what you are muttering about," Patricia said petulantly. "But you must do something. What if Matthias is killed in the duel with Lord Vanneck?"

"Calm yourself, Patricia. I will think of a plan."

Patricia hesitated. "You could refuse to marry my brother. I realize that people would talk, but I do not see how jilting him could do any more damage to the reputation of a lady who is already known as Immodest Imogen."

"You may be correct, but I assure you that my refusal to go through with the marriage would not stop Colchester from meeting Vanneck."

"Why would he fight a duel over a lady who has refused to wed him?"

"You do not know your brother very well, do you?" Imogen said. "Believe me, he intends to proceed with the duel regardless of the circumstances. He has committed himself. His sense of honor will ensure that he meets Vanneck. In any event, I have given him my word that I will marry him today. It was Colchester's only request. I could not deny him."

"Lady Lyndhurst said that you would do anything to gain the title," Patricia blurted out.

Imogen shot her a fulminating glance. "The next time you are tempted to quote Lady Lyndhurst's opinions, you might recall that she is the one who got us all into this tangle."

Patricia stared at her, briefly speechless. She found her voice on another sob. "No, that is not true. She never intended this result. She wished only to help me."

"I do not have the time to argue the matter. Lady Lyndhurst will have to wait. I have more important things to attend to at the moment." Imogen went to the door, opened it, and called down the hall. "Mrs. Vine? Would you please come here at once?"

Patricia gazed at her, bewildered. "What are you about?"

"Do not concern yourself," Imogen snapped, angry and disgusted. "You have caused enough trouble. I suggest you return home and try to stay out of mischief until this is finished."

"What do you intend to do?"

"Begone, Patricia. I have a great deal to accomplish before I marry your brother this afternoon."

Patricia succumbed to another spate of tears. "If Matthias dies tomorrow morning, you will be an extremely wealthy widow. It is not fair."

Imogen whirled around and strode back across the room. She grabbed Patricia by her elbows and yanked her to her feet. "Is that what this is all about? Are you worried about your brother only because you fear that if he is killed tomorrow morning I shall inherit his fortune and you will be left penniless?"

Patricia looked stunned. Her eyes widened. "No, that

is not what I meant. I do not want anything to happen to my brother because he is all that I have left in the world. I am terrified that he will be killed in the duel."

"Are you?" Imogen searched her face intently. "Do you truly care about him?"

"If you are asking me if I love him the way a sister ought to love her brother, then I must admit that I do not." Patricia twisted her hankie between her fingers. Her mouth curved bitterly. "How can I love Matthias when I know that whenever he looks at me he sees his own un- happy past?"

"I'm certain that is not true, Patricia. Perhaps, when you first arrived on his doorstep, he was taken aback, but—"

"You know perfectly well that he took me into his home only because he felt he had to honor the promise he gave Papa. How can I have a deep affection for him when I know that his goal is to marry me off as quickly as possible?"

"He is not going to force you into marriage."

"Papa always told me that if worse came to worst, Matthias would look after me. But if he dies in a duel I shall be forced to return to my uncle's house. And . . . and my dreadful cousin will be there. He will try to touch me and, oh, dear God, I cannot bear to contemplate what will happen."

"Hmm." Imogen absently patted Patricia's shoulder while she tapped one toe on the carpet.

Patricia wiped her eyes. "What are we to do?"

"You will do nothing. I shall handle this. Good day, Patricia." Imogen gave her a small push toward the door.

Patricia blotted her eyes and walked numbly out into the hall. In spite of the problems she had created, Imogen suddenly felt a twinge of sympathy for her. "Patricia?"

"Yes?" Patricia paused to glance back. She looked utterly wretched.

"When this is over, you and I shall have a very long

talk. In the meantime, do not allow your nerves to make you ill. I have trouble enough on my hands."

Mrs. Vine trudged into view. She dried her hands on her apron and grudgingly ushered Patricia into the hall and out the front door. Then she turned reluctantly toward Imogen.

"Ye wanted me, ma'am?"

"Yes, Mrs. Vine. I want you to send a message to the nearest public stable. Inform the proprietor that I wish to purchase clothing suitable for a groom. Make certain that the garments will fit a person of my size."

Mrs. Vine gazed at Imogen as if she had gone mad. "Ye want to buy clothing for a stable lad? But we don't have a stable. Nor any lads, come to that."

Imogen managed a cool smile. "I plan to attend a masquerade, Mrs. Vine. I thought it would be amusing to go dressed as a stable boy."

"Well, it's no worse than the instructions I got from a tenant a couple o' years back." Mrs. Vine sounded surprisingly philosophical. "He used to send me out to fetch him ladies' gowns. He wanted the whole works, fancy shoes, hat, wig. Everything a real lady would wear."

Imogen was briefly intrigued. "You rented to a gentleman who went to masquerade balls dressed as a lady?"

"Oh, he didn't go to no masquerade balls dressed up like that. He liked to wear the pretty things around here in the evenings when he entertained his gentlemen friends. Said the clothes made him feel more comfortable. He was particularly fond of plumes and fancy stockings, he was. His friends all came dressed in gowns and pretty hats too. They enjoyed themselves, they did. And me tenant always paid the rent in a timely manner."

"Indeed." Imogen considered that for a moment. "Each to his own, I suppose."

"That's what I always say. Long as I get me rent, it don't make no difference to me how a body dresses." Mrs. Vine shuffled off toward the kitchen.

∘   ∘   ∘

*M*atthias heard the door of the library open very quietly. He signed the last of the documents he had had his solicitor prepare earlier in the day and set it on the stack of papers in the center of his desk. "Yes, Ufton? What is it?"

"It's me," Imogen said softly. "Not Ufton."

Matthias put aside the quill. He looked up and saw Imogen leaning back against the door, her hands behind her, gripping the knob. She was dressed in a chintz wrapper and a pair of soft slippers. Her hair was anchored beneath a little white cap. She looked as if she should have been in bed.

The anticipation that had been simmering within him all day suddenly came to the boil. His wife. His Anizamara. She had been his lady for almost four hours, but this was the first opportunity they had had to be alone together since the quiet ceremony. When a man was obliged to prepare for both a wedding and a duel within the same twenty-four-hour period, he found himself astonishingly busy.

Matthias smiled at her. "Go back upstairs, Imogen. I'm almost finished here. I shall join you shortly."

She ignored him. "What are you doing?"

"Taking care of one or two small matters."

Imogen walked to the desk and glanced down at the pile of papers in front of him. "What sort of matters?"

"The usual. I wrote some instructions to my estate managers. Made a few entries in my journal. Tidied up my will. Nothing of major import."

"Your *will*?" Fresh alarm flared in Imogen's eyes. She clutched the lapels of her robe very tightly. "Dear heaven, Matthias, surely you do not expect to . . . to . . ."

"No. I fully expect to be home before you are even out of bed. Your concern is touching, my sweet, but entirely misplaced."

"It is not misplaced. Matthias, you have told me often enough that you are not inclined toward dangerous or adventurous activities. You are a man of delicate sensibilities. You know very well that your nerves are not strong."

He grinned, feeling remarkably cheerful. "If it's any consolation, rumor has it that Vanneck's nerves are even weaker than my own."

"What is that supposed to mean?"

"That he is highly unlikely to appear at the appointed hour. He is a coward, Imogen."

"But you cannot depend upon his cowardice."

"I think we can." Matthias paused. "My reputation occasionally has its uses."

"But, Matthias, what if he knows that your reputation as Cold-blooded Colchester is based on inaccurate rumors and false gossip. What if he knows that you are not the man Society thinks you are?"

"Then I shall be obliged to trust that my own poor nerves will be strong enough to see me through this affair."

"Damnation, my lord, this is not amusing."

He rose to his feet and started around the end of the wide desk. "You are quite right. This is our wedding night. We should no doubt approach it with some degree of solemnity."

"Matthias—"

"Enough, madam." He lifted her into his arms. "There will be no more talk of duels. We have far more important matters to discuss."

"What could be more important?" she demanded fiercely.

"I believe that I should like to hear again that you love me."

Her eyes widened. "You know that I do."

"Do you?" He carried her to the closed door.

"Of course I do. For heaven's sake, I would never have agreed to wed you otherwise."

He smiled slightly. "Will you kindly get the door?"

"What? Oh, very well." She reached down to turn

the handle. "But, Matthias, we must talk. There is a great deal I wish to say to you, my lord."

"No doubt. But I would rather hear you say it in bed."

He carried her through the doorway and crossed the hall to the wide staircase. Guilt lanced through him as he started up the carpeted steps.

He was well aware that he had used the heated passions of the moment to coerce Imogen into marriage. She was terrified of the risk she believed he would take at dawn. The night before she had been overwrought by Vanneck's assault. Her emotions had been in a turmoil. She would have agreed to anything he asked. *Because she loved him.*

He had ruthlessly taken advantage of the situation. She was his now. But Matthias knew that when the business of the duel was finished and life returned to normal, so would Imogen's emotions.

He feared she would not thank him then for having manipulated her into this marriage. He remembered what he had said to her in the museum. *Passion and Zamar.*

It would be enough, he vowed. It had to be enough.

Chapter 12

Matthias held himself back until she was clinging to him, beseeching him, demanding that he fulfill the promises he had made with his hands and his questing mouth. He lay cradled between her sweetly rounded legs and kissed the inside of Imogen's quivering thighs. He was dazzled by the rich scent of her desire. The heat of her damp passage scalded his fingers.

If things went terribly wrong at dawn, he wanted Imogen to remember this night for the rest of her life.

"Matthias. No. *Yes.* Dear heaven, you should not, you must not. This is surely another one of your secret Zamarian lovemaking techniques. I cannot bear it."

Her breathless words and soft gasps constituted the most erotic song Matthias had heard. He could not get enough of the ravishing music. He strung kisses along her inner thigh to the plump petals that guarded her secrets. He parted her gently and bent his head to take the firm little bud between his lips.

"Dear heaven, Matthias." Imogen clenched her fin-

gers in his hair and arched herself. "Please. *Please.* Yes."
She shuddered and cried out.

Matthias heard the blood roar in his veins. He raised
his head to watch Imogen's face as she claimed her satisfaction in his arms.

Things would not go wrong at dawn, he vowed silently as he eased himself up along the length of her body.
He had to return to Imogen. Nothing else, not even the
treasures of ancient Zamar, was as important to him.

She was twisting so beneath him that he had to steady
her hips with a hand that glistened with her own dew. He
held Imogen still and pushed himself gently past the tight
muscles that guarded the hot passage. She closed around
him. The last of his self-mastery disintegrated.

"Tell me again that you love me," he whispered
hoarsely as he sank himself into her.

"I love you. I love you." She clung to him in the
darkness.

Lost in her sensual warmth, Matthias allowed himself
the joy of swimming in a sunlit sea.

He plunged deeper into Imogen's welcoming body.
Her tiny convulsions had not yet ceased.

In the end, the shudders that racked him left him
precariously balanced on the fine line between pain and
euphoria. They stole his breath and left him damp, weary,
and replete.

And alive.

Once more he had eluded the clutches of the shadowy phantoms of his past.

Matthias waited until Imogen finally fell into a
deep, exhausted sleep before he eased himself from the
warmth of the bed. The first spectral light of a fog-
shrouded dawn crouched at the window. The ghostly illu-
mination revealed Imogen curled beneath the quilt. Her
hair cascaded across the pillow. The little white cap had
fallen to the floor sometime during the night. Her long,

dark lashes rested feather-light along her high cheek-bones.

The wonder of Imogen struck him again with fresh impact. She might very well be pregnant with his babe.

Another wave of powerful emotion washed through him. This time it was a fierce sense of protectiveness. He stood looking down at Imogen for a moment, stoking the new fires that burned within him with memories of the night and dreams of the future.

It occurred to him that since he had met Imogen he had begun to think more and more of the future rather than of the past.

Matthias reluctantly turned away from the bed and walked into the dressing room. He smiled slightly to himself as he recalled the endless arguments, pleas, and threats he had endured during the night. It was certainly gratifying to know that Imogen did not want him to risk his neck, not even for the prospect of securing the vengeance she had sought for so long.

He had been tempted to reassure her that his nerves were up to the task of dealing with a man such as Vanneck, but he had resisted. In the first place, he doubted that she would have believed him. Imogen was convinced that he was a man of delicate sensibilities. He saw no reason to disabuse her of that notion.

His greatest source of unease was that Imogen would one day realize that his reputation was based on fact, not fiction. Matthias dreaded the dawn of that day far more than he dreaded this one.

Inside the dressing room he lit a candle and reached for his breeches. There was no need to wake his valet. A man did not require an intricately folded cravat or his best linen shirt for such an occasion.

He dressed with swift efficiency and then pulled on his boots. Carrying the taper, he let himself out of the dressing room. He was relieved to see that Imogen was still asleep in his big bed. She had pulled the quilt up over her head, but he could make out the rough outline of her body beneath the covers.

He intended to be home before she awoke.

The town house was as silent as a Zamarian tomb. Matthias made his way downstairs. The sound of wheels and hooves in the street told him that his coachman had followed the instructions he had been given last night.

Matthias set the candle on a hall table. He took his greatcoat from the small room at the foot of the stairs, slung it over his arm, and opened the front door.

A gray shroud of fog cloaked the streets. The carriage was just barely visible at the bottom of the steps. The horses were wraiths in the mist.

If the fog did not clear by the time he reached his destination, he and Vanneck would have a difficult time making out each other's form from twenty paces. Assuming Vanneck showed in the first place, which was highly unlikely.

Matthias was mildly surprised that he had not received a message from his seconds notifying him that the duel had been canceled. The considered opinion of his friends was that Vanneck would quit London rather than face a dawn appointment. The man was not known for his courage. But there had been no word.

Matthias glanced up at his coachman as he strode down the front steps. "Cabot's Farm, Shorbolt."

"Aye, m'lord." Shorbolt, bundled up against the cold in a many-tiered cape and a hat pulled down over his eyes, gestured to the young stable lad who held the horses' heads. "Let 'em go, boy. His lordship's in a hurry."

"Aye." The boy, whose face was concealed by a scruffy scarf and a slouchy cap, jumped back from the bridles and scrambled up onto the box beside Shorbolt.

Matthias vaulted into the carriage and settled back against the seat. Shorbolt gave the horses the signal to set off into the fog.

The streets of London were never truly quiet, not even at dawn. Elegant equipages filled with drunken gen-

tlemen returning from the stews and gaming hells passed
Matthias's carriage. The first of the farm carts was already
making its way to the city markets. The last of the
nightmen, their wagons laden with the contents of cesspits, drove past on their way to the outskirts of Town.
Occasionally the rank fumes from their cargoes wafted
through the air.

But eventually the crowded, bustling streets fell away
to reveal fields and meadows draped in mist. Cabot's
Farm was not far outside the city. It had gained a certain
notoriety over the years as a convenient location for dawn
appointments.

Matthias glanced out the window as Shorbolt brought
the horses to a halt at the edge of a meadow. Tendrils of
fog flowed across the scene, creating skeletal ghosts out of
leafless trees. A curricle loomed in the distance on the far
side of the grassy field. It was horsed with two grays.

Vanneck was here after all. Cold anticipation uncoiled
deep inside Matthias.

The stable lad clambered down from the box to take
charge of the horses. Something hit the ground with a dull
thud.

" 'Ere now, watch yerself, ye clumsy lad," Shorbolt
grumbled. "That's me tool kit ye just dumped in the dirt."

"Sorry," the boy said in a very low voice.

"No call to be jumpy," Shorbolt went on with a gruff
kindness. "It ain't yerself who's goin' to be facin' a bullet
this mornin'."

"Yes, sir. I know that." The boy's voice was barely
audible.

"His lordship can 'andle 'imself. Ye needn't fear that
you'll be lookin' for a new post later today. Now, 'and me
kit back up 'ere and then go take the beasts' heads like a
good lad. The poor creatures don't much care for the
sound o' gunshots."

"Don't blame 'em," the boy muttered.

Matthias ignored the byplay between Shorbolt and
the stable boy. He opened the door of the carriage and

got out. No one emerged from the curricle. The hood of the small two-wheeled carriage was raised against the cold. Matthias could not see the face of the man inside. There was no sign of Vanneck's seconds. The horses stood placidly munching grass as if they had been there for some time.

Matthias was reaching for his watch when he heard the sound of an approaching carriage. He glanced up as it rumbled into view through the fog. The coachman brought the horses to a halt nearby. A familiar figure threw open the door and jumped down onto the damp grass.

"Colchester." Fairfax, tall, thin, and dressed in the height of fashion, flashed a grin as he walked forward to greet Matthias. "You're a bit early, man. Expect you're eager to get back home to your lady wife, eh?"

"Very eager." Matthias glanced at the elegantly carved wooden box Fairfax carried. "I trust you have made certain that the powder is dry?"

"Do not concern yourself. I've taken excellent care of your pistols." Fairfax nodded toward the carriage. "Jeremy and I brought along the doctor in case he's needed."

"Where is Jeremy?"

"Right here." Jeremy Garfield, a short man with merry eyes and a shock of blond hair, descended sedately from the carriage. "Morning, Colchester. I trust you'll get this over with quickly so that I can go home to my bed. Been up all night. Why must these affairs always be conducted at dawn? Ungodly hour of the day for this sort of thing."

"It's an ungodly business," Fairfax offered cheerfully. "Well, at least the fog has lifted sufficiently to allow Colchester to take good aim at Vanneck. Assuming he shows, which ain't likely."

Matthias inclined his head toward the curricle in the distance. "It would seem that Vanneck is even more eager than I am to conclude the matter."

Jeremy snorted at the sight of the small carriage. "So

he put in an appearance after all. That's a bit of a surprise. Where are his seconds?"

Fairfax eyed the curricle. "His seconds gave me the impression Vanneck would leave Town rather than face you."

Matthias started toward the curricle. "Let us see what is keeping him."

"Fear, most likely." Jeremy trotted to catch up with Matthias. "Whole world knows Vanneck lacks bottom. Man's an out-and-out coward. Must have spent the night pouring courage from a bottle."

Matthias did not respond. He glanced absently at the stable lad as he strode past his carriage. The boy was watching him intently from beneath the brim of his battered cap. The scarf was still wrapped closely around his face to ward off the dawn air.

Awareness went through Matthias. A chill that had nothing to do with the fog made him frown. He tried to place the stable lad. He was suddenly very certain that he had not encountered this particular boy in his stables. Yet there was something disturbingly familiar about him. It had to do with his stance and the way he held his head.

"Very odd, if you ask me," Fairfax said.

Matthias was briefly distracted from the small, niggling puzzle of the stable lad. He glanced at his friend. "What's odd?"

"Whole thing." Fairfax looked around. "Jeremy and I met with Vanneck's seconds last night. They both stated that if Vanneck did not leave Town, they would be here to examine the pistols."

Matthias heard soft, hesitant footsteps behind him. He looked back over his shoulder and saw that the stable lad had left the horses to follow the three of them as they made their way toward Vanneck's curricle.

" 'Ere now, where d'ye think yer goin', boy?" Shorbolt yelled. "Come back 'ere. This ain't yer affair."

The lad halted and glanced uncertainly back at Shorbolt. The sense of familiarity deepened within Matthias. He noticed the elegant line of the boy's spine that not even the old coat could disguise. For an instant he refused to believe what his eyes told him. And then disbelief flashed into fury.

"Hell's teeth," Matthias whispered.

Fairfax scowled at him in alarm. "Something amiss, Colchester?"

He took a deep breath. "No. Nothing." He pinned Imogen briefly with his gaze, letting her see the anger that was seething in him. Her eyes widened as she registered the fact that he had recognized her.

"You and Jeremy go talk to Vanneck," Matthias said softly to his friend. "Discover what's keeping him. I want to have a word with one of my staff concerning the horses."

"Be back in a moment," Fairfax promised. "Come along, Jeremy. Let us see if Vanneck's courage has evaporated already."

Matthias waited until the two were out of earshot. Then he whipped around to find Imogen standing a short distance behind him. He walked slowly, deliberately, toward her, reminding himself with every step that above all, he must keep her identity a secret from Vanneck and the others.

The flames of rage within him were not fed solely by the knowledge that Imogen had taken yet another risk with her reputation. Matthias knew that his anger was based on a gathering sense of anguished desperation. Imogen would learn the truth about him if she saw him put a bullet into Vanneck. All her pretty illusions about his delicate sensibilities and weak nerves would be shattered once and for all.

Imogen took a single step back as Matthias reached her. Then she braced herself. Her chin rose. "Matthias, please, I had to come with you."

"What the bloody hell do you think you're about?" He wanted to shake her. "Have you gone mad? Do you

have any notion of what would happen to your reputation
if word of this charade got out?"

"My reputation has never been of particular importance to me, sir."

"Well, it is to me." It was the only logical argument
he could summon in that bleak moment. "You're the
Countess of Colchester now, and you will damn well act
like it. Get into the carriage."

"But, Matthias—"

"I said, get into the carriage and stay there until this is
over, do you hear me? I shall deal with you later."

Imogen drew herself up in a way that Matthias was
coming to know all too well. "I will not allow you to go
through with this stupid duel."

"Just how do you intend to stop it?"

She glowered. "I shall convince Vanneck to apologize. If he does so, you will be obliged to cancel the duel. I
have studied the rules for this sort of thing, and I know
very well that an apology ends the matter."

"There is nothing Vanneck can say that will convince
me to let him go unpunished for what he tried to do to
you," Matthias said very softly. "Nothing at all."

"But, Matthias—"

"Get into the carriage."

"I cannot let you do this."

"You cannot stop me."

"*Colchester,*" Fairfax shouted across the meadow.
"You'd better come here and see this for yourself."

Matthias glanced impatiently at his friend. "What is
the problem, for God's sake?"

"Bit of a muddle here, Colchester," Jeremy called.
"Changes everything."

"Damnation." Matthias turned briefly back to Imogen. "Wait for me in the carriage." He strode off without
bothering to see if she had obeyed him.

The gray geldings harnessed to the curricle continued
to crop grass as the small crowd gathered. Matthias saw
that the horses' reins had been secured to a fallen branch.

Jeremy's face was troubled. Even Fairfax looked more sober than usual.

"Where is Vanneck?" Matthias asked as he reached the curricle.

Jeremy cleared his throat. "Inside."

"What the devil is he doing? Writing his will?"

"Not exactly," Fairfax said.

Matthias peered into the cab and saw the slumped figure sprawled against the seat. Vanneck's head had fallen to one side. His eyes were open, staring sightlessly at nothing. He wore a cloak but he no longer needed any protection against the cold. A large quantity of blood stained the front of his shirt.

"One would hope," Matthias said, "that he had already tended to the matter of his will."

"But who shot him?" Imogen demanded as the Colchester carriage set off from Cabot's Farm. She prided herself on possessing sturdy nerves, but she was obliged to concede that the dizzying course of events and emotions that she had endured during the past few hours had left her feeling shaken.

"How the devil should I know?" Matthias lounged in the corner of the seat and contemplated Imogen with a dark, brooding expression. "Given his unpleasant nature, I suspect that there are any number of candidates. I would send a bouquet to the appropriate party if I knew his identity."

"Whoever it was must have known about the duel. The killer went to the trouble of driving Vanneck's curricle all the way out here to Cabot's Farm and left the body for you to discover."

"The list of people who knew about the duel no doubt includes half the ton."

"But why would someone leave Vanneck's body at the scene of his dawn appointment?"

Matthias shrugged. "Fairfax no doubt had the right

of it. He suspects that Vanneck was attacked by a high-wayman shortly after he arrived at Cabot's Farm. Jeremy agrees with him. It's as sound a speculation as any."

"A highwayman. I suppose that is a possibility."

"A distinct possibility."

Imogen considered that. "It all seems very odd."

"Indeed. Almost as odd as learning that one's bride has a penchant for disguising herself as a stable lad."

She blinked. "Really, Matthias, that is a very small matter compared to Vanneck's murder."

"Not to me."

"I fail to see how you can concern yourself with such a trivial incident, when we are faced with something so extremely serious and perplexing."

"You'd be astonished at how I can focus on the triv-ial." Matthias's voice was laced with silky menace. "I have a talent for it."

Sympathy welled up in Imogen. "I realize that you have been through a great deal this morning, sir. We both have. I must confess that even my nerves are somewhat disordered. It is perfectly understandable that you, with your more anxious temperament, are quite overset by all that's happened. Nevertheless—"

"Overset?" Matthias's gloved hand flexed in a subtle movement that resembled the motion of a hunting cat's paw. "That does not begin to describe my present mood, madam. In case it has escaped your notice, I am bloody furious."

Imogen blinked. "Furious?"

"You seem to have no notion of the damage that could have been done. Fortunately only my coachman re-alizes that you are not a stable lad and, as he wishes to retain his post, he will keep his mouth shut. But it was due to the devil's own luck that Fairfax and Jeremy Garfield were so astounded by the sight of Vanneck's body that they failed to notice that you were dressed for a masquer-ade."

"Matthias, please—"

"It was even more fortunate that Vanneck was already dead and that his seconds did not arrive on the scene. I can only imagine the gossip, had you been discovered."

Realization finally settled on Imogen. "So that is the problem."

He gave her a scathing look. "You do not consider your eagerness to play ducks and drakes with your reputation a problem?"

Imogen turned to gaze out the window. She tried and failed to suppress the pain his words caused. "Sir, you knew when you married me that I was not concerned with social consequence or position. Furthermore, I did not believe that you cared about Society's opinion either."

"Damnation, Imogen, this goes too far."

Hurt and angry, she whirled back around to face him. "If you truly desired a wife who would conform to the ton's notion of a proper countess, you should not have wed Immodest Imogen."

"Bloody hell, madam. The only wife I want is you." Matthias moved so quickly that Imogen did not even realize his intent until his hand closed around her wrist. He tugged her off the seat and settled her against his chest.

"Matthias."

His arms closed around her with the force of iron bonds. "What you did this morning did far more to overset my nerves than the prospect of meeting Vanneck. Do you comprehend me?"

"All you seem to care about is my reputation, my lord."

"Do you think it so odd that a man might object to having his wife attend a duel?"

"I knew it." Imogen felt tears form in her eyes. "You should have married a more suitable lady. We are doomed, you and I, and it is all your fault, sir. I tried to warn you."

"Doomed?"

"Oh, do stop interrupting, Colchester. I have had quite enough of your pithy little lectures." She fumbled in the pockets of the unfamiliar trousers, searching unsuccessfully for a handkerchief. "You have chained yourself for life to a female who will cause you nothing but scandal and humiliation."

He yanked a square of white linen from one of his own pockets and thrust it into her hands. "It is not scandal and humiliation that I fear."

"Yes, it is. You have just said so. You told me that we had passion and Zamar in common, but that is obviously not enough." Imogen blew into the handkerchief. "Not nearly enough."

"Imogen, you don't understand."

"I am well aware that I must take some of the blame for this disaster. I ought to have had the courage and the common sense to refuse your offer. But I allowed my heart to rule my head, and now I must pay the price."

Matthias's eyes hardened. "So you regret our marriage, then?"

"As I said, my lord, we are doomed. As doomed as ancient Zamar."

"*Enough.*" Matthias seized her arms. "I lied when I said that I feared for your reputation."

She looked up warily. "What do you mean?"

His jaw could have been hewn from stone. "Listen to me, Imogen, for I am going to explain this once and once only. I was forced to challenge Vanneck after what he did to you. I had no choice. But in truth, I believed that he would be too much of a coward to show this morning. I fully expected to be able to return to you with the news that there had been no duel."

She frowned. "I see."

"I thought myself quite clever, if you must know. I had anticipated that Vanneck would have been forced to leave London because of the day's events. He would have been ruined in Society, just as you had originally intended. And the whole thing would have been accomplished with no risk to your person."

"Good heavens," Imogen said, awed. "That was indeed very clever of you, Matthias."

"But when I saw Vanneck's curricle, I assumed my scheme was in a shambles. I knew I would have to proceed with the duel. And then I realized that you were present in the guise of a stable lad. I faced both death and the prospect of a great scandal and, well, I fear you were right. It was all too much for my delicate nerves. I lost my temper."

"Death and scandal." She softened at once. "Oh, Matthias, I do understand. I should have realized how much you had on your mind." She managed a wan smile. "I must confess, I have been more than a little anxious myself for the past day or so."

Matthias touched her cheek. "If Vanneck did kill Lucy, she has been avenged. It's over, Imogen."

"Yes. It is, isn't it?" The realization seemed strange, almost unreal. She had lived with the desire to avenge Lucy for so long that it was difficult to believe that vengeance, in the form of a highwayman, had finally been delivered. "I never intended that you risk your life to help me punish Vanneck, however."

"I know." Matthias put his arm around her and drew her against him.

"I wanted to protect you."

"I am quite safe, my dear."

"But it was a very near thing, my lord."

"Not really."

"Yes, it was," she insisted. "For all we know, Vanneck intended to show up for his dawn appointment. His curricle was there at Cabot's Farm, after all. He must have meant to—"

"Hush." Matthias brushed his mouth against hers. "We will never know what he intended and it no longer matters. As I said, it's over."

Imogen was about to argue the point, but at that moment the carriage rumbled to a halt in front of the town house. "We're home."

"With any luck, the household will still be asleep and we can go quietly back to bed," Matthias said. "I for one could use a nap to restore my rattled nerves."

"Perhaps a cup of tea would help calm you." Imogen glanced out the carriage window and saw the door open at the top of the steps. Ufton appeared. "Oh, dear."

Ufton was not alone. Two footmen, the cook, the housekeeper, and a maid crowded close behind him. They all wore expressions of anxious foreboding as they waited for the occupants of the carriage to descend.

"Hell's teeth," Matthias said as one of the footmen raced down the steps to see to the carriage door. "The whole bloody lot of them are awake."

Patricia appeared amid the cluster of servants. Imogen saw the look of fearful anticipation on her face as she waited for the carriage door to open.

"Your sister is obviously very anxious about your welfare, my lord," Imogen said with warm satisfaction. "I knew she would be."

"More likely she's anxious about the future of her quarterly allowance and the roof over her head. She no doubt feared that she would be forced to move back into her uncle's house if I cocked up my toes at Cabot's Farm this morning."

Imogen scowled at him. "Now, Matthias, that is not fair. You are her brother and she was naturally concerned."

Matthias gave her a derisive glance over his shoulder as he got out of the carriage.

"Matthias." Patricia started down the steps. "Are you all right?"

"Of course I'm all right. Don't I appear to be all right?"

"Well, yes." Patricia came to an awkward halt. Her eyes flew from Matthias to Imogen, who was still seated inside the carriage. She bit her lip and turned back to her brother. "I . . . I heard the rumors. I was very concerned."

"Were you?" Matthias asked politely.

Patricia's face threatened to crumple.

Imogen smiled reassuringly through the carriage window. "I'm sure that if my aunt were here, she would say that it was quite correct under the circumstances to give your brother a hug, Patricia. He won't mind a small display of sisterly affection, even though the servants are watching. Will you, Matthias?"

"What the devil are you talking about? *Umph.*" Matthias broke off abruptly as Patricia put her arms around him and gave him a quick squeeze.

"I am very glad you did not get yourself killed, sir." Patricia's words were muffled by Matthias's coat. She released him before he could say anything. She blinked several times in an embarrassed fashion.

For his part, Matthias appeared thoroughly disconcerted. But he pulled himself together with his customary aplomb and glowered at the assembled household. "Haven't you all got work to do?"

"Of course, my lord," Ufton murmured. "But first, on behalf of the staff, may I say that we are all extremely pleased to see you in such, er . . . ."

"Such excellent health?" Matthias supplied very dryly. "Thank you. But I fail to see what all the fuss is about. Surely a man may take his new bride for an early morning drive without causing such dire concern among those in his employ."

Ufton cleared his throat. "Yes, my lord. We had not realized that Lady Colchester had accompanied you."

"Of course I accompanied him, Ufton," Imogen said as Matthias swung her down out of the carriage. "I am an early riser."

Ufton and the staff gazed, astonished, at the bizarre sight of their mistress garbed as a stable lad.

Imogen beamed at the small crowd gathered on the steps. "I vow, these brisk morning drives certainly whet the appetite. Is breakfast ready?"

Chapter 13

"There is an amusing rumor making the rounds today, Colchester." Alastair Drake dropped lightly into the chair across from the one Matthias occupied.

It would have to be Drake who brought the first wave of gossip, Matthias thought. Alastair was a member of the Zamarian Society, but until recently Matthias had dismissed him as one of the many dilettantes who dabbled in the lore of ancient Zamar purely for reasons of fashion.

The discovery of Alastair's past connection to Imogen, however, had altered Matthias's attitude toward him from one of complete disinterest to one of total disgust. That in and of itself did not mean much. Matthias harbored a deep disgust toward most of those who thrived on the cruel and ruthless games played among the ton.

"I rarely listen to gossip." Matthias did not look up from the *Morning Post*. "I find that it is both inaccurate and boring."

It was early by Town standards, barely eleven o'clock. The club was still quiet. Until Alastair had arrived, the only sounds had been the occasional clink of silver and

china as coffee and tea were served to the few hardy individuals abroad at this hour. Most of the gentlemen of the club had not made it home from a night of whoring, gaming, and drinking until close to dawn. They were still sleeping off the sore heads brought on by overindulgence. Others were opening their eyes to vague memories of a fortune lost at cards.

"Actually, there are two rumors floating on the Thames this morning," Alastair continued. "The first is that you married Miss Waterstone by special license late yesterday."

"That is no rumor." Matthias glanced up briefly. "There is an announcement in the *Morning Post.*"

"I see." Alastair's gaze was unreadable. "My congratulations."

"Thank you." Matthias went back to his paper.

"The second rumor is almost as amazing as the first."

Matthias did not inquire about the second rumor. He knew Alastair would be unable to resist telling him.

"Word has it that Vanneck had a dawn appointment today," Alastair said.

"Indeed." Matthias turned the page. He could only hope that Imogen's name was not linked to the thing.

"It is said that Vanneck kept the appointment."

"Astonishing."

"Perhaps, but what is even more amazing is that the duel was conducted before any of the seconds arrived. Most unusual." Alastair paused. "Apparently Vanneck did not survive the affair."

Bloody hell, Matthias thought. So that was the direction in which the gossip flowed. At least no mention had been made of Imogen's presence. "That sort of thing can happen in the course of a duel."

"Yes, indeed. Especially when there are no witnesses to assure that matters are conducted according to the rules. They say poor Vanneck was shot dead before he even got out of his curricle. His opponent apparently wished to take no chances on the outcome."

Matthias accepted the inevitable conclusions with something close to relief. He had been so concerned with Imogen's reputation that he had forgotten about his own. Cold-blooded Colchester had struck again, so far as the ton was concerned.

The rumors that he had shot Vanneck in cold blood would no doubt be served up as scandal broth for a few days, but they would soon fade. There was no evidence to support them, and no one was likely to be sufficiently concerned with Vanneck's death to keep the tales alive for long. They would go the way of all the other Cold-blooded Colchester stories. Matthias had survived such gossip in the past. He would do so again. The important thing was that Imogen not be made to endure more malicious talk. He was her husband now. He had the right and the duty to protect her.

Alastair waited for a moment, his gaze greedy with speculation. Eventually he sighed and got to his feet. "I can see that you are not interested in my news, Colchester, so I shall leave you to your morning paper. Kindly give my regards to the new Lady Colchester."

"I shall convey your felicitations, Drake." Matthias turned another page and mentally consigned Alastair's good wishes to Hades.

He had no intention of mentioning Drake to Imogen. He was still uncertain of her feelings for Alastair. She did not show any signs of carrying a torch, but there was no point courting trouble.

Matthias did not refold his newspaper until Alastair left the coffee room. When he sensed that he was alone again in front of the fire, he tossed the paper onto a side table. He propped his elbows on the arms of his chair, linked his fingers, and looked deep into the dancing flames.

Imogen had given him a promise of love, but Matthias knew that he could not depend upon it too heavily. After all, he had more or less blackmailed her into marriage at a moment when she had been terrified for his life.

He had been out in the world for a long time. He knew very well that intense emotions had a way of encouraging people to make all sorts of wild, reckless declarations. If, or perhaps he should say, *when* Imogen discovered the truth about him, she might turn against him.

He gazed into the depths of the fire and saw the old ghosts grinning at him with their skeletal mouths. They knew just how precarious his newfound happiness was, how easily it could be destroyed. And when it all came crashing down around him, when he was forced to retreat back into the shadows, they would be waiting for him.

He clenched one hand into a fist on the arm of the chair. There was still passion, he told himself. And there was still Zamar. Perhaps they would prove to be enough.

Perhaps not.

He was still staring into the heart of the blaze a long while later when Fairfax hailed him from across the room.

"Colchester. Thought I might find you here." Fairfax's perpetually cheerful expression was tinged with a line or two of concern. He moved to stand in front of the fire. "I say, anything wrong?"

"No." Matthias glanced up at him. "Why do you ask?"

"Had an odd expression on your face, that's all." Fairfax warmed his hands at the hearth. "Never mind. Came to tell you that there are rumors all over Town about Vanneck's death."

"Save your breath. I've already heard them. They'll fade quickly enough."

Fairfax cleared his throat. "That might well be true. Under normal circumstances."

"What makes the present circumstances anything other than normal?"

"The new Lady Colchester," Fairfax said succinctly. He leaned down and lowered his voice even though there was no one nearby. "Don't mean to tell you how to conduct your personal affairs, but have you considered how she will react if she hears this particular tale?"

A very belated light dawned in Matthias's brain. He'd cautioned Imogen not to admit to anyone that she had even heard the rumor of a dawn appointment, let alone that she had accompanied him to Cabot's Farm. But he had not specifically told her how to react if she overheard others discussing the rumors of the duel.

The problem with Imogen was that one had to be extremely specific in one's instructions. She had a way of going off on unexpected tangents.

Matthias clamped his hands around the arms of his chair and shoved himself to his feet. "Excuse me, Fairfax. I've got to go home. I want to have a talk with my wife."

"I fear it's a bit too late for a husbandly chat over breakfast."

"What are you talking about?"

Fairfax's grimace was both sympathetic and amused. "I stopped by your town house before I came here. Your man Ufton said something about Lady Colchester having just set off on a shopping expedition."

"Good God." The horrendous possibilities loomed before Matthias, leaving him momentarily transfixed.

"One can only hope that the gossip has not yet reached the ladies of the ton." Fairfax took out his watch and glanced at the time. "They will be descending upon Oxford Street and Pall Mall even as we speak."

"Not reached the ladies? Are you mad?" Matthias strode toward the door. "The rumors will have reached them along with their morning chocolate."

"*I* was so worried when I realized that Matthias had left the house before anyone had arisen," Patricia confided as she walked beside Imogen. "I was certain that he would be killed. I vow, I shall have nightmares about this entire affair for weeks."

"Nonsense. It is over and done and the less said the better." The morning's events had established a tentative new bond between Patricia and herself, Imogen realized.

It was not surprising, she thought. After all, they both cared about Matthias. "Remember what Colchester said. We are to act as if nothing out of the ordinary has occurred."

"I understand. But I still do not comprehend why you were with him when he returned. And why on earth were you dressed as a stable lad?"

"I went along to make certain that the duel did not take place, of course," Imogen explained. "I could not allow Colchester to risk his neck because of me."

"But what did you think you could possibly do to halt the affair?"

"I had formulated any number of plans," Imogen assured her. "But as it happened, I was not obliged to employ any of them."

"Only because Vanneck got himself shot by a highwayman or a footpad." Patricia shuddered. "What a bizarre thing."

"Very bizarre. But I for one will not mourn him."

"Imogen?"

"Yes?"

"Thank you," Patricia whispered.

Oxford Street was a lively scene. It was nearly noon, prime time for the serious business of shopping. Elegantly dressed ladies paraded from one window to the next in search of the latest fashions. They were followed by maids and footmen burdened with packages and parcels.

"Lady Colchester." A middle-aged woman dressed in an expensive gown and a fashionable bonnet gave Imogen a cool smile. Her beady eyes were filled with avid speculation. "Congratulations on your recent marriage, madam. I saw the notice in the morning papers."

"Thank you, Lady Benson." Imogen made to move off down the street.

"I also heard that there has been a most unusual occurrence regarding a mutual acquaintance," Lady Benson continued quickly. "Lord Vanneck was found shot to death this very day. Quite early in the morning, I believe. Have you heard?"

"Sorry. Don't know a thing about it. I'm afraid I don't have time to chat. You must excuse us, Lady Benson." Imogen urged Patricia toward the nearest shop door. "We have an appointment with . . . uh." She glanced at the small wooden sign overhead. "With Madame Maud. Excellent modiste, you know. I trust I shall see you this evening."

"Of course." Lady Benson's eyes narrowed. "You and Colchester will definitely be the main attraction at the best parties tonight. Perhaps we shall be able to talk later."

"Perhaps." Imogen whisked Patricia through the door of the dressmaker's shop. She was relieved to see that there were no customers in the front of the small establishment.

"We don't have an appointment with Madame Maud," Patricia whispered.

"I am aware of that." Imogen whirled to peer out the window. "But I did not want to get into an extended discussion with Lady Benson. She is a notorious gossip. Just the sort Colchester frets about."

"Yes, I know," Patricia said in a very low voice. "Lady Lyndhurst has mentioned her. Imogen, where is the proprietor of this shop? There is no one here."

"Madame Maud is no doubt in the fitting room with a client." Imogen breathed a sigh of relief as Lady Benson walked off down the street. "Good. She's gone. We can go on to the glovemaker's. Let's be on our way. I want to stop at the bookshop before we go home."

At that moment a woman's voice rose shrilly from the back room. "Never say that Colchester murdered Vanneck in cold blood, Theodosia. I do not believe it."

"They do not call him Cold-blooded Colchester for nothing, Emily," Theodosia retorted in a tone of morbid excitement. "Personally, I am only too well aware of the fact that he is perfectly capable of killing a man. Lord

Vanneck was one of many. There was my dear Jonathan. And you must have heard the rumors about Rutledge's mysterious death."

"Well, yes, of course I have. The Rutledge Curse and all. But, Theo, Jonathan Exelby was killed years ago. And Rutledge died in far-off Zamar. This affair with Vanneck occurred this very morning on the outskirts of the city."

"I know Colchester's true nature better than anyone, and I can assure you that . . . *ouch*. Do be careful with those pins, Maud. You stuck me."

"Pardon, madam," the modiste mumbled.

"Colchester is said to be an excellent shot," Emily observed thoughtfully. "Why would he kill Vanneck before the duel? Why not simply wait and shoot him in front of the proper witnesses?"

"Who knows? Perhaps there was a quarrel before the seconds arrived," Theodosia said. "One thing is certain, Colchester will never go to the gallows for his crimes. He is devious and far too clever."

"And he is an earl," Emily noted pragmatically. "Speaking of devious, I wonder what deep game he is playing with Immodest Imogen. The engagement made some sense. Everyone knows he would stop at nothing in order to get his hands on a valuable Zamarian artifact. But marriage?"

"A marriage need not last forever," Theodosia said grimly. "It is not all that difficult to murder a wife."

It was too much. A white-hot rage boiled up within Imogen. "How dare they talk about him in such a fashion?"

Patricia glanced uneasily at the curtain that separated the fitting room from the front area of the shop. "Perhaps we should leave."

"Not until I have had a few words with Theodosia Slott." Imogen rounded the counter and stalked toward the fitting room.

Patricia hurried after her. "Imogen, wait. I'm not sure

my brother would approve. You know very well that he warned us not to speak of this affair."

"I have been pushed too far." Imogen grasped the heavy curtain and jerked it aside. Three startled gasps greeted her.

Theodosia stood in front of a mirror. Her friend Emily sat on a chair, watching, as Theodosia was fitted for a new ball gown.

Madame Maud, looking extremely harried, knelt on the floor to mark the hem of her client's gown.

"A moment, *s'il vous plaît*, madam," the modiste said around a mouthful of pins.

"There is no rush." Imogen met Theodosia's startled gaze in the mirror. "I merely wished to correct Mrs. Slott. She is putting about false information."

"Miss Waterstone." Theodosia's mouth opened and closed in dismay. "I mean, Lady Colchester. I did not hear you come in."

"Obviously," Imogen snapped. "You were too busy spreading lies and falsehoods about my husband."

Patricia plucked at Imogen's sleeve. "I think we should leave."

Imogen ignored her. She turned to Theodosia's companion. "Good day to you, Mrs. Hartwell."

"Good day, Miss . . . er, Lady Colchester." Emily Hartwell offered a weak smile. "Congratulations on your marriage."

"Thank you." Imogen pinned Theodosia again in the mirror. "Now, about those lies concerning Colchester."

"They are not lies." Theodosia had recovered from her initial shock. She raised a defiant chin. "No one will ever prove a thing, but anyone acquainted with Colchester's character knows that it is very likely he shot poor Vanneck before the duel could be properly conducted."

"That is absolute nonsense, Mrs. Slott," Imogen said. "As it happens, there were witnesses to the entire affair, and they will be delighted to testify to my husband's innocence should it become necessary."

Emily gasped. Her hand went to her throat. "I had not realized that there were witnesses."

"Imogen, please, we must be off." Patricia sounded frantic. "Appointments, you know."

"In a moment, Patricia." Imogen glared at Theodosia. "It will not be necessary for anyone to testify concerning Colchester's innocence because the notion that he might be guilty is utterly ludicrous."

"Do not be too certain of that, Lady Colchester," Theodosia retorted. "The whole world knows that your husband has a very dangerous reputation."

Emily was horrified. "Theodosia, please, what are you saying? Colchester will be furious if he hears that you are accusing him of murder. You must be careful."

"Yes, Mrs. Slott," Imogen said smoothly, "I would advise you to be extremely cautious in your accusation."

Theodosia blinked several times. A hint of uncertainty replaced some of the righteous indignation in her eyes. She cast a quick, uneasy glance at her companion. "I am not making any accusations. I am merely commenting on the obvious."

"Indeed?" Imogen set her hands on her hips and tapped one toe. "I fail to see anything obvious except, of course, that you had as much reason to shoot Lord Vanneck as anyone else. And more cause than most."

"*What?*" Theodosia's mouth fell open in scandalized outrage.

"You cannot be serious." Emily stared at Imogen, horrified.

The modiste froze, her mouth still full of pins.

"Imogen," Patricia whispered desperately. "Please. We must go."

Before anyone could move, a familiar voice spoke from the front room of the shop.

"Do go on, Lady Colchester," Selena murmured as

she glided into the fitting room. "I cannot wait to learn why Theodosia killed Vanneck before the duel."

"Lady Lyndhurst." The modiste was becoming frantic. "A moment."

Everyone in the small room turned to look at Selena. "I did not kill anyone," Theodosia wailed.

Imogen scowled. "I did not say that Theodosia shot Vanneck. I merely pointed out that she had as much reason as any number of people. Given that fact, she ought to be careful when it comes to making accusations."

"I never said that Colchester murdered Vanneck," Theodosia cried. "I said he *may* have done so. That's all."

Selena smiled faintly at Imogen. "Why would Theodosia shoot him just before the duel?"

"To make it appear that Colchester had murdered him in cold blood," Imogen said calmly.

Theodosia's face worked in desperate rage. "But why would I do such a thing?"

Imogen pursed her lips and considered the question. "Perhaps because you hoped that the ensuing gossip would drive Colchester from London."

"What do you mean?" Theodosia demanded.

"It is somewhat awkward for you to have him hanging about, is it not, Theodosia? After all, every time he appears in Society, there is the risk that he will let the truth be known."

Selena's brows rose. "What truth would that be, Imogen?"

"Why, that Theodosia has been living on falsehoods for years," Imogen said. "No one ever fought a duel over her. Her friend, Mr. Exelby, left Town to seek his fortune in America after he was caught cheating at cards in The Lost Soul. And as for that nonsense about Colchester seeking to take Exelby's place in your bed, well, that is ludicrous."

Theodosia gave her a seething look. "How dare you imply that I have been lying to my friends."

"The only person who might wish to set the record

straight is Colchester himself," Imogen continued. "You could not risk that, could you, Theodosia?"

"What do you mean?" she demanded.

"So long as he remained out of Society, your secret was safe. But lately Colchester has reentered the social whirl. Only think what he could do to your position in the ton were he to start discussing the true events surrounding Exelby's departure from London. You would be made to look ridiculous."

"This is an outrage," Theodosia howled. "I will not stand for it."

"And I will not abide any more of your silly accusations against my husband," Imogen said coldly. "The next time you are tempted to imply that he may have killed Vanneck, stop and think that you could be made to appear the guilty party."

"You cannot do this to me," Theodosia hissed.

Imogen gave her a scornful look and then spoke to a stunned Patricia. "Come along. We must stop at the glovemaker's and then I want to pay a visit to the bookshop."

She swung around briskly. And ran straight into Matthias, who lounged in the entrance of the fitting room.

"Umph." Imogen staggered. For a second she could see nothing but green straw. She realized that her wide-brimmed bonnet had been knocked askew by the impact and had fallen forward over her eyes. She grabbed the brim and shoved it out of the way.

Matthias smiled slightly and reached out to adjust the bonnet. "Allow me."

"Good heavens, Colchester." Imogen hastily retied the bonnet strings. "I didn't see you. What on earth are you doing here in Madame Maud's shop?"

Matthias surveyed the frozen tableau in the fitting room with gleaming eyes. "Perhaps I have developed an interest in fashion."

Selena appeared vastly amused. Emily's eyes darted anxiously about, as though she sought an escape.

Theodosia made a very odd, strangled noise and collapsed to the floor in an untidy heap.

"Hmm." Imogen peered at the fallen woman. "I do believe that this time her swoon is quite genuine. Perhaps you should get out your vinaigrette, Mrs. Hartwell."

*T*he tall clock ticked heavily in the corner of the library. For some reason Matthias was intensely aware of the sound as he sat facing his wife and sister across the width of his desk. He studied the pair, trying to think how best to begin his lecture.

Patricia would not be a problem, he decided. She already looked thoroughly uneasy about the outcome of this little interview. Matthias suspected that her chief fear was that he would throw her out on her ear because she had inadvertently disobeyed his instructions not to discuss the duel.

Imogen was another matter. She faced him with a disgruntled expression that did not bode well. Any apprehension she may have felt was buried beneath her sense of righteous indignation.

Matthias folded his hands on his desk. He looked at Imogen. "Perhaps I did not make myself clear this morning."

"You made yourself perfectly clear," Imogen assured him grandly. "You told me that I was not to discuss the events surrounding Vanneck's death with anyone."

"May I ask why you chose to disobey me?"

Patricia cringed at the tone of his voice. Matthias ignored her.

Imogen gave him a frosty glare. "I did not disobey you, sir."

"Then would you kindly explain just what the devil you were discussing in that dressmaker's damned fitting room?"

Patricia crushed the hankie she held.

Imogen bristled. "It was not my fault that I happened

upon Theodosia Slott spreading lies and falsehoods. All I did was put a stop to them by pointing out that there were any number of people besides you, my lord, who could be made to look guilty of Vanneck's murder."

"You damned near accused her of killing Vanneck."

"Not exactly," Imogen said carefully.

"Yes. Exactly."

"Well, even if one could interpret my words in that manner, it was only what she deserved." Imogen scowled ferociously. "Aunt Horatia assures me that Mrs. Slott has spread all sorts of malicious tales about you for years. And she as good as accused you of Vanneck's murder in that fitting room. Is that not true, Patricia?"

Patricia gave a start at hearing her name brought into the discussion. Somewhat to Matthias's surprise, however, she managed to answer Imogen's question.

"Yes," she said very softly. "It's true."

"There, you see?" Imogen flashed him a triumphant look. "The gossip would have been all over Town by tonight if I had not intervened."

"The gossip is already all over Town. Madam, you may be brilliant when it comes to deciphering the formal script of lost Zamar, but you are hopelessly naive where Society is concerned."

Imogen was briefly diverted. "Brilliant?"

Matthias flattened his hands on the desk and got to his feet. It was not easy to scold her for leaping to his defense, but it had to be done. "Dammit, Imogen, I told you to ignore anything that you overheard regarding Vanneck's death."

"I could not ignore Theodosia Slott's accusations. I did not want them going any further."

"Nobody, including me, gives a damn about Theodosia Slott's opinions," Matthias said through his teeth. "Don't you understand? I am far more concerned with your reputation."

"I have told you that I do not give a bloody damn for my reputation."

"Well, I do. How many times must I remind you that you are my wife now? You will act accordingly."

"Is that all you can think about?" she flung back. "How the new Lady Colchester should behave?"

"Hell's teeth, madam, I will not have your name linked to Vanneck's death."

"And I will not have yours linked to it either, my lord."

"The only way to deal with the inevitable gossip is to ignore it," Matthias said. "Believe me, I am an expert on the subject."

"I do not agree with you. In my opinion, one must fight fire with fire."

"We will fight this particular blaze my way," Matthias said bluntly. "The tales will fade with time. They always do. Henceforth, you will follow my instructions to the letter. You are not to utter another word concerning Vanneck or his death to anyone outside this house. Do you understand me, madam?"

Patricia jumped to her feet. "Do stop shouting at her, Matthias."

Matthias stared at her in astonishment. So did Imogen.

Patricia's expression was a mixture of fear and determination. She clenched her hands very tightly. "I think it is grossly unfair of you to talk to Imogen in this manner, Colchester. Indeed, she was only trying to defend you when she confronted Mrs. Slott."

"This does not concern you, Patricia," Matthias said. "Sit down."

"*Patricia.* How kind of you." Imogen shot up from the chair. She threw her arms around Patricia. "No one has ever defended me in such a fashion. How can I thank you for interceding on my behalf?"

Patricia looked taken aback. She patted Imogen somewhat awkwardly on the shoulder. "It's all right, Imogen. I was forced to speak up. Colchester is being most unfair."

"Damnation." Matthias sank wearily back down into his chair.

Imogen stepped back from Patricia and whipped a hankie out of her reticule. "You must excuse me." She blotted her eyes. "I am overcome with emotion."

She rushed toward the door, opened it, and vanished into the hall.

Matthias drummed his fingers on the desk as the door closed behind Imogen. "She does have a way of ending a conversation that she is not enjoying."

"You really should not have lectured her in such a nasty manner," Patricia muttered. "She was only attempting to defend you."

Matthias eyed her with brooding interest. "When did you become one of Imogen's supporters? I thought you disapproved of her."

"I have changed my mind about her," Patricia said stiffly.

"I see. In that case, it would seem that we have a mutual goal."

Patricia looked wary. "What is that?"

"We must both exert a great deal of effort in order to keep her out of trouble."

"I do not think that will be easy," Patricia said slowly. "Nothing is ever simple where Imogen is concerned."

Chapter 14

That evening, during the middle of the Reedmore ball, Imogen came to the conclusion that there was definitely something amiss with Patricia.

Alastair smiled gallantly at Imogen and abandoned any attempt to lead her in a long, gliding circle around the dance floor. "I assume you gave the map showing the location of the Queen's Seal to Colchester as a wedding gift. Tell me, was he suitably grateful?"

"Actually, we have not discussed the map." Imogen gave Alastair a vague smile and glanced to the side to see who was dancing with Patricia this time.

Hugo Bagshaw. Again.

Imogen nibbled on her lower lip. This was the second time that evening Hugo had led Patricia out onto the floor. Matthias would not be pleased.

The strains of the waltz drifted from the ballroom balcony, where the musicians gamely battled the heat generated by hundreds of chandelier candles and an almost equal number of people. The affair was already accounted

a crush, the highest accolade that could be paid by Society.

Imogen knew that Horatia considered Patricia an even greater success. She had told Imogen earlier that she was greatly relieved that the recent rumors concerning Colchester had done no harm. Indeed, the fresh gossip concerning the duel and the hasty wedding had served to make the Colchester women even more intriguing to the jaded members of the ton.

"Imogen?" Alastair sounded impatient.

"I beg your pardon?" Imogen forced herself to smile at him. Dancing with Alastair was somewhat boring, but at least there was never a struggle. Dancing with Matthias, on the other hand, was always something of a skirmish.

Imogen had accepted Alastair's invitation to dance just as she had agreed to dance with a number of other gentlemen only because it was the most convenient way of keeping track of Patricia. Horatia had voiced some concerns earlier about the efforts of certain known rakes to lure Patricia out into the gardens.

Imogen said nothing to Horatia or to Matthias, but she had become increasingly worried about Patricia since the duel. There was a moodiness about her that had begun to alarm Imogen. She knew that the Colchester bloodline harbored a tendency toward dark imaginings, but Patricia's current behavior appeared more anxious than usual.

Imogen had begun to wonder if she should discuss the situation with Matthias. The only reason she had hesitated thus far was that she knew he was not fond of conversations about the family tendency toward anxious forebodings and weak nerves.

Alastair must have realized that he had lost Imogen's attention again. Annoyance flickered briefly in his eyes. It vanished quickly, however, and was replaced by bland amusement. "I am surprised that Colchester has not already made plans to search for the Queen's Seal."

"I expect we shall get to the matter one of these

days," Imogen said carelessly. She tried for another glimpse of Patricia and Hugo. The pair had disappeared, swallowed up by the crowd on the dance floor. "Bloody hell." She steered Alastair back across the floor.

Alastair's mouth compressed with irritation. "What did you say?"

"You are taller than I am, Mr. Drake. Can you see Colchester's sister?"

Alastair gave the crowd a cursory glance. "No."

"I do hope young Bagshaw has more sense than to drag her out into the gardens." Imogen came to a halt in the middle of the dance floor and stood on tiptoe to see over the heads of the nearest dancers. "Ah-ha. There they go. You must excuse me, Alastair."

"Devil take it," Alastair muttered, furious at being abandoned in the middle of the dance floor. "You do not have the least notion of how to behave properly in Society. Lucy was right. You're a walking joke, Lady Colchester."

Lucy's name stopped Imogen as nothing else could have done. She whirled around to stare at Alastair. "What did you say?"

"Nothing." The brief flare of fury faded swiftly in Alastair's gaze. He glanced around uneasily, clearly embarrassed by his predicament. "Run along and see to your duty as a chaperone."

"What did you say about Lucy?" Imogen staggered slightly as another couple, unable to change course quickly enough, plowed into her. She scowled at the pair. "I'm trying to have a conversation here."

"Yes, we can see that, Lady Colchester," the gentleman said wryly. "Perhaps it would be easier to conduct your discussion off the dance floor." The lady in his arms looked slyly amused.

Imogen flushed. "Yes, of course." She turned back to discover that Alastair had disappeared in the crowd. "Damnation. Where did he go?"

Matthias's strong, elegant fingers curled firmly around her wrist. "Perhaps I can be of some assistance."

"Matthias." Imogen smiled in relief as he drew her into his arms. "What are you doing here? I thought you intended to spend the evening at your club."

"I took a fancy to dance with my wife." Matthias surveyed the room over the top of her head. "What happened between you and Drake a moment ago?"

"What? Oh, nothing important. He said something about Lucy. I tried to make him repeat it, but he vanished when I turned around to speak to those people who crashed into me."

"I see."

"I believe he was annoyed with me because I left him standing in the middle of the dance floor," Imogen confessed.

"I have no difficulty with that notion," Matthias said. "But I'm curious as to why you abandoned him. Did he attempt to take the lead?"

"No, it wasn't that. I wanted to find Patricia. I had lost sight of her in the crowd."

"She's in the buffet room with Hugo Bagshaw. I saw her a moment ago."

"Oh." Imogen searched his face. "I collect that you are not pleased."

"No, I am not."

"I know that you are convinced that Mr. Bagshaw is looking for a way to avenge himself against you, but I trust you will not make a scene tonight. Patricia would be mortified. I think that she is developing some very tender emotions for him."

"In that case, I had better move quickly."

"Now, Matthias, you must not be hasty."

Matthias's brows rose. "What would you suggest that I do?"

"I think that you should talk to Mr. Bagshaw in private."

"Excellent notion. I shall take him aside and warn him to stay away from Patricia."

"Not that sort of talk. For heaven's sake, Matthias, warning him off will not do any good."

"You may be right." Matthias grew thoughtful. "I do believe he's becoming more reckless in his attentions to Patricia."

"The important thing is that Patricia must not be hurt by what is going on here. I think you should tell Mr. Bagshaw the full truth about his father's death."

"I doubt that he gives a damn about the truth. He was raised on a pack of lies."

"I think you could make him confront the truth, Matthias. He must accept it someday or else he will go through life nursing a hatred for you that will eat at his own soul."

Matthias's arm tightened around her. His eyes were grim. "What makes you think that I can force young Bagshaw to deal with the truth about his father?"

"Because you have been through a similar situation with your own father," Imogen said gently. "You of all people understand something of what festers inside him. You know what it is to be rejected by your father."

"Bagshaw's father did not reject him. He committed suicide because of his financial problems."

"I suspect that the result was very much the same for Hugo. Rejection can take many forms, my lord. You and Hugo were both left alone at a very young age to deal with the consequences of your fathers' actions."

Matthias said nothing.

Imogen met his eyes. "You found your salvation in the search for Zamar. I fear Hugo will not be so fortunate. You must guide him, Matthias."

"I have better things to do than try to talk sense into young Bagshaw."

Imogen caught sight of Patricia and Hugo at the edge of the crowd. She saw the shy, eager expression on Patricia's face and then she saw Hugo glance across the room toward Matthias. There was no mistaking the seething anger in the younger man's eyes.

"No, Matthias," Imogen said softly. "I do not think that you have better things to do."

$\mathcal{M}$atthias lounged, arms folded, in the doorway of the gaming room of The Lost Soul and watched Hugo roll the dice in a round of hazard. A hoarse shout went up as another player claimed the winnings. Hugo clenched his hand. His face was a mask of fury and recklessness. He was losing.

The hour was late and the hell was crowded with a mix of young bloods, dandies, and world-weary rakes. A smoky haze of urgency and unhealthy excitement hung over the tables. The room reeked of sweat, ale, and perfume. Little had changed since he had owned the place, Matthias reflected. Perhaps the nature of gaming hells was immutable.

"Good evening, Matthias. Come to play, or just to pay a visit to some old shades?"

Matthias glanced at the short, round man who had joined him in the doorway. "Hello, Felix. You must be in good spirits tonight. A lively crowd."

"Indeed." Felix folded his hands over the ornately carved handle of his cane. His cherubic smile dimpled his plump cheeks and created good-natured creases at the corners of his shrewd eyes. "I shall see a tidy profit off this night's work."

Ten years earlier Matthias had hired Felix Glaston to manage The Lost Soul. Felix had an uncanny talent for numbers. He also had a knack for collecting information. The combination of skills had made him extremely valuable to Matthias. Together they had created one of the most notorious and most popular hells in London. Their success had made them both very wealthy.

When Matthias had gathered the funds he needed to finance the first expedition in search of Zamar, he had sold The Lost Soul to Felix. Glaston had been prospering in the role of owner ever since. He now lived the life of a wealthy merchant.

The two men, from dramatically different social stations, had forged a bond of friendship that still held. A bond that still shocked Society. A gentleman might lose his fortune in a gaming hell, but he would not dream of consorting with the owner of one.

Another shout went up at the table where Hugo stood. Hugo's face grew more rigid.

"Looks like young Bagshaw will be under the hatches by dawn," Felix observed.

"Are you going to intervene?"

"Naturally." Felix chuckled. "I have maintained your wise policy of never allowing a customer to lose his estates or his entire fortune at my tables. It's been good for business."

"Does young Bagshaw always play so wildly?"

"No. In truth, he rarely plays at all, from what I hear. And certainly not in this house. You know he still blames The Lost Soul for his father's death."

"I am aware of that."

"Yes, of course, you would know that better than anyone," Felix murmured. "I comprehend that you have had a busy week, Colchester. My felicitations on your marriage, by the way."

"Thank you."

"And on surviving yet another duel."

Matthias smiled grimly. "It was not difficult this time."

"Vanneck, I understand, did not even fire a shot. Dead when you arrived at Cabot's Farm, I'm told."

"Your information is, as always, astonishingly accurate, Felix."

"I pay enough for it." Felix made a dismissing motion with his plump, beringed hand. "A bit odd though."

"What is?"

"Vanneck being at the scene. According to my

sources, he dismissed his staff yesterday afternoon without notice. Apparently he planned to take an extended journey on the Continent."

"Interesting."

"I suppose some public-spirited footpad or a highwayman was responsible for removing Vanneck from this mortal plane?"

"I'm not so certain of that."

Felix glanced at him. "Why do you doubt it?"

"Because when we found him in his curricle, he was still wearing his rings."

"Curious."

"Very."

Felix frowned as Hugo seized the dice. "I suppose I really must see to young Bagshaw. I doubt that he has the stamina or the temperament for this kind of play. I wonder what drives him to such recklessness tonight."

"I believe that tonight is the anniversary of his father's suicide."

"Ah, yes. That would explain it."

Matthias watched Hugo throw the dice with feverish speed. He could almost hear Imogen whispering in his ear. *You found your salvation in the search for Zamar. I fear Hugo will not be so fortunate.*

Matthias thought of the look he had seen on Patricia's face as she stood at the buffet table with Hugo. There was no doubt that she had developed a *tendre* for Bagshaw.

One way or another, Hugo had to be sorted out.

Matthias came to a decision. "I shall handle Bagshaw for you tonight, Felix."

Felix shrugged his well-padded shoulders. "Be my guest."

Matthias made his way through the crowd to where Hugo stood at the table, poised for another toss of the dice.

"If you don't mind, I'd like a word with you, Bagshaw," Matthias said quietly.

Hugo stiffened. "Colchester. What the devil do you want?"

Matthias looked into Hugo's seething gaze and noted yet another ghost. This particular specter was unlike those he routinely saw in the flames. This apparition was one he occasionally encountered in his shaving mirror.

"I'm told that you and I have something in common," Matthias said.

"Leave me alone, Colchester. I have nothing to discuss with you." Hugo made to turn back to the gaming table. Then he paused, his mouth twisting into a taunting smile. "Unless, of course, you're here to challenge me to a duel. I comprehend that you conduct your dawn appointments in a somewhat unusual manner."

A sharp hush fell across the table. The other players watched Matthias and Hugo with glittering interest.

"You will come with me," Matthias said very softly to Hugo. "Or we will have this conversation right here in front of your companions."

Hugo gave him a derisive smile. "I'll wager that this concerns my attentions to your sister. Well, well, well. I wondered when you'd notice that she and I have become very good friends."

"It's about your father."

"*My father?*" Hugo dropped the dice. They bounced across the green felt. "What the hell are you talking about?"

Matthias took advantage of Hugo's shock to seize hold of his arm. He led the younger man up out of the hot, smoky hell and into the clear, crisp night, where the hired carriage waited.

"*M*atthias is going to challenge poor Hugo," Patricia wailed as the Colchester carriage made its way through the clogged streets. "How could he do such a thing? It is so very unfair. Hugo will not stand a chance against him. Matthias will kill him."

"Rubbish," Horatia said firmly. "I'm sure Colchester has no intention of shooting anyone, least of all young Mr. Bagshaw."

"Quite right, Aunt Horatia." Imogen leaned forward in the seat. "Patricia, listen to me. I have told you several times already that Matthias is not going to challenge Mr. Bagshaw. He is only going to speak to him."

"Threaten him, more likely." Tears glistened in Patricia's eyes. "He is going to tell Hugo that he must never dance with me or speak to me again."

"No, I don't think so."

"How can you know what Colchester will do? He does not approve of Hugo. He has warned me to stay away from him."

"The friendship that has sprung up between you and Mr. Bagshaw worries Colchester because he is uncertain of Mr. Bagshaw's motives," Horatia said. "And not without some reason, if I may say so. Your brother is right to be concerned."

"Hugo cares for me," Patricia said. "That is his only motive. And he is perfectly respectable. Matthias has no right to raise objections."

Imogen rolled her eyes. "I have explained to you that Hugo blames Matthias for what happened to his father several years ago. Matthias is going to attempt to tell Hugo the truth tonight."

"What if Hugo does not believe him?" Patricia whispered. "They will quarrel. You know how men are. One of them will challenge the other and there will be a duel."

"There will be no duel," Imogen announced. "I will not allow it."

Patricia seemed not to have heard her. "It is the curse."

"Curse?" Horatia frowned. "What on earth are you talking about?"

"The Rutledge Curse," Patricia said. "We have been studying it in Lady Lyndhurst's salon."

"The Rutledge Curse is utter nonsense," Imogen said very firmly. "There is no curse involved in this situation."

Patricia turned her head to look at her. "I fear that you are wrong, Imogen."

$\mathcal{M}$atthias studied Hugo's angry, defiant face in the flickering light of the carriage lamp. He tried to think where to begin a conversation that he privately considered pointless.

"I have discovered over the years that it is often more satisfying to blame someone for an injustice than it is to accept the truth of the matter," he said.

Hugo's mouth thinned. "If you are going to tell me that you had nothing to do with my father's death, save your breath. I will not believe a word you say."

"Nevertheless, as we are here together, I may as well say the words. Now then, here are the facts surrounding your father's death. You may do with them what you will. He did not lose his fortune in a game of cards. He lost it in a poor business investment. He was one of many."

"That is a lie. My mother told me the truth. My father played cards at The Lost Soul on the night he died. You quarreled with him. Do not deny it."

"I don't deny it."

"It was after that game that he went home and put a bullet in his brain."

Matthias looked at him. "Your father was drinking heavily that night. He sat down at a table with several other gentlemen. He wanted to enter the game. I asked him to leave the club because I knew that he was too deep in his cups to even hold his damned cards."

"That is not true."

"It is true. I also knew that he had been informed of a serious setback in his finances that very day. In addition to being drunk, his spirits were very depressed. He had no business making any wagers that night."

"You took advantage of his condition," Hugo said furiously. "He told others."

"Your father was enraged with me when he left the club because he had planned to recoup his fortunes at my tables. But if he had played, you may be assured he would have lost even more than he'd already forfeited in the shipping venture."

"I do not believe you."

"I know." Matthias shrugged. "I told my wife that you would not accept my word on the matter. But she insisted that I try to explain what had happened."

"Why?"

"She worries that Patricia will be hurt if you attempt to use her to avenge yourself against me."

Hugo's hand clenched around his walking stick. He stared out the window. "I have no intention of hurting Lady Patricia."

"I am, of course, pleased to learn that." Matthias flexed his fingers absently. "Because if anything were to happen to my sister, I would be obliged to take action. I am responsible for her."

Hugo turned his head swiftly to stare at Matthias. "Are you warning me to stay away from Lady Patricia?"

"No. I confess that I had intended to do just that, but Lady Colchester advised against it. I am, however, warning you not to use my sister in any scheme of vengeance that you may have concocted. If you feel that you must blame me for your father's suicide, then come after me directly. Deal with me man to man. Do not hide behind a lady's skirts."

Hugo flushed. "I am not hiding behind Patricia's skirts."

Matthias smiled fleetingly. "Then there is nothing more for us to discuss. I shall inform my wife that we had this pleasant little chat and perhaps she will give me some peace."

"Do not tell me that you did this just to please your

lady wife. That does not sound at all like you, Colchester."

"What would you know about me?" Matthias asked softly.

"I know what my mother told me after my father died. I know of the rumors surrounding your association with Rutledge. I know that you were accounted wild and reckless. That you shot a man named Exelby several years ago. Some say you killed Vanneck in cold blood only this morning. I know a great deal about you, sir."

"So does my wife," Matthias mused. "She has heard all the tales that you have heard. But she married me regardless. What do you think prompted her to do that?"

Hugo looked taken aback. "How would I know?" He cleared his throat. "Lady Colchester is said to be an Original."

"She is that. Definitely one of a kind. And I suppose there's no accounting for taste." Matthias pulled himself out of his brief reverie. "She told me that you and I have something in common."

"What could we possibly share?" Hugo demanded scornfully.

"Fathers who chose not to take responsibility for their sons."

Hugo stared at him. "That is outrageous. The most outrageous thing that I have ever heard."

"An hour ago I told my wife that she was talking nonsense. But now that I've pondered the matter further, I do believe she has a point."

"What point?"

"Does it occur to you, Bagshaw, that your father and mine both left their sons to pick up the pieces of the messes that they themselves had created?"

"My father did not create a mess," Hugo retorted passionately. "You ruined him at cards."

"As I told Imogen, this was a complete waste of time." Matthias glanced out the window and recognized the neighborhood. The hackney coachman had followed instructions.

"So it was," Hugo said sullenly.

Matthias rapped on the roof of the carriage to signal the coachman to halt. "I believe I shall walk from here. I need some fresh air."

Hugo glanced out the window, confused. "This is not your address."

"I am aware of that."

The hackney rumbled to a halt. Matthias opened the door and got out. Then he turned to look back at Hugo. "Remember what I said, Bagshaw. Pursue your vengeance if you feel you must. But do not use my sister as a shield. You are not your father. Something tells me that you are made of sterner stuff than he was. You can face your problems as a man."

"Damn you, Colchester," Hugo whispered.

"You might start by making a few inquiries of your father's old solicitor. He can tell you what really happened to the family finances." Matthias started to close the carriage door.

"Colchester, wait."

Matthias paused. "What is it?"

"You forgot to warn me that I must not pay my addresses to your sister."

"Did I?"

Hugo scowled. "Well?"

"Well, what? I have other matters to attend to this evening, Bagshaw. You must excuse me."

"Are you telling me that I will be welcome in your house?"

Matthias smiled slightly. "Why don't you pay a visit and find out for yourself?" He slammed the door and walked off down the street without a backward glance.

He was in a quiet, respectable area of Town. The dark expanse of a long, narrow park loomed between two rows of modest town houses. A few of the residences were dark, but windows were still lit in the majority. The rumors had been correct on one point, Matthias thought. Vanneck's fortunes had definitely plummeted. Until a few months ago Vanneck had lived in a much larger house in a wealthier neighborhood.

The notion of paying a late night visit to Vanneck's residence had occurred to him that afternoon as he reflected again on the events of the morning. Matthias had said nothing to Imogen of his plans because he suspected that she would have insisted on accompanying him.

He came to a halt and studied the twin rows of town houses. The one in which Vanneck had lived was darkened.

Matthias stood on the street for a long time, reflecting on the various possibilities that presented themselves. Eventually he walked around the corner and found the shadowed alley that would lead him to the back of Vanneck's town house.

There was sufficient moonlight to allow Matthias to find his way to the gate that opened onto the small garden. The hinges squeaked in the darkness.

He closed the gate as gently as possible and went through the garden to the kitchen door. Fortunately, he was able to see very well at night. The ability had come in handy over the years.

He was surprised to discover that the kitchen door was open. The departing servants had evidently forgotten to lock up securely before they left for their own homes.

Matthias stepped into the kitchen and paused to allow his eyes to adjust to the deeper shadows. Then he removed the candle he had brought with him from the pocket of his greatcoat. He lit it.

Shielding the weak flame with one hand, he started down the long hall that divided the first floor of the house. He was not certain what he was looking for, but he intended to start his search in Vanneck's study. It was the most logical place to begin.

He found the cluttered chamber on the left side of the hall. Vanneck's desk was littered with a jumble of papers. Matthias glanced at the inkstand and saw that the lid was open on the small bottle of ink. A quill pen lay nearby. It was as if Vanneck had been interrupted in the midst of writing a letter or a note.

Matthias set down the candle and picked up the first sheet of foolscap. He paused when he noticed several small, dark stains on one of the papers. He held the paper closer to the light. Not ink spots. It was possible that the dried droplets had been caused by spilled tea or claret, but Matthias did not think that was the case.

He was almost certain that the stains were dried blood.

Glancing down, he saw a much larger, more ominous-looking patch on the carpet near the toe of his boot.

Something stirred the hair on the nape of his neck just as he bent down to take a closer look at the dark stain. He did not need the almost inaudible scrape of a shoe on the carpet to warn him that he was not alone in the study.

He flung himself to the side just as something very large and very heavy slammed downward toward his head. There was a splintering crash as a heavy candlestick struck the edge of the desk.

Matthias twisted and came up out of the crouch just as his attacker raised the candlestick for another blow.

Chapter 15

Matthias avoided the second swing of the candlestick by no more than scant inches. He did not allow his assailant time for a third attempt. He slipped to the side, using one of the movements he had learned from an ancient treatise on Zamarian fighting methods.

Before his opponent could alter course, Matthias kicked out with his booted foot. The blow slammed his attacker back onto the top of the desk. Quill, papers, and inkstand cascaded off the far side.

The attacker grunted heavily and scrambled to get off the desk. He was hampered by his cloak and a thick woolen scarf wrapped around the lower half of his face. His hair was covered by a cap that was jammed securely onto his head.

A rustle of sound in the hallway alerted Matthias just as he was about to launch himself across the desk. There was not one, but two people in the house with him. The face of the second figure was lost in the shadows of a cloak hood and scarf.

Even as Matthias watched, the newcomer raised one

arm. Candlelight glinted on the barrel of a small pistol in a heavily gloved hand. Matthias seized the candlestick that had nearly broken his skull and hurled it toward the figure in the doorway.

The pistol exploded just as the heavy candlestick struck the second attacker in the chest. Matthias heard the ball thud into the oak paneling behind him and knew he now had some time. It would take a few minutes for the second assailant to reload the tiny one-shot pistol.

Matthias leaped over the top of the desk and came down on top of the first man, who was struggling to get to his feet.

The impact sent both men down onto the carpet. They rolled violently into a chair and then back toward the desk. Matthias avoided a bunched fist and raised his own hand for a blow. At the last instant he sensed the approach of the second villain.

Resorting again to one of the Zamarian techniques he had practiced for years, he twisted to the side and uncoiled to his feet. Cold fire lanced through his arm.

He ignored the pain and lashed out with one booted foot in a swift, brutal arc that caught the first man just as he rose from the floor. The man reeled back against the desk.

Matthias readied himself for the next onslaught, but to his surprise, both of his assailants turned and rushed from the study. Their shoes echoed on the tile in the hall as they dashed toward the rear of the house.

Prepared and braced for another attack, Matthias was momentarily disconcerted by his opponents' flight.

He raced out of the study into the hall, but he knew he was too late. He heard the kitchen door slam shut behind his quarry.

"Hell's teeth."

He put out a hand and flattened it against the wall to steady himself while he drew several deep breaths. He was feeling oddly dazed.

Matthias frowned. What the devil was the matter with

him? he wondered. The battle had not lasted more than a few minutes, and he considered himself to be in excellent physical condition.

It occurred to him that the fire in his left arm was no longer an icy flame. It was now a hellish blaze. He glanced down and saw that the sleeve of his coat had been slashed open. There was enough light from the single candle that still burned in the study to see the color of his own blood as it saturated the expensive fabric.

His opponents had been well armed. One had carried a pistol. The other had wielded a knife. Whatever it was that they had sought in Vanneck's house had been very important to them.

Matthias wondered if they had found it.

He ripped off his neck cloth, tied it quickly around his bleeding arm, and then turned back to examine Vanneck's study. He made himself think the way he had trained himself to think when he had searched the ghostly ruins of ancient Zamar.

An hour later Matthias reposed on the dolphin sofa in the comfort of his own library and listened as Imogen flew down the stairs. He grinned in spite of the discomfort he was experiencing as Ufton finished stitching up the knife wound.

"*Injured?*" Imogen's voice penetrated the closed door of the library with no difficulty. Matthias would not have been astonished to learn that passersby outside in the street heard her. "What the bloody hell do you mean, he is injured? Where is he? How badly is he hurt? Has Ufton sent for a doctor?"

Imogen's rapid string of questions was punctuated by the staccato beat of her footsteps on the stairs. "Ufton is tending him? Ufton? *Ufton?* Ufton is a butler, for heaven's sake, not a doctor."

"Madam is concerned," Ufton noted as he carefully secured the white bandage around Matthias's arm.

"Apparently." Matthias closed his eyes and leaned his head back against the sofa. He smiled to himself. "Odd, having a wife around the house."

"No offense, my lord, but Lady Colchester is a trifle more odd than most wives."

"Yes, I suspect she is," Matthias said.

He listened contentedly as Imogen continued to hurl orders and demand more information.

"See to it that his bed is turned down at once," she said to someone. "You. Charles, yes, you. Prepare a litter of some sort that we can use to carry his lordship upstairs."

Matthias stirred and reluctantly opened his eyes. "I suppose one of us had better stop her before she converts the entire house into a hospital."

Ufton blanched. "Pray, do not look at me when you suggest that someone should attempt to halt Lady Colchester's chosen course of action, sir."

"I have never before known you to lack nerve and fortitude, Ufton."

"I have never before been obliged to deal with a lady of madam's peculiar temperament."

"That makes two of us."

Outside in the hall, Imogen's voice rose. "That is blood on the tile, is it not? Colchester's blood. Dear God. Bring bandages. Water. And a needle and thread. Hurry, for God's sake."

"Brace yourself, Ufton." Matthias glanced toward the door. "She is almost upon us."

Ufton sighed as he tended to the bandage.

The library door slammed open and Imogen, garbed in a chintz wrapper and a frilly little white cap, rushed into the room. Her wide, alarmed eyes went instantly to the sofa. Matthias tried to look both heroic and tragic.

"Matthias, what on earth has happened?" She skidded to a halt near the sofa. Her eyes flew to the white bandage around his left arm and then to the torn, blood-stained shirt that lay wadded up on a tray. Matthias could have sworn that she paled.

"It's all right, Imogen," he said. "Calm yourself, my dear."

"Dear heaven, this is all my fault. I should never have sent you off alone in a hackney carriage tonight. The streets are so dangerous. If only you had come home with the rest of us. Whatever was I thinking of when I told you to talk to Mr. Bagshaw?"

Matthias raised his hand, palm out. "You must not blame yourself for this, my dear. As you can see, I am not at death's door. Ufton has had some experience with this sort of thing. He is far more competent than the average London doctor, I assure you."

Imogen glared suspiciously at Ufton. "What sort of experience?"

Ufton looked down his austere nose. "I accompanied his lordship on his travels abroad in search of ancient Zamar. Accidents and adventures of all varieties were rather commonplace. I became quite adept at attending to wounds, broken bones, and the like suffered by our companions both on board ship and during the excavations."

"Oh." Imogen looked briefly nonplussed. Then she nodded, seemingly satisfied. "Well, if you are certain that you know what you are about, Ufton, I suppose we can rely upon you."

"Yes, we can," Matthias assured her. "Ufton has always had a flair for medical matters. During our travels he picked up all sorts of interesting techniques and recipes for medicines."

"What sort of techniques and recipes?" Imogen asked.

Ufton cleared his throat. "As an example, I poured brandy into his lordship's wound before I closed it. Many sailors and military men believe that strong spirits ward off infection."

"How very interesting." Imogen gave a dainty sniff.

"I collect that you also poured some of the brandy down his lordship's throat. Was that part of the treatment?"

"Absolutely critical," Matthias murmured.

Ufton coughed discreetly. "I also held the needle in the heart of a flame before setting my stitches. It is a technique favored in the East."

"I have heard of it." Imogen crouched to study the white bandage on Matthias's arm. "The bleeding appears to have stopped."

"The cut was not terribly deep," Ufton said. His voice softened slightly in gruff reassurance. "His lordship will be feeling quite fit in a day or two."

"That is wonderful news. I am so relieved." Imogen jumped to her feet and threw her arms around Ufton. "How can I ever thank you for saving Colchester's life?"

Ufton froze, an expression of acute horror on his face. "Uh, madam. If madam pleases, this is most . . . most unusual." He broke off to turn desperate, pleading eyes toward Matthias.

"I think you had better release him, Imogen." Matthias suppressed a grin with effort. "Ufton is not accustomed to such displays of gratitude. I have always rewarded him with money, you see. I believe he prefers that arrangement."

"Oh, yes. Of course." Imogen released Ufton and quickly stepped back. "I beg your pardon, Ufton. I did not mean to embarrass you." She gave him a brilliant smile. "But I want you to know that I am in your debt for what you have done here tonight. If there is ever anything I can do, you must tell me."

Ufton turned a strange shade of red and swallowed heavily. "Thank you, madam, but I assure you, my long-standing association with his lordship makes such an offer entirely unnecessary. He would do the same for me were the situation reversed, as indeed it was on one or two occasions."

Imogen was clearly intrigued. "He sewed up a wound for you?"

"It was a number of years ago. Unfortunate incident in a tomb." Ufton backed hastily toward the door. "Well then, I'd best be off now. I'm sure that you and his lordship have matters to discuss."

Ufton turned and fled.

Imogen waited until the door had closed behind him and then she sank down on the sofa next to Matthias. "Tell me everything. Were you attacked by a footpad?"

"I do not believe *footpad* is the correct term."

Imogen's eyes widened with sudden horror. "Never say that young Mr. Bagshaw lost his temper and assaulted you?"

"No."

"Thank heavens. For a moment there I wondered if perhaps he had gone quite mad when you spoke to him."

"Bagshaw is reasonably sane so far as I know. He was not at all interested in what I had to say, however."

"Oh, dear." Imogen sighed. "I had so hoped that he would come to understand . . . Well, never mind. That is another problem. Tell me the whole tale, Matthias."

"It's a long story." He shifted slightly and winced as his wounded arm protested.

Imogen's eyes were eloquent. "Is the pain very bad?"

"I believe I could use another dose of brandy. For my nerves, you know. Would you mind fetching me a glass?"

"Yes, of course." Imogen sprang from the sofa and hurried to the brandy table. She seized the decanter with such force that the elegantly cut crystal stopper flew off and bounced on the carpet. She ignored it to pour not one but two hefty measures.

She brought the glasses back to the sofa, handed one to Matthias, and sat down beside him. "I vow, this whole thing has been somewhat unsettling." She took a large swallow of her brandy and promptly began to cough.

"There, there, my dear." Matthias slapped her lightly between her shoulders. "The brandy will soothe your overwrought nerves."

She glared at him over the rim of the glass. "My

nerves are not overwrought. I have exceedingly strong nerves. I have explained that to you on several occasions."

"Well, then perhaps it will do something for mine." Matthias took a fortifying swallow. "Where to begin? Ah, yes. I had my little chat with Bagshaw, as I told you. When it was finished I got out of the carriage and, to my surprise, found myself on the street in front of Vanneck's residence. Former residence, I suppose I should say."

"You just happened to alight in that neighborhood? How very odd."

"I was certainly astonished. At any rate, I decided that as long as I was in the vicinity, I would have a look around his study."

Imogen nearly dropped her glass. "You did *what*?"

"There is no reason to shout at me in that manner, my dear. Surely you realize that I am in a very delicate state due to my recent unnerving experiences."

"I did not mean to raise my voice. It was just that I was quite startled. Matthias, perhaps you should not be sitting up in that fashion. It will no doubt make you feel faint. Why don't you rest your head on my lap?"

"Excellent notion."

Imogen put her arm around his shoulder and eased his head down onto her leg. "There. That's better."

"Infinitely." Matthias closed his eyes and savored the warm, lushly rounded shape of her thigh beneath his head. Surreptitiously he inhaled her scent. His body tightened in response. "Where was I?"

"Vanneck's study." Imogen scowled down at him. "Why on earth did you go there?"

"I simply wanted to have a look around. The circumstances of his death have been worrying me a bit. You know how I fret about things."

Imogen gently massaged his brow. "You should have talked to me about your concerns before you did anything rash."

"I did not know if there was anything to be concerned about. Which, as I said, was why I let myself into Vanneck's study."

"Did you find anything unusual?"

"Bloodstains."

Imogen's hand paused on his forehead. "Bloodstains? Are you certain?"

"Quite certain. A fair amount of blood was spilled in Vanneck's study recently. There was a large patch on the carpet. No one had bothered to clean it up, which indicates that it happened shortly before his death." Matthias paused. "And probably after he dismissed his servants."

"He dismissed his servants? When?"

"Yesterday afternoon, I'm told."

"But, Matthias, that means that he no doubt intended to leave Town rather than face you."

"Yes. But to continue, one of the papers on his desk was stained with several drops of blood. As it happens, the page was dated. It looked as though Vanneck had just begun to write a letter, when he was interrupted."

"What was the date on the paper?"

"Yesterday, the day before the duel."

"Amazing." Imogen sat very still and stared into the fire. "Do you think he was shot right there in his own study last night before he was to meet you at Cabot's Farm?"

"I'd say that's a likely possibility." Matthias followed her gaze. He wondered absently if Vanneck's ghost would appear in the flames, and then concluded that it would not. That particular specter would not haunt him, he thought.

"But that would mean that he was not killed by a footpad or a highwayman. A housebreaker, perhaps?"

"Surely no casual thief or robber would bother to drag his victim to the site of the duel," Matthias said. "He would not even know about Vanneck's dawn appointment."

"Very true." Imogen frowned intently. "But that would imply—"

"Precisely." Matthias adjusted his position on her thigh, hoping to attract her attention back to his brow. "I think it's safe to conclude that Vanneck was killed by someone who knew him well enough to know about the duel. The murderer probably sought to shift the blame in my direction by carting Vanneck's body out to Cabot's Farm."

Imogen tapped one finger against Matthias's uninjured shoulder. "But that means someone in Vanneck's circle of acquaintances must be the killer."

Matthias hesitated. "I believe that there were two people involved."

"Two? But how do you know that?"

"Because when I went into Vanneck's house tonight," Matthias said, "I interrupted two people in the act of searching the premises. They had gotten there ahead of me and they did not appreciate my arrival on the scene."

Imogen's fingers suddenly clamped around his injured arm. "That is how you were hurt? One of those two people stabbed you?"

Matthias sucked in his breath. "I appreciate your concern, my sweet, but that's my damaged arm."

"Oh, my God." She released him instantly, her eyes widening in anguished apology. "I forgot. I was carried away by your news."

"I understand. A case of rattled nerves will do that to a person."

"There is nothing wrong with my nerves. Now, go on with your tale."

"Suffice it to say that there was an extremely undignified scuffle during which one of the two other people in the house used a knife on me. I could not identify either villain because they both wore cloaks and had scarves wrapped around their faces. I regret to say that they both escaped."

"Matthias, you could have been killed."

"I wasn't. Now then, that is the boring part of the

story. The more interesting bit has to do with what I discovered after my two companions fled into the night."

He had not required the brandy for the pain of his wound, Matthias thought. He had needed it to give him the strength to risk his future on the throw of the dice. He knew himself for a fool. It was as if he were some brainless moth that could not resist the flame.

"You stayed to search the house after you had been injured? Colchester, how could you do something so stupid? You should have come straight home."

Searching the study was not the stupid part, Matthias thought. *The stupid part comes now.*

"I did not hang around Vanneck's study for more than a few minutes," he said. "Just long enough to find that journal."

Imogen's brows drew together in a severe line. "What journal?"

"That one there on the table beside you."

Imogen glanced at the thin leather-bound volume. "Is it Vanneck's?"

"No. It belonged to your friend Lucy."

"Lucy?" Imogen studied the journal with a perplexed gaze. "I don't understand."

"Vanneck had it cleverly hidden in a secret compartment of his desk."

"But why would he bother to conceal it?"

"I have no notion." Matthias gave her a considering glance. "But it did occur to me that the two people I surprised in Vanneck's house may have been searching for it."

"Why?"

"We will not know the answer to that question until one of us reads it." Matthias set his back teeth. "As Lucy was your friend, I suggest that you do the honors."

Imogen looked troubled. "Do you think it is right to read her journal?"

"She is gone, Imogen. How can it hurt her?"

"Well—"

"You and I have made a career out of studying the messages left by those long since dead and in their graves."

"You speak of the records left by the ancient Zamarians. Lucy was not from Zamar."

"What is the difference? The dead are dead. It does not matter how long they have been in that condition." *Their ghosts can linger for a lifetime.*

Imogen reached out to touch the volume. "It seems as though we would somehow intrude on Lucy's privacy if we were to read her journal."

"We will most certainly intrude upon it. But I want to know why Vanneck thought the thing important enough to conceal and why two other people may have searched his house for it tonight."

"But, Matthias—"

"Let me be blunt, Imogen. If you do not want to read your friend's journal, I will read it for you."

The library door opened again before Imogen could respond. Matthias turned his head and saw Patricia standing in the opening. She stared at him with a stricken expression.

And then she screamed. A shrill, high, bloodcurdling screech that Matthias suspected reached the rafters. He winced and covered his ears with his hands.

"It's all right, Patricia," Imogen said crisply. "Matthias will recover quite nicely."

"It is the curse." Patricia put her hand to her throat. "Blood has been spilled. *Just as the curse predicted.*"

She turned and fled across the hall. Through the open door Matthias watched as she raced up the stairs as though all the demons of Zamar pursued her.

"It has occurred to me that my sister was destined for a career on the stage," Matthias muttered. "What the devil was she on about? What was that rubbish concerning a curse?"

"She said something about it earlier this evening." Imogen frowned. "Apparently she and the other young ladies who attend Lady Lyndhurst's salon have been studying the Rutledge Curse."

"Hell's teeth. I thought Selena had more sense."

"I doubt that Lady Lyndhurst believes in it herself," Imogen said. "I'm sure that to her it's just an amusing game. But young ladies of Patricia's age and delicate sensibilities sometimes take that sort of thing too seriously."

"Those damnable delicate sensibilities," Matthias said with a sigh. "Always causing problems for those of us who are plagued with them."

Imogen lay awake long after Matthias fell asleep. She turned restlessly, seeking a more comfortable position in the massive bed. Minutes became eons. The shaft of icy moonlight that streamed through the window shifted slowly across the carpet. She was intensely aware of Matthias slumbering beside her, but she felt very much alone as she pondered the prospect of reading Lucy's journal. For some reason that went beyond the question of privacy, she was reluctant to open it.

But she also knew that she would not get any sleep at all if she did not confront the journal. Matthias would read the thing if she did not do so. There was no point trying to avoid the inevitable.

Imogen slipped out of the warm bed. She pulled on her wrapper, stepped into her slippers, and turned to look down at Matthias. He was sprawled on his stomach, his face turned away from her. His bare shoulders looked sleek and powerful against the white sheets. The moonlight gleamed on the silver fire in his black hair. It occurred to Imogen that there was something about Matthias that seemed well suited to the night.

A chill of premonition went through her. She recalled the dark figure of her dreams, he who was both Matthias and Zamaris. A man trapped in the shadows.

She turned quickly away from the bed and walked

through the cold moonlight into her own bedchamber. She closed the connecting door behind her.

Lucy's journal lay on the table near the window. Imogen picked it up and pondered it for a long while. Her reluctance to open it seemed to intensify even as she held the slim volume. It was as though some unseen force attempted to restrain her.

Annoyed by her own dark imaginings, she sat down in the reading chair and lit the lamp.

$\mathcal{M}$atthias waited until he heard the connecting door close softly. Then he turned onto his back, folded his uninjured arm behind his head, and gazed up at the shadowed ceiling.

He knew that Imogen had gone into her own bedchamber to read Lucy's journal. If there were answers to be found in the volume, she would discover them.

From what Horatia had said, Matthias gathered that Lucy had not been such a fine friend. It was obvious that Lady Vanneck's kindness to Imogen had had a dark side. He told himself that the worst that could happen was that Imogen would be obliged to face some unpleasant truths about Lucy.

But he knew that he lied to himself. Learning the truth about Lucy was not the worst that could come of this.

The worst that could happen was that Imogen would learn the truth about him.

Matthias hesitated until he could wait no longer. The dreadful silence from the adjoining room threatened to drive him mad. He shoved aside the quilt and got out of bed. A powerful sense of urgency hit him with the force of a blow. He had been a fool. Perhaps it was not too late to save himself.

He found his black robe, struggled briefly to get his injured arm into the sleeve, and then abandoned the attempt. Flinging the robe around his shoulders as though it were a cape, he went to the connecting door.

He paused, took a deep breath, and opened the door.

A chill of intense regret swept through him at the sight of Imogen seated in the chair near the window. Lucy's journal lay facedown in her lap. Matthias knew without being told that his suspicions about the contents of the wretched volume had been accurate. He stood gripping the doorknob, bleakly aware of a terrible sense of doom.

"Imogen?"

She turned to look at him. Her cheeks were wet with tears.

"What is it?" he whispered.

"Lucy was having an affair." Imogen's voice broke on a sob. "I suppose, given her unhappy marriage, that is not so surprising. And I do not blame her for seeking her happiness elsewhere. Truly, I do not. But, oh, Matthias, why did she use me? I thought she was my friend."

He felt his gut clench. He had known it would be something like this. "Lucy used you?"

"That was why she invited me to visit her three years ago." Imogen dabbed at her eyes with a hankie. "Indeed, that was the only reason she wanted me here in London. She hoped to prevent Vanneck from learning of the affair, you see. She was afraid that he would cut off her funds. Perhaps send her to rusticate in the country. He was furious with her already because she had not given him an heir."

Matthias walked slowly toward Imogen. "I see."

"Lucy writes that she could not abide Vanneck's touch. She married him for his title and his money." Imogen shook her head as though she could not fully comprehend what she had learned. "She is quite forthright about it all."

Matthias stopped in front of Imogen. He said nothing.

"She thought that if I were her constant companion

here in Town, Vanneck would assume that I was the object of her lover's affections."

Matthias put the pieces of the small puzzle together in his mind. "Alastair Drake."

"What?" Imogen slanted a sidelong glance at him as she blew her nose. "Oh, yes. It was Alastair, of course. He was her paramour. She seems to have loved him with a great passion. She writes that she intended to run off with him, but until the time came to do so, she wanted to be able to be in his company as much as possible."

"And you made it possible for her to be in Drake's company without arousing Vanneck's suspicions."

"Yes." Imogen dried her eyes with the edge of her hand. "Alastair conspired with her to make it appear that I was the lady who had captured his affection. Vanneck and everyone else, including me, believed him. He certainly gave a . . . a convincing performance. For a while I even considered . . . Well, that does not matter now."

"I'm sorry that you had to learn the truth in this manner."

"Do not blame yourself, Matthias. You could not have known what I would discover in Lucy's journal." She gave him a small, sad smile. "I have been obliged to conclude that you were right. It seems I am rather naive in some respects. And gullible."

"Imogen—"

"It is astonishing, when I think about it. All that time that I spent in Alastair's company and I never once sensed that he was in love with Lucy. I never guessed that he was using me to meet with her openly as well as secretly. No wonder she was in such fine spirits whenever the three of us went about together."

"I'm sorry," Matthias whispered. He could think of nothing else to say. He reached down to haul her gently up out of the chair.

"Matthias, how could I have been so foolish?" Imogen leaned her head against his chest. "She wrote such unkind things about me. She mocked me. It is as though I never knew Lucy at all."

Matthias had no words with which to comfort Imogen or himself. He folded her close and gazed out into the night.

He wondered if he really did possess weak nerves. Then again, perhaps the savage sense of despair that had turned his insides to ice was the price one paid for trampling on the fragile flower of innocence.

Chapter 16

Two days later Imogen paced Horatia's small parlor, a teacup in her hand. "I still cannot bring myself to believe that I was so entirely mistaken in my judgment of her."

"I know you do not wish to think ill of Lucy." Horatia, seated on the sofa, watched Imogen with deeply troubled eyes. "You imagined her to be a friend, and it is your nature to be fiercely loyal to those you care for."

"She *was* my friend. I did not imagine it." Imogen paused in front of the window and gazed out into the street. "She was kind to me when we were neighbors in Upper Stickleford."

"You were kind to her. You were forever inviting her to stay the night."

"She gave me her gowns."

"Only after they had gone out of fashion," Horatia muttered.

"Fashion was not important in Upper Stickleford."

"It was to Lucy."

Imogen ignored the comment. "She often came to

visit and share a cup of tea with me after my parents died."

"She visited you because she was constantly on the verge of expiring from boredom. Life in the country was not to her taste."

"We talked of ancient Zamar."

"You talked," Horatia said deliberately. "I fear Lucy only pretended to take an interest in Zamar."

Imogen whirled around so quickly that her teacup clattered in its saucer. "Why do you say that?"

Horatia heaved a small sigh. "I will admit that I did not know your friend Lucy well, but what I did learn of her character was not inspiring."

"Gossip," Imogen insisted. "Nothing but gossip."

"I am sorry, my dear, but all indications were that she was selfish, willful, reckless, and possessed of a strange, unpredictable temperament."

"She was desperate to escape her uncle's house. George Haconby was a most unpleasant man. My parents never cared for him."

"I know," Horatia admitted.

Imogen remembered Lucy's eyes the first night she had come to the door and asked to spend the night. "Haconby frightened her, especially when he was in his cups. There were many times when she begged to stay with me rather than be alone with him."

"And you took her in." Horatia lifted one shoulder in a tiny shrug. "Imogen, I certainly do not wish to quarrel with you about the matter. Lucy is dead. Nothing is to be gained from probing her past at this late date."

"No, I suppose that is true."

Horatia watched her with an expression of grave disapproval. "You say you learned about this liaison between Lucy and Mr. Drake from Lucy's journal?"

"Yes. I know it was not right to read it, but Colchester was convinced that it might contain some clues about why Vanneck was shot. I am two-thirds of the way through it, but thus far I have found no information that would explain murder."

Horatia frowned. "I thought Vanneck was killed by a highwayman."

"We are not entirely certain of that. In any event, Colchester said that if I did not read the journal, he would. I felt I had an obligation to Lucy to protect her personal writings from a stranger's gaze."

"Indeed. And may I ask how Colchester came into possession of this journal?"

Imogen cleared her throat. "He, er, discovered it when he paid a call at Lord Vanneck's residence."

"Why on earth did he go to Vanneck's house?"

"He has been concerned about some of the details surrounding Vanneck's murder," Imogen explained. She thought quickly. "He believed he would learn something of the truth if he talked to some of the servants."

"I see."

Imogen did not like Horatia's skeptical tone of voice. "Perfectly natural, given his circumstances," she said quickly. "After all, gossip has linked Colchester's name to Vanneck's murder. But I do wish he had informed me of his intentions."

Horatia's brows rose. "I'll grant you that Colchester is in a rather awkward situation. But that is nothing new for him."

Imogen glared at her. "He wished to clear his name and put the gossip to rest."

"I fear that is an impossible task and I suspect he knows it," Horatia said dryly. "People have always enjoyed gossip about Cold-blooded Colchester. A little thing such as the truth of the matter is unlikely to change that."

"Do not call him cold-blooded."

"My apologies." Horatia did not sound the least apologetic. She sounded quietly furious.

Imogen frowned in consternation. "Aunt Horatia? What is wrong?"

"Nothing important, my dear," Horatia said smoothly.

"Let us return to the matter at hand. You say Colchester discovered Lucy's journal and gave it to you to read?"

"Yes. I intend to finish it tonight. But I doubt I shall learn anything other than what I already know. Poor Lucy was clearly obsessed with Alastair Drake. She was determined to run off with him. She dreamed of going to Italy, where the two of them could be free to celebrate their love."

"I presume that while in Italy, Lucy wished to live in the style to which she had become accustomed?"

"She notes in her journal that Alastair appeared to have a liberal income."

"Indeed."

"But he was unwilling to take her to Italy." Imogen recalled the tone of rising desperation in Lucy's journal entries. "She was distraught. She loved him very much, you know."

"Did she?"

"She wrote that Vanneck often flew into a rage because she tried to refuse him whenever he attempted to exert his marital rights. He forced himself on her on several occasions." Imogen shuddered. "And I can well believe it. At one point she actually took steps to rid herself of Vanneck's babe which she did not want to bear. There is something in the journal about consulting a woman in Bird Lane who dealt in such services."

"I see."

"I believe that Vanneck either learned of the abortion or discovered her plans to leave him."

"And became so enraged that he murdered her?"

"Yes." It was a neat summary of events, Imogen told herself. But every time she repeated it, she thought of how Vanneck had strongly denied any involvement in Lucy's death.

"Well, if Vanneck killed Lucy, he has paid for his crime," Horatia said.

"Yes, but who killed him?" Imogen asked quietly.

"We shall likely never know."

"You are right, I suppose." Imogen gazed out at the row of town houses across the street.

"Is something else troubling you, my dear?"

"I have been contemplating a theory about Lucy's behavior for two days," Imogen said slowly.

"What is that?"

"It occurs to me that she might have been ill."

"Ill?"

"A form of madness, perhaps." Imogen swung about to face Horatia with a sense of growing certainty. "That would explain so much. Her recklessness. Her desperation. Her strange moods."

"Oh, Imogen, I really don't think—"

"It makes sense, Aunt Horatia. I suspect that she suffered much at the hands of her uncle, perhaps more than she ever admitted. Perhaps it affected her mind. It was no doubt a condition that gradually worsened through the years. No wonder she seemed so different after she left Upper Stickleford."

"I am not at all certain that she was so very different," Horatia said.

Imogen paid no attention. She was consumed by a growing enthusiasm for her new theory. "Now I understand why she plotted to use me to conceal her affair with Alastair Drake. Don't you see, Aunt Horatia? By the time I came to stay with her here in London, Lucy was desperate. She was no longer herself."

Horatia gazed at her for a long time. "Perhaps you are correct, my dear."

"It is the only reasonable explanation," Imogen said firmly. "Lucy was never very strong. The dreadful treatment that she received, first from her uncle and then from her husband, no doubt made her unbearably anxious and distraught. It destroyed her in the end, just as surely as the laudanum. Yes. An illness of the brain explains everything."

A sense of peace descended on Imogen. She had not been wrong about her friend after all. Lucy had been ill and desperately unhappy. She had not been in her right mind when she had written those cruel things about Imogen in her journal.

Imogen alighted from the carriage and went up the town house steps with a far lighter heart than she'd had when she set out for her aunt's house. Nothing would bring Lucy back, but the warm memory of her friendship was safely enshrined once again in Imogen's heart. Poor Lucy. How she had suffered.

The door opened at the top of the steps. Ufton stood in the opening.

"Welcome home, madam."

"Thank you, Ufton." Imogen smiled at him as she untied her bonnet strings. "Is Colchester in the library?"

"No, madam. His lordship has gone out."

Imogen was alarmed. "Gone out? Where?"

"He did not say, madam."

"But what of his wound? Surely he should be resting here at home."

Ufton closed the door behind her. "His lordship is not inclined to take advice in such matters, madam."

"I shall speak to him about it the moment he returns."

"Of course, madam." Ufton hesitated. "Will you be needing the carriage this afternoon?"

Imogen, one foot on the bottom of the stairs, paused to glance back at him. "No. I do not plan to go out again. Why do you ask?"

Ufton inclined his head. "I merely wanted to be certain that you did not require transportation. Lady Patricia mentioned that she wished to pay a call on Lady Lyndhurst. I thought we might need two carriages today."

"That won't be necessary." Imogen smiled and hurried on up the stairs.

When she reached the landing, she strode down the carpeted hall to her bedchamber. She was determined to finish Lucy's journal that afternoon. Now that she had a clear understanding of Lucy's illness, she would be able to study the volume with a more detached, analytical eye. She had been so sunk in melancholy by what had appeared to be Lucy's betrayal of their friendship that she had not been thinking at all clearly.

She opened the door to her bedchamber and swept into the room. She tossed her bonnet onto the bed and then came to a startled halt.

She was not alone in the bedchamber. Patricia stood near the window, clutching Lucy's journal. She gazed at Imogen with a stricken expression.

"Patricia?" Imogen took a step toward her. "What on earth are you doing in here? Why have you got that journal? It belongs to me."

"Imogen, please forgive me. I know you must think me a terrible person, but I pray you will understand when I tell you that I have no choice."

"What on earth are you talking about?"

"The Rutledge Curse."

"Not that ridiculous curse business again."

"Don't you see? Matthias was nearly killed the other night because of it. I am the only one who can put an end to this before someone dies."

"Rubbish."

"It's real, Imogen. We all promised not to discuss it, but I have been so anxious. I cannot bear it any longer. Everything is happening just as the inscription on the tablet predicted."

"What tablet?" Imogen asked sharply.

"Lady Lyndhurst has some ancient Zamarian clay tablets. The curse is written on one of them."

"Impossible. Calm yourself, Patricia." Imogen took another step toward her and paused as a thought struck her. "What has the Rutledge Curse got to do with my friend's journal?"

"I overheard you and Matthias discussing it. I know

he took it from Vanneck's house the night he was wounded. That was why he nearly died."

"What do you think happened?" Imogen asked cautiously.

"Don't you see? Vanneck was a victim of the Rutledge Curse. This journal is linked to him. Matthias took it from his house and was nearly killed because the journal is tainted with the curse. Everything that was Rutledge's is tainted."

"Oh, for heaven's sake, Patricia—"

"I cannot allow this to go any further. Someone has to stop it. Lady Lyndhurst has studied Zamarian curses. She will know what to do."

"Nonsense." Imogen walked to the bed to retrieve her bonnet. "I have heard quite enough about the Rutledge Curse. It is time to put an end to the foolish gossip."

Patricia watched uncertainly as Imogen retied her bonnet strings. "What do you plan to do?"

"Isn't it obvious?" Imogen gave her a bracing smile. "I shall attend Lady Lyndhurst's salon with you today, Patricia. I want to see the curse that is inscribed on that clay tablet for myself."

$\mathcal{M}$atthias arrived home shortly after the Colchester carriage had departed. He had sought refuge from his bleak thoughts first at his club and then in Tattersall's auctioneering yard. But not even the prime horseflesh paraded in front of the crowd of eager buyers had elevated his mood.

He was disappointed but distinctly relieved to learn that Imogen was not home. He ached to hold her in his arms, but a part of him dreaded looking into her eyes. He feared the dawn of truth far more than the shadows of the night. He was accustomed to ghosts, after all.

He walked into his library, annoyed by the unfamiliar mix of emotions that swirled within him. It occurred to him that he had experienced a remarkable variety of strange sensations and moods since the day he met Imogen.

He untied his cravat, tossed it aside, and sat down at his desk. Opening a thick Greek text that contained references to a mysterious island, he tried to lose himself in his researches. He was convinced that the isle in question was actually ancient Zamar. If he was right, it would confirm some of his speculations concerning trade and commerce between the Greeks and the Zamarians.

The Greek words, which he read as easily as he read English, seemed jumbled on the page. He found himself having to go back to the beginning to read through the passage a second and third time. He was distracted and restless as he tried to focus on the text.

> It is said that the people of this far isle are skilled
> in the study of mathematics. They make calcula-
> tions to determine the height of buildings and
> mountains. They predict the rise and fall of the
> tides.

It was no use. Every time he looked at the words in front of him he saw a ghostly image of Imogen's anguished eyes as she told him what she had read in the journal. He could almost feel the dampness of the tears she had shed. Matthias had lain awake for a long time during each of the past two nights. He had been racked by a sense of impending doom. It was a doom that he had brought down upon himself.

Why had he forced Imogen to read the journal? Over and over again he had asked himself the same damning question. He did not know the answer.

Matthias closed the volume on his desk and rubbed the back of his neck. An deep sense of weariness stole over him. He was a thoughtful, logical man when it came to his studies of ancient Zamar. But he could not seem to comprehend his own actions. What the devil was happening to him? he wondered.

The knock on the library door interrupted his grim musings.

"Enter."

Ufton appeared. "Mrs. Elibank to see you, sir."

"Horatia? I wonder what she wants. Send her in, Ufton."

Horatia swept into the library, an expression of barely restrained fury on her face. She appeared more formidable than Matthias had ever seen her. He got to his feet slowly, somewhat warily.

"My lord."

"Good day, Horatia." He studied her as she took a chair on the other side of his desk. "Did Ufton inform you that Imogen is not at home?"

"I came to see you, Colchester."

"I see. Is something wrong?"

"I will not beat about the bush, my lord," Horatia said coldly. "Why did you give Lucy's journal to Imogen?"

"I beg your pardon?"

"You heard me. You found Lucy's journal, did you not?"

"Yes."

"And you gave it to Imogen," Horatia said. "You must have suspected that she would not find any comfort in it and that she might very well be hurt by what she would learn. Why did you give it to her?"

Only a lifetime of habit and practice enabled Matthias to keep his expression unreadable. Deliberately, he lounged back in his chair. "Lucy was Imogen's friend. It seemed natural that Imogen should be the one to read it."

"Rubbish. You gave that journal to Imogen because you wished to destroy her illusions about her friend. Do not trouble to deny it."

Matthias said nothing.

"Just as I thought." Horatia leaned forward and fixed

him with a furious gaze. "What did you hope to gain by crushing Imogen's image of Lucy? What cruel purpose possessed you?"

"You were the one who first informed me that Lucy was not the fine, noble friend Imogen believed her to be. I have made a few discreet inquiries of my own since I returned to Town. All of them verified what you said regarding Lucy's character."

"What of it?"

Matthias toyed with a quill pen. "It is always wise to confront the truth, don't you think? In the end, one must deal with it."

"Lucy was the only friend Imogen had after her parents' death. Imogen would have been utterly alone in Upper Stickleford had it not been for Lucy. She has a right to her illusions about her."

"Lucy and that damned Alastair Drake used Imogen to conceal their illicit liaison. You call that friendship?"

"No, I do not." Horatia narrowed her eyes. "But what good have you wrought by forcing the truth upon Imogen at this late date?"

"There are some questions about Vanneck's death that need to be answered." Matthias studied the nib of the pen. "I thought some of those answers might lie in Lucy's journal."

"You could have read that journal in private, my lord. There was no need to tell Imogen about it, let alone blackmail her into reading it."

A painful sensation that might have been anguish or rage ripped through Matthias. "I did not blackmail her into reading that damned journal."

"It appears to have been a case of blackmail to me, sir. She said that you threatened to read it if she did not. She thought to protect Lucy's privacy."

"Damnation, Horatia. I did what I felt was best. Imogen needed to confront the truth about Lucy."

"Bah. The truth is not the issue here. You deliberately tried to demolish Imogen's cherished memories of her only friend. Sir, allow me to tell you that you deserve to be called Cold-blooded Colchester. What you did was callous and unkind. I wondered when your true nature would show itself. Unfortunately, it has surfaced too late to save my niece from what will no doubt prove to be a disaster of a marriage."

The quill pen snapped in half. Startled, Matthias looked down at the broken bits he held in his fingers. Very carefully he placed them on the desk. "You are, of course, entitled to your opinion, Mrs. Elibank."

"One can only wonder at your motives." Horatia rose from the chair and looked down her nose at him. The very old, very blue blood that flowed in her veins was much in evidence. At that moment it was not difficult to see that she enjoyed a connection to a marquess.

Matthias surged to his feet. He met Horatia's eyes across the width of the desk. "I had no motive other than to bring out the truth."

"I do not believe that for a moment. Damnation, sir, I was actually convinced that you cared for my niece. How could you do this to her?"

Matthias clenched one hand into a fist, whirled around, and slammed the other against the wall. "Has it occurred to you, madam, that I may have grown weary of living a damned lie with my own wife?"

There was a short, heavy pause.

"What in the name of heaven do you mean?" Horatia asked quietly.

Matthias fought to pull himself together. He drew a deep breath and wrapped himself in the armor of his self-mastery. "Never mind. It is not important. Good day to you, Mrs. Elibank. Ufton will see you out."

Horatia stared at him for a moment and then, without a word, she turned and walked toward the door.

Matthias did not move until Horatia was gone. Then

he went to the window and stood looking out into the garden for a long time.

He finally had the answer to the question he had been asking himself. He now knew precisely why he had given Lucy's journal to Imogen.

He had ripped the veils from Imogen's eyes not because he had wanted to force her to confront the truth about Lucy. He had done so because he wanted her to face the truth about him.

What he had said to Horatia in that burst of frustrated rage a moment before had been all too painfully honest. He could not continue to live a lie with Imogen. He needed to know if she could care for him once she had faced the reality of his own nature. He needed to know if she could love Cold-blooded Colchester.

Imogen was too intelligent not to realize what he had revealed about himself when he had forced her to read the journal. She was I. A. Stone, after all.

*O*mogen surveyed the other members of the Zamarian salon as they sat in a half circle around their elegant hostess. The first thing she noted about the group was that with the exception of Selena and herself, it was composed entirely of very young ladies. Imogen was willing to hazard a guess that not one of the brightly garbed females sitting in the circle was above nineteen years. Many were younger and in their first Season.

Selena, dressed in a blue gown trimmed with blue roses, smiled graciously at her guests as her housekeeper served tea.

Imogen realized that until that day she had seen Selena only from a distance or at night, when she appeared in the chandelier-lit ballrooms of the ton.

It was no secret that candlelight was far more flattering to a lady than sunlight. Nevertheless, Imogen was surprised to note that Selena suffered more than most in the glare of the sun. The light of day rendered the lady hailed as the "Angel" somehow harder and colder than one would have expected. Her celestial-blue eyes made Imogen think of glittering sapphires rather than the heavens.

The salon guests were clearly enthralled by their fashionable hostess. They chattered and giggled and gossiped excitedly as they waited for Selena to signal the beginning of the afternoon's activities.

Selena held court with the air of a fairy-tale queen. The accoutrements of a high-minded philosophical salon surrounded her. Several impressive leather-bound volumes were stacked on a nearby table. A wooden box containing shards of pottery and some ancient glass bottles were arranged next to the books. An object wrapped in a black velvet case lay on the table. Bits and pieces of Zamarian artifacts, none of them particularly notable in Imogen's opinion, were scattered artfully about the drawing room. There was a rather poor copy of a statue of Anizamara near the window.

Patricia leaned close to Imogen and lowered her voice. "Lady Lyndhurst keeps the tablet with the curse inscribed on it in that velvet cover. She says it is the most valuable item in her collection."

"I see." Imogen eyed the velvet-shrouded tablet as she accepted a cup of tea from the housekeeper.

Selena clapped her hands lightly and the small group fell into a respectful silence. She smiled coolly at Imogen.

"Lady Colchester, this is a pleasant surprise. I am delighted that you could join us today. May I ask what drew your attention to our little gathering?"

"Just curious," Imogen said. "Lady Patricia has told me how much she has enjoyed your Zamarian salon."

"We can hardly compete with your learned husband's discoveries and writings," Selena murmured. "As a matter of fact, I was under the impression that Colchester considered that only fashionable dilettantes and amateurs attended salons such as mine."

"I will not stay long." Imogen put down her teacup. "Lady Patricia tells me that you have been studying the Rutledge Curse."

"That is true." Selena's gaze flickered to Patricia. Something that might have been anger flashed in her icy blue eyes. It vanished almost instantly behind a mask of cool charm. "But it was supposed to be a secret investigation."

Patricia stiffened in her chair and cast an anxious glance at Imogen.

Imogen frowned at Selena. "You must not blame Patricia. I stumbled onto the truth this afternoon. As you know, I have a certain interest in things Zamarian."

"You refer to the Queen's Seal and the map your uncle left you in his will." Selena's smile was mocking.

"Indeed. But now that I am married to Colchester of Zamar, my interests extend well beyond the seal. I wish to examine the tablet that is inscribed with the so-called Rutledge Curse. I understand it is in that velvet case."

A brittle silence settled on the drawing room. The elegant young members of the salon exchanged uneasy glances. They were obviously not accustomed to seeing Selena's authority challenged.

Selena hesitated. Then she gave a small, graceful shrug. "As long as you are here, you are welcome to study it. But I must warn you that the curse is written in Zamarian. Only a handful of people in all of England can decipher it."

"I am aware of that." Imogen rose from her chair, took two long steps toward the table in front of Selena, and picked up the black velvet case before anyone realized what she intended.

There were several small, shocked gasps from the onlookers as Imogen unwrapped the tablet.

Selena's eyes narrowed as she watched Imogen remove the ancient clay tablet. "The gossip concerning your rather eccentric manners is correct, I see."

Imogen ignored her. She looked down at the heavy tablet. "How astonishing. This is a real Zamarian tablet."

"What did you think it was?" Selena snapped.

"I was prepared to discover that it was a forgery. But it is definitely quite authentic."

"Thank you for your opinion," Selena said coldly. "Now, if you are quite finished—"

"But I'm not finished." Imogen looked up from the tablet. "The tablet is definitely from ancient Zamar. Hardly surprising. I understand that it is fashionable to have one or two in one's library. But the inscription on it is not a curse."

"I beg your pardon," Selena snapped.

"I fear that you have been sadly misinformed, Lady Lyndhurst."

Selena flushed furiously. "How would you know what that inscription says?"

"I can read Zamarian script, both formal and informal." Imogen smiled coolly. "This would be amusing if it were not for the fact that some people have taken the notion of a curse far too seriously."

"Amusing?" Selena was incensed. "What do you mean by that?"

"The inscription on that tablet is nothing more than a bill of sale," Imogen announced. "To be precise, it records the exchange of two measures of wheat for one ox."

"That is a lie." Selena shot to her feet. Her voice rose with her. "How could you possibly know anything of Zamarian script?"

There was a slight movement in the doorway. Everyone in the drawing room turned to see Matthias. His stance was deceptively casual.

"My wife reads ancient Zamarian script as well as I do," Matthias said softly.

Imogen swung around so quickly that her reticule, which dangled from a satin cord, flew out in a wide arc. It struck a teacup and sent it crashing to the carpet. Several young ladies seated in the path of the splashing tea leaped to their feet with cries of dismay.

"Colchester." Imogen smiled. "I didn't see you there. Perhaps you would care to give your opinion on this silly tablet?"

Matthias inclined his head in a graceful nod that conveyed both amusement and unmistakable respect. "Your translation is correct. That tablet is an ancient Zamarian business document. In short, a bill of sale."

Chapter 17

Matthias vaulted into the carriage and took the seat across from Imogen and Patricia. He glanced reflectively at the front door of Selena's town house as the vehicle moved off into the street. This visit in search of Imogen and Patricia constituted the first time he had ever stepped foot inside the Angel's residence. He felt as though he had just plucked Imogen and Patricia from a spider's web.

"This is a surprise, my lord," Imogen said cheerfully. "What made you come in search of us? Is something wrong?"

"No." Matthias settled back against the cushion and turned to face her. He forced himself to examine her closely, searching for signs of melancholy, anger, or resentment.

He saw none. Much to his amazement, Imogen's customary excellent spirits appeared to have revived. The shadows that had darkened her eyes for the past two days had miraculously evaporated. She had evidently recovered from the crushing blow he had delivered. He was not certain what to make of that fact.

Patricia looked at Imogen and then at Matthias. Her eyes brimmed with puzzlement and hope. "Was that inscription on the clay tablet truly nothing more than an ancient bill of sale?"

Imogen patted Patricia's gloved hand. "Yes, indeed. Most of the Zamarian clay tablets that the fashionable use to decorate their studies and libraries are ancient records of business transactions, or other equally mundane matters." She looked at Matthias. "Is that not right, Colchester?"

"Yes." Matthias glanced at Patricia. "I assure you, Imogen is expert at reading Zamarian script. I saw the symbols for wheat and oxen on that tablet myself, from where I was standing. The message was definitely not a curse."

"I don't understand," Patricia whispered. "So many dreadful things have occurred lately. The duel. Lord Vanneck's death. And then, two nights ago, you were nearly killed, Matthias. I was certain that Lady Lyndhurst was right when she said that the Rutledge Curse had struck again."

"The Rutledge Curse is rubbish," Matthias said. "It was invented by a group of cork-brained dilettantes in the Zamarian Society shortly after word reached them that Rutledge had died in the labyrinth. One can only hope that the Polite World will soon grow bored with ancient Zamar and return to its interest in Egypt."

"Not likely," Imogen scoffed. "How could ancient Egypt possibly compete with lost Zamar? Besides, we already know everything there is to know about Egypt."

Matthias was briefly distracted by that notion. "I'm not so certain. If someone ever succeeds in deciphering the inscriptions on that chunk of black basalt that they are calling the Rosetta Stone, there could well be a renewed interest in ancient Egypt."

Imogen wrinkled her nose. "I shall always prefer the wonders of Zamar."

"You are nothing if not loyal, my dear," Matthias said softly.

Patricia looked down at her hands. "Lady Lyndhurst claimed that she could translate Zamarian script. She said she could read the inscription on that clay tablet. Why would she lie about such a thing?"

"Lady Lyndhurst enjoys playing games." Matthias did not bother to conceal his disgust. "Henceforth, you will both keep your distance from her."

Patricia shuddered. "I have no wish to attend any more of her salons."

Imogen's brows snapped together. "Patricia, there is something I want to ask you. It was your idea to take Lucy's journal to the salon this afternoon, was it not?"

Matthias's insides went cold. "What's this about the journal?"

Patricia stiffened at his tone. "I am very sorry about the journal. I thought that what I was doing was for the best."

Matthias opened his mouth to repeat his demand for an explanation but Imogen silenced him with a quick, tiny shake of her head. Reluctantly he subsided. It had occurred to him on one or two occasions lately that Imogen's methods of dealing with Patricia were more effective than his own.

Imogen smiled at Patricia. "It's quite all right. No harm was done. I merely wondered if you had mentioned the journal to anyone since it, uh, came into our possession."

Matthias raised his brows at her tactful description of what some might term outright theft.

"Oh, no," Patricia assured her. "I told no one about it."

Imogen watched her intently. "No one suggested that you take the journal to Lady Lyndhurst's salon this afternoon?"

Patricia shook her head with great certainty. "Of

course not. How could anyone else have known that Matthias had taken it from Lord Vanneck's house?"

"Indeed," Imogen said very casually. "Who could have known other than the three of us?"

Patricia visibly relaxed. "I concluded that I had to take the journal to Lady Lyndhurst after I got a message from one of my friends in the salon."

That bit of news was too much for Matthias's self-control. He pounced before Imogen could stop him. "Someone sent you a message about the journal? Who was it?"

Patricia's eyes widened. "I'm not certain. The message I received this morning was not signed. But it carried the secret seal that the members of the salon use whenever they communicate with each other."

"Secret seal?" Matthias winced. "What nonsense. Why the devil didn't you show me that damned message? When did it arrive? Did you recognize the handwriting?"

Patricia retreated into the corner of the carriage seat. She looked at Imogen with a beseeching expression.

Imogen glared at Matthias. "I pray you will be silent, my lord. You are complicating matters."

"Damnation." Matthias wanted to shake the answers out of Patricia. As that approach was clearly not an option, he turned the brunt of his rapidly thinning patience on Imogen. "Make no mistake, madam, I intend to discover just what is going on here."

"I know you do and you shall," Imogen said in her apple-crisp tones. "But we will all get through this far more quickly if you allow me to discuss the matter with your sister in a calm, reasonable fashion."

Matthias drummed his fingers on the side of the carriage frame. She was right and he knew it. "Very well. Get on with it, then."

Imogen turned back to Patricia. "Pay no attention to him. Men are inclined to be impatient. Now then, this message that you said you received. Did it specifically mention the journal?"

"No, of course not." Patricia was obviously perplexed. "How could anyone have known that we had it?"

"How indeed," Matthias said dryly. "Perhaps you jotted a few notes to your friends in the salon? Properly sealed with the secret seal, of course."

Patricia's eyes glistened with tears. "I just told you that I did not tell a soul."

Imogen gave Matthias another repressive glare. "My lord, if you possess half the intelligence I have always credited you with, you will cease interrupting."

Matthias set his teeth but he kept silent.

Imogen smiled encouragingly at Patricia. "Now then, tell us about the note you received."

Patricia eyed Matthias warily, no doubt fearful that he would renew his aggressive efforts to wring the information out of her. When he said nothing, she looked at Imogen. "The message claimed that we must all beware of the Rutledge Curse, lest it fall on the household of one of the members of the Zamarian salon. I realized at once that Matthias had been the latest victim."

"Naturally. A perfectly logical conclusion," Imogen said.

Matthias scowled at her, but he managed to hold his tongue.

"Did the note say anything else?" Imogen asked quickly.

"Only that anyone who possessed any object that might have once belonged to Vanneck was in the greatest danger." Patricia hesitated. "The curse will have tainted everything that he owned, you see."

"Hardly subtle," Matthias said scornfully. "Hell's teeth, someone knows about the journal."

Imogen gave him another warning glance before resuming her gentle inquisition. "You realized that one of Vanneck's possessions was indeed under our roof, did you not, Patricia? Namely the journal."

"Yes." Patricia looked bewildered. "I knew that neither you nor Matthias would believe me if I tried to explain about the curse. You both dismiss it. I had to do something. Matthias had nearly been killed. Who knew how the curse would strike next? I thought that Lady Lyndhurst would have some notion of what to do with the journal, as she is an expert on ancient Zamar and she believed in the Rutledge Curse."

"Damnation," Matthias muttered. "Selena is no expert on anything except fashion."

Imogen kept her attention fixed on Patricia. "I understand why you felt you had to take action, but your brother is quite right. The Rutledge Curse is nonsense. I fear that Lady Lyndhurst was playing a rather unpleasant little game with you and the other members of her salon."

Patricia sighed. "But, Imogen, I don't understand. If there is no curse, how can one explain all of the strange events of late?"

"Coincidence," Imogen said easily. "They happen all the time."

"*C*oincidence be damned," Matthias growled twenty minutes later as he stalked into the library behind Imogen. "There is far more than mere coincidence involved in this matter, and well you know it."

"Yes, Matthias, but I do not see any reason to alarm Patricia." Imogen glanced at the closed door of the library as she stripped off her bonnet and gloves. "She is anxious enough as it is. And given the family tendency toward lurid and dreadful imaginings, I think it best that we not frighten her."

"It strikes me that there is bloody good cause for a few lurid and dreadful imaginings in this situation." Matthias flung himself down into the chair behind his desk and watched with brooding eyes as Imogen began to pace the room. "What is this all about?"

"I'm not certain. But it's obvious that Lucy's journal is very important to someone."

Matthias narrowed his gaze as he freed his thoughts

to make connections between seemingly unconnected events and people. "Selena?"

"She is certainly a possible suspect." Imogen appeared to have no trouble following his leaps of logic. "She is the one who pretended to interpret the Rutledge Curse, after all."

"Why would she want the damned thing?"

"I have no notion. As far as I know, Lucy and Selena were only barely acquainted three years ago. Lucy never spoke of her, except occasionally in passing."

"Indeed."

Imogen gave him a sharp, searching glance. "Do you see some connection that I have missed?"

"Do you recall the night that we shared an extremely memorable embrace in a certain garden?"

Imogen turned a charming shade of pink. "Yes, of course. You insisted that we become engaged because of it."

"I did not insist upon the engagement simply because of the embrace, delightful though it was."

Imogen paused briefly in her pacing. "You insisted upon it because we had been seen by Selena and Alastair Drake."

"Precisely. It's not much to go on, but it is an interesting tidbit of information, is it not?"

"But it was just a coincidence that they happened to be taking a stroll in the garden together that night and discovered us in such a . . . such a . . ." Imogen cleared her throat. "Such a compromising situation."

"As I just told you, I am not inclined to believe that there is anything coincidental about this entire affair."

"Very well, let us start with some assumptions." Imogen clasped her hands behind her back and resumed her pacing. "Someone knows that you took the journal from Vanneck's house. That unknown person attempted to trick Patricia into bringing it with her to the salon today. That individual could well have been Selena, although there is no reason to believe she would have any interest in the journal or that she would have any way of knowing that we possess it."

"Perhaps the person behind this was one of the other members of the salon."

Imogen shook her head. "Not likely. You saw them, Matthias. They are all young ladies of Patricia's age. For most, this is their first Season in Society. They would have still been in the schoolroom three years ago. None of them would have even been acquainted with Lucy."

"A relative of one of the young ladies, perhaps?"

"Possible." Imogen frowned. "But unlikely. It comes back to the same problem. How could any of them have known that you took the journal from Vanneck's study?"

"You're forgetting that there were two other people in Vanneck's house the other night in addition to myself," Matthias said. "I could not see their faces because they had gone to a deal of trouble to conceal themselves. But they must have seen me."

"Good heavens. You're right."

"They may have assumed that I was after the journal simply because that's what they were searching for themselves," Matthias continued. "They considered it valuable and likely concluded that I also knew of its importance."

"But you had no notion of its worth."

"I did not enter the house to look for anything in particular, but the two people I encountered there could not have known that. I took that blasted journal only because it was obvious Vanneck had deliberately concealed it." Matthias hesitated. "And because I saw that it had belonged to your friend Lucy."

"You do have a remarkable ability for uncovering that which is hidden," Imogen mused.

"We all have our small talents. The skill served me well in lost Zamar." Matthias wondered glumly if she sensed his lies of omission. He had not taken the journal solely because it had been hidden or even because it had belonged to Lucy. He had taken it because he had known that his fate was somehow tied to it.

But Imogen seemed intent on pursuing the logic of the problem under discussion, not the murky questions of his particular choice of self-imposed doom.

"The two villains who attacked you may have gone back into the house after you left to continue their search," she suggested. "When they failed to discover the journal, they may have concluded that you had found it and taken it."

"Perhaps they simply hid outside the house and watched as I left with the journal in my hand. There was enough moonlight to see quite clearly the other night."

"I don't know, Matthias. None of it makes sense unless there is something of grave import in Lucy's journal. But what could that be? Vanneck was the only one who would have cared about Lucy's affair with Alastair Drake. Surely no one else would be concerned at this late date. It all happened three years ago."

Matthias steeled himself for the question he had to ask. "Have you finished reading the journal?"

"Almost." She glanced out the window into the garden. "I have made slow progress, I fear. Lucy's writings have been somewhat painful to read."

Matthias picked up the small knife he used to trim the nibs of quill pens and began to fiddle with it. "Imogen, I doubt you will believe this, but I regret forcing you to read that damned journal."

"Nonsense." She gave him a reassuring smile. "You did what you thought best and you were quite right. We need to know what the journal contains that makes it so valuable to someone else."

He tossed the blade down onto the desk. "You're amazing, do you know that? Absolutely astounding. Good God, can you not deal squarely with the truth when you run headlong into it? You're I. A. Stone, after all."

She came to a halt in the middle of the room and stared at him in openmouthed astonishment. "What is wrong? Why are you angry, my lord?"

"How can you be so bloody damn intelligent on the one hand and so incredibly naive on the other?"

She gave him an odd smile. "Have you considered that I am not quite so naive as you believe, Matthias? I simply see some truths from a different perspective than you do."

"There can be only one truth in any given situation."

"I do not agree, my lord. Only recall how often you and I have argued in print about a particular point concerning Zamarian history. In those instances we both interpret the script in an identical fashion but we attribute different meanings to it. Two views of the same truth."

"Don't you understand?" he said through his teeth. "This has got nothing to do with ancient Zamar. As long as we are discussing truth, let us have one thing clear between us."

"What is that?"

Matthias was appalled at what he was doing. He should stop right now, he thought. He was a fool to say another word. He had apparently had a narrow escape in the matter of the journal. He should thank his lucky stars for his good fortune and cease digging this bottomless pit for himself.

Imogen had convinced herself that he had given her the journal to read because there was no alternative. If he had any sense, he would allow her to go on believing that. It was folly to push his luck in this absurd manner. But he could not stop himself. He leaped into the dark chasm he had excavated.

"Surely you realize that I was aware of what you were likely to learn about Lucy's character when I gave you her journal," he said.

"You made certain assumptions about Lucy based on old gossip. You assumed I would do the same after I read her journal."

"They were more than assumptions. You were hurt by what you read. Bloody hell, I saw your tears, Imogen."

She tilted her head to one side and contemplated him

in a thoughtful manner. "Aunt Horatia admitted today for the first time that she, too, had been aware of Lucy's odd behavior."

"Odd behavior?" Matthias gave a crack of humorless laughter. "That is putting an extremely kind twist on the matter. She was a heartless jade."

"She was deeply troubled. I was her friend for several years before she went to London. I do not deny that certain changes came over her after she left Upper Stickleford."

"Changes?"

"I confess I was concerned, especially when she ceased to write. But I thought that those changes were caused by her marriage."

Something in her voice alerted Matthias. "You've altered your opinion? You no longer believe that Vanneck was responsible for Lucy's unhappiness?"

"Vanneck had a great deal to answer for," Imogen assured him. "But I now believe that Lucy had other problems."

"What the devil are you talking about now?"

"I have been thinking about what I have read in her journal thus far. As I told Aunt Horatia, I have come to the conclusion that Lucy was ill."

Matthias was stunned. "Ill?"

"I believe that her state of mind was not a healthy one. She was always plagued by a high-strung temperament. At times she suffered from bouts of melancholy. But her moods became far more volatile after she married Vanneck. The tone of her journal reflects her increasing agitation. And there is no doubt but that she became obsessed with Alastair Drake."

Matthias gazed at her in stark disbelief. "Let me be certain that I comprehend this fully. You have concluded that Lucy may have been mad?"

"Not in the manner that we associate with those poor souls who end up in Bedlam. She did not see things that were not there nor did she hear strange voices. Her writings in the journal are quite lucid. Indeed, when I visited her here in London she was always rational. But I see now that something was very wrong. Her consuming passion for Mr. Drake does not seem . . ." Imogen hesitated, obviously searching for the right word. "Healthy."

"She was committing adultery," Matthias observed derisively. "Perhaps that worried her. After all, she had not yet given Vanneck his heir. He would have been furious if he had learned of her indiscretions. The good wives of the ton always provide their lords with an heir before they take up a career of illicit liaisons."

"No, there is more to it than a concern that Vanneck would discover the affair. She wanted Alastair Drake with a single-mindedness that does not seem natural. She was furious because he did not agree to run off with her."

Matthias got to his feet behind the desk. "If I listen to any more of this babble, I shall likely go mad myself. Imogen, your aunt came to see me today."

"Aunt Horatia paid a call upon you?" Imogen gave him a quizzical look. "How odd. I went to see her this morning. She did not mention that she intended to speak to you."

"It was no doubt your visit to her that inspired hers to me." Matthias's jaw ached from the tension that gripped every muscle in his body. "After you talked to her she realized at once, although you did not, just what I had done when I gave you Lucy's journal."

"I do not understand."

"That much is obvious." Matthias flexed his hands and flattened them on top of his desk. He leaned forward slightly and forced himself to look straight into Imogen's clear eyes. "I made you read Lucy's journal because I wanted you to face certain facts about your so-called friend. I wanted to force you to see her for what she was. God help me, I practically blackmailed you into reading the damned book, even though I knew you would be hurt by the truth. It was a cruel, callous act on my part."

Imogen's eyes never wavered. "I do not believe that for one moment."

"Damnation, it's the truth," Matthias said savagely. "Look at me, Imogen. See the truth. Surely you must realize that in giving you Lucy's journal, I demonstrated just how cold-blooded I am."

"Matthias—"

"The day we met you said that I was not the man you had believed me to be. You were right." Matthias did not take his eyes off her. "You did not know then just how right you were."

A terrible silence fell on the library.

The chamber was suddenly filled with ghosts. They surrounded Matthias, mocking him with their voiceless mouths, scorning him with their empty eye sockets. Their soundless laughter rang in his ears.

Why destroy her illusions? They served you well enough, did they not? You did not hesitate to warm your ice-cold soul with the heat of her sweet passion. You reveled in the false image of yourself that you saw in her eyes. Why could you not leave well enough alone? Now you have ruined everything.

Matthias did not need the old specters of his haunted past to tell him that he was a fool. But there was no going back. He had told Horatia the truth that morning. He could not live a lie. Not with Imogen.

"What are you trying to say, my lord?" Imogen asked carefully.

"Do not be obtuse. I am called Cold-blooded Colchester for a reason. I earned that name, Imogen. I am not the kind, noble, high-minded man you believe me to be. I do not possess delicate sensibilities or refined emotions. I proved it when I forced you to read Lucy's journal. A kind, thoughtful husband would not have blackmailed his wife into learning the truth about a woman she once called friend."

Imogen studied him for an eternity with eyes that

seemed to burn through his skin. Matthias braced himself for the endless night that waited to engulf him.

And then Imogen smiled. It was the smile of Anizamara herself. It glowed with the warmth of the sun.

"It strikes me that you have taken this whole thing much too seriously, Colchester," Imogen said. "I suppose that is only to be expected of someone who possesses such a sensitive temperament."

"Too seriously?" Matthias went swiftly around the desk and seized her by her arms. "What is the matter with you? What sort of mirror does it take to show you what I am?"

She reached up to touch his cheek with trembling fingers. "I have already explained that you and I do not always see the truth in the same light."

His hands tightened on her arms. "What truth do you see when you look at me?"

"I see many truths. The most important of them all is that you and I are very much alike in some ways."

"For God's sake, we are opposites, not kindred spirits."

"You once told me that we had passion and Zamar in common, if you will recall."

Desperation and hope swept through him with the force of a wild, uncontrolled fire. "We share those things, but they do not make us soul mates. They do not make us *alike.*"

"Ah, now, that is where you are wrong, my lord." Imogen's eyes were brilliant with an unreadable emotion. "You are a man who prides himself on responding to logic, so let us consider this in a logical fashion. We shall consider passion first. It speaks for itself, does it not? I have never felt what I feel for you with any other man."

"You have never lain with any other man. How can you know what you would feel with someone else?" He could barely speak the words. The image of Imogen in the arms of another man now that she had given herself to him was excruciatingly painful to contemplate.

"Hush, my lord." Imogen closed his mouth with her fingertips. "I do not need to experience the act of love with another to know that what you and I share is quite unique. But enough on that point. Let us proceed to the subject of our shared interest in Zamar."

"You think that our mutual interest in ancient Zamar binds us together in some grand, metaphysical manner? Madam, you have been reading too much Coleridge and Shelley. There are a hundred members of the Zamarian Society who share our interests. I assure you, I do not consider myself bound to any of them, metaphysically or otherwise. I do not give a bloody damn if I never see a single one of them again so long as I live."

"Matthias, don't you understand? It is not the *study* of Zamar that joins our spirits on the metaphysical plane. It is the fact that we both sought its secrets for the same reason."

"What reason is that?"

Imogen stood on tiptoe and brushed her mouth against his. "Why, to escape the loneliness, of course."

Matthias was bereft of speech. The shattering truth of her simple observation hit him with the force of dawn on the lost island of Zamar. Everything was suddenly illuminated in a light that was so spectacularly clear, it seemed unnatural.

He had used his quest as a means of holding his ghosts at bay. It had not occurred to him that Imogen might have been battling her own gray specters.

"Don't you see?" Imogen persisted softly. "The search for the secrets of ancient Zamar filled up the empty places in our lives. It gave us passion and purpose and goals. What would we have done without Zamar?"

"Imogen—" He swallowed heavily.

"I know what Zamar is to you, Matthias, because it is the same thing to me. Indeed, I owe you more than I can ever repay because you did what I could not do. You discovered that lost island. Your researches and writings opened doors that I was in no position to open. You will never know what your explorations did for me. They brought a grand mystery to Upper Stickleford. I gloried in the search for solutions to the enigma of Zamar."

Matthias finally found his voice. "It is not enough."

She stilled in his grasp. "You said that it was enough, my lord. You said that it was a better basis for marriage than most couples had."

"I meant that it is not enough to explain why you persist in crediting me with a nobility that I do not possess. Surely you did not marry me because I found ancient Zamar. What if Rutledge had returned after the second journey instead of me? What if he had opened the doors for you? Would you have married him?"

Imogen grimaced. "No, of course not. I've told you why I married you, Matthias. I love you."

"You said that only because you thought I was in danger of getting myself killed in a duel. You were distraught that night. Emotional. Fearful. Agitated."

"Nonsense."

"And, God help me, I took advantage of your overwrought condition to coerce you into marriage."

"How dare you, sir? You did no such thing. I was in full command of my faculties when I agreed to marry you. How many times must I explain that I have excellent nerves? I do not become overwrought. The fact is, I loved you then and I love you now."

"But, Imogen—"

Her eyes narrowed. "You are the most stubborn man I have ever met in my life. I cannot believe that I am standing here arguing with you about my feelings for you. One would think that we were quarreling over some obscure reference in a Zamarian scroll."

Matthias stared at her. "I find your love for me to be far more incomprehensible than any mystery of ancient Zamar."

"Some truths one must simply accept because they are self-evident, my lord. Love is one of those truths. I have given you my love. Will you take it or reject it?"

Matthias looked into her clear blue-green eyes and saw no ghosts. "I may be stubborn, but I am not stupid. I accept your gift. God help me, it is more valuable than anything I discovered in the library of lost Zamar. I swear to you that I will cherish and protect it."

She smiled a mysterious smile that held all the secrets of his past, present, and future. "I would not have given you my love if I had not believed that you would take excellent care of it."

He wasted no more time attempting to comprehend the womanly secrets of her smile. He pulled her into his arms and crushed her mouth beneath his own.

Chapter 18

Imogen heard a rasping, inarticulate groan and realized it
had come from Matthias's soul. He swept her up into his
arms and carried her to the dolphin sofa. His eyes met
hers as he set her down amid the silken pillows. She saw
the unmistakable gleam of desire mingled with an almost
unendurable longing in his gaze.

She was both astounded and intrigued. "Matthias?
What are you about? Surely you do not intend to . . . to
make love to me here? Now?"

"I have often sat in that chair behind my desk and
wondered how you would look lying naked here on this
sofa. It was a form of self-inflicted torture."

"Good heavens."

"I have been waiting for an opportunity to make my
fantasy a reality." Matthias lowered himself down onto the
cushions beside her and reached for her. "I believe today
is the day."

"But it is the middle of the afternoon and we are in
the library."

Matthias nibbled her earlobe as he began to unfasten

her gown. "The ancient Zamarians often made love during the day."

"They did?"

"Most assuredly." Matthias loosened the bodice of her gown. "I have it on the best authority."

"That would be your own authority, would it not? You are the foremost expert on the subject of ancient Zamar."

"I am delighted to hear you admit it, I. A. Stone." He bent his head to kiss the swell of one breast.

Sweet anticipation swirled inside Imogen. "Lovemaking in the afternoon. How very unusual. You did write that the Zamarians were an uninhibited lot."

"For want of a better word." He reached down to tug Imogen's skirts up to her waist.

Delightful sensations bloomed inside Imogen. She felt light-headed, almost giddy. She had given Matthias her love and he had vowed to cherish it. Colchester was a man of his word. He was also, she told herself, a man who could learn how to love.

It was up to her to teach him.

At that moment he found the hot, moist place between her thighs with his powerful, elegant hands and all thought of the future fled temporarily from Imogen's brain. She surrendered to his exotic Zamarian lovemaking techniques with joyous abandon. Matthias stroked her until she was breathless. Until she shivered in his arms. Until she twisted and turned in his embrace.

She fumbled with his breeches, freeing his rigid staff. He pushed himself between her fingers and shuddered with pleasure when she caressed him.

"I love you," she whispered.

"Oh, God, Imogen." Matthias rolled on top of her.

He drove himself into her, crushing her into the pillows. She clung to him, glorying in the weight and strength in him. Her fingers sank into the muscles of his shoulders.

When he found his release deep inside her, Imogen heard him whisper her name.

It was enough for now.

Lucy's journal ended with unnerving abruptness. An ominous sense of foreboding descended on Imogen as she read the last few entries.

My dear, charming Alastair is the most handsome of men, but he shares the common weakness of his sex. He talks too much in bed and his chatter concerns naught but himself. He no doubt assumes that I did not notice his small slip of the tongue the other night. Perhaps he thinks that I did not comprehend the implications of what he said as he succumbed to the ennui that afflicts men in the aftermath of spent desire. He may have actually convinced himself that he did not say it aloud. But I am no fool. I heard and I understood. Alastair is my true love and I will force him to acknowledge that we are meant for each other. We shall go to Italy and live the golden, glorious life of lovers who are destined to be together.

I am so consumed with excitement that I can scarcely breathe. My hand shakes as I write these words. The Bow Street runner I hired to investigate Alastair's small indiscretion has finally returned from the north. The information he has provided is more useful than I had dared to hope. My naughty Alastair is not at all what he professes to be. I am certain that he will do anything to keep the truth from Society. Anything. When I tell him the price of my silence, he will surely pay it. He may be angry at first, but when we are safe in Italy he will come to the realization

that we are fated to be together for all eternity.
He will forgive me eventually for what I am
obliged to do. It is for his own good.

A chill went down Imogen's spine as she closed the
journal. She sat quietly for a long while, gazing unseeingly
out the window of her bedchamber.

There was no question about it, she thought. Toward
the end, Lucy had been living more and more in a strange
world of her own creation. Reality and fantasy had
blended to such an extent that she could no longer tell
where one stopped and the other began. Her obsession
with Alastair Drake had driven her beyond logic and reason. Perhaps Lucy had not been truly mad, but she certainly had not been entirely rational.

Imogen rose from her chair. She tucked Lucy's journal under her arm and went slowly downstairs to find
Matthias.

He was right where she had left him less than two
hours earlier, seated behind his desk, deep into a Greek
text. He looked up as she walked into the library.

"Imogen." He started to smile and then he saw the
journal. All hint of emotion disappeared from his ghost-
gray eyes. He got slowly to his feet. "You have finished
it."

"Yes."

"Well?" He watched her as she came to stand before
him on the opposite side of the desk. "Was it worth the
anguish, my dear?"

Imogen gave him a rueful smile. "I suspect the pain
was worse for you than it was for me, Matthias."

"Not bloody likely. Lucy was your friend, not mine."

"Yes, but you have been tormenting yourself because
you asked me to read her journal. The talons of self-inflicted guilt are extremely sharp, are they not, my lord?"

Matthias raised his brows. "I confess that I have not
had much experience with them until recently. I cannot
say that I care for the sensations they cause. Have mercy,

madam. I may deserve the torment, but I trust that you
will put me out of my misery as quickly as possible. Did
you learn anything of importance, or was it all for
naught?"

"I think I know why someone is after the journal.
And possibly who is after it. Lucy discovered some dark
secret about Alastair Drake."

"Drake?" Matthias frowned. "What sort of secret?"

"I don't know. She did not write it down in the journal. But it must have been something very important, because she hired a Bow Street runner to investigate it."

"How very interesting," Matthias said softly.

"Her last entry concerns the runner's report. Whatever he told her seems to have confirmed some suspicion
she held. She intended to use the information to blackmail
Mr. Drake into taking her to Italy."

"What a poor, benighted fool she must have been."
Matthias shook his head. "Anyone acquainted with him
can see that Drake is a creature of London Society. He
thrives on it. He would never willingly abandon Town
life."

Imogen gripped the journal very tightly. "I doubt that
Lucy understood that. I certainly did not."

Matthias shrugged and said nothing.

Imogen glowered at him. "If you make a single comment on the subject of my supposed naiveté, sir, I shall
lose my temper."

"I would not dream of saying a word."

"Very wise of you, my lord." Imogen cleared her
throat. "In any event, as I told you, Lucy was not herself
toward the end."

"You may be right on that point. Surely no rational
female would have concocted such a crazed plan. She
gave no hint of this secret she discovered?"

"No." Imogen blushed at the memory of what Lucy
had written. "Only that it was something Mr. Drake accidentally allowed to slip during one of those curious peri-

ods of extreme exhaustion that appear to envelop members of the male sex following an encounter."

"An encounter with what?" Matthias's brow cleared. "Oh, I see. Drake didn't have the brains to keep his mouth shut while his breeches were off, is that it?"

"That is a rather crude way of expressing it."

"But accurate, you must admit."

"I suppose so." Imogen tapped her toe on the carpet. "You do realize the implications of this information, do you not, my lord?"

A keen, predatory intelligence glittered in Matthias's eyes. "Of course. Your friend may, indeed, have been murdered. But the killer could easily have been Alastair Drake rather than Vanneck."

"Yes." Imogen sank slowly into a chair. She stared at the journal in her lap. "Mr. Drake might have concluded that he had to kill her in order to keep her from revealing his secret. What a strange notion. For three years I have assumed that Vanneck murdered Lucy. It is very difficult to imagine Mr. Drake as a killer."

"I have no particular difficulty imagining it," Matthias muttered. "But it's that damned secret that interests me. I wonder if it would be possible to locate the runner Lucy hired three years ago. I would like to interview him."

Imogen glanced up. "That is an excellent notion, Matthias."

"I shall send a message to Bow Street immediately." Matthias sat down and reached for a pen. "In the meantime, I believe I shall pay a visit to someone else who may have knowledge of this matter."

"Surely you are not going to confront Mr. Drake? We do not have enough information yet."

"Not Drake. That shining beacon of Zamarian scholarship, the Angel."

"You intend to speak with Lady Lyndhurst?" Imogen frowned. "Why?"

"I feel certain that she is somehow connected to this

matter." Matthias finished his short note and put down the pen. "I think she was the one who attempted to get her hands on the journal this afternoon."

"Quite possibly, my lord. She may know something more than we do." Imogen sprang to her feet. "I shall accompany you."

"No, you will not." Matthias eyed her with determination. "You will wait here until I return."

"I cannot allow you to go off by yourself in search of information, Matthias. Only consider the disastrous situation you got yourself into when you searched Vanneck's house without my assistance. You could have been killed on that occasion."

"I seriously doubt that Selena will attempt to murder me in her own drawing room." Matthias was amused. "She's a lady, not a ruffian from the stews. Women of her sort rely on their charms to achieve their goals."

"Hmm. No offense, my lord, but I am not certain that we can depend upon your experience in the matter. My mother once told me that men frequently underestimate women."

"I am always careful never to underestimate you, madam."

Imogen wrinkled her nose. "Very well, then. Since you insist there is no danger, it follows that there is absolutely no reason I should not accompany you to Lady Lyndhurst's, my lord."

Matthias paused in the act of sealing the note. "I can see that I shall have to take more care with my logic in future."

"Do not blame yourself, sir." She cast a thoughtful glance at the Zamarian sofa. "After all, we arose from the conjugal couch only a short while ago. Perhaps you have not yet recovered fully from the debilitating ennui that strikes the male of the species in the aftermath of the amorous embrace."

Matthias's teeth flashed in a wicked grin. "You do have an unsettling effect on my delicate sensibilities. Very well, you may accompany me to pay a call upon Selena, but you will allow me to conduct the interview. Is that understood?"

Imogen gave him her most beatific smile. "But of course, my lord. I would not dream of attempting to take charge of this matter when you are so obviously in command of the situation."

Matthias looked distinctly skeptical. "Indeed."

*L*ess than half an hour later, a disgruntled housekeeper opened the door of Selena's town house. She glowered at Imogen and Matthias. "What can I do for ye?"

"Please inform Lady Lyndhurst that the Countess and Earl of Colchester wish to speak with her about an urgent matter," Matthias said coldly.

"Lady Lyndhurst is not at home," the housekeeper grumbled. "Don't know when she'll return."

It occurred to Imogen that it was nearly five o'clock. "Has she gone for a drive in the park, perhaps?"

The housekeeper gave a bark of harsh laughter. "Not unless the fancy has taken to packing its bags afore it sets out for the park."

"Are you telling us that Lady Lyndhurst has packed up and left Town?" Matthias asked.

"Aye, that's what I'm sayin'."

"But we were just here a few hours ago," Imogen protested. "She held her Zamarian salon earlier today."

"She shooed all them young ladies out the door the moment you two left," the housekeeper said. "And then she set the staff to packing as fast as they could. Never seen the like."

"Did Lady Lyndhurst mention her destination?" Matthias asked.

"Not to me, she didn't." The housekeeper shrugged broad shoulders.

"Damnation," Matthias muttered.

Something in the housekeeper's tone caught Imogen's attention. She recalled the tales that Mrs. Vine had related concerning her former tenants and their secret lives. "Did Lady Lyndhurst remember to pay the quarterly wages to the staff before she left?"

"No, she did not." Indignation flared in the housekeeper's eyes. "Typical of that sort. After three years of loyal service, she takes herself off without bothering to pay any of us."

Imogen slid a sidelong glance at Matthias. "My husband would be happy to reimburse you and the rest of the staff if you could give us some notion of where Lady Lyndhurst went."

"Imogen, what the devil are you about?" Matthias demanded. "I never said—"

"Hush, my lord." Imogen kept her attention on the housekeeper. "Well? Do we have a bargain?"

A hopeful gleam appeared in the housekeeper's eye. "Expect her brother will likely know where she's gone."

"Her brother?" Imogen gazed at the woman in astonishment. "I was not aware that Lady Lyndhurst had a brother."

"That's because the two of 'em kept it quiet," the housekeeper said slyly. "I learned about it by accident right after I went to work for Lady Lyndhurst. No one pays any attention to staff. Act as if we're invisible. But we got eyes and ears, same as the fancy. I overheard the pair of 'em talkin' one day when he came to visit."

"What is the name of Lady Lyndhurst's brother?" Matthias inquired softly.

The housekeeper looked shrewd. "I'll be happy to tell ye, sir, once me and the staff have got our wages."

"Never mind," Matthias said. "I believe we can hazard a guess concerning the identity of Lady Lyndhurst's brother. There is only one likely candidate for the post."

Inspiration struck Imogen. "Alastair Drake?"

The housekeeper's face crumpled. "Ain't that just like the fancy. Spend a fortune on clothes and horses and then turn all clutch-fisted and cheeseparing when it comes to paying the poor folk that work for 'em."

"Give her the money for the quarterly wages, my lord," Imogen instructed.

Matthias glowered. "Why should I do that?"

"Colchester, this is no time to be stubborn. Pay her the money."

Matthias sighed in resignation. "Very well." He turned back to the housekeeper. "As I have just agreed to pay for information that I already possess, perhaps you will be so good as to confirm it?"

Relief shone in the woman's face. "Lady Lyndhurst's brother is Mr. Alastair Drake, all right. Don't have any notion why the two of 'em wanted to keep their family connection a secret. What possible difference could it make to anyone?"

"An excellent question," Imogen murmured.

"Thus far, we seem to be collecting far more questions than answers," Imogen remarked as Matthias handed her up onto the phaeton box. "So Mr. Drake and Selena are brother and sister. I wonder if that is the secret Lucy discovered."

"She may have learned of the relationship," Matthias said as he picked up the reins. "But it does not seem worthy of blackmail, let alone murder."

"Not unless Mr. Drake and Selena concealed their connection in order to hide another, more dangerous secret." Imogen grabbed at the crown of her wide, shell-trimmed bonnet as the horses set off. "I wonder if Mr. Drake also left Town this afternoon."

"That should be easy enough to confirm. I shall drive past his lodgings. I believe they are in Hollowell Street."

"How do you come to know that, Matthias?"

"I made it my business to learn a few things about Drake shortly after we came to London," he said grimly.

Imogen was suddenly deeply intrigued. "Why on earth did you make inquiries about him?"

"Let us just say that the sight of you in his arms that day I called upon you and your aunt raised a number of interesting questions."

Imogen gazed at him in astonished wonder. "Never say that you were jealous of Alastair Drake, Matthias."

"Of course not." Matthias fixed his attention on his horses' ears. "Jealousy is a ridiculous, immature passion suited only to smoldering poets and very young men."

"Of course, my lord." He had definitely been jealous, Imogen told herself. She smiled complacently. "What do you propose to do if Mr. Drake has disappeared?"

"Take precautions." Matthias's eyes narrowed. "I do not care for the feel of this situation, Imogen. Something is very wrong."

"I agree."

A few minutes later Matthias halted the phaeton in front of 12 Hollowell Street. No one responded to the knock on Alastair's front door.

A glance through the undraped windows revealed a chaotic scene inside the rooms at Number 12. Alastair Drake had obviously packed his belongings in a hurry.

"They're both gone. It is incredible." Imogen led the way back into Matthias's library a short while later. "But why? What made them so uneasy that they felt they had to leave Town?"

"The fact that we possessed the journal and had no intention of letting it fall into Selena's hands," Matthias said. He yanked impatiently at the knot of his cravat. "After that scene in Selena's drawing room today, she obviously concluded that we had either discovered the same secret Lucy had uncovered, or that we would soon do so."

"She must have notified Alastair." Imogen frowned in thought. "And the pair of them panicked and left Town?"

"Perhaps."

She glanced up swiftly, alarmed by Matthias's ominous tone. "What do you mean, perhaps?"

Matthias went to stand in front of the window, the ends of his snowy white cravat draped casually around his neck. "There is every likelihood that Drake killed Lucy because she had learned his secret. He may also have shot Vanneck for the same reason."

"But Vanneck would have inherited Lucy's journal three years ago. Why wait until this year to murder him?"

Matthias braced one hand on the windowsill. "Who knows when Vanneck actually discovered the journal or when he got around to reading it?"

"A few months ago he sold his large house and bought a new, smaller residence," Imogen reminded him. "Perhaps the journal came to light when his staff packed up his household for the move."

"Quite possibly. There is something else though. Lucy did not reveal this deep, dark secret in her journal. She only alluded to having discovered it and stated that she planned to use it to blackmail Drake. The secret itself is not actually written down in that damned book."

"True." Imogen clasped her hands behind her back and began to pace the library. "But the fact that Vanneck had concealed the journal in his study implies that he knew it was important."

"And the fact that Selena and Drake want it indicates that they believe that Lucy did write down the secret. How would they know otherwise if they have never read the journal?"

"Excellent point," Imogen whispered. "What if Vanneck had only recently discovered the journal, as you suggest? What if he learned that Selena and Alastair had something to hide but did not know what it was?"

"Vanneck might very well have tried a bluff. He may have let Drake think he knew the secret that Lucy had discovered and attempted to blackmail him, just as Lucy had done. And Drake killed him, just as he killed Lucy."

"Yes. A brilliant deduction. That makes perfect sense, Colchester."

"Thank you. Coming from I. A. Stone, that is praise indeed." Matthias turned away from the window and walked toward his desk. "One thing we know for certain is that the journal is dangerous. Until we know why, I intend to make sure that both you and Patricia are protected."

Imogen was startled. "Surely you do not believe that your sister and I are in jeopardy? Selena and Alastair have left London."

"So they would have us believe. I do not intend to take any chances." A knock on the library door interrupted Matthias. "What is it, Ufton?"

"A Mr. Hugo Bagshaw to see you, sir," Ufton said calmly.

"Bagshaw?" Matthias scowled. "That young man has a wretched sense of timing. Tell him that I am not at home."

Hugo came to stand behind Ufton in the doorway. He was dressed to the nines and he clutched a small bouquet in one hand. He glowered furiously at Matthias. "I knew you were only trying to cozen me when you told me that I would be welcome to pay my addresses to your sister. Why didn't you have the decency to be honest about it? Why feed me all that rubbish about how you and I had something in common?"

"Hugo." Imogen smiled warmly and held out her hands in greeting as she hurried across the room. "Do come in. We are delighted to see you. Is that not so, Colchester?"

"I have a few other matters to attend to at the moment," Matthias said evenly. "Or have you forgotten our other small problem?"

"Of course not," she assured him. "But I do feel that Hugo should be made welcome."

"Some other time," Matthias growled.

"Hah." Hugo's brows were a solid line across his nose. "You don't mean that. You're just trying to get rid of me, Colchester."

"*Hugo.*" Patricia's delighted voice rang out from the top of the stairs. "I mean, Mr. Bagshaw. What are you doing here? Have you come to call?"

"Yes, I have," Hugo said very loudly. "But it seems I am not welcome."

"That is not true," Imogen said crisply. "Ufton, please get out of the way so that Mr. Bagshaw can enter the library."

"As you wish, madam." After a fleeting glance at Matthias, Ufton stepped aside.

"Oh, *Hugo,*" Patricia cried as she pattered lightly down the stairs. "Of course you are welcome."

Imogen smiled at Ufton. "Have a tray of tea brought into the library, please."

"Yes, madam." Ufton inclined his head in a stiff little bow and started to retreat.

"Don't bother." Hugo drew himself up proudly. "It would appear that I will not be staying."

"On the contrary"—Imogen cast a repressive look at Matthias—"I have just explained that you are most welcome. Please be seated, Hugo." She sharpened her tone. "Now."

Hugo appeared slightly taken aback. He blinked once or twice and then edged cautiously into the library.

Matthias resigned himself to the inevitable. He sat down behind his desk and regarded the crowd in the doorway with a considering expression. "By all means, Bagshaw, take a seat. As it happens, I have need of your assistance."

"Assistance?" Hugo eyed him warily. "What the devil are you talking about, Colchester?"

Matthias smiled grimly. "At the moment, Patricia has more use for a bodyguard than she does a beau. I have been told that you have been practicing your marksmanship quite diligently at Manton's and that you have engaged Mr. Shrimpton to teach you the fine points of boxing."

Hugo turned a dull shade of red. "What of it?"

"I realize that you no doubt intended to use your new skills against me, but I have a more practical suggestion. What do you say, Bagshaw? Do you care to play the knight-defender for my sister?"

"Whatever are you talking about, Colchester?" Patricia demanded.

"Yes, what on earth do you mean?" Imogen asked.

"It's very simple," Matthias said. "I do not want either you or Patricia to leave this house unless you are escorted by myself or Bagshaw. Ufton will serve in a pinch, but he has a number of other duties. I would prefer that he be left free to discharge his responsibilities."

Hugo stared at Matthias, clearly fascinated by this turn of events. "Are you saying that there is a threat to the ladies of this household, Colchester?"

"Yes," Matthias said. "That is precisely what I'm saying. I do not yet know how great the threat is. I intend to determine that at the earliest possible moment. In the meantime, I want to enlist the assistance of a man I can trust. Well, sir?"

Hugo glanced at Patricia, who blushed. He straightened his shoulders and raised his chin. "I would be honored to serve as Lady Patricia's defender."

Patricia looked at him with a worshipful expression. "Oh, Hugo. How very brave and noble of you."

Hugo flushed. Then he apparently recalled the bouquet he held. He thrust it toward her. "For you."

"Thank you." Patricia smiled as she came forward to take the flowers.

Imogen sidled closer to the desk and gave Matthias an approving smile. "Well done, my lord," she murmured out of the side of her mouth. "You have made two people very happy."

"Thank you, my dear, but I assure you, it's all in a day's work for a man who possesses my degree of delicate sensibilities and exquisite depth of feeling."

Chapter 19

She was standing in Uncle Selwyn's black-draped library. Ebony candles burned low. Dark hangings drifted over her head. The eyes of the sepulchral masks watched her from the walls. The scene had become chillingly familiar, but she realized that something was different this time.

She turned, searching for Matthias in the shadows. Then she noticed that there were two sarcophagi rather than one in the chamber. Both of the heavily carved lids had been removed. She froze in horror as two figures sat up inside the coffins. Selena and Alastair. They laughed silently, their eyes cruel and mocking. Then they pointed skeletal fingers toward the cloaked figure of a man sprawled on the carpet. Imogen went forward with a sense of dread, afraid of what she would discover. His face was turned away from her but she could see the swath of silver in his night-dark hair.

"It's entirely your fault, you know," Alastair said as he got out of the coffin. "He would never have been dragged into this amusing little play if you had not assigned him a role in it."

"Entirely your fault," Selena concurred. *She rose from her sarcophagus and stepped onto the carpet.*

Imogen came awake very suddenly. Ghostly fragments of the terrifying dream clung to her thoughts. Her skin was damp. So were her eyes. She took several deep breaths in an attempt to quell the sense of panic that assailed her. Strong nerves, she reminded herself. She had very sturdy nerves.

For a moment she lay motionless in the darkened bed. Something was wrong. Dreadfully wrong. Then she realized that she was alone. She could not feel the familiar, comforting heat of Matthias's large body or the weight of his muscled arm across her breasts. Fear seized her.

"Matthias."

"I'm right here, Imogen."

She sensed rather than heard him move. She sat up quickly, clutching the sheet to her throat. Matthias was silhouetted against the window. He came toward her through the darkness, his face concealed in shadow. There was just enough moonlight to reveal the streak of silver in his hair. It looked exactly as it had in the dream.

"I'm so sorry," she whispered. She squeezed her eyes shut in an effort to blot up the remainder of the dream and the tears. "This is all my fault. I should never have brought you into it."

"What damnable nonsense is this?" Matthias sat down on the edge of the bed and gathered her into his arms. "Calm yourself, my dear. Are you all right?"

"I had a dream. A nightmare." She rested her face on his shoulder. The woven silk of his black dressing gown was reassuringly rough against her cheek. "It was similar to one I've had on previous occasions, but this time Selena and Alastair were in it."

"Not surprising under the circumstances." Matthias stroked her hair. "I've had a few unpleasant visions concerning that pair myself tonight. The only difference is that mine occurred while I was lying awake in bed. But such dreams will end once I've located Drake and his sister."

"Matthias, I never meant to put you in danger. It was wrong of me to ask you to help me. I had no right—"

"Hush." He bent his head and kissed her into silence. Imogen trembled and clung to him.

Matthias lifted his mouth from hers and smiled slightly. "I shall tell you something now, Imogen. Something very important, so listen closely." He framed her face between his hands. "You could not have kept me out of this."

"I don't understand. If I had not held you to that promise that you made to Uncle Selwyn, none of this would have happened. You would have been safe."

"From the moment I met you, nothing could have kept me from becoming involved in your life, do you understand?"

"But, Matthias—"

"Absolutely nothing."

"But if I had not summoned you to Upper Stickleford—"

"I would have found you soon thereafter. I had already determined to discover the identity of I. A. Stone. It would not have taken me long. So you see? It would all have been the same in the end."

"Oh, Matthias, you are so kind, but I—"

"No," he interrupted roughly. "I'm not kind. But I want you more than I have ever wanted anything in my life."

His mouth came down on hers again, overwhelming her protests with the potent force of his sensual hunger. Imogen struggled briefly and then, with a small sigh, allowed herself the rare luxury of surrender.

Sometimes it was very pleasant to let Matthias take charge, she reflected. Then again, sometimes she had little choice. He did seem to have a natural tendency to take the lead in a number of activities besides the waltz. And as she was inclined to do the same, it was safe to say that their lives together would not be dull.

When Matthias raised his head, his eyes were fierce. "You will not speak of regrets or guilt again, do you understand? I regret nothing and I will not allow you to feel any regret either."

Imogen shivered and nestled closer. He wrapped her in the cloak of his strength and warmth.

"Do you think that you will be able to find the Bow Street runner Lucy hired?" she asked after a while.

"I hope to hear something tomorrow, but I have decided not to invest all of my expectations in that quarter. It would be extremely useful to interview the runner, but there are other ways to obtain information. In the morning I shall explore one of them."

"What do you plan to do?"

"Pay a call upon Felix Glaston."

"Your former partner?"

"Yes. Information flows through The Lost Soul the way the River Styx flows through Hades, and Felix is an adept fisherman. He might be able to catch something of interest in his net."

Imogen raised her head. "I shall look forward to making Mr. Glaston's acquaintance. He must be a most interesting individual."

"You wish to meet Felix?" Matthias was startled. "Impossible. Your aunt would surely murder me if I introduced you to him. And no one would condemn her."

"My aunt has nothing to say about the matter."

"Imogen, be reasonable. Felix operates a gaming hell. A lady does not pay social calls upon men who own business enterprises such as The Lost Soul."

"You operated that same hell yourself at one time."

"That was several years ago, and I can assure you that in those days you would not have been able to call upon me either." His mouth twisted. "At least not without damaging your reputation beyond any hope of repair."

"Do you think that would have stopped me?"

Matthias groaned. "Knowing you, no. But that is not the point. It is simply not done for a lady to enter the residence of a man who runs a gaming hell."

"Rubbish. When did you become such a keen arbiter of proper behavior and good manners, my lord?"

"Imogen—"

"Cold-blooded Colchester and Immodest Imogen have certain reputations to maintain. I trust that you do not intend to turn into a stuffy, straitlaced prig now that you have assumed the duties of a husband, Matthias. It would be a dreadful disappointment."

"Would it, indeed?"

"You know very well that I do not care what the Polite World thinks. Why should I, when it has always thought so little of me?"

Matthias laughed in the darkness. "Once again my common sense is undone by your bold logic, madam. Very well, I shall take you with me to meet Felix on the morrow. Something tells me that the two of you will get along famously."

*M*atthias was thoroughly amused by the stunned expression on the face of Felix's butler. The poor man swallowed heavily several times before he managed to repeat the names of the visitors.

"Lord and *Lady* Colchester, did you say, sir?"

"You heard me, Dodge," Matthias replied dryly.

"Lady Colchester?" Dodge repeated very carefully. "Are you quite certain, sir?"

"Dodge, are you implying that I do not know the identity of my own wife?"

"No, of course not, m'lord," Dodge stammered.

Imogen gave him a blinding smile.

"Beg pardon." Dodge was transfixed by Imogen. "I shall announce you both at once. If you will excuse me."

Dodge bowed himself back into the hall, turned, and

promptly slammed the door in Matthias's and Imogen's faces.

"Mr. Glaston's butler seems a trifle unnerved," Imogen observed.

"He's seen me standing on Felix's doorstep often enough," Matthias said, "but I can assure you, he's never before opened the door to a countess."

Imogen gazed at the closed door. "He did not actually open it, if you will note. At least not for long."

"He was flustered. No doubt he will soon realize that he left us standing on the front step and rush back to make amends."

At that moment Dodge yanked the door open again. He was sweating profusely. "Beg your pardon. So sorry. Accident. Wind caught the door. I pray you will both come in out of the cold. Mr. Glaston will see you at once."

"Thank you, Dodge." Matthias took Imogen's arm and escorted her into Felix's grand front hall.

"This way, madam." Dodge went to stand in the doorway of a firelit library. He cleared his throat very loudly. "Lord and *Lady* Colchester to see you, sir."

"Colchester." Felix rose from his chair with the aid of his cane. "This is a surprise." He turned a speculative gaze on Imogen. "Dodge tells me that your new bride has accompanied you."

"Allow me to present my wife." Matthias was aware of a surge of satisfaction as he said the simple words. "Imogen, this is my old friend, Felix Glaston."

"I am delighted to make your acquaintance, Mr. Glaston." Imogen held out her hand as though she had just been introduced to a high-ranking gentleman of the ton. "Colchester has told me a great deal about you."

"I see." Surprise flared in Felix's eyes. For a few seconds he looked as though he did not know quite what to do with Imogen's hand. Then he swiftly took it and bent over her gloved fingers with the air of a cultivated courtier. "I am honored. Please, won't you both be seated."

Matthias saw Imogen into a chair near the fire and then sat down across from her. He watched Felix wince as he lowered himself cautiously into his own chair. He noticed that his friend had his gnarled hands wrapped very tightly around the head of the cane.

"Leg acting up?" Matthias asked quietly.

"It's the weather." Felix sighed heavily as he leaned the cane against the arm of his chair. "I think I can safely forecast rain in the next few hours."

"My aunt has an excellent remedy for rheumatism and other pains in the extremities," Imogen said conversationally. "I shall ask her to write out the recipe for you."

Felix blinked. "That is very kind of you, Lady Colchester."

"Not at all." Imogen smiled. "It is Aunt Horatia's own personal recipe. She created it herself."

"Very kind," Felix repeated. He looked as dazed as Dodge had appeared a few moments earlier.

Matthias concluded that it was time to take command of the situation. If he did not act quickly, his old friend was likely to turn into a blithering idiot.

"We have come upon a matter of some urgency," Matthias said.

Felix tore his attention away from Imogen's face. "Urgency? What sort of urgency?"

"A matter of life and death," Imogen announced.

Matthias grimaced. "My wife has a somewhat lurid turn of phrase on occasion, but I assure you the matter is serious enough. I have a question for you, Felix."

Felix spread his hands. "Ask it, my friend. If I know the answer, I shall be happy to supply it."

"What do you know of Alastair Drake?"

"Drake?" Felix scowled in thought. "He appeared in Town about three years ago, I believe. Plays cards at The Lost Soul on occasion. Come to think of it, he has not been there much of late. Why?"

"Did you know that he is Lady Lyndhurst's brother?" Imogen asked.

Felix quirked a brow. "No. Is it significant?"

"We want to know why the pair of them have kept their connection a secret," Matthias said. "For starters, I wish to discover where they lived before they took up residence in London."

Imogen leaned forward eagerly. "Were you by any chance acquainted with Lord Lyndhurst, Mr. Glaston?"

Felix exchanged glances with Matthias. "I do not believe so," he said.

Imogen looked at Matthias. "Did you know him, Colchester?"

"No," Matthias said thoughtfully. "I never met the man."

"How very odd. Between the two of you, I would have thought that you would have met most of the gentlemen in London at one time or another. I am told that sooner or later they all show up at The Lost Soul." Imogen paused. "Do you suppose that there ever was a Lord Lyndhurst?"

Felix's eyes creased at the corners. "An excellent question."

"Yes, it is," Matthias said. "Should have thought of it myself."

"Indeed." Felix steepled his fingers. "You have married a very clever lady, Colchester. My congratulations. I am delighted to see that you have found yourself someone who can bring you up to scratch on occasion."

"I most certainly will not be bored," Matthias murmured.

Imogen gave Matthias a warm smile. "Colchester and I have a great deal in common."

"I can see that you do." Felix settled more comfortably into the depths of his chair. "Well, then, it should not be difficult to learn the answers to your questions. I shall look into the matter immediately."

Imogen's eyes lit with gratitude and excitement. "That would be wonderful, Mr. Glaston. How can we ever thank you?"

Felix eyed her thoughtfully. "By staying for a cup of tea, Lady Colchester. I have never taken tea with a countess."

"I'm certain that it will not prove nearly so entertaining as tea with the owner of a gaming hell," Imogen said. "Indeed, when Colchester informed me that we were to call upon you, I confess I rather hoped that we would be paying a visit to your place of business. I have never seen a hell."

Felix stared at her in amazement. Then he looked at Matthias.

Matthias shrugged.

Felix turned back to Imogen. "Perhaps some other time, Lady Colchester," he began smoothly.

Imogen brightened. "That would be lovely. Would tomorrow be convenient?"

"Don't even think about it," Matthias said grimly.

Imogen smiled at Felix. "Pay no attention to him, Mr. Glaston. My husband suffers from an overanxious temperament. Delicate sensibilities, you know."

Felix gave her his most cherubic grin. "I suspect that you will have a bracing effect upon his nerves, madam."

$\mathcal{T}$he message from Bow Street was waiting when Imogen and Matthias returned home. Ufton delivered the news as he ushered them into the hall.

"The runner you seek was killed nearly three years ago, m'lord. Shot dead by a highwayman whom he was attempting to arrest."

Matthias glanced at Imogen. "More likely murdered by Alastair Drake."

A chill went through Imogen. "Yes. After Lucy died, the runner would have been the only other person who knew his secret. He would have had to get rid of him."

o   o   o

*H*oratia glanced across her cozy parlor and smiled at the sight of Patricia and Hugo. The pair were seated at a small table, absorbed in a game of cards.

"I must say, they make a handsome couple," Horatia murmured to Imogen. "But I find it amazing that Colchester has given Mr. Bagshaw permission to pay his addresses to Patricia. The whole world was certain that Hugo and Colchester were fated to engage in a duel before the end of the Season."

"It only goes to show how often Society misjudges a situation," Imogen said.

Hugo had taken his new responsibilities very seriously. For the past few days he had made himself available to escort Patricia and, on those occasions when Matthias was otherwise occupied, Imogen, wherever they wished to go. He had endured hours of shopping, afternoon drives in the park, and endless evenings spent in stuffy ballrooms.

Patricia had confided that her gallant defender had taken to carrying a small pistol on his person. "Just in case," she explained to Imogen. The information had made Imogen somewhat uneasy, but she supposed it was wise for Hugo to go about armed. She wondered if Matthias did the same.

It should have all been quite exciting, Imogen reflected, but, in fact, life had quickly become exceedingly tedious and confining. Patricia seemed happy enough to have Hugo escort her everywhere, but Imogen was beginning to chafe beneath the restrictions Matthias had imposed. She had never been obliged to wait upon a gentleman's convenience before she made plans. She did not care for the experience.

Unfortunately, in spite of Felix's predictions, it had proven considerably more difficult to obtain information on Alastair Drake and Selena than anyone had suspected. It was as though the pair had simply materialized upon the London scene three years earlier. They had the money to keep up appearances and the social polish to ensure themselves a welcome in the best drawing rooms. No one had questioned their pasts.

Four days had passed with no firm word of the pair. Rumors abounded, however, and Felix Glaston had sent several messages imparting tidbits of information. None of it could be confirmed. The strain was beginning to affect the entire household.

Matthias had become increasingly restless and irritable. He prowled his library and growled at the servants. At night he spent hours at the bedchamber window, gazing out into the darkness. It was only in the moments immediately after he had made love to Imogen that he seemed to find some peace. And that contentment was short-lived.

For her part, Imogen had begun to dread falling asleep. Her dreams of blood and sarcophagi had grown more frequent and more disturbing. She awoke, shivering, two or three times a night to find herself wrapped tightly in Matthias's arms.

The entire affair had become quite maddening, even for someone with strong nerves.

That morning Matthias had announced at breakfast that he intended to meet with Felix at The Lost Soul. When Imogen had mentioned that she would like to accompany him, he had adamantly refused to even consider the notion.

Trapped at home, Imogen and Patricia immediately made plans to escape the house for a few hours. Imogen suggested that they both go to the museum at the Zamarian Institution. She longed to lose herself in her researches for a time. Patricia had complained that she would collapse from boredom if she was forced to spend an entire afternoon among the dusty relics of ancient Zamar.

After a spirited discussion of the alternatives, they had agreed to pay a visit to Horatia. Patricia had sent a message to Hugo informing him that his services as an escort were required. He had dutifully appeared at the appointed time and had whisked them off to Horatia's town house.

"What will you do if Colchester is unable to locate Lady Lyndhurst and Mr. Drake?" Horatia asked with a troubled frown.

"The situation cannot go on forever," Imogen said. "I certainly do not intend to endure much more of this imprisonment."

"Imprisonment?" Horatia's brows rose above her spectacles. "That rather overstates the case, don't you think?"

"It would be different if Matthias would allow Patricia and me the same freedom to come and go that he has accorded himself," Imogen complained. "But that is not the case."

"Ah, well, I'm certain that it will all be over soon."

"I trust so. Colchester has promised to escort me to the Zamarian museum on two different occasions during the past four days and both times he has broken the engagement because his friend Mr. Glaston sent him a message. It is very irritating."

Horatia hesitated and then lowered her voice. "The current situation aside, are you happy in your marriage, my dear?"

"I beg your pardon?" Imogen pulled her thoughts away from Matthias. "What an odd question. Why do you ask?"

"You are an unusual woman, Imogen. And Colchester is hardly a typical gentleman of the ton. I had some understandable concerns."

"I am well content with my marriage. The only thing that warrants concern is finding Alastair and Selena. Until that is done, no one in our household will sleep well."

"It is rather unsettling to think that there is a murderer running about," Horatia said.

"Knew a murderer once," Mrs. Vine announced matter-of-factly as she came through the doorway with a tray of tea. "Rented this house five, maybe six years ago. Right proper gentleman, he was. Very clean in his habits compared to some of the tenants I've had here."

Everyone in the parlor turned to stare at Mrs. Vine.

Imogen found her voice first. "You kept house for a murderer, Mrs. Vine?"

"I did indeed. Didn't know it at first, of course." She set the tray down on a table and began to arrange the cups. "Always paid his rent on time, he did. I was sorry to lose him as a tenant."

"How did you learn that he was a murderer?" Hugo demanded, fascinated.

"Unfortunate confrontation in the hall one night," Mrs. Vine said with a sigh of sincere regret. "It was me night off and I'd been to visit me sister that evening. But instead of stayin' with her until mornin' as I generally did, I decided to come back here. Ran into Mr. Leversedge in the hall, I did. Unexpected like, y'see. He had just returned home a few minutes afore me. He was draggin' a body down into the basement."

"Good Lord," Horatia breathed, transfixed. "He hid the bodies in the basement?"

"Did his work on the nights I was off visitin' me sister. Took the bodies down into the basement to cut 'em up so's they'd fit nice and neat into boxes. Then he hauled the boxes out of the city and got rid of 'em."

"My God." Patricia covered her mouth with one hand. Her eyes widened in horror. "What did you do when you found him in the hall with his victim, Mrs. Vine?"

"Weren't nothin' for it, what with the body there and all." Mrs. Vine shook her head sadly. "Couldn't ignore it, even if he had been the best tenant I'd ever had. Had to trot right back down the steps and summon the watch. I'll never forget Mr. Leversedge's last words to me though."

"What were they?" Imogen asked.

"He said, 'Don't worry about the blood in the hall, Mrs. Vine. I'll clean it up.' As I said, a very tidy gentleman."

∘ ∘ ∘

The following morning Matthias stood with Imogen in the center of the Zamarian museum and surveyed the dusty antiquities heaped before them. Imogen's smile of satisfaction hid a goodly measure of triumph. Matthias knew it was because she had won the small skirmish that had taken place at the breakfast table.

He had been opposed to wasting the morning there in the museum, but he had not been able to come up with a suitable excuse for avoiding it. Felix had sent no word of any new rumors. Furthermore, as fond as she appeared to be of the pair, it was obvious that Imogen was not about to tolerate another day of shopping or visiting in the company of Patricia and Hugo. In the end, Matthias had surrendered. It occurred to him to wonder if he would ever be able to deny Imogen anything once she had set her heart upon it.

"We shall start on the far side of the room, Matthias." Imogen tied a white apron around her waist. "Would you care to take notes, or shall I?"

"I'll take the notes while you examine the items," Matthias said as he removed his greatcoat. "You may as well be the one to get your hands dirty. I'm already convinced that there is nothing of great importance buried in this rubble that Rutledge sent back."

"Now, Matthias, you cannot be certain of that until it is all properly catalogued." She made her way through the broken statuary and stone coffins toward the heavy wooden crates stacked against the wall. "Who knows? Perhaps we shall find the Queen's Seal in one of those boxes."

"Not bloody likely," Matthias said softly. He hung his greatcoat on a hook. There was a soft clank as the pocket brushed against the wall.

"What was that noise?" Imogen asked.

"I put a pistol in the pocket of my coat," Matthias explained as he rolled up the sleeves of his white linen shirt.

Imogen frowned. "You've taken to carrying a pistol too?"

"It seems a reasonable precaution under the circumstances."

"Matthias, you don't really believe that Alastair will return to London, do you? Surely he and Selena will stay as far away from us as possible. I'll wager that they have fled to the Continent."

"I don't know what they will do, and neither do you." Matthias met her eyes. "It would appear that they have murdered three times already. We cannot be certain that they will not attempt to kill again."

"But what would be the point of killing us?"

"If we are dead, there is no one to link them to the murder of Lord and Lady Vanneck, let alone to that runner. They would be free to resume their life here in Town. And I have told you before that Drake and his sister are creatures of the ton. They will not willingly give up the style of life to which they have become accustomed."

"But surely they cannot simply resume their places in Society after all that has happened. There may not be any proof of their guilt, but there will be a great deal of gossip."

"They can survive a little gossip about murder." Matthias smiled faintly as he sat down on the edge of an open sarcophagus. "I did."

"You have a point." Imogen yanked a large square of canvas off a jumble of clay tablets. She tossed the shroud aside and picked up the first tablet in the heap. "Still, I must tell you that I cannot possibly live such a restricted life for much longer. Patricia does not seem to mind, but it will soon drive me into Bedlam."

Matthias was amused. "It may interest you to know that the sort of restrictions I have placed upon you and Patricia this past week amount to no more than the ordinary limitations most ladies accept readily enough here in Town."

"Well, I certainly do not intend to accept them for

long." Imogen bent over at the waist to examine a tablet. "Matthias, there is something I have been intending to ask you."

He studied the enticingly rounded curves of her derriere. "Ask, madam. I am at your service today." He contemplated the prospect of lifting her skirts while she was in such an inviting position. He could always explain that it was another exotic Zamarian lovemaking position.

"Do you know what actually did happen to Rutledge?"

The question sent a jolt of surprise through him. It took a moment to recover. He drew a deep breath. "Yes."

"I thought that might be the case." Imogen straightened and began to stack the tablets with great precision. "Well, my lord? Are you going to tell me?"

Matthias gazed thoughtfully at the notebook he had brought along to record Imogen's observations. "Rutledge tried to murder me. He died in the attempt."

"Good heavens." Imogen swung around so quickly that her elbow struck the stacked tablets. She reached out quickly to steady the pile. Her eyes were fixed on his face. "You do not jest, do you?"

"Not about this. We were exploring one of the corridors in the labyrinth. I had taken the lead. Rutledge always said that I was far better at that sort of thing than he was."

Matthias had come upon the stone staircase without any warning. One moment he was in the narrow confines of the cramped underground corridor, the next he was hovering on the brink of an endless flight of stairs hewn from solid rock.

"What is it?" Rutledge demanded from behind him. He sounded hoarse and out of breath.

"Another staircase." Matthias held the lamp higher, but the light could not penetrate the darkness at the bottom of the steps. It was as though the staircase plunged down into hell itself. "It looks treacherous. We'll need ropes to descend."

"Go on," Rutledge ordered. "We don't need the ropes."

"It's not safe. I cannot even make out the bottom of the passage."

It was the sound of Rutledge sucking in his rasping breath that alerted Matthias. He turned to see what was wrong. Rutledge was rushing toward him, a spade raised to strike.

"Rutledge, no."

"I said you don't need the bloody ropes." Rutledge's face was contorted with fury. He swung the spade downward.

Matthias moved, but there was very little room to maneuver in the narrow passageway. He took the blow on his shoulder rather than on his skull. It stunned him and sent him staggering back to the top step. For an instant he teetered on the brink of eternity. Then he dropped the lamp, caught his balance, and threw himself forward toward the man who had once been his closest friend.

"Die, damn you," Rutledge screamed. "I don't need you any longer. You have served your purpose."

The spade came up again. Matthias seized the wooden handle. He yanked it out of Rutledge's hands.

"You have to die." Rutledge charged him, blinded by rage.

Matthias flattened himself against one stone wall. Rutledge groped for him and missed. His own momentum carried him to the top of the staircase.

For a few seconds Rutledge seemed to hover there, scrabbling futilely for purchase. Matthias started toward him, intending to catch hold of him and drag him back into the safety of the corridor.

But he was too late. Rutledge plummeted over the edge and fell into the endless darkness at the bottom of the stone steps. His scream echoed off the corridor walls for a very long time.

o   o   o

"But why would he do such a thing?" Imogen asked softly, bringing Matthias back to the present.

Matthias studied a leering clay mask that was propped against the side of the sarcophagus. "He had been acting oddly ever since I had made a rather valuable discovery two days earlier."

"The library?"

"No. Something else. It doesn't matter now. We had formed an agreement. When it came to the individual artifacts, we would each keep whatever we uncovered. But Rutledge was obsessed with the item I had found. He was willing to kill to possess it." Matthias raised his eyes to meet Imogen's. "The thing is, I would have given it to him if he had simply asked for it."

Imogen fitted her hands to her hips and began to tap the toe of her little half-boot. "Do you think, perhaps, that Rutledge went mad, as poor Lucy did?"

"No," Matthias said evenly. "I think he used me from the very beginning. He realized even sooner than I did that I might have actually located the clues that would lead me to Zamar. He made himself my friend. Gave me access to his library. Accompanied me on the journey. And then he tried to kill me when he had no further use for me."

"But he was your friend."

"I choose my friends more carefully these days." Matthias grimaced at his own youthful naiveté. "Fool that I was, I was actually honored that Rutledge had such faith in my researches. For some reason that I have never been able to comprehend, I wanted his approval."

A gentle understanding appeared in Imogen's eyes. "Perhaps he gave you what your father—" An ominous scrape of stone on stone interrupted her. She whirled to stare at the looming artifacts around her. "What on earth was that?"

Matthias put down the notebook and got slowly to his feet. "I believe we have company."

Alastair Drake rose from the depths of a half-covered

sarcophagus on the opposite side of the room. "I have always wondered what happened to Rutledge."

"Drake." Matthias watched Alastair step from the coffin.

"So you pushed him down a flight of stairs, eh, Colchester? Very clever." Alastair smiled the smile that had made him so popular in the best drawing rooms and aimed the pistol in his hand at Matthias. "Pity you will never be able to tell the tale yourself."

"Alastair." Imogen stared at him with openmouthed shock. "What are you doing here?"

"I should think that was obvious," Alastair said.

"Indeed." Matthias glanced regretfully at his great-coat, which was hanging well out of reach. He cursed himself silently for having left the pistol in the pocket. "Where is your charming sister?"

"Right here, Colchester." Selena stepped gracefully from behind a sheet of canvas that had concealed several statues. She had a small, elegant pistol clasped in her gloved hand. "We have been waiting for the two of you to join us. We have been watching your town house for several days, knowing sooner or later an opportunity would present itself."

Alastair smiled at Imogen. "I'm sure you will be pleased to learn that you and your husband will end your studies of ancient Zamar in a suitable fashion. You will be hailed by one and all as the latest victims of the Rutledge Curse."

Chapter 20

Imogen's chest felt very tight. She realized that she had stopped breathing. She glanced anxiously at Matthias. He still lounged against the edge of the sarcophagus as though nothing out of the ordinary had occurred. His face was a cold, enigmatic mask. This was the man who had earned the epithet Cold-blooded Colchester, she thought. Now she knew why.

She wondered how she could ever have concluded that Matthias suffered from a weakness of the nerves.

His ghost-gray eyes briefly met hers. The icy resolve in him raised the hair on the nape of her neck. She knew that if it were possible to escape this situation, Matthias would arrange for them to do so.

This was Colchester of Zamar. Imogen felt a certain sense of vindication. She had not been mistaken. She had always known that he was a man of action.

Imogen started to breathe again. They were comrades, companions, partners. She must be ready to do her part in whatever plan Matthias was formulating.

"I suppose it was too much to hope that the pair of

you would take yourselves off to the Continent," she said with what she prayed was a tone of disgust.

"And abandon everything that we have worked so hard to achieve?" Selena's smile was very thin. "Don't be a complete fool. My brother and I have gone through far too much to gain our present positions in Society. We do not intend to lose our new roles because of a silly blue-stocking eccentric such as yourself, Lady Colchester." She looked at Matthias. "Or because of your rather more dangerous husband."

Imogen nodded seriously, as though Selena's words had been enlightening. "I see. Colchester said something along those lines, but I told him that you were far too clever to hang about after all that has occurred."

"Obviously, you overestimated their intelligence, my dear," Matthias said softly.

Anger blazed in Alastair's gaze. He raised the barrel of the pistol with a short, jerky movement that betrayed his agitated state. "Silence, you arrogant, interfering bastard. In a short while you and your lady will be occupying one of these very convenient Zamarian coffins. I think that with a bit of squeezing we can just manage to fit you both into the same sarcophagus. A romantic notion, is it not?"

"That's your plan?" Matthias's mouth twisted with sardonic amusement. "You intend to stuff us into one of these things?" He patted the edge of the stone sarcophagus.

Alastair frowned at the small movement. His expression eased when Matthias's hand stilled. "It will work."

"You're more of an idiot than I thought, Drake," Matthias said. "I do have one or two friends in London, you know. They will soon reason out what happened and they will know who is responsible."

"Not bloody likely." Alastair narrowed his eyes. "Even if someone, say your good friend Felix Glaston, deduces what happened, he will not be able to prove a damn thing. He won't even be able to find your bodies."

Imogen stared at him. "What do you mean?"

Alastair smiled. "The sarcophagus containing you and Colchester will be carted out of this chamber late tonight in a nightman's wagon. You will journey out into the country together with the contents of several cesspits. I have hired a group of stout villeins from the stews to handle the matter. They are not the sort to ask questions. And they certainly will not raise the lid of a sealed coffin to peer inside."

"You will both disappear into an unmarked grave in some farmer's field," Selena said. "Very simple. Very tidy."

"It will not be that easy," Imogen said fiercely. "Our coachman will return for us within two hours. When he does not find us, he will have the entire Zamarian Institution searched."

"A message has already been sent to your residence stating that you will not be needing the carriage again this afternoon." Alastair's eyes were bright with a feverish excitement. "Your butler has been informed that as it is such a fine day, you have decided to walk home."

Matthias looked briefly interested. "What makes you think anyone will believe that?"

Selena gave him a satisfied smile. "Two people will be seen leaving the Zamarian Institution this afternoon. The gentleman will be wearing your black greatcoat, hat, and boots, my lord. The woman will be dressed in Lady Colchester's distinctive Zamarian-green gown and her very unfashionable bonnet."

Imogen scowled. "You're going to leave here wearing our clothes?"

"And disappear into the London crowds, never to be seen again." Selena made a negligent movement with her free hand. "More victims of the Rutledge Curse."

"There will be talk," Imogen insisted. "Colchester is right. His friends will ask questions."

"Questions that will never be answered," Selena assured her. "Society will thrive on speculation and gossip for a time and then the entire affair will fade away. Alastair and I will return to Town in a few months and resume our usual routine. No one will link us to your disappearance."

"Or to the death of Lady Vanneck?" Matthias stirred slightly, as though he needed to stretch a bit. His boot brushed the clay mask that rested against the side of the coffin.

Alastair started at the small movement. His eyes went to Matthias's boot. Then he relaxed. "So you reasoned that out, did you? Very clever."

"It was not difficult after I read Lucy's journal," Imogen said. "You killed her because she was trying to blackmail you into running off with her to Italy."

Alastair grimaced. "Lucy had ceased to be amusing. I tried to end the affair in the usual fashion, but she would not leave me alone. She became obsessed with the notion of going off to Italy, although why the devil she thought I would want to accompany her is beyond me."

"Lucy would not leave Alastair alone." Selena's hand tightened on the handle of the pistol. "And then she tried to blackmail him. We had to do something."

"Fortunately, she did not discover that Selena and I were related, but she managed to learn something of what had happened in the north." Alastair shrugged. "Too much."

"There was nothing for it but to get rid of her," Selena explained. "And the runner she hired to investigate."

Imogen looked at Alastair. "You, I presume, were the highwayman who killed that poor Bow Street runner?"

"I made a rather dashing sight wearing a cape and a brace of pistols, if I do say so myself," Alastair drawled. "But Lucy was more of a problem. The stage had to be properly set for her death so that neither Selena nor I would be implicated. You may be certain that we wrote that scene with great care."

"And you cast me in the leading role," Imogen said bitterly.

Matthias folded his arms across his chest. "It is just as

we had concluded, my dear. They arranged the thing so that the gossips would hold you and Vanneck responsible for Lucy's so-called suicide."

"If it's any consolation, Vanneck was just as much an unwitting player as yourself, Lady Colchester," Selena said. "He went to that bedchamber with the expectation of meeting his current paramour."

"Would that have been you, by any chance?" Imogen asked.

"Indeed." Selena smiled again. "By a stroke of luck, Lucy never uncovered my connection to Alastair nor my part in what had happened in the north. It's obvious that she made no mention of me in her journal, because after Vanneck found it a few months ago, he attempted to blackmail only Alastair."

Imogen thought she heard the merest hint of a question in Selena's tone, as though she expected confirmation. Selena was not entirely certain that the journal did not mention her, Imogen realized.

Imogen glanced at Matthias out of the corner of her eye. He moved his head once in a slight negative motion. He did not want her to reassure Selena. As though she could read his mind, Imogen suddenly comprehended that he intended to use the journal to bargain for their lives.

"The night that you and Vanneck met in that bedchamber," Selena continued, "Alastair arranged to pass by in the hall with a companion. My brother was, as everyone knows, suitably shocked and horrified to discover you in such a compromising position."

Imogen whirled to confront Alastair. "You and your companion immediately put about the rumor that Vanneck had seduced his wife's closest friend. Then you somehow convinced Lucy to take too much laudanum."

"It was not difficult," Alastair assured her. "I told Lucy that the glass contained a new tonic for her nerves. She had grown extremely anxious and fearful. She took the stuff without question."

"And everyone called it suicide," Imogen whispered.

"Congratulations." Alastair executed a small, mocking bow. "You have finally got it right."

"A pair of bloody actors," Matthias said softly.

"As it happens, that is correct." Selena laughed. "How did you guess? Alastair and I both trod the boards in the north. But three years ago we determined to write our own parts and play them here in London. We have performed brilliantly, if I do say so myself."

Matthias uncrossed his arms and gripped the edge of the sarcophagus on either side of his thighs. The new shift in his position caused Alastair to stiffen again.

Matthias regarded him with amused contempt. "When you staged your second murderous little play, you again attempted to cast Imogen and Vanneck in leading roles, did you not? You also added me to your company of players. I was to be Vanneck's executioner."

"That was how the scene was written," Selena said. "But Vanneck refused to act his part."

"If one of you had thought to consult with me," Matthias said, "I could have told you that Vanneck was not the type to show up on time for a duel."

Fury flashed in Selena's celestial-blue eyes. "I knew that he was weak, but I did not realize that he was such a complete coward until it was too late. I went to see him the night before the duel to act the part of the tearful, distraught former lover."

"You wished to assure yourself that everything was going according to plan," Matthias said. "I can imagine your chagrin when you saw that he was preparing to leave Town rather than face me."

"It was worse than you know," Selena retorted. "When I arrived, I saw that he had just sat down to write a letter to Imogen. He had learned that she blamed him for Lucy's death. He intended to tell her that he suspected that Alastair had murdered Lucy. He thought that information might convince Imogen to restrain you,

Colchester. I still shudder to think of what might have happened if I had not visited him that evening."

"You shot him yourself, did you not?" Matthias said easily. "Right there in his study."

"I had no choice," Selena said. "He was about to escape to the country."

Imogen was outraged. "After you killed Vanneck, you summoned Alastair and together the two of you managed to get the body into the curricle. You left him at the scene of the duel, hoping that everyone would assume that Colchester had killed him in cold blood."

Alastair shrugged. "Or, at the very least, that he had been murdered by a footpad. It did not particularly matter so long as Vanneck was dead."

Matthias shifted position again. The toe of his boot once more tapped the clay mask. This time Alastair did not appear to take any notice.

Imogen realized that Matthias had made a number of such small, inconsequential motions during the past few minutes. Such restlessness was at odds with his usual air of controlled stillness.

His gaze met hers for a fleeting moment. She had no difficulty reading the warning in his eyes. It was clear that he was planning some desperate action.

In that instant of silent communication Imogen suddenly understood the reason for the series of seemingly unimportant movements. Matthias was attempting to lull Alastair and Selena into growing accustomed to such slight motions from him.

"One thing has puzzled me," Imogen said slowly. "Why did you wait so long to kill Lord Vanneck? You murdered Lucy three years ago."

Selena's eyes darkened. "The bastard did not discover Lucy's journal until quite recently. No one knew that it even existed until a maid found it packed away with Lucy's things. It came to light when Vanneck moved into his new town house."

"For three years Selena and I assumed our secret was

safe." Alastair grimaced. "Then, a couple of months ago Vanneck came to me and said he had found Lucy's journal and that he knew what she had known. He said that if I made regular payments, he would maintain his silence. I was forced to comply while Selena and I devised a way to get rid of him."

Selena smiled at Imogen. "And then you conveniently descended upon the ton with that crazed tale of a map and an ancient Zamarian artifact. What's more, you had Colchester dancing attendance upon you."

Alastair glanced at Matthias. "I must confess, Selena and I were amazed when you showed a serious interest in Imogen and her map. When you went so far as to seduce her and announce your engagement, we knew that you believed that her map was genuine. There was no other explanation for such a ridiculous alliance."

"You think not?" Matthias asked gently.

Selena paid no attention. "As you were evidently serious about getting your hands on Imogen and her map, we soon saw a way to use the rivalry between you and Vanneck to bring about Vanneck's demise."

"There was still the problem of the journal," Matthias said. "You had to get rid of it. You searched Vanneck's house to find it."

Alastair scowled. "And encountered you. But how did you know about the journal?"

"Ah," said Imogen. "An excellent question." She took a small step back until she stood next to the tower of clay tablets that she had stacked a few minutes earlier. "And how many other people know about it?"

"Bah. We shall find a way to get it once you have disappeared."

"Perhaps," Matthias said.

"It should not be difficult to convince your grieving sister to get rid of the cursed journal," Selena murmured.

Matthias smiled. "Do not be too certain of that. I have made arrangements to see that the journal falls into the right hands should anything happen to me or my wife."

"I don't believe you," Selena spat out.

Matthias raised his brows but said nothing.

Alastair frowned. "Selena?"

"He is bluffing, Alastair. Pay him no heed. We will get the journal."

"You might be interested in learning how we discovered the existence of Lucy's journal," Imogen said coolly. "It was no accident, you know."

Alastair and Selena both rounded on her with glittering expressions. It was clear they had not considered that point.

"What the devil are you talking about?" Alastair demanded.

Selena glared at her. "Vanneck must have told you about it."

"Actually, no," Imogen said. "It was not Vanneck."

"Then who?" Alastair shouted.

Selena flicked him a repressive glance. "Calm yourself, Alastair."

"Damnation, Selena, don't you see? Someone else knows about the journal."

"No. She's lying."

For an instant Selena and Alastair were occupied with the fresh concern. Matthias chose that moment to move again. This time there was nothing casual or restless about the action.

He reached down and seized the heavy clay mask that had been propped against the edge of the sarcophagus. He hurled it with deadly accuracy straight toward Alastair.

"What are you . . . ?" Selena reacted first, swinging around to aim the pistol at Matthias. "No. *Alastair*. Look out."

Alastair started to turn, but his reaction was too slow. He gave an inarticulate cry and raised his arm. The heavy mask was only partially deflected by his defensive reaction. It struck him with enough force to send him staggering backward. The pistol flew from his hand. Matthias raced toward him.

"Bastard." Selena's beautiful face contorted with rage. She started to pull the trigger.

Imogen swept out her hand, striking the stack of Zamarian tablets. They toppled toward Selena, startling her before she could pull the trigger.

"You clumsy, cow-handed oddity." Selena whirled back to face Imogen. "You have caused all this trouble."

Imogen turned to flee. Her knee struck the edge of the sarcophagus. She stumbled and fell just as Selena pulled the trigger.

Imogen felt something cold brush her arm as she sprawled ignominiously forward into the stone coffin. Behind her she heard the sounds of a violent scuffle. Selena screamed in raw fury.

Imogen sat up. For some reason her left shoulder did not function properly. She concentrated on using her right arm to pull herself out of the coffin.

She saw with horror that Alastair and Matthias were circling each other warily. Light glinted on the knife blade Alastair gripped. Selena was crouched low in an attempt to seize the pistol Alastair had dropped.

"This time I'm going to kill you, Colchester," Alastair snarled. He feinted with the knife.

Matthias lashed out with his leg in a strange sweeping movement that caught Alastair on the side of his thigh. Alastair yelled in pain and lurched to the side.

Imogen saw that Selena had almost gotten hold of the fallen pistol. "Oh, no, you don't." She heaved herself out of the coffin and launched herself at Selena, colliding with her in a jarring thud.

The force of Imogen's momentum propelled both her and Selena straight into the towering statue of Zamaris. The impact sent a shudder through the heavy figure. Its poorly repaired arm cracked at the shoulder. Stone grated ominously on stone.

"Imogen, get back," Matthias shouted.

Imogen rolled to the side in a flurry of skirts. A fraction of a second later the great arm of Zamaris crashed to the floor.

Selena was not able to get out of the way in time. The stone arm struck her shoulders, pinning her to the floor. She gave a short, broken cry and then lay still.

Imogen sat up slowly. There was a strange buzzing sound in her brain and her shoulder hurt. She realized she must have scraped it when she fell into the sarcophagus.

Silence gripped the chamber. She turned to look for Matthias and saw that he was getting to his feet beside Alastair's still form.

"Matthias." Imogen struggled to rise. "Are you all right?"

"Yes. What about you?"

"Quite"—Imogen sucked in her breath as pain lanced through her—"fit."

"My dear, you never cease to amaze me." Matthias started toward her. His gaze fell on Selena. "Is she dead?"

"I don't think so." Imogen glanced at Selena. "Unconscious, I believe. What about Alastair?"

"The same. It looks as though they will both live to stand trial for their crimes." Matthias frowned. "Are you sure you're all right, Imogen?"

"Yes, of course." It took an effort of will to get to her feet. She was forced to grab hold of Zamaris's leg to steady herself. "I have told you often enough that I am not inclined toward nervous weakness."

"I envy you your stout nerves, madam." Matthias smiled ruefully. "Personally, I am feeling somewhat overwrought."

Imogen swallowed heavily. "Do not expect me to believe that, sir. You have greatly misled me in the matter of your poor nerves."

"On the contrary. The realization that you were very nearly killed just now will be enough to send me to my bed for a fortnight." Matthias's eyes darkened suddenly. "Imogen, your *shoulder*."

"Calm yourself, sir. I merely scraped it a bit on the edge of the sarcophagus."

"The devil you did." Matthias's eyes were pools of silver ice as he hurried toward her. "Selena shot you."

Imogen glanced down at her injured shoulder and saw the blood. "Oh, dear. So she did." And then the real pain struck. Searing, flaming, mind-dazzling pain.

For the first time in her life, Imogen swooned. Matthias caught her before she hit the floor.

Imogen surfaced from the darkness to find herself in Matthias's arms. She heard him issue orders to two workmen on the steps of the Zamarian Institution. Something about summoning the watch and securing the two people in the museum.

The world spun again when Matthias lifted her into a hackney coach. She turned her face into Matthias's shoulder and gritted her teeth. His arms tightened around her.

After what seemed a century of pain, she realized that the coach had come to a halt. Matthias carried her up the steps of the town house. The door opened.

Raised voices sounded from the vicinity of the drawing room. A violent quarrel was in progress, Imogen realized.

"Take your hands off her," Hugo snarled. "Or I'll smash your face."

"She's my niece," another man roared. "I'll do what I like with her."

"Patricia is not going anywhere with you," Hugo vowed. "Stand aside. I am prepared to defend her to the death."

"Ufton," Matthias bellowed. "Where in the name of God are you?"

"Here, sir," Ufton said. "Sorry, sir. Didn't hear you at the door. We've got a bit of a problem on our hands."

"It can wait. Imogen has been shot."

Imogen opened her eyes and saw Ufton peering down at her with deep concern. "Hello, Ufton." She was startled at the weakness in her own voice.

"Bring her into the library at once," Ufton said.

Voices rose again in the drawing room.

"That must be Patricia's dreadful uncle, Mr. Poole," Imogen whispered. "He's here, isn't he, Ufton?"

"Says he's come to take Lady Patricia back to Devon with him," Ufton explained as he opened the library door. "Mr. Bagshaw objects."

Imogen smiled. "Good for Hugo."

At that moment another fierce shout went up inside the drawing room. A tall, thin man with greasy hair crashed through the open doorway and sprawled on the hall floor.

For a moment the man lay, stunned, on the marble tile. Then he shook his narrow head and scowled up at Matthias with malevolent eyes. Yellow teeth flashed in his whiskers. He reminded Imogen of a rat.

"I say, you must be Colchester." The man sat up, rubbing his jaw. "I'm Poole, Patricia's uncle. Come to take the chit off yer hands, m'lord. That young bastard in there says you told her she could stay with you."

Hugo came to stand in the doorway. Patricia hovered anxiously behind him.

"It's the truth." Hugo massaged the bruised knuckles of his right hand as he looked down at his victim. Then he met Matthias's eyes. "You gave Patricia your word that you would not send her back to this vermin, did you not, Colchester?"

"Yes, I did." Matthias walked into the library with Imogen in his arms. "Get rid of him, Bagshaw."

"With pleasure."

Imogen caught a blurred glimpse of Hugo as he reached down to haul Poole to his feet.

"Don't touch me." Poole reared back out of reach.

He skittered across the tile toward the front door. Hugo pursued him.

Patricia hurried across the hall as Hugo slammed the front door behind Poole. "What's wrong with Imogen?"

"Lady Lyndhurst shot her." Matthias settled Imogen gently down onto the dolphin sofa.

"Dear heaven," Patricia whispered. "Is she going to . . . to be all right?"

"Yes," Matthias said. The single word had the weight of a vow sealed with his own blood.

Imogen reclined against the arm of the sofa and managed what she hoped was a reassuring smile. "I'm going to be fine. There is no call for all of you to look so anxious."

"Let me see what we have here." With an effort, Ufton managed to get Matthias out of the way so that he could examine the wound.

"Well?" Imogen demanded. The world was no longer spinning. She was feeling better by the minute, she thought.

Ufton nodded, looking quite satisfied. "Just a superficial wound, my lady. You'll be fit in no time." He reached for the brandy bottle. "If you'll take a good, long swallow, madam?"

Imogen blinked. "What an excellent notion, Ufton."

She allowed him to pour a large measure of the strong brandy down her throat. The liquid burned all the way to her stomach, but it sent a pleasant warmth through her veins. When she was finished she blinked again and gave Matthias a beatific smile. He did not return the smile. If anything, his expression became even more grim.

"If you'll steady her, sir?" Ufton said softly.

Matthias sat down on the arm of the sofa and took hold of Imogen. He braced her against his leg, his hands gentle but unyielding.

"Forgive me, Imogen," he said.

"For what?" Imogen scowled up at him. "You have done absolutely nothing offensive, my lord. Indeed, you were most heroic this afternoon. It was quite thrilling. I always knew that you were, at heart, a man of action, sir."

Ufton poured brandy into the raw wound. Imogen shrieked and fainted for the second time in her life.

Chapter 21

Three days later Imogen was again ensconced on the Zamarian sofa, chatting with Horatia, when Patricia breezed into the library.

"How are you feeling, Imogen?" she asked as she removed her bonnet.

"Very well, thank you," Imogen said. "My shoulder has given me a few twinges, but on the whole it is healing nicely, thanks to Ufton and his brandy treatment."

"Do not remind me." Patricia grimaced as she dropped her flower-trimmed bonnet on a nearby table. "I vow, I shall never forget the expression on Matthias's face when he held you still so that Ufton could pour the brandy into your wound."

Imogen brightened. "What sort of expression was that, would you say?"

"He looked as if he yearned to murder someone." Patricia sat down and reached for the teapot. "At that moment I realized how he came by the name Cold-blooded Colchester."

"I expect that he was concerned about me," Imogen

said. She had hoped that Patricia would describe Matthias's expression as one of impassioned, heartfelt anguish for the pain he had known she was about to experience. But *murderous* was sufficient, she told herself bracingly. It implied great depth of feeling.

Horatia looked at Patricia, who was flushed and sparkling. "You appear to be in excellent spirits this afternoon, my dear. Enjoy your drive?"

"Oh, yes." Patricia's blush deepened. "Very much. Hugo is a true master of the ribbons. We were the center of attention in the park. By the way, Imogen, he sends you his regards and regrets that he will not see you this evening at the Sheltons' soiree."

Imogen wrinkled her nose. "Matthias has forbidden me to stir from the house for a fortnight. He has been absolutely adamant on the subject. Thus far I have had no success in persuading him to change his mind."

"He says you gave him a dreadful fright the other day." Patricia finished pouring the tea and set down the pot. "He told me that he fully expects that his delicate sensibilities will take weeks to recover."

"Hmm." Imogen sipped her tea. "Lately it has occurred to me that Colchester lays claim to anxious nerves and delicate sensibilities only when it is convenient for him to do so. He seems quite oblivious of them the rest of the time."

Patricia laughed. "I believe you may be correct. Pity you will miss the parties and balls this week though. You and my brother are going to be the chief topics of conversation at every affair in Town. Today in the park Hugo and I were stopped again and again. Everyone wanted to know about the dreadful events in the Zamarian museum."

Horatia chuckled. "I suspect that is the principal reason Colchester has insisted that Imogen cannot accept any invitations for a fortnight. He has no interest in satisfying the curiosity of the ton."

"You are absolutely correct, Horatia," Matthias said

from the doorway of the library. "I have better things to do than make polite conversation about a matter that has so deeply affected my nerves."

"Ah, there you are, Colchester." Imogen smiled at him. "We have been waiting for you. Did your friend Felix have the information you sought?"

"He did." Matthias crossed the room and leaned down to give her a quick, possessive kiss on the mouth.

"What information?" Patricia demanded.

Imogen glanced at her. "Why, the answer to the question of what happened in the north, of course. Mr. Drake and his sister refuse to confess to anything, you know. They have guessed, correctly, that Lucy never actually wrote down the dark secret she uncovered."

"But with the information that Imogen and I had plus what Felix Glaston had discovered, I have finally managed to put the whole story together." Matthias sat down on the sofa next to Imogen and glanced at Horatia. "You will no doubt find this rather interesting."

"Why is that?" Horatia asked.

"Remember the lurid tale of the infamous Demon Twins of Dunstoke Castle?"

"Of course." Horatia's eyes widened. "Never say that Mr. Drake and Lady Lyndhurst are the evil twins."

"That is precisely the case," Matthias said.

Patricia frowned in confusion. "But they aren't twins."

"Not all twins are identical," Imogen reminded her as she reached for the teapot to pour a cup for Matthias.

"Just so." Matthias frowned. "Here, let me do that. You are not to exert yourself yet." He took the pot from Imogen's hand. "Selena and Drake escaped the fire they set to kill old Lord Dunstoke, just as the rumors claimed. What is more, they got out with Dunstoke's hoard of gems and jewels. They have been living off the profits for the past three years."

Imogen's imagination leaped to fill in the missing parts. "They assumed new identities and moved to London. They had the money to keep up appearances and the acting skill to play the parts they had chosen. No one thought to question them."

Matthias agreed as he poured his own tea and sat back. "But when they reached London they learned that everyone in Society was talking about the Demon Twins. An unknown brother and sister appearing on the scene would have been suspect. So, as an added measure of caution, they decided to keep their relationship a secret."

"And then had to go on maintaining the secret after the gossip had died down," Horatia murmured. "They could hardly announce that they were brother and sister after letting people think otherwise for several months."

"Exactly," Matthias said. "But then Drake began the affair with Lucy. At some point he made the slip of the tongue that made her suspicious. Probably said something about the theater or about his own acting talent. Whatever it was, it was enough to make her hire a runner, who, in turn, must have learned something of interest."

Imogen grew thoughtful. "And three years later Lord Vanneck found Lucy's journal. He did not learn the precise nature of the secret, but he realized that there *was* a secret of some sort. It was enough. He needed money, so he decided to try blackmailing Alastair."

"He convinced Drake that he knew what Lucy had known, and in the process he signed his own death warrant," Matthias concluded. "The Polite World was everything to Drake and his sister. They were willing to kill to protect the positions they had created for themselves."

Patricia shuddered. "Will they hang, do you think?"

"Transported to Australia, most likely," Matthias said. "It's the usual fate for that sort, now that we can no longer ship convicts to America."

Imogen grimaced. "Something tells me Selena and Alastair will do very well in the colonies."

∘   ∘   ∘

She was standing in a black-draped bedchamber this time. Somehow she knew that it was nearly midnight. The windows were open. Cold night air caused the candles to flicker. There was no sign of Matthias. She turned slowly, calling his name. There was no answer.

She was suddenly seized by a sense of panic. She had to find Matthias. She hurried out of the bedchamber and ran through Uncle Selwyn's funereal house. Desperation and dread consumed her. If she did not find him, they would both be lost forever in this dreadful mausoleum. . . .

She searched every dark room in the mansion until only the library remained. She looked at the closed door, afraid to open it. If Matthias was not inside, she would never find him. They would both be alone forever.

Slowly she reached out her hand to twist the knob. . .

"Good morning, my dear," Matthias said.

The fragments of the dream dissolved in a heartbeat. Imogen opened her eyes and saw Matthias standing at the foot of the bed. He had a small, ornately carved chest tucked under one arm and a copy of the *Zamarian Review* in his hand.

"Sorry to awaken you," he said. "But I thought you'd like to know that the newest edition of the *Review* has just arrived. You will never guess what that arrogant, presumptuous, overbearing I. A. Stone has dared to write this time."

Imogen yawned and sat up against the pillows. She examined Matthias surreptitiously. He looked very solid and quite real. He was dressed in his shirt-sleeves and breeches. Sunlight gleamed on the icy silver in his hair. His eyes were the clear gray of an early dawn.

She suddenly realized that there was a great deal of light pouring through the window. "Good heavens, what time is it?"

"Not quite ten o'clock." Matthias looked amused.

"That is impossible. I never sleep late." She glowered

at the clock on the dresser and saw that it was, indeed, five minutes until ten o'clock. "It is your fault. You kept me up until all hours last night, sir."

He gave her a devilish grin. "Your insistence upon practicing half the positions illustrated in my Zamarian marriage instruction scroll inspired me, my sweet."

Imogen blushed at the memory of his passion and her own. "Not half. Merely a select few that appeared especially interesting."

"All of those positions that featured the lady on top, as I recall." Matthias's grin widened. "But never fear, my dear. You know how it heats my blood when you take command." He walked around the bed and handed her the *Zamarian Review*.

"You woke me up to show me my own article?" she asked, beginning to take an interest. She opened the *Review*.

"Well, no, actually. That was not why I awakened you."

"Oh, look, Matthias, the editors printed my article ahead of yours."

"Yes, I know," he said. "But as to why I woke you, Imogen—"

"This is the first time that they have actually printed one of my articles in front of yours," she said with gathering enthusiasm. "Perhaps they have finally come to the conclusion that my observations are as well reasoned and as interesting as your own, my lord."

"I intend to speak to them about the matter. They seem to have forgotten that I founded that damn journal." Matthias sat down on the edge of the bed. "But first there is something I wish to give to you, my dear."

"One moment, sir. Let me see if there are any letters concerning my last article on the relationship of Zamaris and Anizamara in Zamarian mythology."

"I have something for you, Imogen."

"Ah-ha. Here is a letter from that idiot Bledlow. I

knew he would try to dispute my arguments." Imogen paused. "What did you say?"

He smiled faintly. "I have a gift for you."

"How lovely." She sensed that he was trying to tell her something very important. "Is it in that chest?"

"Yes." He put the carved box into her hands.

Slowly she opened the lid and peered inside.

Nestled against black velvet was a magnificent object about the size of her hand. It was fashioned of gold, heavily inscribed on one side in the formal script of ancient Zamar. The other side was crusted with gems and crystals of singular beauty. They glowed with such brilliant clarity that Imogen could scarcely believe that they were real.

"The Queen's Seal," she breathed.

"You are looking at the artifact that caused Rutledge to attempt to murder me."

She searched his eyes. "You have had it all this time? You kept it hidden away and allowed the legends to grow?"

He lifted one shoulder in a small shrug. "Yes. I suppose it represented a ghost."

"Why have you given it to me?"

He touched her cheek with his elegant fingers. "Because you saved me from the ghosts. You are my Anizamara."

"Oh, Matthias. I do love you so." Imogen tossed the priceless seal aside and reached for him.

"I am glad to hear that." Matthias managed to grab the seal just before it tumbled off the bed and fell to the floor. He set it down very carefully on the nightstand. "Because I love you too. I will love you for the rest of my life and beyond."

"Is that a promise, my lord?"

"Yes. The most important one that I have ever made."

Imogen wrapped her arms around his neck and pulled him down on top of her with joyous enthusiasm. The whole world knew that Colchester always kept his promises.

Author's Note

"*H*orrid" novels—chilling tales of romantic gothic horror—were enormously popular in
the early 1800s. The most successful authors in the
genre were women. Everyone, including such nota-
bles as Jane Austen and Percy Shelley, read the
books. Not everyone approved of them, however.

The critics deplored the taste for thrills and dark
mysteries. But novels with titles such as *The
Mysterious Hand, or, Subterranean Horrors* and *The
Enchanted Head* found a wide and enthusiastic
audience.

In the end, the critics managed to keep most of
the horrid novels and their authors out of the
respectable literary establishment. But no amount
of criticism could dampen the enthusiasm of the
readers. The archetypal nature of the stories proved
too powerful to subdue.

We seldom study the horrid novels in English

literature classes today, but that does not mean that their influence is not strongly felt. The authors left a lasting impact on modern popular fiction. The genres of romance, science fiction, fantasy, suspense, and horror are especially indebted to them.

Incidentally, one horrid novel did make it into the modern era. The critics at the *Quarterly Review* savaged it when it was first published in 1818, but today everyone knows the title. That novel was Mary Shelley's *Frankenstein*.

Sometimes it takes only one book.

LOOK FOR AMANDA QUICK'S NOVEL

SLIGHTLY SHADY

Coming soon from Piatkus Books

Turn the page for a preview!

PROLOGUE

$\mathcal{T}$he intruder's eyes blazed with a cold fire. He raised a powerful hand and swept another row of vases off the shelf. The fragile objects crashed to the floor and shattered into a hundred shards. He moved on to a display of small statues.

"I advise you to make haste with your packing, Mrs. Lake," he said as he turned his violent attention to a host of fragile clay Pans, Aphrodites, and satyrs. "The carriage will leave in fifteen minutes, and I promise you that you and your niece will be aboard, with or without your luggage."

Lavinia watched him from the foot of the stairs, helpless to stop the destruction of her wares. "You have no right to do this. You are ruining me."

"On the contrary, madam. I am saving your neck." He used a booted foot to topple a large urn decorated in the Etruscan manner. "Not that I expect any thanks, mind you."

Lavinia winced as the urn exploded on impact with the floor. She knew now that it was pointless to berate the lunatic. He was intent on destroying the shop and she lacked the means to stop him. She had been taught early in life to recognize the signs that indicated it was time to stage a tactical retreat. But she had never learned to tolerate such annoying reversals of fortune with equanimity.

"If we were in England, I would have you arrested, Mr. March."

"Ah, but we are not in England, are we, Mrs. Lake?" Tobias March seized a life-size stone centurion by the shield and shoved it forward. The Roman fell on his sword. "We are in Italy and you have no choice but to do as I command."

It was useless to stand her ground. Every moment spent down here attempting to reason with Tobias March was time lost that should be spent packing. But the unfortunate tendency toward stubbornness that was so much a part of her nature could not abide the notion of surrendering the field of battle without a struggle.

"Bastard," she said through her teeth.

"Not in the legal sense." He slammed another row of red clay vases to the floor. "But I believe I comprehend what you wish to imply."

"It is obvious that you are no gentleman, Tobias March."

"I will not quarrel with you on that point." He kicked over a waist-high statue of a naked Venus. "But then, you are no lady, are you?"

She cringed when the statue crumbled. The naked Venuses had proved quite popular with her clientele.

"How dare you? Just because my niece and I got stranded here in Rome and were obliged to go into trade for a few months in order to support ourselves is no reason to insult us."

"Enough." He whirled around to face her. In the lantern light, his forbidding face was colder than the features of any stone statue. "Be grateful that I have concluded that you were merely an unwitting dupe of the criminal I am pursuing and not a member of his gang of thieves and murderers."

"I have only your word that the villains were using my shop as a place to exchange their messages. Frankly, Mr. March, given your rude behavior, I am not inclined to believe a single thing you say."

He pulled a folded sheet of paper from his pocket. "Do you deny that this note was hidden in one of your vases?"

She glanced at the damning note. Only moments ago she had watched in stunned amazement while he shattered a lovely Greek vase. A message that looked remarkably like a villain's report to his criminal employer had been tucked inside. Something about a bargain with pirates having been successfully struck.

Lavinia raised her chin. "It is certainly not my fault that one of my patrons dropped a personal note into that vase."

"Not just one patron, Mrs. Lake. The villains have been using your shop for some weeks now."

"And just how would you know that, sir?"

"I have watched these premises and your personal movements for nearly a month."

She widened her eyes, genuinely shocked by the infuriatingly casual admission.

"You have spent the past month *spying* on me?"

"At the start of my observations, I assumed that you were an active participant in Carlisle's ring here in Rome.

It was only after much study that I have concluded you probably did not know what some of your so-called customers were about."

"That is outrageous."

He gave her a look of mocking inquiry. "Are you saying you *did* know what they were up to when they came and went in such a regular fashion?"

"I am saying no such thing." She could hear her voice climbing but there was little she could do about it. She had never been so angry or so frightened in her life. "I believed them to be honest patrons of antiquities."

"Did you indeed?" Tobias glanced at a collection of cloudy green glass jars that stood in a neat row on a high shelf. His smile was devoid of all warmth. "And how honest are you, Mrs. Lake?"

She stiffened. "What are you implying, sir?"

"I'm not implying anything. I am merely noting that most of the items in this shop are cheap replicas of ancient artifacts. There is very little here that is truly antique."

"How do you know?" she shot back. "Never say you are an expert in antiquities, sir. I will not be taken in by such an outlandish claim. You cannot pass yourself off as a scholarly researcher, not after what you have done to my establishment."

"You are correct, Mrs. Lake. I am not an expert in Greek and Roman antiquities. I am a simple man of business."

"Rubbish. Why would a simple man of business come all the way to Rome in pursuit of a villain named Carlisle?"

"I am here on behalf of one of my clients who employed me to make inquiries into the fate of a man named Bennett Ruckland."

"What was the fate of this Mr. Ruckland?"

Tobias looked at her. "He was murdered here in Rome. My client believes it was because he learned too much concerning the secret organization that Carlisle controls."

"A likely story."

"Nevertheless, it is my story and mine is the only tale that matters tonight." He hurled another pot to the floor. "You have only ten minutes left, Mrs. Lake."

It was hopeless. Lavinia took two fistfuls of her skirts and started up the stairs. But she paused midway as a thought struck her.

"This business of making inquiries into murders on behalf of your clients—it seems a rather odd sort of profession," she said.

He smashed a small Roman oil lamp. "No more odd than selling false antiquities."

Lavinia was incensed. "I told you, they are not false, sir. They are reproductions designed to be purchased as souvenirs."

"Call them what you wish. They look remarkably like fraudulent imitations to me."

She smiled thinly. "But as you just said, sir, you are no expert in rare artifacts, are you? You are merely a simple man of business."

"You have approximately eight minutes left, Mrs. Lake."

She touched the silver pendant she wore at her throat the way she often did when her nerves were under a great strain. "I cannot decide if you are a monstrous villain or merely deranged," she whispered.

He looked briefly, chillingly, amused. "Does it make any great difference?"

"No."

The situation was impossible. She had no choice but to concede the victory to him.

With a soft exclamation of frustration and anger, she whirled and rushed on up the stairs. When she reached the small, lantern-lit room, she saw that, unlike herself, Emeline had made good use of the time allotted to them. Two medium-size and one very large trunk stood open. The smaller trunks were already crammed to overflowing.

"Thank goodness you are here." Emeline's words were muffled, as her head was inside the wardrobe. "Whatever took you so long?"

"I was attempting to convince March that he had no right to toss us out into the street in the middle of the night."

"He is not tossing us into the street." Emeline straightened away from the wardrobe, a small antique vase cradled in her arms. "He has provided a carriage and two armed men to see us safely out of Rome and all the way home to England. It is really very generous of him."

"Rubbish. There is nothing at all generous about his actions. He is playing some deep game, I tell you, and he wants us out of his way."

Emeline busied herself rolling the vase into a bombazine gown. "He believes we are in grave danger from that villain Carlisle, who used our shop as a place to send and receive messages from his men."

"Bah. We have only Mr. March's word that there is any such villain operating here in Rome." Lavinia opened a cupboard. A very handsome, extremely well endowed Apollo gazed out at her. "I, for one, am not inclined to put much faith in anything that man tells us. For all we know, he wants the use of these rooms for his own dark purposes."

"I am convinced he has told us the truth." Emeline stuffed the cushioned vase into the third trunk. "And if that is the case, he is right. We are indeed in danger."

"If there is some villainous gang involved in this affair, I would not be surprised to discover that Tobias March is their leader. He claims to be a simple man of business, but it is obvious to me that there is something distinctly diabolical about him."

"You are allowing your ill temper to influence your imagination, Lavinia. You know you are never at your most clearheaded when you allow your imagination to run wild."

The sound of shattering pottery echoed up the staircase.

"Damn the man," Lavinia muttered.

Emeline paused in her packing and tilted her head slightly, listening. "He certainly is intent on making it appear that we were the victims of vandals and thieves, is he not?"

"He said something about destroying the shop so this villain Carlisle would not suspect he had been discovered." Lavinia wrestled with the Apollo, struggling to get it free of the cupboard. "But I believe it is just another one of his lies. The man is enjoying himself down there, if you ask me. He is quite mad."

"I hardly think that is the case." Emeline went back to the wardrobe for another vase. "But I will admit it is a good thing we stored the genuine antiquities up here so we could keep them safe from street thieves."

"The only bit of luck in this entire affair." Lavinia wrapped her arms around Apollo's chest and hauled him out of the cupboard. "I shudder to think what might have happened if we had put them on display alongside the copies downstairs. March would no doubt have destroyed them too."

"If you ask me, the most fortunate aspect of this thing is that Mr. March concluded we were not members of Carlisle's ring of cutthroats." Emeline shrouded a small vase in a towel and stored it in the trunk. "I tremble to think what he might have done to us had he believed us to be consorting with the real villains and not just innocent dupes."

"He could hardly have done worse than to ruin our only source of income and throw us out of our home."

Emeline glanced at the old stone walls that surrounded them and gave a delicate sniff. "You can hardly call this unpleasant little room a home. I shall not miss it for a moment."

"You will most certainly miss it when we find ourselves penniless in London and forced to make our living on the streets."

"It will not come to that." Emeline patted the towel-wrapped vase she held. "We will be able to sell these antiquities when we return to England. Collecting old vases and statues is all the rage, you know. With the money we receive for these items we shall be able to rent a house."

"Not for long. We will be fortunate to make enough from the sale of these objects to support ourselves for six months. When the last of them is gone, we will be in desperate straits."

"You will think of something, Lavinia. You always do. Just look at how well we managed when we found ourselves stranded here in Rome after our employer ran off with that handsome count. Your notion of going into the antiquities business was nothing short of brilliant."

Lavinia managed, by dint of sheer willpower, not to scream in frustration. Emeline's boundless faith in her ability to recover from every disaster was quite maddening.

"Give me a hand with this Apollo, please," she said.

Emeline glanced doubtfully at the large nude statue Lavinia was attempting to haul across the room. "It will take up most of the space in the last trunk. Perhaps we ought to leave it behind and pack some of the vases instead."

"This Apollo is worth several dozen vases." Lavinia stopped halfway across the room, breathing hard from the exertion, and changed her grip on the figure. "He's the most valuable antiquity we've got. We must take him with us."

"If we put him in the trunk, we won't have room for your books," Emeline said gently.

A sick sensation twisted Lavinia's insides. She stopped abruptly and looked at the shelf filled with the books of poetry she had brought with her from England. The thought of leaving them behind was almost too much to bear.

"I can replace them." She took a tighter hold on the statue. "Eventually."

Emeline hesitated, searching Lavinia's face. "Are you certain? I know how much they mean to you."

"Apollo is more important."

"Very well." Emeline stooped to grasp Apollo's lower limbs.

Booted footsteps rang on the staircase. Tobias March appeared in the doorway. He glanced at the trunks and then he looked at Lavinia and Emeline.

"You must leave now," he said. "I cannot risk allowing you to remain here even another ten minutes."

Lavinia longed to hurl one of the vases at his head. "I am not leaving Apollo behind. He may be all that stands between us and life in a brothel when we return to London."

Emeline made a face. "Really, Lavinia, you mustn't exaggerate so."

"It's nothing short of the truth," Lavinia snapped.

"Give me the bloody statue." Tobias came toward them. He hoisted the sculpture in his arms. "I'll put it into the trunk for you."

Emeline smiled warmly. "Thank you. It is rather heavy."

Lavinia gave a snort of disgust. "Don't thank him, Emeline. He is the cause of all our troubles tonight."

"Always delighted to be of service," Tobias said. He wedged the statue into the trunk. "Anything else?"

"Yes," Lavinia said instantly. "That urn near the door. It is an exceptionally good piece."

"It will not fit into the trunk." Tobias gripped the lid and looked at her. "You must choose between the Apollo and the urn. You cannot take both with you."

She narrowed her eyes, suddenly suspicious. "You intend to take it for yourself, do you not? You plan to steal my urn."

"I assure you, Mrs. Lake, I have no interest in that damn urn. Do you want it or the Apollo? Choose. Now."

"The Apollo," she muttered.

Emeline hurried forward to stuff a nightgown and some shoes in around the Apollo. "I believe we're ready, Mr. March."

"Yes, indeed." Lavinia gave him a steely smile. "Quite ready. I can only hope that one of these days I shall have an opportunity to repay you for this night's work, Mr. March."

He slammed the lid of the trunk. "Is that a threat, Mrs. Lake?"

"Take it as you will, sir." She seized her reticule in one hand and her traveling cloak in the other. "Come, Emeline, let us be off before Mr. March decides to burn the place down around our ears."

"There is no call to be so disagreeable." Emeline picked up her own cloak and a bonnet. "Under the circumstances, I think Mr. March is behaving with admirable restraint."

Tobias inclined his head. "I appreciate your support, Miss Emeline."

"You must not mind Lavinia's remarks, sir," Emeline said. "Her nature is such that when she is feeling hard-pressed she is inclined to become somewhat short of temper."

Tobias settled his cold-eyed gaze on Lavinia again. "I noticed."

"I pray you will make allowances," Emeline continued. "In addition to all of the other difficulties tonight, we are obliged to leave her books of poetry behind. That was a very difficult decision for her. She is very fond of poetry, you see."

"Oh, for pity's sake." Lavinia swung her cloak around her shoulders and strode briskly toward the door. "I refuse to listen to any more of this ridiculous conversation. One thing is certain, I am suddenly quite eager to be free of your unpleasant company, Mr. March."

"You wound me, Mrs. Lake."

"Not nearly so deeply as I could wish."

She paused on the staircase and looked back at him. He did not look wounded. Indeed, he looked magnificently fit. The ease with which he hoisted one of the trunks testified to his excellent physical condition.

"Personally, I'm looking forward to going home." Emeline hastened toward the stairs. "Italy is all very well for a visit, but I have missed London."

"So have I." Lavinia jerked her gaze away from Tobias March's broad shoulders and stomped down the stairs. "This entire venture has been an unmitigated disaster. Whose idea was it to travel to Rome as companions to that dreadful Mrs. Underwood in the first place?"

Emeline cleared her throat. "Yours, I believe."

"The next time I suggest anything so bizarre, I pray you will be so kind as to wave a vinaigrette under my nose until I come to my senses."

"It no doubt seemed quite a brilliant notion at the time," Tobias March said behind her.

"It did indeed," Emeline murmured in very neutral tones. " 'Just think how delightful it will be to spend a season in Rome,' Lavinia said. 'Surrounded by all those wonderfully inspiring antiquities,' she said. 'All at Mrs. Underwood's expense,' she said. 'We shall be entertained in grand style by people of quality and taste,' she said."

"That is quite enough, Emeline," Lavinia snapped. "You know very well it has been a very educational experience."

"In more ways than one, I should imagine," Tobias said rather too easily, "judging by some of the gossip I have heard concerning Mrs. Underwood's parties. Is it true they tended to evolve into orgies?"

Lavinia gritted her teeth. "Granted there were one or two minor incidents of an unfortunate nature."

"The orgies were somewhat awkward," Emeline allowed. "Lavinia and I were obliged to lock ourselves in our bedchambers until they ended. But in my opinion, matters did not become truly dire until we woke up one morning to discover that Mrs. Underwood had run off with her count. That course of action left us stranded and penniless in a foreign clime."

"Nevertheless," Lavinia continued forcefully, "we managed to come right again and we were doing quite nicely until you, Mr. March, chose to interfere in our personal affairs."

"Believe me, Mrs. Lake, no one regrets the necessity more than I," Tobias said.

She paused at the foot of the stairs to take in the sight of the shop full of shattered pottery and statuary. He had destroyed everything, she thought. Not a single vase had been left unbroken. In less than an hour, he had ruined the business it had taken nearly four months to establish.

"It is inconceivable that your regret equals my own, Mr. March." She tightened her grasp on her reticule and walked through the rubble toward the door. "Indeed, sir, so far as I am concerned, this disaster is entirely your fault."

Also available from Piatkus

THE THIRD CIRCLE

Amanda Quick

Leona Hewitt has secretly made her way into Lord
Delbridge's private museum to find a relic stolen from her
family. But someone else is in the dimly lit gallery on the
same errand. Psychic mesmerist Thaddeus Ware is
accustomed to fearful reactions from others but Leona
shows no trace of hysteria in his presence. She exerts a
rather hypnotic power over the hypnotist himself and,
determined to keep the crystal they recovered, she gives him
the slip at a rundown London inn. Thaddeus knows the
menace Leona is courting by absconding with the crystal.
Lord Delbridge has already killed to acquire it and now
intends to find Leona. And, with the stolen crystal in their
possession, the danger is only beginning . . .

978-0-7499-3918-2